Hunted

BOOKS BY SHALINI BOLAND

VAMPIRES OF MARCHWOOD SERIES

Hidden

Taken

PSYCHOLOGICAL THRILLERS

The Secret Mother

The Child Next Door

The Millionaire's Wife

The Silent Sister

The Perfect Family

The Best Friend

The Girl from the Sea

The Marriage Betrayal

The Other Daughter

One of Us Is Lying

The Wife

My Little Girl

The Couple Upstairs

The Family Holiday

A Perfect Stranger

The Daughter-in-Law

SHALINI BOLAND

SECOND SKY

Published by Second Sky in 2023

An imprint of Storyfire Ltd.
Carmelite House
50 Victoria Embankment
London EC4Y 0DZ
United Kingdom

www.secondskybooks.com

ISBN: 978-1-83790-022-0
eBook ISBN: 978-1-83790-021-3

For Neil
The funniest, kindest little brother
I could've wished for

PROLOGUE

Dying... I must be dying.

Alex lay on the cold wet grass. His skin burned with fever, and yet he felt so cold. Like ice. Ice and fire. He shivered. His teeth chattered. What had happened? Why did he feel so awful? His body was soaked with rain and sweat. He didn't even have the strength to open his eyes. They ached. His whole body ached. Maybe if he slept, he would feel better. Yes, sleep would be good. If he could let the darkness take him for a while, perhaps he would wake up feeling better? Or perhaps he would not wake up at all...

CHAPTER ONE

The creature's earliest memory was of the frozen Northlands. Of ice and snow. Of crystalline cold, and glistening air. Of a time when the howling wind was its only lullaby.

It had the sense of being born of the landscape. A raw, wild thing which dreamed itself into existence. But that was long ago. Millennia had passed since that distant time.

Now. Now, it was something else...

CHAPTER TWO

CHRISTMAS DAY

Madison opened her eyes. It was pitch black in the room, the shutters closed tight against the morning. She wondered what the time was. There was no way of knowing without flicking on her bedside light to see the clock. But she didn't want to move. Not just yet. Maddy thought back to this time last year. When she'd found her brother Ben in the cellar, half-dead. When she'd got so mad, she had tried to kill Alexandre... So much had happened since then. So many terrible and amazing things. A half-smile tugged at the corner of her mouth.

She slid down under the duvet and closed her eyes again. It was so good to be back home after everything she'd just been through. To be safe and warm with her strange but wonderful family. Maddy basked in the glow of her feelings. The sheer comfort and familiarity of Marchwood made her smile once more and turn her body to Alexandre who lay fully dressed on top of the covers.

'Mm,' she sighed, as his arm came around her waist. 'Happy Christmas.'

'Merry Christmas, Madison,' he replied, dipping his head to find her mouth.

Maddy kissed him back. A long, slow morning kiss that she never wanted to end. She twined her arms about his neck and pushed her body closer. Too close. Not close enough. After a moment, he eased himself away and broke off the kiss. 'We should go down and find the others,' he said.

'No. Not yet.'

Alex leaned back and turned on the lamp. Propping himself up on one elbow, he bent to kiss the tip of Maddy's nose. 'It's almost eight o'clock, lazybones,' he murmured. 'I heard Ben get up ages ago.'

'I'm not being lazy,' she replied. 'I'm just enjoying being here. Back there... I thought... I thought I'd never get home. That I'd never be with you like this again. After everything that's happened. I just want to hold on to each second, before it disappears. D'you know what I mean?'

'I do. I know exactly what you mean.' He kissed her again as she threaded her fingers through his thick dark hair, grazing his scalp with her nails.

Suddenly, Maddy gasped and pulled away. She had just realised something awful.

'What?' Alex said, his body tensing. 'What is it, Madison? What's wrong?'

'I can't believe it,' she said.

'*What?* Tell me.'

'I... I didn't get you a Christmas present! I didn't get anyone a present.'

Alex relaxed his shoulders and laughed. 'Mon Dieu, I thought you were going to tell me something terrible.'

'It *is* terrible. And it's not funny!' Maddy slid out from under him and sat up. 'Great Christmas this is going to be with no presents.'

'Well, Christmas shopping can be a little tricky when you're being held hostage, or fighting thousand-year-old vampires. I think you'll be forgiven. We only arrived home yesterday.'

'I suppose so.'

'I have no gifts to give either. But at least we're together, and safe. That is the best gift of all, don't you think?'

'Yes.' Maddy relaxed and smiled at her previous momentary panic. Presents weren't important. Alex was right, being alive and together was definitely the most important thing. Plus, no one else would have had time to go shopping either. 'Come on, then.' She finally pushed off the duvet and sat up. 'Let's go downstairs and find the others.' Sliding out of bed wearing just an oversized T-shirt, the cool air made her bare legs turn to gooseflesh. She padded over to the chest of drawers, pulled out a pair of fleecy jogging bottoms, wriggled into them and pulled a ratty old sweatshirt over the top of her head. Then, she slid her feet into a pair of chunky cable-knit socks and ran her fingers through her hair. She would shower and change after breakfast. For now, she was suddenly itching to see her brother and give him a great big hug.

'Get up, lazy,' she said to Alex with a grin. 'Let's go.'

'Me? Lazy? You're the one who—'

'Yeah, yeah, whatever. Come on, stop making excuses and get up.' She squealed as a pillow flew through the air and thwacked her on the side of the head. Alex was already out of the door, and probably downstairs by now. 'That's not fair!' she yelled after him. 'You can't use vampire superpowers to beat me downstairs!' His laughter floated back up the stairs and she grinned, heading for the door.

Seconds later, when Maddy walked into the kitchen, Alex and his vampire siblings, Isobel and Jacques, were already sitting in the room laughing and chatting in French. They switched to English as soon as she entered.

'Merry Christmas!' Isobel said, rising to her feet in a swish of pale blue silk. She was adorned in a beautiful nineteenth-century gown with pearls at her wrist and throat. Jacques, too, was in one of his original suits.

'Wow,' Maddy murmured. 'You guys look amazing. Like something out of a movie.'

'Thank you,' Isobel dipped a little curtsey.

'Belle made me wear it,' Jacques said with an eye-roll. 'Apparently we have to wear our finest clothes for Christmas.' Jacques had taken to the relaxed twenty-first-century lifestyle since his awakening with glee, fully embracing the language, clothing and entertainment. He wasn't impressed at having to dress so formally once again.

'Look at the state of me in my sweats!' Maddy blushed, feeling totally inadequate.

'I'm glad you're not dressed yet,' Isobel said. 'I have a gown that would look perfect on you. Would you mind? I thought it would be fun to dress up as it's a special day. But we don't have to. If you'd rather not...'

'No, no, that would be cool. We could do that. Not sure if Ben will go for a suit, though.'

'I'm sure he will get into the spirit of things, if everyone else is,' Isobel replied, clapping her hands.

'You've made my sister's year,' Alex said to Maddy.

'And what of you, brother?' Isobel added. 'You look like you've been thrown from a horse and dragged through the desert.'

'Charming,' Alex replied, glancing down at his crumpled suit and running a hand through his dark, unruly locks. 'Don't worry, I'll dress up for you, darling sister. Where's Freddie? Is he all right today? It must be hard for him, without Leonora.'

'He'll be up any minute,' Jacques replied.

Freddie and Leonora were Ben and Madison's ancestors, who had also become vampires during the nineteenth century while on an archaeological dig in Cappadocia with Alexandre's family. These days, Madison and Ben were the only humans living in the beautiful Marchwood House, but they willingly shared it with their vampire family who they had discovered the previous year bricked up in the basement.

'Where's Ben?' Maddy asked. 'Out on his bike, I guess. Or gone to feed the deer?' Marchwood House had extensive grounds, including woodland, meadows and its very own deer park. Having come through the care system, Maddy and Ben still couldn't quite believe they owned such a grand residence, having inherited it only seventeen months ago from their distant, long dead – or so they thought – ancestors.

The front door slammed.

'Ben?' Maddy called out.

Seconds later, their housekeeper, Esther, puffed into the kitchen, her face flushed and her eyes bright. She took in the sight of everyone in the kitchen and scowled, without passing comment on Isobel and Jacques' lavish attire. 'Right, you lot, out. I can't cook Christmas lunch with everyone cluttering up my kitchen.' Esther and her husband, Morris, lived in a cottage in the grounds of Marchwood. They knew all about the history of the place. Esther's family had been tasked with guarding the vampires until a descendant could be located. Once Madison and Ben moved in, Esther and Morris had taken the orphaned siblings under their wings, in their own unique, grumpy way.

'Merry Christmas, Esther,' Alex said, planting a kiss on her ruddy cheek.

'Yes, well, Merry Christmas, I suppose.'

'You suppose?' Maddy smirked. 'Can I at least stay to make a cup of tea? I'm gasping for a cup. And a slice of toast would be—'

'No. Out, out, out! I'll bring you your tea and toast into the drawing room. And where's young Ben? I suppose he'll be wanting porridge.'

'He's gone out,' Maddy replied. 'Be back any minute, I hope.'

Esther made a harrumphing noise in the back of her throat

and stood with her hands on her hips while she waited for everyone to vacate the cosy warmth of the kitchen. Maddy had long ago given up trying to offer their surly housekeeper any help. The kitchen was Esther's domain and she liked it that way. Occasionally, she might tolerate Ben helping with a few chores, but generally that was her limit.

As Maddy followed the others out of the kitchen, she had a sudden thought and popped her head back around the kitchen door. 'Esther...'

'Hmm?' Esther replied, her back to Maddy as she rummaged around in one of the cupboards.

'Thank you,' Maddy said.

Esther paused for a second and grunted something unintelligible before continuing her rummaging.

'You know,' Maddy continued, 'for your help... and Morris's help. And for looking after us and everything. Thank you.'

The older couple had recently discovered that Freddie's sister, Leonora, had betrayed Madison and the others. Morris had put himself in considerable danger to keep Ben and Maddy safe. Madison knew she owed the two of them a lot. Not to mention the fact that they did an amazing job of keeping them fed and watered. Esther and Morris were only meant to look after the house until it was returned to its rightful owners. But Maddy and Ben needed them, without parents of their own, and they'd become part of the fabric of the house.

'Yes, well, Christmas dinner will be ready at two p.m. sharp,' Esther replied, ignoring Maddy's thanks. 'So if you could all be seated in the dining room by five to two.'

'Will you and Morris eat with us?'

'Well.' Esther straightened up and smoothed down her apron. 'I don't know about that. Morris and I are—'

'Have you got other plans?' Maddy asked.

'Not plans as such, no, but—'

'Great. You can eat with us, then. We can all sit down together. And me and Ben will help you serve.'

'I don't want you two getting in my way.'

'Good,' Maddy said firmly. 'That's settled.' As Maddy retreated from the kitchen, the front door slammed behind her.

'Hey, Mads.'

'Shortie!' she cried, swirling around towards her brother who was shedding his coat and hat.

'Happy Christmas,' he said.

'Happy Christmas, Benny boy.' She pulled him into a hug, and he tipped his tousled head towards her so she could kiss the top of it. 'Where've you been?'

'Just cycled down to see how the deer were doing. Took them some greens. The old stag's really tame. He's actually eating out of my hand now.'

'Cool. Will he eat from *my* hand, do you think?'

'He might. He doesn't really know you, though. We could try.'

'After lunch?'

'Yeah. Brilliant.'

'Is it cold out?' she asked, loving how much enthusiasm Ben had for their home and grounds.

'Nah. It's okay.'

'Esther's making porridge if you're hungry.'

'Yeah, starving.'

After a decadent morning of lazing around and allowing Isobel to deck them out in nineteenth-century finery, everyone finally sat down at the dining table. Ben in a suit and Madison wearing a crimson gown and a beautiful gold necklace – a heart-shaped ruby inside a wreath of rose-cut diamonds and tiny round garnets. It had been Alex's mother's necklace, and Isobel said that, with her colouring, it looked better on Maddy than on her, so she should keep it. Maddy kept touching it, feeling as though she were playing a part in some lavish TV costume drama.

The already impressive dining room had been decorated to within an inch of its life. Candles glimmered on the polished dark wood table, giving off the spicy-warm aroma of citrus fruit and pine needles. Colourful Christmas crackers and gold-trimmed napkins took their place beside sparkling crystalware, gleaming plates and heavy silver cutlery. Sprigs of holly and mistletoe adorned the walls, and russet-and-scarlet flames blazed in the inglenook fireplace. To complete the festive scene, a faint chorus of pre-recorded traditional Christmas carols swirled around them.

Seated to her left, Alex kept glancing at Madison. Brushing her cheek with the tip of a finger, or squeezing her hand, and smiling into her eyes with a tenderness that made her melt. This, right here, was a happiness so rare and pure that Maddy expected to awaken back in her London foster home any minute, the whole experience having been a beautiful yet impossible dream. She still couldn't believe that she'd inherited this magical, beautiful house, and that it had led her to Alex and to her new family. Something she'd never dared to dream of for her and Ben.

She grinned at her brother who sat opposite, dressed in one of Freddie's suits, looking like a proper nineteenth-century gentleman. He pulled a stupid face at her, trying to hide his embarrassment. Maddy attempted to give him a gentle reassuring kick in the shin but couldn't quite stretch her leg under the wide expanse of table, so she settled on sticking her tongue out at him instead.

It was a bright blustery day outside, but the shutters were pulled tightly closed and the curtains drawn, giving the illusion of night. No one mentioned the fact that half the dinner party wouldn't be eating because, of course, vampires didn't eat in the same way as humans did. Everyone simply wanted to enjoy the day. The conversation was light and fun, with no talk of the dramatic events of the past month. Only Freddie was a little more subdued than usual. The absence of his sister, Leonora, must have weighed on his mind. But her name wasn't uttered by anyone. It was as though the day was a bubble, separate from the terror and violence they'd so recently experienced. A warm cocoon of family and normalcy and love. Even Esther, dressed in a tweed skirt and smart white blouse, dropped her stern face and while she didn't exactly smile, she didn't exactly scowl either. Morris was positively jovial by comparison.

Maddy would have savoured each second for longer. Would have revelled deeper in the easy warmth and comfort. She would have laughed louder and captured each perfect moment in her memory with more clarity and meaning, had she known what was approaching. As it was, she would remember this Christmas Day as one of the happiest of her life. For how could she have foreseen the dark, dark times that were about to descend?

CHAPTER THREE

It regarded the house and its occupants. Fascinated and absorbed by what it saw through the myriad panes of glass. The lights winking on and off. The bright colours and the constant chatter.

It mimicked their smiles and touched a hand to its own mouth to feel the upward curve of flesh.

It had been too long since it had felt the thrill of the hunt. Could it remember what to do? Now it gave a true inward smile. Of course it could remember.

Soon it would be time. But not yet.

No.

This was enough for now. To watch...

And wait.

CHAPTER FOUR

Full to bursting from an over-indulgent Christmas dinner followed by an afternoon of snacks, chocolate and other treats laid on by Esther, Maddy trudged up the stairs to change into something more comfortable than the figure-crushing gown Isobel had squeezed her into that morning. The dress was torturous. Imagine having to dress like that 24-7? No thanks. Maddy had to admit, she did feel glamorous and gorgeous – not at all like herself – but the thought of unlacing the crippling bodice made her so-o-o happy. She absolutely should not have had that last piece of Christmas cake. She paused on the stairs to rub her complaining stomach.

Esther had outdone herself. There was so much food, she and Ben would probably be eating turkey and goose until February. Maddy was sure Esther had catered for all eight of them, despite knowing that four would not be touching a single morsel. Today, Maddy had almost forgotten what the others really were. That they were not human, they drank blood, that they were essentially killers who chose not to kill. Instead, they sustained themselves by drinking from humans who were at death's door, easing their transitions with bliss instead of pain.

The events of the past few weeks had shown Maddy what her vampire family was actually capable of. Their powers were incredible. And yet, weren't humans just as dangerous? Granted, they couldn't do as much damage without weapons, but they still had dual natures, just as there were evil vampires, there were good ones, too. Just as there were evil humans, so there were good ones. But this wasn't the time to be pondering the natures of vampires and human. No. She had to get out of these clothes before they did her ribcage permanent damage. Plus Ben was waiting for her to feed the deer.

As she continued up the wooden staircase, Maddy caught her breath, sure she'd glimpsed somebody's shadow on the half-landing above. But everyone was downstairs, weren't they? The light from the hall below struggled to reach this far up the stairs, and she couldn't really see things properly. She stared again, but there was no one there. With a shiver, she continued upwards, past the empty half-landing and onto the upper staircase, suddenly desperate to reach the light switch. Part of her wanted to turn around... to double check. But, what if someone was actually there? She felt clammy, aware of her heart pumping double time.

She shouldn't be so pathetic. Probably just ate too much that was all. Too much rich food giving her palpitations. She lived in a houseful of vampires, for goodness' sake, and now she was jumping at imaginary shapes and shadows. *Pull yourself together, Madison Greene*, she told herself. She stopped at the top of the stairs, gave herself a mental shake, turned around... and screamed.

'Alex, you scared the life out of me!' Maddy stabbed at the light switch with her forefinger and sank down onto the top step in relief, her legs soft and her heart still pounding. Alexandre had followed her up the stairs and was now staring with a bemused smile on his face.

'I didn't mean to startle you,' he said, crouching next to her.

Maddy put a hand to her chest. 'I thought there was someone up here, but it must have been a trick of the light. And then I saw you and nearly had a heart attack. I don't know what's wrong with me. Why am I so jumpy?'

'There's no one here,' Alex replied, helping her to her feet. 'I would know if there was. And there's nothing wrong with you. It's not surprising you're nervous after everything that's happened these past weeks – being kidnapped by the Cappadocian vampires, chased across the snowy plains, and then coming within a whisper of death. Most people would have taken to their beds for a month after going through such an ordeal. But you... you've handled it all so incredibly well. I'm not sure I would have been so calm had I been a human in your situation.'

'Yeah, well, I still feel like an idiot for overreacting.' Maddy's heartbeat slowed as she gazed into Alex's concerned eyes. 'I think this dress is cutting off the circulation to my brain and making me hallucinate.'

Alex placed a hand on Maddy's forehead. 'Hmm, yes, you are feeling a little warm around the temples. We should get you out of that gown at once.'

'Alexandre! Are you taking advantage of my mental state for your own benefit?'

'Yes. Yes, I am.' Alexandre grinned.

Any residual fear Maddy may have had dissolved as Alex swung her up into his arms in a swish of petticoats and satin, as if she weighed nothing, and carried her through into their room – the opulent red-and-gold bedroom that had once belonged to her ancestors, Leonora and Freddie's parents. Alex lay Maddy down on the brocade coverlet of the four-poster bed, where she instantly sat up again.

'Get me out of this thing,' she gasped, gesturing at her dress. 'With pleasure.'

Maddy groaned with relief as Alex's deft fingers released

her from the nineteenth-century instrument of torture. 'That feels so good.'

'It looks good, too,' he said, his eyes travelling over her underwear-clad body.

Annoyingly, Maddy blushed. Alex wrapped his arms around her and brought her in close to him. Their kiss made Maddy forget everything else. It was just the two of them, his mouth on hers, and the deep sensations within her body. He picked her up and she wrapped her legs around his hard vampire body.

'Maddy!' Ben's voice swept up the stairs. 'Mads? You coming?' Madison loved being with Ben and having her new extended family around her, but sometimes she wished it could be just her and Alex. If only for a few days at least. With no interruptions or obligations. Just the two of them, together. Would that ever happen? She felt Alex's smile beneath her own, and reluctantly uncoiled her legs from around his waist.

'Just a minute!' she yelled back. 'I'm coming.'

As dusk fell, Maddy and Ben walked briskly down the driveway towards the deer park, Ben carrying a plastic bag of vegetable peelings in one hand and a torch in the other in case the light faded completely before they headed home again.

'It's good to be back here, Shortie,' Maddy said.

'Can you stop calling me that, Mads?'

'What? Shortie?'

'Yeah. It's kind of embarrassing.'

Maddy thrust out her bottom lip, making a sad face. 'Aww, Shortie.'

'Well, okay,' Ben said with a sigh, 'but not in front of my friends.'

Maddy grinned and squeezed his cheeks. 'I can't promise, but I'll try.'

'We're here.' Ben unlatched the gate. 'Morris said the deer have been at Marchwood for hundreds of years. Our ancestors used to hunt them. I wonder if Freddie used to. He better not try that now.'

Maddy followed her brother through the gate, and they headed across the grass. 'How're we gonna find them?' Maddy asked. 'They could be anywhere. This place is massive.'

'You just have to keep walking and calling. They'll come eventually.' Ben called out to them and Maddy copied his call, feeling faintly ridiculous. His face was animated, eyes bright in the fast-fading light, and Maddy felt a sudden rush of love. It was amazing to see him so settled and happy. She hoped recent events hadn't traumatised him too much. Ben wasn't one for talking about his problems. She had to ease things out of him.

'How are you doing, Benny boy?' she asked in between calls.

'All right.'

'No.' Maddy stopped walking and laid a hand on his shoulder to make him look her way. 'No, I mean it. Really. How are you doing? After everything you've been through over the past few weeks. It must've been horrible for you stuck here without us, not knowing who to trust.'

'Me?' Ben's eyes quirked upwards. 'How am I doing? What about you, Mads? You're the one who was kidnapped by vampires. They nearly killed you.'

'I'm fine. But stop changing the subject. We're supposed to be talking about you.'

'Shh.' Ben put a finger to his lips. 'Look,' he whispered.

Maddy followed the line of his finger to the edge of the woods and saw dark shapes emerge from the foliage. Ben reached into the carrier bag and pulled out a handful of cabbage leaves, thrusting his hand towards the shyly approaching creatures. It looked as though they were on tiptoe as they daintily made their way across the grass to them. Maddy felt a little nervous. She hadn't done this for a while. They were quite big and there were a lot of them.

'Are you sure this is safe?' she whispered. 'They won't... charge at us or anything?'

Ben gave a snort. 'I think you're thinking of a bull.'

'Well, I dunno, do I? They're wild animals, aren't they?'

'Hold your hand out and take some of this.' Ben laid some leaves on the flat of Maddy's palm. 'Now call out softly.'

Maddy did as she was told. As the twenty or so deer approached, she held her breath. They were so beautiful, with their shaggy red coats and shiny button eyes. They looked as nervous as she felt, but it didn't stop them coming to say hello. One had already reached Ben and had taken the proffered cabbage in one delicate swipe. Now another approached Maddy, its muzzle soft as velvet as it lifted the leaves from her hand. Maddy's heart gave a little leap and she grinned. This was definitely as awesome as Ben had promised it would be.

Twenty minutes later, their bags empty, Maddy and Ben said farewell to the herd and made their way back across the field towards the driveway. The sun had set, and Ben switched on the torch to illuminate their journey, their warm breath clouding their faces.

'Shall we come back and give them some more?' Ben asked.

'What, *now*?'

'Yeah.'

'You come back if you like, Shortie. I'm going to be a slob and veg out in the lounge for the rest of the evening.'

'Did you enjoy feeding them, though?'

'I loved it. Thanks for bringing me out here.'

'I think I might like to work with animals when I'm older,' he added. 'Be like a vet or something.'

'That's a brilliant idea. You'd make an amazing vet.'

'D'you think so?'

'I know so.'

'Cool.'

Once back inside, Maddy shed her coat and joined the

others in the lounge while Ben visited Esther in the kitchen to beg for more deer fodder. Maddy had enjoyed feeling them, but now she was looking forward to relaxing in the warmth.

In the drawing room, a fire blazed in the hearth and the television played, but Alexandre barely registered the blur of gaudy images or the grating sounds of canned laughter. The others, however, were transfixed by the comedy show; Freddie and Jacques giggling and snorting at the characters' antics. He envied them their exuberant release valve of emotion. Esther and Morris appeared happy enough, each seated on a wingback chair, chuckling at the screen, sipping at their almost-empty glasses of sloe gin. And Isobel with a half-smile on her face as her eyes flicked from the television screen to the boys' beaming faces. She, too, seemed at peace. Ben had gone back out to feed more of his beloved deer. And, like a contented cat, Madison had fallen asleep curled up next to Alex on the velvet sofa. Her head on his chest, her breathing slow and regular. Relaxed. But Alexandre couldn't relax. Hadn't been able to relax since they got home from Cappadocia. He was coiled up tighter than a rattlesnake about to bite. The threat of danger had wrapped itself around him like a choking shroud.

For Madison's sake, he had feigned happiness today. Tried to give her the Christmas she deserved. He had thoroughly ruined the day for her last year – what with almost killing her brother and everything – so it was only fair he should try to make it up to her this year. But the pressure of pretending everything was fine was almost too much to bear. His brain was spinning too fast, buzzing and whirring, trying to come up with a foolproof plan to keep them all safe. However, since Alex had rejected his demand to bend the knee and join him in Turkey, the Cappadocian Emperor now had Alexandre and the other

Marchwood vampires locked in his sights. How could Alexandre fight against such a powerful adversary? It was only a matter of time before the enemy came for him. Came for them all.

Not for the first time, Alex wished he had someone else to confide in. How he yearned to hear the reassuring tones of his father, with his no-nonsense advice and guidance. Or to be soothed by the gentle voice of his mother, saying she would always be there for him no matter what. Only she wasn't there anymore. Neither of his parents was. They were long dead and buried. It was just him, with his younger siblings to care for. And poor Freddie, whose sister, Leonora, had betrayed them all. Alex actually missed Leonora a lot. He had come to think of her like a sensible sister, his voice of reason... until she wasn't anymore. She was now the voice of madness. Becoming a vampire had changed her more than it had changed any of them. She had lost herself.

And Madison... God, how he loved that brave, feisty girl, but he didn't want to burden her with his fears. He knew she would want to know his thoughts, would be angry that he kept them from her. But he couldn't worry her with this. Not so soon after her ordeal. It wouldn't be fair. It was up to him to protect them all. His family. Yet how was he supposed to keep them all safe? He simply wasn't strong enough. Not against the Cappadocian vampires.

Perhaps they should all leave Marchwood. Escape to another part of the world where no one knew them. But where? And was anywhere *truly* safe? They would always be looking over their shoulders. Never be able to feel entirely free. No. The only way to deal with the threat was to face it head on. But they had tried that once already. And they had failed. Could they succeed if they tried again?

Alex shifted in his seat. He needed to get out of the house. To be alone. To order his thoughts. Gently shifting Madison away from his body, he stood up and eased her back down on the sofa, on two plump pillows. She gave a soft sigh but didn't wake. Isobel looked up enquiringly.

'I'm going for some fresh air,' he said.

'Very well.' She turned back to the television, and Alex left the room.

As soon as he stepped outside into the blissfully dark night, Alexandre felt the chill of something bad. Of something he didn't want to know. He gave a low growl and wished he could return to the drawing room. To turn back the clock a few moments and sit in blissful ignorance of whatever was happening out here. But he had no choice. He would have to press on through the dark.

CHAPTER FIVE

Its rapturous surveillance had been interrupted. The creature sensed the intruders' intent. A cold, bright murderous intent that would bring them joy. Would they approach the house and make for the coven leader? The creature could not allow that to happen. It had already marked its prey and would not permit another to spoil the hunt.

For the hunt must happen with the proper ritual. Slowly, methodically, carefully. Until all the elements were in perfect alignment. Nothing could disrupt it. Not after having waited for so long. The creature was too weak. Its power diminished after years of starvation.

Something like anger flitted through its body, and it came to a decision. It would have to intervene. It would have to stop them.

CHAPTER SIX

Alexandre ran. It only took a matter of seconds to reach the deer park, but it felt like an eternity. They had all been slaughtered. Around thirty of the magnificent creatures lay on their sides with their throats slit, scattered about the wet meadow like some grotesque modern-art installation. The stag lay among them, neck twisted up, antlers like dead branches. The sweet metallic tang of fresh blood assaulted Alexandre's nostrils like a knife to his own throat. But that wasn't what made Alexandre stop and almost fall to his knees. No. It was the sight of the fallen figure in the centre of the bloody scene.

Please, God. No.

Alex moved quickly, but he felt as though he were in a dream. Not willing to confirm what he knew was true, but unable to stop moving. Now he stood above the body on the grass and stared in mute horror. His knees buckled and he sank to the ground. The frigid moisture from the grass soaked his trousers and seeped through to his skin. His hand shook as he reached out to touch Ben's face. Cheeks pale but still warm. Only his hands were ice cold. The boy lay on his side, eyes closed, torch by his side, its beam shining across the grass into the woods.

Alexandre didn't need to take Ben's pulse to know his young friend was mortally wounded. Alex's appearance must have interrupted the attacker, for the knife was still embedded in Ben's chest. The boy had maybe a minute or two left before his life was gone. Alex knew he must get him back to the house as quickly as possible. He wanted to cry and scream into the black and bloody night. But his grief and anger would have to wait. Instead, he narrowed his eyes and scented the air, but the blood-soaked deer corpses masked everything beyond. Whoever had done this barbarous act was gone. Despite the use of a knife, it was most definitely the work of an immortal. No human could have come and gone quickly enough to elude detection from a vampire. This was not a warning. This was a message. First, they had taken Madison. Now they had attacked Ben. From kidnap to murder... there was nowhere left to go after that. It was kill or be killed.

As he scooped Ben into his arms, the scent of fresh human blood in such close proximity blindsided him. Alex staggered, resisting the urge to bend his head and drink. He tightened his jaw and clamped his teeth. How could the thought of such vileness cross his mind? He tried to shake these thoughts as he turned back towards the house, hating himself for his base instincts. As he ran with the warm weight of his young friend in his arms, the lights from the windows up ahead blurred with crashing waves of self-disgust, making him suddenly yearn to join Ben in unconsciousness. His dear friend's blood had been spilt and Alex wanted some of it for himself. He was indeed a demon. A devil, bringing death and destruction wherever he went. He had failed to keep Madison safe. And now her brother was dying.

In a moment, Alexandre would have to tell the girl he loved that her brother was grievously harmed. That he would certainly lose his life. Ben was her world. Her only true family. Madison would be devastated. How could he begin to tell her this impossible news?

Isobel, Freddie and Jacques were on their feet before Alex entered the sitting room, Ben's limp body in his arms.

'Eh? What?' Morris and Esther glanced from the TV to the vampires, confused.

Curled on the sofa where Alex had left her only twenty minutes earlier, Madison still slept, safe in ignorance. Was it really such a short time ago that he had left the house? It felt like days.

'What has happened?' Isobel hissed, crossing the room in less than a second. 'No! Not Ben!' She put a hand to Ben's face and looked into Alexandre's eyes for some kind of reassurance that he would be all right.

Alex shook his head and looked away, ignoring the questioning faces around him, his heart heavy as a rock, hollow as a dead tree.

The room fell quiet, all eyes on Madison who still slept.

'Maddy,' Alex murmured. 'Madison, wake up.' The fire spat and crackled as a seam of pine resin caught alight, flooding the room with its Christmassy aroma, momentarily masking the scent of blood.

Maddy stretched and opened her eyes. Her face lit up at the sight of Alexandre, but her smile vanished immediately as she saw Ben in his arms.

All words of comfort choked in Alex's throat. A single red tear slid down his cheek.

'Alex! Why are you carrying Ben? What the hell's going on? What's that knife doing... *No!*' She leapt to her feet and put her hands on her brother's face, stared in horror at the knife in his chest.

Alexandre's stomach lurched as he saw the maelstrom of

fear and panic in her pale blue eyes. 'I'm sorry,' he said. 'I'm so, so sorry.'

'Not Ben,' she whispered. 'Tell me he's okay, Alex. Tell me he's okay.' She gazed up at him, with a pleading look that broke his heart.

He shook his head. 'He's still breathing. But... it's not good. I was too late to stop them. I'm so, so sorry.' His words were inadequate, as he knew they would be.

Maddy's knees gave way, but Isobel was there to gather her in her arms. A hailstorm of questions came at Alex from everyone, but he only had time for Madison now. As Alex lay Ben down on the sofa, Maddy disentangled herself from Isobel's arms. 'We need to get help,' Madison cried, turning to face Alex, and then back to her brother.

'Ben! Ben, wake up. It's me, Ben.' She kissed his cheek and lifted one of his eyelids. 'Call bloody 999,' she yelled at Alex. 'Don't just stand there. We need an ambulance.'

'He won't make it, Madison,' Alex said, hating himself for saying the words. Wishing they weren't true. 'It's a mortal wound.'

'Where's my phone?' she muttered. 'Any of you got a phone on you?' she shrieked. 'Call 999.'

'Madison, I'm sorry, but he will be gone before they even arrive,' Alex said. 'I can sense his life slipping. He has a minute at most.' Alexandre knew she wouldn't listen to him, and he didn't blame her.

When she looked back up at him, there was fresh rage glittering in her eyes. 'Vampires?' she asked.

He nodded.

'The bastards stabbed him!' she cried. 'They bloody stabbed him. My baby brother! How could they even... This can't be happening. It can't be true,' she gasped. 'Why? Why would they do this? He's nothing to do with any of this... madness. He's a child, for God's sake.'

Alex couldn't speak. Couldn't tell her that the Cappadocian vampires didn't care who Ben was. Didn't care what age he was. That they had no regard for human life. All they cared about was power – keeping everything under their control. And if Alex and his family would not bow down to them, they would kill them one by one, starting with the least important and working their way up. If Alexandre didn't stop them, he would be forced to watch as they worked their way through his family and friends. Until every last one of them was dead. Including him.

'Do something!' she pleaded. 'One of you! Any of you! Save my brother.' She straightened up and tried to shoulder her way past Alex. 'I'm getting my phone. It's... I think it's in the kitchen.'

Morris caught her arm as she passed him. 'If Alex is right, then there's no time. Let me have a look at the little fella. I'm no doctor, but I know what's what.'

She glared at him, and then her shoulders sagged. 'Okay, Morris. But you better be able to save him.'

The others parted to let Morris through, Maddy close behind him.

He crouched down, put a finger under Ben's chin and tipped it back. Then he looked down at the knife which had penetrated Ben's coat and clothing. Morris drew a chunky penknife from his trouser pocket and flipped out a pair of scissors which he used to cut away Ben's clothing from around the handle of the protruding knife.

'This dagger's old... an ancient weapon,' Morris said as he worked. 'Leather grip, brass guard and pommel. The owner of this won't be best pleased to have left it behind. You get a look at the bugger, Alex?'

'No. But it was one of our kind.'

The pale skin on Ben's chest was now visible, almost

translucent. Shocking to see, with such a large weapon sticking out of it.

'It went straight in,' Morris said. 'No twisting. No bruising from the guard. But the blade on this must be at least eight inches. It's a miracle the lad's still breathing. I'll warrant there's internal bleeding and a whole lot more besides.' He looked up at Maddy. 'We can't take this weapon out of him, love. That'll kill him instantly.'

'So what can we do?'

Morris didn't reply.

'I said, what can we do?' Her voice rose up into a wail.

'What's this?' Morris said. He was pulling at the wound where the knife had split the skin.

'What are you doing, Morris?' Alexandre leant forward to see that Morris had something between his thick fingers, his lined face further creased into a frown.

'What is it?' Maddy tried to snatch the thing from Morris's hand, but Alex got there first.

A scrap of blood-stained paper. A note. Alexandre read it aloud:

> *You will come*
> *Or one by one*
> *Your lives shall be undone*

No one spoke as the words sank in. This confirmed everything Alexandre had feared. The Cappadocians wanted them to join with them. If they refused, this was to be their fate.

'I don't care what the stupid note says,' Maddy cried. 'Alex, you can get him to the hospital, can't you? Carry him there! You can move like lightning, so—'

'I would have done it if I could,' Alexandre replied. 'But it's too late for that. And the movement would only have made things worse.'

'Isn't it at least worth trying?' Maddy cried. 'I'll call an ambulance, then. Should've done that straight away.' She turned, but Morris straightened up and put a hand on her shoulder, holding her back.

'It's no use, love. Best let him go peaceful. Be beside him when he passes. I'm sorry. Truly I am. I love the lad like my own.' His voice broke at this last admission. He turned and walked back towards Esther who was leaning against the door-frame for support, grief clouding her normally sharp, clear eyes.

'No, Morris,' Maddy cried. 'Come back. You said you could save him. That you knew... stuff.' Maddy's eyes held fear and horror and all the pain a person could know. Alex could hardly bear to look at her. And then she turned her stricken eyes on him.

'Save him, Alex,' she said. 'You can save him. *Please.*'

'Me?'

'Yes.' Her eyes lit with a fevered hope. '*You.*'

'You know I would if I could, but—'

'Turn him,' she cried. 'Into one of you. You can do it.'

Alexandre recoiled. 'You can't mean... I've never—'

'Doesn't matter if you've never done it before,' she replied. 'It was done to you. So you can do it to him.'

'He's still a child,' Isobel interjected. 'He would remain a child forever. He might not want—'

Maddy turned on her. 'So you'd rather he was dead? Is that it?'

'No, of course not, but—'

'What if it was Jacques?' Maddy cried. 'Wouldn't you try everything you could?'

Isobel shook her head but didn't reply.

'Do it!' Maddy cried, turning her head wildly to look at them all. 'One of you, try to save my brother!'

'I'll try, Mads,' Jacques said, taking a step forward.

'No,' Alex growled, grabbing his brother's arm as he made his way towards Ben.

Maddy tried to peel Alexandre's hand off Jacques's arm. 'Get off him, Alex. He's trying to save my brother. Which is more than you're doing!'

Her words stung, but Alex knew it was only the grief speaking. 'Maddy, I only meant to say *no* to Jacques, because *I* will do it. If you really think this is what you want, I will try. But please think about it a moment more. You are grieving. You're angry now. You are making a decision that will affect him for eternity. He is still only a boy. Only fourteen years of age. He would remain a boy forever. Would Ben want that? As the years pass, will he resent remaining a child?'

'None of that even matters!' she cried. 'All that matters is that you can bring him back. Ben is dying. He's *dying*. And you have the power to stop that. So just try! You have to try. He can't not be here. Please. I'm begging you. After all the bad stuff that keeps happening, make something good happen. Make being *what you are* something good.'

The way she said *what you are* made Alexandre feel ashamed. He caught Jacques's eye and could tell his brother felt the same way. *What they were* were monsters. A coven of vampires gathered around the body of a mortal boy. Leave him to die, or turn him into one of them. Could they even do it? Was it possible?

He glanced back at Esther and Morris. The fire cast wavering shadows across their faces as tears rolled down their cheeks. He had never seen them remotely ruffled by anything before. But, it was true, the older couple loved Ben like he was family. It was impossible *not* to love the boy. He had a way of getting under your skin. Alex raised an eyebrow at them, questioningly. Esther nodded and Morris gave a small shrug. They too were giving permission.

Alexandre knelt before Ben's body. He felt the weight of

collective apprehension in the warm room. The intoxicating smell of blood making him dizzy. He was scared he might lose control. But then he pictured his young friend alive. The vibrant boy with his sweet and kind sensibility and cheeky sense of humour. Alex bent his head, lifted Ben's wrist, unsheathed his fangs, split the delicate skin, and began to drink.

But as the blood flowed, Alex knew it wouldn't work. Ben was barely alive. His warm spirit was departing. His body was here, but his blood was cooling and nothing on this earth would bring him back.

Finally, Ben's fluttering heart grew still. His eyes remained closed. But Alexandre continued to drink, unwilling to stop and face Madison with the look that would break her heart.

CHAPTER SEVEN

There were two of them. Good, strong vampires of ancient lineage. Not leaders, but warriors. It was not in the creature's nature to dispose of such specimens in this ill-thought-out manner, especially not after centuries of drought. It seemed... a waste. But it could not risk them upsetting its hunt.

Moving with cunning and guile, blending, chameleon-like, into the dark winter landscape, with a single thought, the creature was beside the two vampires. They had already slaughtered the animals and were preparing to deal the child a mortal blow. Their hearts were pleased, and they were thirsty for death. But Alexandre was now approaching. These two would try to kill him. The creature must be quick.

Before the vampires could discern what had happened, the creature had disarmed one of them and used its own blade to sever its head from its body. As the other vampire plunged its knife into the child, the creature gave it the same treatment. Both vampire bodies exploded into pale grey dust.

The creature blew their ashes to the wind, before disappearing back into the darkness.

CHAPTER EIGHT

The night was finally still. Quiet and dark and shrouded in pain and disbelief. Madison had cried herself to sleep. Sobbed into Alex's shoulder, his shirt salted with her grief. Even now, asleep in their bed, she moaned and whimpered as though tortured. Alexandre could not bear it. But bear it he must, for he had brought this terror and heartache to her door. He could not turn from the knowledge. The taste of Ben's blood was still fresh in his mouth, both sweet and repellent in equal measure. The boy's death making his own body sing with life.

What must he do now? How could he fix this? Not for the first time he considered the possibility of all of them fleeing to the other side of the world. But no. He must face it and fix it. Or die trying.

Morris and Esther had returned to their own house, amid protestations that it was unsafe. In the end, Jacques and Freddie had accompanied them across the meadow, ensuring they reached their cottage safely. The others were now mourning below in their basement suite. None thought it wise to leave the house again tonight. Not while they were under attack. Alex didn't think the Cappadocians would try anything else so soon.

They would give Alex and his family the opportunity to consider the message and act accordingly. But there was no way Alex would live under *their* rule. That would be no life at all.

Images of Ben came to Alex unbidden, and he wished he could sleep to obliterate their brightness. He remembered how helpless and alone he himself had felt when he had thought his own siblings as good as dead. At least then he had had some modicum of hope that they would awaken. Madison had none. She had nothing but an empty heart and time to grieve. How would they recover from this?

A slight thud made him start. An eyelash flicker. A beat. The pulsing of blood in newly formed veins. The beginning of life.

Could it be?

Alexandre sat up, carefully disengaging his arm from beneath Madison's sleeping form, peeling back the covers and sliding out of bed without a sound. But before he could reach the bedroom door, it opened.

Alex realised he was holding his breath. He released it with a rush of gratitude.

'Ben.'

Alive. Yet not alive.

So, it hadn't failed after all. It had worked. Ben was one of them. And, by the look of him, he was thirsty. Ben's eyes were fixed on his sister with a grim determination. The boy still wore his clothing – his coat and shirt cut open, to reveal a pale, unscarred chest. No sign of any knife wound. Earlier, after his heart had ceased beating, Morris had removed the knife, and Alex had carried Ben upstairs and laid him on his bed. Now the boy was here.

Alex couldn't believe their hasty, desperate plan had worked. He felt a rush of pride and a sense of... ownership. He, Alex, had done this. He had brought Ben back from death. He moved towards his newly awakened friend, but Ben paid him no heed.

'Ben,' Alex whispered. 'Ben, stop. Come with me.'

But Ben didn't appear to be listening. 'Thirsty,' he hissed, in a voice that sounded nothing like the boy he knew. Ben took another step towards his sleeping sister.

Alex glanced back at Maddy, terrified she would awaken and offer her blood to her brother. Alex knew what this would cost her. She would be ill for days. She may not even recover from it. He couldn't risk that happening.

Now, behind Ben on the landing, stood Isobel, Jacques and Freddie. Alexandre raised a finger to his lips and inclined his head at Ben. As one, the vampires converged on the boy. Alex covered Ben's mouth with his hand to prevent him crying out, and somehow they got him down the stairs and out of the front door. Alex had him restrained in his arms. Ben wasn't fighting against him, but he was straining in the direction of the shuttered house, his eyes drawn upwards to the only human in the vicinity.

They probably had a couple of hours until dawn. Enough time to find a warm body for Ben to drink from. Someone in pain and close to death. Someone whose passing they could ease.

'Belle, will you stay here?' Alex asked. 'In case Maddy wakes up. I don't want her to wonder where I am. Or go to Ben's room and find him gone. And we need to keep Maddy safe in case Ben somehow escapes us.'

'Of course,' Isobel replied. 'Where will you take him?'

'Not far. We'll find someone close by and bring Ben back as soon as we're able.'

'Madison will be so happy.' Belle beamed. 'I can't believe it actually worked. Shouldn't we wake her now?'

'Not until he's fed,' Alex replied.

'D'you think Ben will mind?' Freddie asked. 'I mean, that he's a...'

'I don't know,' Alex replied. 'It's a bit late for that. He is what he is.'

'I think he'll love it,' Jacques said. 'He's always wanted to do all the things we can do.'

'We can talk about it later,' Alex replied. 'Right now, he's in an agony of thirst. We have to help him. Don't you remember how it felt?'

Isobel shuddered. 'I would rather forget. At least Ben has us to help him through it. Our experience was somewhat different.'

Alexandre remembered the terror and shock of being turned by those vicious underground creatures, and the later agony of changes to his body. The pain of being alive again. He knew exactly how Ben was feeling. Inhuman. The pull to drink drowning out all other thought and reason.

'We'll come with you,' Freddie said. 'Help find someone for him.'

'Good,' Alex said. 'But we must stick together. Whoever tried to kill Ben, may still be out there somewhere. Belle, you must stay inside the house. Don't leave for anything.'

She nodded and left. The front door closed with a loud *thunk* behind her.

'Come,' Alex said, his heart suddenly ballooning with joy that Ben wasn't dead. 'Let's go.'

Her face felt swollen and raw. Like she'd been punched. She tasted her own tears and realised she'd been crying in her sleep. Please let this be a terrible nightmare. Let it not be true. Hadn't she had enough pain in her life? Her father gone, her mother dead, and now this. Her beautiful brother. Why couldn't she die too? Put an end to it all. Stop the hurting.

Madison opened her eyes. Where was Alex? Her eyes lighted on the note on his empty pillow.

I wanted to let you sleep. Come down to the basement the moment you wake. We need to talk. It's important.

Alex was wrong. Nothing was important anymore. She scrunched up the note. There was nothing to talk about. Her brother had been murdered and she was probably next on the hit list. But she didn't care about that. She couldn't face talking to them. Going over what had happened. What they should or shouldn't do. None of that even mattered anymore. How could it? Ben was dead. Her sweet, funny, kind baby brother was gone. The last real member of her family. It had been the two of them against the world. He had been her responsibility and she had let him down. Big time. She needed to get out of this place. To walk? No, she needed to drive fast, with her music turned up loud enough to drown out all thought. And she didn't want to speak to anyone. Her grief was too raw.

Leaving her nest of covers, she stumbled across the room to draw back the curtains. But the room still lay in darkness so she fiddled with the latch and opened the shuttered French windows which clattered against the outside walls. Bright swathes of sunlight enveloped her, stinging her swollen eyes, and she raised a hand to shield them against the glare. The frigid morning air shivered her skin and burned at her throat. It was wrong for the sun to be shining today. It should be raining. Pouring. There should be a storm lashing at the windows. Rolling thunder and angry lightning. Not this sunshine and brightness. It was... disrespectful. Wrong.

Madison stood for a moment, trying to remember what life had been like this time yesterday. So recent, and yet a lifetime ago. But she couldn't think back that far. All she saw in her mind was Ben's small bare chest with that great huge knife sticking out.

Without bothering to shower, or even brush her teeth, she pulled a pair of sweats over her pyjamas and tugged a hoodie over her head. Leaving her bedroom, she turned towards Ben's room and reached for the door. But she couldn't bear it. She was too scared to go in. To see her brother's small, lifeless body. Instead, she briefly rested her forehead on the wooden door and took a breath. Wiping stray tears from her eyes, she straightened up and jogged downstairs.

The roads were still empty. Maddy glanced at the dashboard clock: 7.47 a.m. It was Boxing Day morning, which meant soon everyone would be out and about, driving to parks, meadows, forests and rivers to walk off the excesses of yesterday's Christmas dinner. But, for now, the winding roads were hers, and she pressed her foot harder on the accelerator, swinging into the bends and fishtailing out again on the icy tarmac. There was nothing to stop her putting her foot right down to the floor, closing her eyes and driving into a tree. But, for now, the sound of one of Ben's thrash metal mixes on the stereo was keeping her going. The distorted feedback and screaming male vocals channelling her anger and heartbreak.

She remembered yelling at everyone else last night. Blaming them all for Ben's death, because they were vampires, and they had brought danger to their doorstep. But really, it was because of her; she should never have let Ben go outside on his own last night. He had asked Maddy to go back out with him a second time to feed the deer, but she had turned him down. She'd been more concerned with getting back to Alex and the warmth of the living room. She was a terrible sister. It was her fault he was dead.

An orange light appeared on the dash. The fuel light. Damn. Her wallet was at home, but even if she had money on her, Maddy couldn't face going into a petrol station and talking to anyone. Her plan of driving into oblivion was ruined. She took her foot off the gas and stomped on the brake in annoyance, not bothering to pull over to the side of the road. The engine cut out and she yanked at the handbrake. Suddenly the music was too much. Too raw. Too distressing. Maddy had always teased Ben when he'd played it, she'd given a weak imitation of someone headbanging and pulled stupid faces at him while he rolled his eyes and stuck a middle finger up at her. Now, she'd give anything to tease him like that again. To have him irritate her with his ridiculous music. Only, it wasn't ridiculous. It was pure, raging emotion and she felt it deep down in her gut. Aching and churning.

Tears came again in a sudden streaming flood – from her eyes, her nose, her heart, her soul. She switched off the wall of noise and rested her head on the steering wheel. Salt water dripping onto the leather grip and sliding between her shaking fingers.

A sudden beeping horn jolted her from grief. The car behind her had no room to get past her hulking Land Rover. She looked in the rearview, prepared to see an angry face, gearing up to storm out and have a slanging match. But the middle-aged woman in the SUV gave her a worried smile and a short wave. Maddy gulped back another sob, wiped the back of her sleeve across her eyes and nose and restarted the engine. It was time to go home and face the horror of the first day without her brother.

Driving back down the driveway, she felt numb. Her brain refused to focus on anything. Nothing made sense. Everything was pointless. As she pulled up outside the house, her heart sank further. Morris was standing on the drive, and it looked as though he wanted to talk to her. With a sigh, she opened the door and stumbled out, her ankle twisting slightly as she half fell into Morris's arms.

'Whoa, easy there,' he said. 'We've been lookin' for you. Didn't you get Alex's note?'

Maddy extricated herself from his arms and gave a slight shrug.

'You need to come with me.'

'Morris, thanks, but I'd rather—'

'Come on.' He pushed her gently towards the front door, up the steps and into the hallway. 'They're waiting downstairs.'

'Fine.' She would have thought they'd respect her right to grieve in private. But no, apparently she wasn't even allowed to do that. In the kitchen, Esther was waiting by the cellar door. She opened it and gestured downward.

Madison glared at her, but did as the housekeeper asked, making her way to the small doorway and stepping through. She would listen to what Alex and the others had to say. About how they were sorry, and how they had all loved Ben, and then she would tramp back up the stairs, climb into her bed, and sleep for a thousand years. The rest of the world could go to hell.

Everyone was gathered at the foot of the stairs. All on their feet, wearing expectant, *happy* expressions. Standing in front of them, was her brother, Ben. Gloriously alive. She stood on the bottom step, unable to move. Wondering if she was dreaming.

'*Shortie*,' Madison gasped. 'Is it you? Are you really not dead?' Was she dreaming?

He grinned. A smile so pure and full of joy it made her chest hurt with happiness. 'Mads, guess what?' he said, his voice strange and musical, like Christmas bells and summer breezes.

'What?' she breathed, the air suddenly knocked from her lungs.

'I'm a vampire!' he cried.

'Yes, you are, Ben.' She laughed. 'You really are.'

CHAPTER NINE

From its vantage point outside the house, the creature could see and hear everything. It knew all the occupants' fears and worries. All their dreams and desires. It would use them to its advantage. Twist and bend them to its will, so that taking its prey would be like running a finger through whipped cream – delicious, with a hint of soft resistance.

But the creature was bone-weary; it would have to move quickly. Alas, not enough energy to savour the hunt. Not enough power to finish them all. Its earlier encounter had weakened it further. It would have to think fast. Come up with a plan. It needed its prey. And soon.

CHAPTER TEN

If Madison had harboured any doubts about Ben becoming a vampire, right now, in this glorious moment, all those doubts had fled. To have her brother back from the dead was the most incredible gift she could have wished for. Here they were, all of them, safe at home, shutters closed against the sparkling Boxing Day sunshine, and whatever else lay outside.

Maddy scooched up next to Ben on the sofa in the lamp-lit sitting room. She took his hand and squeezed, marvelling at its new, cool hardness. He sat upright on the green velvet. At ease, yet somehow alert and aloof. Tactfully, the others had remained downstairs, giving Maddy and her brother some time alone together. Before they would allow Ben to leave the basement, Ben had first had to assure them he was no longer hungry. That he was in no danger of attacking his sister. He'd looked at them like they were mad. Satisfied he wasn't a threat, Ben and Maddy had been "allowed" to climb the cellar steps together.

'Do you feel weird, Ben?' Maddy now asked. 'Are you okay with all of this?'

He turned to smile at her, and she examined his features, searching for a clue to what was happening behind that smile. It was Ben, and yet, at the same time, it wasn't Ben. He seemed older; less like her little brother. 'I feel a bit strange, yeah,' he said. 'The weirdest thing is that you smell so good. Like... like all my favourite food laid out in front of me.'

Maddy let go of his hand. 'Are you still hungry? Do you need to, er... eat... feed... whatever?'

'Nah, I'm okay. And anyway, I'd never want your blood, Mads. No matter how bad I got. I'd never, ever... you know that, right?'

'Yeah, course I do.' She gave a nervous laugh and paused, wanting to ask more, but feeling faintly squeamish about the whole thing, which was odd because she hadn't really thought too much about the other vampires' feeding habits. She knew how they got their sustenance – Alex had once unknowingly fed from her – but it wasn't something she and Alex chose to discuss at length. He and the others tried to keep this part of their nature separated from her. 'Did you... get some food last night? Did Alex take you out hunting?'

'We found this woman in a nursing home,' Ben replied. 'Alex said she was dying and in terrible pain. He said if I drank she would sleep and the pain would leave her.'

'So...'

'Yeah.' He winced. 'I drank from her. I was pretty hungry. And, well, it felt amazing. She was crying in agony when we got there, and then when I, you know, she drifted off into a peaceful sleep.'

'She died?' Maddy tried to picture the scene in her head.

'No,' Ben replied. 'Alex said we aren't allowed to drink so much that they die. We have to stop before that. I could kind of sense her blood flowing and her heart beating. Alex found me a couple more like that. It's difficult to stop drinking once you start, but the others were there to stop me if I couldn't, you know, stop myself. Afterwards, I felt like I could do anything. Like I could fly.'

Madison wasn't sure how she felt about her brother engaging in such a horrific activity. She hadn't considered it in this much detail before. The moral implications hadn't struck her quite as forcefully when she thought of Alex doing it, so why should she feel any differently about Ben?

Probably because he was her fourteen-year-old brother.

'Ben,' she began. 'Last night... before... outside, with the deer. What happened?'

Ben shrugged, sighed and turned away from her. His face closing down.

'Can you talk about it?' she pressed gently.

'Can we... d'you mind if we don't?' he replied. 'I don't really want to think about it. Not yet.'

Maddy gave a small noise of assent. She was beyond happy that he wasn't gone, that she hadn't lost him forever. But she was also worried about him. Surely, he'd have to speak about what happened sooner or later. It wasn't good to keep such a traumatic event bottled up. It would be better if he talked things through. He'd been murdered by vampires. It must have been terrifying. She'd have to read up about the best thing to do for shock and trauma. Did vampires even go into shock, or was that a human thing? Maybe Ben would be okay at dealing with that sort of thing, now he was a vampire. She should talk to one of the others about it. They'd been through something equally terrible. They could relate. Ben might open up to Freddie or Jacques.

'So,' she said, shaking off an avalanche of worries, 'a vampire, eh?'

'Can you believe it, Mads?' He turned back to her, his eyes gleaming, and she glimpsed the old familiar Ben. 'I can't wait until tonight,' he said, 'to go outside. I'm going to run superfast, climb trees, pick up heavy stuff and chuck it across the fields.'

Maddy laughed. 'Pick up heavy stuff? Sounds awesome.'

'Shut up. You know what I mean.'

'Yeah, picking up heavy stuff is cool.' She widened her eyes and pretended to look impressed.

'I'll pick *you* up and stuff you up the chimney in a minute,' he retorted.

Maddy leaned over and gave him a hug, wiping away an escaping tear. 'I love you, bro,' she whispered in his ear.

'Love you, too, sis.'

As dusk settled across the land, Ben's excitement was palpable. Maddy sipped her tea and smiled across the plush basement room at Ben, Freddie and Jacques chattering like magpies, discussing what they were going to do this evening. Becoming a vampire hadn't dampened his natural exuberance. In actual fact, he seemed more hyper than ever.

'Can we go out yet?' Ben asked for the gazillionth time.

'Soon,' Isobel replied, putting down the book she was reading. She caught Maddy's eye, and they exchanged a smile.

Maddy still had clawing doubts about letting Ben out of the house. There were killers out there, somewhere. Her smile melted as anxiety took over again.

'Don't worry,' Isobel said softly. 'There are no vampires near here. We would sense them.'

'You didn't sense them yesterday.'

Isobel bowed her head. 'We did, but we were too late. And then they vanished without a trace. Tonight, Ben will not be alone. There will be at least two others with him at all times. And he is stronger than before.'

Maddy couldn't argue with that. Ben had spent most of the day destroying things with his bare hands – firewood, a chair, a telephone directory, a broken DVD player... If Maddy hadn't put her foot down, she was sure everything in the house would have been torn or karate-chopped in half by now.

Maddy's heart missed a beat when the doorbell rang. Who could that be?

'Travis,' Alexandre said. 'And three more.'

'Can I...' Ben started.

'NO,' everyone chorused.

'You can't tell anyone what's happened, Ben,' Maddy said, giving him a hard stare.

'I know *that*. I was going to say, can I answer the door. I haven't seen Travis for ages.'

'Sounds like Esther's already answered it,' Alex said. 'She'll send them away.'

Suddenly, Maddy realised she would like to see Travis, especially if he'd brought Kerri and Taff with him. It would be fun to see them. Take her mind off all the weird, dark stuff that was going on. She stood up.

'I'm going to let them in. See if they want to stay for a cuppa. We need some light relief. Some normality. What do you guys think?'

There were a few murmurs of assent. Alex caught her eye. She raised her eyebrows, questioning, and he shrugged in response.

'Just for a while,' she said. 'With all that's going on, who knows when we'll see them again.' She headed for the stairs up to the kitchen. 'You guys come up in a minute once the front door's closed.' Maddy glanced at Isobel's floor-length gown. 'And it might be a good idea to wear something twenty-first century.'

Fifteen minutes later, they were all sprawled in the living room, having given their tea, coffee and cake orders to Esther, who had insisted on preparing a lavish tea before she left for the evening.

'Nice suit, Alex,' Taff said in his Welsh lilt. 'D'you always dress so sharp at home?'

'Thank you,' Alexandre replied. 'Madison keeps buying me

jeans, but I don't really like them. The denim is very thick and stiff. Suits are a softer fabric, infinitely more comfortable.'

Taff and Travis stared at Alex, mouths slightly gaping. 'Yeah,' Taff finally replied. 'Nice one, man. Nice one. Don't let your woman tell you how to dress. You gotta stand up for your rights.'

Kerri spluttered with laughter. 'Like I didn't pick out your whole wardrobe, Taff! You crack me up.' Taff gave her a playful shove. 'But I like where you're coming from, Alex', she continued. 'Most men don't make an effort. It's nice to see a guy in a good suit. What do you reckon, Nadia?'

Travis's new girlfriend smiled and nodded. 'I like suits,' she said, so quietly they could barely hear her. Everyone, including Maddy, was having a hard time keeping their eyes off the stunning blonde next to Travis. No offense to Travis, he was a good-looking guy, but Nadia was in a whole other league. She was tall and slender with smooth skin, razor cheekbones and blue eyes. Her clothes were casual and understated – jeans, boots and a cream turtleneck, the complete opposite of Kerri's flamboyant green mini dress and fake fur jacket. Travis himself wore the expression of someone who'd just won the lottery. Like the cat who'd got the cream, the fish, the steak, the chicken and every other delicacy in the feline world. The grin on his face was so wide, it seemed his face would split in half. Maddy couldn't blame him. Even Alex was glancing at Nadia more times than Maddy was comfortable with. But there was no way she was going to turn into one of those jealous females who didn't let their man look at another woman. As long as looking was *all* Alex did.

'So, where did you two meet?' Maddy asked.

'We literally bumped into each other in town this morning,' Travis replied. 'I was walking past the supermarket as Nadia was coming out with two shopping bags. I walked right into her, and all her shopping went everywhere. So, being a gentleman, I picked it up, and asked if she wanted to go for a coffee.' He grinned, and everyone laughed. 'We got talking and realised we had all this stuff in common. Like music and skating and stuff. Don't we, babe?' Travis turned to her and winked, and she touched his cheek in response.

Maddy resisted raising her eyebrows. She would not have put Nadia as a skater girl. Not at all. But she did seem to be really into him. Madison pushed away a different wave of jealousy. Travis had had a crush on Maddy ever since they first met, and she felt odd seeing him so besotted with someone else. She also felt possessive. Travis was a good friend, and she'd hate to see him have his heart broken. Not to be mean or anything, but Nadia really did look way out of his league. She was in the supermodel category. But, then again, she also appeared to really like him, and she seemed sweet and friendly. Hopefully, they'd be good together. At least she only had eyes for Travis; people were usually transfixed by Alex, yet Nadia hadn't taken her eyes off Travis all night.

Ben really liked Travis and Taff and everyone, but he was itching for them to be gone. He wasn't able to do any vampirey stuff with all these people hanging around. Plus, Kerri kept giving him these weird stares, saying he looked different. He realised she was now asking him another question.

'You do look good, Ben,' she said. 'Have you had your hair cut?'

Ben had to stop himself replying: *No, not my hair, but I did get stabbed in the chest last night, and now I'm a vampire.* Kerri would think he was joking, but Maddy and the others would go mental if he said anything like that. They wouldn't see the funny side at all. He was also trying not to lean in too close to Kerri. She smelled so good he could almost taste her. Ben could smell the blood in all the humans' veins, and it was difficult to keep control when he knew he could just lean across and drink from them. You could see how vampires easily turned into monsters. They needed so much self-control. At least he wasn't hungry like he'd been yesterday. The smell wasn't driving him crazy anymore. Well, not too crazy anyway.

'Honestly, you look so different, Ben.' Kerri turned to Maddy. 'Your little brother's gonna be such a heartbreaker when he's older.'

Maddy smiled and changed the subject. Ben could sense how on edge his sister was. Her voice was fractionally higher than normal, and her right leg was jiggling up and down. Alex kept putting his hand on her knee to stop it shaking. Ben would never have noticed stuff like that before. Now he noticed everything. But he couldn't concentrate on anything anyone was saying; he was still too preoccupied with the look and sound and smell of everything. It was like his senses had been hibernating his whole life, and now they were clear and sharp. He could even make out sounds way down in the woods. If he concentrated, he could hear individual animals – foxes and rabbits and owls. He wondered if it was like this for dogs, with their hearing and scenting abilities. But then dogs couldn't see very well. Ben felt like he now had hawk vision, bat hearing and a wolf's sense of smell. Cool.

Finally, what seemed like hours later, Travis and the others got up to leave. Ben made polite goodbye noises and tried not to appear too keen to see them go. Once they were back in Travis's yellow van, the taillights a distant glow, Ben turned to Freddie and Jacques.

'Yes, okay,' they chorused before he'd even said a word. 'Let's go outside, then, and check out your new skills.'

'Be careful,' Maddy warned. 'It could be dangerous out there.'

'Don't worry, Mads. I'll be fine.'

She wasn't happy, but at least she didn't try to stop him.

As they headed out into the dark, Alex and Isobel were issuing them with reams of instructions, but Ben wasn't listening. His attention was on the clear, beckoning night. Previously, night-time had always been so... black. So dark and unseeing. Now, it was just the opposite. The darkness felt like the light. His vision cut through it so he could see everything in his line of sight as though it was daylight outside. He felt completely in control of his body and of the landscape around him. Like he could bend anything to his will. Like he was part of it and it was part of him. A smile lit him up from the inside and he took off at speed. Running across the short grass and into the woods. Subconsciously, he had made the decision to head in the opposite direction to the deer park. Although yesterday felt like a world away, he had no wish to be reminded of those violent events. He knew Morris had already disposed of the slaughtered deer carcasses – 'Let's just say, the locals will be eating venison for quite a while to come,' Morris had said in answer to Ben's questioning. Ben hadn't enquired any further. Now he pushed these gruesome thoughts from his mind.

Ben moved so fast, he skimmed the ground, yet miraculously he could still see everything clearly, his vision unblurred by his speed. He knew where each footfall landed and avoided every obstacle in his path as easily as if he were walking. But he realised that to human eyes he was too fast to appear as anything other than a brief shadow or blur. What a thrill.

Freddie swept past him, and Ben smiled, taking up the challenge and pushing himself faster. They were in the woods now, Jacques at his side. Ben took a giant leap and reached upward, grabbing a high tree branch with ease. Then another, and another, until he was nearly at the top of the treeline. He jumped and landed on a sturdy branch of the next tree, disturbing birds, sending them squawking and shrieking into the sky.

'Sorry,' he called, laughing as he went. His hands didn't even hurt from the rough bark and twigs that tried and failed to scrape his skin. He really was invincible. What would happen if he let himself fall? Would he break a bone? Die? He didn't quite have the courage to try that. Instead, he leapt from tree to tree, making his way to the edge of the wood, and there, from the top of a beech tree, he jumped down. Through the rushing air he flew, to alight on a grassy bank without so much as a jolt to his bones, or a gasp for breath.

Jacques and Freddie had altered course to follow him, and now they too leapt in graceful arcs from the forest to land by his side, ruffle his hair and congratulate him on being a fully-fledged awesome vampire.

CHAPTER ELEVEN

SCYTHIA, 514 BC

Kelermes eased back his hide covering and sat up. The fire had burned out and icy tendrils wound their way about him, but he didn't mind the cold; it helped to shake off sleep. Morning light filtered down through the open crown of the low *yurta* – their huge, light travelling tent. With the absence of night, there was no promise of sunshine, just a hard white winter's light promising a difficult day ahead. The unnatural quiet of the morning could mean only one thing – snow. It would seem the Sky God, Tar, had seen fit to send winter early this year, and they were unprepared.

From the sound of it, he was the first awake; soft snores punctuated the heavy silence. Already fully clothed, Kelermes stood and stretched his arms above his head, almost grazing his fingertips on the thick, felt ceiling. They would have to dismantle the yurtas today. He hoped the snow hadn't fallen too thickly, or it would be slow going to pack everything up. He pulled on his soft deerskin boots, tucked his trousers securely into them, and then, silently, so as not to wake his fellow soldiers, he reached down for his belt and fastened it around his waist, hooking it closed and running his fingers over the smooth horn belt plate. From the rope on the wall behind him, he reached for his sword, bow case and whip, securing them in place on his belt. Lastly, he bent to check his dagger was still securely attached to his left leg. It had been his grandfather's and was slightly curved in the Chinese manner. His mother had made him a present of it before he had left to fight, and he kept it on him at all times.

To his shame, Kelermes had not been born into a Scythian warrior clan. His family were humble cattle-farmers – nomadic like all their people. However, his maternal grandfather had been a king's archer before dying young in battle. A born horseman, fighter and bowman, Kelermes had inherited his grandfather's blood. The curved dagger would always be special to him, and was the only link to his family, whom he would likely never see again as they lived in the northern lands, far from these dangerous borders.

Across the tent, on the eastern side of the room, the women's side, he caught sight of pale arms stretching upwards. Laodice was awake, too. She turned her head towards him, her blonde curls running loose down her back, and he winked at her with a sudden lightness of being. She would make the day less boring, less arduous. She always did. It wouldn't be long before he could vie for her hand in marriage. As was law, their women were unable to marry until they had slain three enemies. Laodice only had to make one more kill, and then he could ask for her. As soon as he had first sighted her last year, he had yearned for her to be his. Aged seventeen, he was the fiercest warrior of his age group, and she almost matched him in her valour and ferocity. With legions of Persians coming after them, it was inevitable she would send one or more to the afterlife very soon. But it wasn't a given that Laodice would be his woman. There were plenty of others who would wish to claim her as a wife.

'Snow?' she mouthed at him across the forms of their

sleeping brothers and sisters. She too had sensed the change of light inside the yurta, the muffled quality of the air that signified snow had arrived.

Kelermes screwed up his face and nodded.

Laodice shrugged her shoulders and mouthed something else, but he couldn't make out what she was saying. He tilted his head to the door, and she nodded, rising from her bedroll and bringing it with her, as she followed him out through the tent flap into a frozen world of whiteness. Outside, Kelermes nodded to Abaris who, relieved of guard duty, grunted a morning greeting and made his way back inside the tent, rubbing his hands together as snow crunched under his boots.

Simultaneously, Kelermes and Laodice shaded their eyes and squinted out across the Silys River. Kelermes scratched at his dense, blond beard. Soon, the eddying water would grow a thick skin of ice, and then those damned Persians would be able to cross the river wherever they chose. The Scythians were giving the Persians a hard enough time, though. He smiled to himself as he recalled the numerous surprise attacks they'd carried out over the past few months. Attack, retreat. Attack, retreat. Those Persian dogs never saw them coming. And then before they had time to blink, he and his Scythian comrades were galloping off again. As the Scythians retreated, they employed scorched-earth tactics, leaving a barren land with poisoned water supplies for their Persian enemy. It must be driving them crazy with frustration, not to mention hunger and thirst. Served them right. If they stayed in their own lands, they'd keep their necks. If they kept coming, Kelermes and his brethren would be happy to keep up their ploys and skirmishes, gathering enough scalps to build a tower to the heavens.

Snow would be an inevitable hindrance to both sides. Blessedly, it wasn't yet too deep. A couple of inches at most. Kelermes wondered if this was just a precursor to winter. If Tar might show mercy and melt the snow. Keep the harsh weather at bay for a few weeks more. Or, if this was really winter come to stay. Their cautious but ruthless leader, Aristeas, wouldn't take any chances. He would order them to pack up instantly and head northeastward, eventually moving away from the river before it froze.

Kelermes didn't mind leaving the river. It would be exciting to see more of his countrymen again. And they would be welcomed as heroes. Treated like royalty as they passed through their lands. As long as Laodice had the chance to take another scalp, all would be well. He couldn't bear the thought of having to wait until spring to see if she would choose him. He wanted her now.

'I hope I get the chance to skewer another one of those Persian dogs before we leave,' she said, as though reading his mind. 'Even if I have to sneak off on my own for a couple of hours to ambush one of them.'

He grinned and elbowed her in the ribs affectionately. Could she be hinting that she wanted him as a husband? Or was he reading too much into her comments? He tried to think of a suitable reply, one that didn't make him sound too keen. The last thing he wanted was to appear as a lovesick pup. But he should have seized the moment to speak, for now the tent flap opened and they were joined by Lohant and Orik.

Lohant pushed past Kelermes. 'Out of my way, runt,' he said, before turning to Laodice. 'I'll come with you on your ambush, Lae,' he said. 'Act as a distraction while you take your scalp.'

'I'll hold you to that, Lo,' she replied with a twinkling smile that served as a knife to Kelermes's heart.

'But I hope to be more than a distraction afterwards,' Lohant added, making Kelermes want to punch the smug warrior.

Orik sensed Kel's anger and placed a warning hand on his friend's shoulder.

Within the hour, everyone was awake, packing up the last few bits and pieces of their temporary camp. It should have been a noisy operation, but the snow damped down the sounds, giving everything an eerie, faraway quality. Kelermes clicked his teeth and patted his mare's neck as she knelt for him so he could swing himself easily onto the thick blanket which covered her narrow chestnut back. Once mounted, he clicked his teeth again, the signal for her to stand up. It had taken him days to teach her that trick, but it could be very handy if he was laden down, or happened to injure himself. His steed was called Tabi, named for her shining flame-coloured coat, after the Fire Goddess, Tabiti.

Kelermes turned slightly to rearrange the weaponry hanging from his belt, ensuring each item was within easy reach. He was itching to get moving. Lohant had managed to rile him again, and Kel welcomed the distraction of the journey to calm his frustration. Surely Lae couldn't think that oaf would be a worthy husband.

Once the yurtas had been dismantled and folded down into the cart, and everyone was mounted, Aristeas gave the order for them all to move out. The riders at the rear had long swathes of brush attached to the hindquarters of their mounts to erase their trail of churned-up snow. Like always, it would be as though they were never there. The Scythians moved like ghosts, leaving no traces behind. In this way, their enemies could never track them, never mount an attack. It was always Kelermes and his brethren who would attack on *their* terms.

First, they took a few moments at the Silys to refill their water skins and to water their horses. Then they followed the curving line of the river northwards, moving briskly but unhurriedly. Laodice was up front, while Kelermes stayed towards the rear, casting his gaze right, over the flat, snow-covered steppe, and left, across the steel-grey river. Always searching for movement and irregularities. Always alert. Spring was a world away.

He missed the untamed grasses, the horses sinking up to their knees in a silvery sea of side oats and silkweed. The millions of mullein flowers and the tall forests of hemp and spurge. The air infused with the bitter aroma of wormwood, and the skies awash with the warbling of larks. This winter landscape was different altogether – more open and hostile. Blank and hard. Any softness removed. The frigid air sharp in his throat and lungs. And, with his cheeks raw, and his fingers numb, it felt as though the land had always been this way, and would forever be.

Twenty minutes into their journey, Aristeas's hand came up. The forty-eight warriors came to an immediate halt. Kelermes could hear the bubbling river, the clinking of weaponry and the snorts and pants of the horses. He strained his ears above these immediate noises and heard it – the sound of men. Not far ahead. Probably around the next bend in the river. Aristeas had stopped them just in time.

Their leader gestured to his division to fall back. All but Abaris were to retreat. Kelermes watched the thick-set warrior dismount and slide down the side of the riverbank, keeping out of the icy water, but hugging the steep bank so as not to be detected. He would make his way forward towards the sounds up ahead, and report back soon enough. Kel gently reined his pony around and headed back around the last river bend with the others. As they waited upriver, he caught Laodice's eye. She winked at him and made a quick slicing motion across her throat. His heart lifted – it looked like his chances of winning her were becoming brighter.

They sat astride their mounts, ready to move at a moment's notice. The sky bleached whiter – more snow would fall within the hour. The breath of horses and warriors mingled, a warm cloud hanging in the air. The swish of horse tails drowned by the louder swish of the river. Kelermes took this time to check and double-check his weapons. Every warrior had a formidable supply of arrows at any one time. Kelermes's *gorytos* contained a double-curved bow, and around three-hundred slim, bronze-tipped reed arrows, most of which were barbed with thorns and dipped in poison – a mere graze from one of these could work its lethal magic in less than a day. A few fine-tipped arrows were kept pure and clean for hunting birds; though they were unlikely to see any of their feathered friends today.

Kel wondered how many soldiers lay up ahead. It was the Persians of course. Who else would it be? In any case, everyone here was relaxed, Laodice included. She chatted with some of the other women as they passed around the leather milk bag, taking swigs and passing it on. Not a wrinkle of worry lined their brows; this was simply another day.

Did his comrades truly feel no fear at the inevitable skirmish they were about to embark on? Kelermes reluctantly admitted to himself that he always felt more than a trickle of apprehension before battle. But he would never show this weakness to the others. He would rather die. Perhaps it was because he hadn't always lived this way. He had moved from a civilian life into a military one. His family had been relatively safe away from the borders. Would he too have been more relaxed if he'd been born to this fighting life like the others? He supposed he would never know. Did his comrades' hearts beat a little faster before battle? Did their palms sweat despite the cold? Perhaps they were just as good at feigned nonchalance as he. But he couldn't believe it. He hated that he alone was troubled by apprehension, and he cursed his weakness. Yet, despite his inner battle with nerves, he didn't doubt that this is where he wanted to be – fear or no fear. He was a Scythian warrior, trained to strike terror and death into the heart of the enemy. And that is what he was about to do.

Thirty minutes later, a distant figure clambered up from the riverbank, heading towards them, a black outline against white snow and sky. Collectively, Kelermes and his comrades tensed in readiness. But, as the figure drew closer, they saw it was only Abaris reporting back. He approached at a walk, his face blank, giving nothing away of what lay behind him.

The warrior made straight for Aristeas with his news. The rest of them drew closer as their leader beckoned, his heavily tattooed face stern, totally focused on his second-in-command. Abaris's wife, Savlius, a heavyset woman, formidable in battle but with a warm heart, handed her husband the milk bag, and he took a deep swig of the liquid before speaking.

'Persians,' Abaris confirmed without preamble, and spat on the ground. 'They're crossing the river in rafts. Hundreds of them. Idiots. About a third of them have fallen in. If they'd waited a few days, they could've strolled across the ice.'

Kelermes and his brethren shook their heads and muttered at their enemy's stupidity.

'We should burn their rafts,' Lohant hissed.

'With the Persians tied to them,' added Orik.

Everyone chuckled. Aristeas held up his hand for silence and nodded to Abaris to continue.

'Looks like they're heavily armed. Scrawny, though. I'll bet they're starving. They'll have found nothing to eat between the Ister and the Silys.'

'How many do you estimate?' Aristeas asked.

'At a guess, around a thousand. Only two hundred have crossed so far. All infantry as usual.'

'A pity we didn't arrive earlier. We could've cut down the first wave as they landed. Two hundred is too many for us now.'

At this last statement, there were grumbles of discontent. This many Persians would be rich pickings, guaranteeing them all a prosperous winter. But Kelermes knew Aristeas would never rate those odds – four to one was too risky. He was a good leader. Brave and cunning, but not foolhardy. He had been in the field since the age of fourteen, and now he was a respected thirty-four-year-old warrior, the eldest of them all.

'Sir,' Abaris continued, 'they've sent a detachment out into the steppe. Twenty soldiers on foot – maybe on a recce or sent to loot provisions. They'll be easy to track in the snow, and they can't have gone far. What do you think?'

Aristeas swept a decisive gaze over his eager warriors. 'What are we waiting for?'

The horses immediately sensed their masters' anticipation and began to shift restlessly. Kelermes ran his fingers over the stag tattoo on his forearm, marvelling at how the beast was now part of his body, as smooth as his skin, as though he'd been born with it. It had been his very first tattoo for his very first kill two years earlier. Now, he had almost twenty tattoos, and likely he would have many more by the month's end... if he survived.

Abaris grinned and swung up onto his horse. 'Follow me,' he said to his leader, clicking his teeth and setting off eastwards, away from the river at a canter.

As they headed into the steppe, Kel acknowledged the usual thrill of nerves and anxiety in his belly. More foe to eliminate. Of course he wanted to be here. To be fighting for his people, but for the thousandth time he wished he had been born with the natural bravery his brethren appeared to possess. They charged at the enemy with broad smiles, with excitement and glee. Kel always attempted to emulate their courage, but it didn't sit naturally. He had to pull his courage around him like a cloak that was constantly being tugged from his shoulders by a relentless wind.

He said a muttered prayer to the goddess Tabiti and another to the Father, Papaeus. With their blessings, he would try to banish his fear, and despatch at least two of the enemy. He was paid per head, and he needed the wages if he had any hope of being married this winter.

CHAPTER TWELVE

Watching her brother disappear into the night, Maddy stood in the shadow of Marchwood House. Her stomach lurched as she thought about the fact that Ben would never grow any older. That he would always look like a fourteen-year-old boy. Forever. Would he come to resent it? At least he was happy now, she told herself. At least he was enjoying his transformation. She still didn't know if she'd made the right call. But she did know that given the choice over again, she would ask Alex to do the same thing. She couldn't have let her brother die. Disappear into nothingness. He was Ben. He was meant to live. To be vibrant and funny. To be her little brother. She didn't work properly on her own. She wouldn't have been able to go on. So, maybe she was selfish. She had wanted him turned in order to keep her sane and happy. To keep him with her.

'Stop it,' Alex said, taking her hand and bringing it to his lips.

'Hmm?'

'Ben is fine. You made a good decision. Stop beating yourself up and wondering if you did the right thing.'

'How do you do that? Read my mind?'

'I don't have to. It's written all over your face. The worry.'

'Alex is right,' Isobel added, joining them on the front drive. 'I wasn't so sure it was the right thing to do, last night. But now... Ben is happy. He loves it. It's not a life for everyone. I'm not sure it's such a good life for me, or even for Alex. But Ben and Jacques and Freddie... they were born to it. They are good souls, and they're enjoying the powers without any of the darkness it can bring. They are untainted by it.'

'Do you really think so?' Maddy turned to her, wanting to believe what she said.

'I do.'

'For now, anyway,' Alex added.

'What do you mean?' Maddy's momentary relief dissolved.

'Just that our lives are eternal. Who knows what changes we'll go through? Whether we'll always feel the same way we feel now.'

'Alex!' Isobel cried. 'We're supposed to be reassuring Madison, not adding to her doubt.'

'You're right, I'm sorry. I spoke without thinking.'

'It's okay, you're being truthful,' Maddy said. 'I'd rather hear it like it is than have it sugar-coated.'

'You're shivering,' Alex said, pulling her close. 'We should go inside.'

'I don't want to leave them out here. In case...'

'I can hear everything. They'll be fine.'

For a moment Maddy wished she, too, could hear everything. She was at a disadvantage, relying on the others to be her eyes and ears. She felt inadequate. But she didn't have the energy to argue, and she let herself be led back inside.

'Let me make you some tea,' Alex said.

'No offence, Alex, but your tea isn't the greatest. I'll do it.' The words were meant to sound teasing, but they sounded sharper than intended. Like a criticism. Suddenly she wanted to cry. But she gritted her teeth instead.

'Charming,' Alex replied as he led her back inside through the huge front door.

Maddy tried to repair her clumsy joke: 'Everything else about you is pretty amazing, though. So don't be too upset about your tea-making skills.'

'Don't call him amazing,' Isobel said. 'You'll give him a big head.' She followed them in, closing the front door behind her. 'He's already an unbearable show-off.'

It was strange coming into the house at this time of night while her brother was out there being *supernatural*, but she would have to shake off her insecurities. This was Ben's life now. She better get used to it. She wouldn't be able to tell him what to do anymore. Well, she could try, but he probably wouldn't listen.

'What do you think of Travis's new girlfriend?' Maddy asked, changing the subject and switching on the kettle. 'Gorgeous or what?'

Isobel sat at the kitchen table and pulled her hair back into an elegant ponytail. 'Travis seems very happy,' she said.

'Alex?' Maddy turned to look at him. 'What do you think?'

'I agree with Belle. He seems very happy.'

Maddy wasn't sure why she wanted to discuss Nadia. Maybe she missed having girly gossips with her friends. Maybe she was being mean. Maybe she just wanted something to talk about that wasn't to do with danger, or vampires, or death. But it didn't seem like that was on the cards; Alex and Belle weren't up for a bitchy gossip. She reached up to grab a mug from the cupboard and dropped a teabag into it.

'At least you won't have to worry about Ben so much now,' Alex said, passing her the milk carton from the fridge. 'He can take good care of himself. He's no longer an easy target.'

'True,' she replied.

'Madison, I will have to go and fight the Cappadocians.

They won't stop coming. I must kill them all. Or, at the very least, I must kill the Emperor.'

'*We* will. Not *you*. *We*,' Isobel added.

'We need a plan first,' Maddy said, sloshing milk into her mug and spilling it in the process. 'You can't just go there and hope to win, like last time.'

'Havva Sahin is our only hope,' Alex replied.

'You mean Sofia? The old lady?' Maddy had trusted her. Liked her, even. The extraordinary woman who had saved her people from the Cappadocian vampires hundreds of years ago. And then, more recently, had saved Maddy from them, too.

'Yes,' Alex replied. 'Although I suppose her real name isn't Havva or Sofia; it's Aelia.'

'Do you believe her story?' Isobel asked. 'Can we trust her?'

'Why would she make something like that up?' Alex said. 'She certainly has the power and strength to prove her tale. She is not a vampire, and yet she looks the same to me as she did one hundred years ago. Yes, I believe her.'

'Me too,' Maddy said, putting her teabag in the bin and plonking herself down opposite Isobel. Alex returned the milk to the fridge and sat next to her. 'And anyway,' Maddy continued, 'Aelia helped me. She sent the other vampires packing. Even that ancient Cappadocian vampire, Mislav, was scared of her, and he doesn't strike me as the type to be scared of anything.'

'So, we'll have to travel back to Turkey, then,' Isobel said, her shoulders slumping. 'Visit Aelia there.'

'Yes. But Ben should stay here,' Maddy added.

'He'll be safer with us in Turkey than alone here,' said Alex. 'We should all stay together.'

Maddy bit her lip and dug her nails into the palm of her hand. She was desperate to keep her brother safe, but it seemed nowhere was safe anymore. Alex was right. If she left him alone at Marchwood, she'd probably worry more.

'If he stays close to Aelia, he'll be fine,' Alex said. 'She's the most dangerous creature of them all. The Cappadocians won't want to risk the sleeping sickness she carries in her blood. They won't want to go anywhere near her.'

'But could she be dangerous for you, too?' Maddy asked. If she really did carry the sleeping sickness in her blood, Maddy wondered if it was possible for Ben or Alex to get infected.

'She's only dangerous as an enemy,' Alex said. 'And I believe she is our friend. Don't you?'

Maddy nodded. 'I guess.' She gave a start as Alex and Isobel scraped their chairs back from the table and rose to their feet. Isobel looked questioningly at Alex.

'What?' Maddy cried. 'Is it Ben? Has something—'

'Shh,' Isobel held her palm up to quiet Maddy.

'Ben is fine,' Alex said. 'It's that girl... Travis's girlfriend. She's in trouble. I'll be back. Belle, stay here with Madison.'

Alex was gone and Maddy made to follow, but Isobel touched her shoulder and shook her head. 'Let my brother deal with it. He'll bring her back if she's in trouble. You can't go out without protection.'

Once again, Maddy was being made aware of the fact that she was the only human at Marchwood, unless you counted Esther and Morris. Therefore, she was the weakest, the biggest liability. Instead of her worrying about her brother, *he* would be the one looking out for *her*. And she wasn't sure quite how she felt about that.

Tracking the pitiful sound of sobbing, Alexandre was outside in moments, and on the winding main road out of Tetbury. A couple of cars flashed past, bass lines thumping, male laughter full of bravado and hormones. He came upon the girl soon after. She was alone, stumbling along beside the drystone wall that bordered Marchwood's grounds. Where on earth were Travis and his friends? Why was the girl out here by herself? Alex stood on the opposite side of the narrow road, not wanting to startle her, or upset her even more.

'Hello,' he said.

She continued walking, head bowed, platinum hair falling in front of her tear-streaked face.

Alex stepped into the middle of the road and matched her pace. 'Hello,' he repeated, only this time fractionally louder. She stopped walking and glanced his way with a gasp. Then she backed up, turned and started running in the opposite direction. But the verge was muddy and uneven, and she made poor progress. Alex didn't want to give chase; the girl was clearly terrified out of her wits. He realised Isobel should have been the one to come out here. Another female would have been far less threatening.

'I'm not going to hurt you,' he called. 'Nadia, it's me, Alexandre. Alex. From the house earlier.'

She slowed a little, but still didn't turn around.

'Nadia! Do you want me to fetch help? Call the police?'

She stopped. 'No! Do not call the police,' she cried. 'I... I have been attacked.' Her voice broke and she gave a strangled sob. Alex noticed that her English was a little stilted. He wondered where she was from.

'Where's Travis?' Alex walked towards her, softly, slowly, like approaching a wild rabbit who might bolt at any moment.

'Travis?' she spat. 'He's the one who attacked me.'

Alex was so taken aback, he stopped walking for a second. Travis? That didn't sound right. As another car came along, Alex moved off the road and onto the grass verge a few paces behind her. 'Travis attacked you?' He took another step towards her as the car sped past.

'Travis is your friend, is he not?' Nadia said warily.

'I've met him on a few occasions,' Alex said. 'But I don't

know him that well. I didn't think him the type to attack a woman. He's Madison's good friend.'

She sniffed and raised her head. Stared at him directly. Alex was mesmerised for a moment by her sheer beauty. Her face was like a porcelain doll's – perfectly proportioned, with huge, tear-filled eyes and bee-stung lips. Alex didn't altogether like the physical reaction he was having. Maddy was his life and his love, and he had never looked at another girl since meeting her. He would never... but this girl, this Nadia, she was truly beautiful. Breathtaking.

'Tell me what happened,' he said.

'I do not know you,' she said. 'You could be part of this, with Travis.'

'Part of what?' Alex said, taking another step closer. 'Come back to the house. My sister's there. She'll look after you. You can use the phone.' The girl was clearly terrified. Something had happened, but he couldn't believe Travis was involved. There must have been some kind of misunderstanding. 'Or shall I leave and fetch Isobel now? Bring her back here?'

'You seem like nice person,' Nadia said, in halting English. 'But so did Travis. How I know I can trust you?'

'What if I sit here, away from you, and then you tell me what happened.' Alex sank down onto the sodden grass and sat cross-legged with his hands in his lap, trying to appear as non-threatening as possible. 'If I was going to attack you, I surely would have done it by now. We're on a deserted road in the middle of the night. No one else is around. But I don't want to hurt you. I want to help.'

'Why you are out here alone?' she asked.

It was a reasonable question. He would have to lie. 'I, uh, had an argument with my girlfriend and needed to clear my head,' he replied, feeling instantly disloyal to Madison.

'Oh. I'm sorry you had argument.'

'It's okay.' The wet grass had soaked through Alex's

trousers. If he was human, he'd be squirming in discomfort by
now. As it was, he was enjoying simply looking at this girl. She
grew more beautiful as each second passed, if that were even
possible.

She took a step towards him. Alex realised he'd been
holding his breath. The air seemed stiller than usual. Charged
with an energy that made him feel like he was soaring. It was
the girl. Could he be attracted to her? No. Madison was waiting
at home for him. Madison was beautiful, kind, funny, clever.
She loved him, and he loved her. They had saved each other.
He didn't even know this girl, this stranger. Nadia.

'What happened with Travis?' he asked, trying to shake
himself out of this disturbing train of thought.

'What always happens with men,' she said. 'He tried kiss
me. That's okay. I kiss him back. But then he tried more. I said
no, but he not listen. Got rough and I punch him in stomach
and run away.'

Alex felt a rush of anger towards Travis. An anger that
made him want to... But that didn't sound like the Travis he
knew. Maybe Nadia had the wrong end of the stick. Or
maybe not.

She was crying again. Her hands curled into fists by her
side. 'Now I don't know what I do. I have nowhere to go. No
job, no home. I—'

'What did you do before you met Travis?' Alex asked.
'Where are you from?'

'I thought Travis was good man. But he just like all others. I
think you may be a good man. Or maybe you like all others,
too?'

She had gradually moved closer to Alex, who remained
cross-legged on the verge. Now, she stood directly in front of
him, her mud-stained boots in his line of sight. He raised his
head, his eyes lingering on her slender thighs, up her body and
finally allowing his gaze to rest on her tragically beautiful face,

framed by that pale blonde hair. Her expression so heartbreaking. So unutterably sad.

'Can I trust you, Alexandre?' she whispered, holding her hand out to him. He took it and let her raise him to his feet. She was much taller than Madison. Her face almost level with his.

'Yes. Of course,' he replied. 'I'll do everything I can to help you.' He let go of her hand, cleared his throat and took a step back. 'Madison and I will see to it that you are okay. Why don't you come back to the house with me? You need to warm up. You must be freezing.'

'Yes. I'm cold. Okay. I come back with you. Thank you, Alexandre. You are kind.'

'Come back to the house, and then, when you're settled, I'm going to pay Travis a visit.' Alex felt an unaccountable anger when he thought of Travis trying to attack Nadia. But surely she'd got it wrong. Maybe Travis had misread her signals. She was a beautiful girl, and she did have a way of looking at you that invited you in. That made you want to... but no, there was no excuse. The boy had obviously gone too far. He needed to learn that kind of behaviour was unacceptable.

'You will visit Travis?' she asked as they began to walk back to Marchwood.

'Yes.'

'But you not tell him I am here with you.'

'No. I won't tell him where you are.'

'Good, because he might come here. He might hurt me.'

Alex felt his pulse quicken in anger once more. 'Not if I've got anything to do with it.'

They walked side by side. Not touching, just a hair's breadth between them. Alex stole a glance at her. At least she was no longer crying. She still shivered, though whether it was through cold or shock or something else, Alexandre couldn't tell; his head was suddenly all over the place.

CHAPTER THIRTEEN

SCYTHIA, 514 BC

The Scythians travelled across unblemished snow, more flakes beginning to fall as they moved in relative silence. Feathers of cold melted on Kelermes's cheeks, on his chin, his nose, his eyebrows. Laodice had kept her position up front, wanting to be among the first to meet their enemy. Some of their brethren would be happy to allow her to make her kill – they knew how important the third kill was to a young woman. But many would be more concerned with their own kill tally, wanting all the scalps for themselves. Twenty Persians was a puny number, not even enough for one each, and there would be great competition to strike the death blows. Kelermes would try to ensure Laodice got her scalp, even if it meant getting in the way of his fellow soldiers and thwarting their attacks. He dug in his heels and pushed Tabi to a gallop to catch up with her, his mounting determination almost banishing any residual fear.

Away from the river, the land became flatter and within minutes they came upon their enemy's tracks leading into the endless steppe. Kelermes and his clan slowed to a trot, automatically fanning out into a semicircle to close in on the Persians. They could see them now, a dark smudge up ahead. Their enemy was outnumbered and outclassed. Kelermes smiled with some relief and noticed the broad grins on his brothers' and sisters' faces, too. Easy pickings.

The Persians had spotted them and now stood in formation, facing outward in a circle, swords drawn, shields aloft. Most of them wouldn't even get a chance to use their weapons, for as the Scythians approached they took up their bows, nocked their arrows and, on the word from Aristeas, unleashed a hail of poison shafts. Most bounced off the Persians' shields but, at least a couple found their mark. Not instant-death blows, but nevertheless. A second wave of arrows flew, and then a third. Now, only about a dozen of the enemy remained upright.

Kelermes was twenty yards away as he released another arrow straight into the eye of a Persian. He closed in, unsheathed his sword and cleaved the wounded man's head from his shoulders. With a whoop, he caught the whirling head and stuffed it, one-handed, into the deerskin pouch attached to his saddle blanket.

The Persians' circular formation had disintegrated, and the Scythians were now hacking down the few who remained. Kel had lost Laodice in the melee, and he scanned soldiers and bodies for her. So much for him helping her. He hadn't had the chance. But he had faith that she would be successful. A Persian was headed his way charging through blood and snow, his sword thrust ahead of him. With deadly speed, Kelermes let another arrow fly. It found its mark in the man's gullet, the Persian's battle cry dying in his throat. Kelermes was so close to the man, the arrow had flown straight through the unfortunate soldier's neck and out the other side.

Just as he was about to take his second scalp of the day, another Scythian lopped the dying Persian's head and took it for himself. It was Lohant. The sullen fellow had no sense of honour or comradeship. Kelermes was about to protest vigorously with the point of his sword, when he caught sight of

Laodice. She had come off her steed and was now engaged in furious hand-to-hand combat with a Persian twice her size.

Despite the Scythian's ferocity, it was an unfair fight. The enemy would surely kill her. Kelermes couldn't let that happen. He immediately left Lohant to his ill-gotten gains, and wheeled Tabi around, urging the mare towards Laodice, whilst readying another poison-tipped arrow.

Even through the thickly swirling snowflakes, he had no doubts about his arrow finding its target. Kelermes could fell a hawk from the sky with a perfectly aimed shaft between its eyes. He loosed his arrow, but before it could find its mark, Laodice had struck the massive Persian with an upper thrust of her dagger into the underside of his chin. Kelermes's arrow struck the top of the soldier's forehead about a tenth of a second later. The huge Persian fell backward to the ground, and with his demise, quiet descended. The Persians were all slaughtered, and it had taken only minutes.

Laodice glanced across and caught Kelermes's eye, but instead of a smile, she threw him a warrior's glare. The silence of the battlefield was momentary, followed by whoops and cheers, a noisy celebration of the Scythians' swift victory. But Kelermes was confused. Why had Laodice thrown him such a look of disgust? Or perhaps he had imagined it.

Kel urged Tabi to cross the several yards to reach Laodice, collecting her horse on the way, a bay mare who was nosing at the snow, unperturbed by the chaos around her. Once he'd reached Laodice, he jumped off Tabi and yanked the dagger out of the dead Persian's chin, wiping the blood on his trousers before handing it back to her with a flourish. Without even a nod of thanks, she took it and slipped it into the sheath at her back. Then she raised her sword in two hands and took the dead man's head in one powerful strike.

'Bravo!' he cried, above the noise of celebration.

She ignored his praise, turned her back on him and shoved

the freshly severed head into the bag hanging from her saddlecloth.

'Have I done something to offend you?' he enquired, his heart beating uncomfortably.

'As if you need to ask,' she snapped.

'I *am* asking,' he said, trying hard not to match her aggrieved tone. For the life of him, he couldn't understand what he had done that could warrant her anger.

Finally, she turned to him, her sapphire eyes burning with fury. 'How dare you try to take my scalp,' she said. 'You knew how important it was for me to make my third kill. To earn the status that you men are awarded from the start. You could see I was engaged in battle, and yet...' Her voice cracked a little. '... and yet you saw fit to loose your arrow and try to steal my scalp for yourself.'

Kelermes took a step backwards, as though she had struck him. 'Steal your scalp?' he echoed. 'But that was not my intention at all. I was only trying to—'

But she had turned away from him. Unwilling to hear that he had only wanted to save her from a seemingly perilous situation. Instead, she mounted her horse and clicked her into a trot, away from Kel and his confusion.

To rub salt in the wound, Lohant now came to her side, saying something to make her laugh. They rode together, talking and comparing scalps. No doubt planning their betrothal, Kel thought bitterly. Did Laodice really believe Kelermes to be the type of warrior who would steal another's glory for himself? Ironically, she was at this very moment laughing with just such a man. For Lohant had only moments ago stolen Kelermes own kill. Some justice.

'Any luck, brother?' It was Orik.

Kel remounted Tabi and pointed to the bag hanging from his horse blanket. 'Two scalps,' he said without enthusiasm. 'But that dog Lohant swiped one of them for himself.'

Orik scowled. 'You should take it back.'

Kel shook his head. 'One is enough for me. Lohant can keep it.'

'You're mad, Kel,' Orik replied. 'If it were me, I would wipe the smile from his face and add his own miserable scalp to my bag.'

'I see you managed to get lucky,' Kel said, changing the subject and pointing to a blood-soaked bag hanging at Orik's side.

'I did the Persian a favour really. He was an ugly brute,' Orik replied with a nod. 'Much like yourself.'

This last comment elicited a faint smile from Kelermes, who could never fail to be cheered by Orik's insults. But now there was too much noise to speak or be heard, as the victory cries of their clan rose into the air, weapons aloft, the smell of blood and snow thick in their nostrils.

Aristeas cut their vocal celebration short. 'Comrades, you have done well. But now, we must gather our spoils with haste. The Persians will soon come looking for their fallen brothers, and that is a battle we will not win.' The warriors heeded their leader, relieving their fallen enemies of weapons, armour and valuables. Within minutes, the dead were stripped and heaped upon the ground, snow swiftly falling to cover the bloody pile. Their own horses and carts were laden down with scalps and booty. Regrettably, two Scythian warriors had been slain and four injured, but not too badly. The Scythians lay their two fallen comrades reverently atop one of the carts. They would be buried later with due ceremony. Then they flung themselves onto their horses and cantered north-east, away from the approaching enemy, snow covering their tracks as they left.

An icy wind grazed Kelermes's cheeks as Tabi flew across the snow. But instead of the usual post-battle feelings of exhilaration and lightness, Kel was awash with gloom and darkness. The attack had not gone at all how Kelermes had hoped. Yes, they had won. Yes, Aristeas was pleased with them. Yes, they had gained a cartful of loot. Yes, Laodice had made her third kill and was now free to choose a husband. But it was all for nothing because he had messed up his chances with her. And now Lohant was riding with her. And he, Kelermes, was riding alone.

As they journeyed northward, the snowfall eventually eased, and the sun made brief appearances through the bleached sky. It gave no warmth but lifted spirits and made the journey a little more pleasant in the unchanging landscape. Kelermes and Orik travelled towards the rear of the party, side by side. Orik had given up trying to get Kel to talk; he just wasn't in the mood. Kelermes felt guilty at casting gloom over his friend's day, but, having tried and failed to explain to Laodice what had happened earlier, he had neither the energy nor inclination to pretend to be sociable, even with his best friend.

Before the battle, he had been excited about his future. He had actually been stupid enough to believe that Laodice might consider him as a husband. Now, with his ill-timed arrow, he had ruined everything. Soon, Laodice would present her scalp to Aristeas, and would formally request their leader's permission to marry. He would lay bets on her choice of husband being Lohant. The man was an oily snake, who shouldn't be allowed within ten feet of Laodice, let alone her marriage bed. But what could Kelermes do to prevent it? It seemed inevitable. There would be a feast, and everyone would celebrate. Everyone, except him.

Kel caught sight of her up ahead with two of her closest friends, Opis and Arga. She didn't appear to be upset that she and Kel had fallen out. Instead, he saw her smiling and chatting, apparently without a care. How could she act so carefree, when he felt as though his heart had been ripped out? Was she really so unaffected by their rift? He marvelled at the unblemished skin on her face, at the piercing blue of her eyes, and at the wild, deep golden curls that tumbled down her back, making him yearn to bury his face and fingers in their softness. He should ride over to her now and make her listen to his side of the story. Explain that he had merely been trying to prevent her death. Beg for forgiveness. But he knew she wouldn't thank his over-protective action. She would see it as a lack of faith in her skills as a fighter. If he approached her now with apologies and explanations, she would cut him down with withering words. Everyone else would witness his humiliation and things would be ten times worse. No. Better to leave things as they were. Accept that he would never have her. Let her go...

They stopped briefly to melt snow for drinking water and eat a few strips of dried meat. Kel didn't want the food, but he forced himself to eat it anyway, even though it stuck in his throat. After a short, uneventful meal, they resumed their journey. The sun would begin to sink in a couple of hours, and they would have to make camp before night fell. On horseback, they would easily outpace the Persians. If they kept up a steady speed this afternoon, they would sleep tonight without fear of being woken by swords and daggers.

Above them, a flock of greylag geese headed south, their honking calls startling Kelermes from his contemplation. He craned his neck upward and narrowed his eyes to squint at their snaking dark silhouettes, stark against the pale sky. The birds were late to leave this year. He didn't bother reaching for his bow – they were too high. Safe from his arrows, worse luck.

'Kolos!' someone cried out.

Kelermes immediately forgot about the geese and turned his attention landward. Up ahead to the left, a herd of about thirty saiga antelope were already panicking at the warriors' approach, racing away with extraordinary speed, their feet hardly seeming to touch the ground, flying across the snow. They were greyish-yellow beasts, with strange, oversized noses. Ugly and, if the truth be known, not the most delicious of creatures, but truly any fresh meat would taste better than the tough dried strips they'd been chewing on for the past couple of weeks. Would Aristeas give the command to hunt? It took about ten seconds for their leader to decide, reaching for his bow and slotting in an arrow. Everyone followed suit and kicked their steeds into pursuit of the fleeing antelope herd.

The *kolos* were swift; too swift for the soldiers' weary horses to catch. But they were creatures that tired easily. So it was simply a case of waiting for a couple of stragglers, and then the hunters would get their meal that night. As they drew closer to the zigzagging beasts, Kelermes spotted the lone male out in front. He had about thirty hornless females in his herd. He could spare a couple. Better to be eaten by a Scythe than a Persian. Sure enough, three of the *kolos* were soon lagging behind – two old and one young – their eyes rolling in fright, emitting a panicked bleating sound like sheep for the slaughter. It didn't take the soldiers long to round them up and put them out of their misery with a few well-placed arrows. Two victories in one day. They cheered once more and hauled the beasts onto one of the carts. Each one must have weighed at least 100 pounds – the warriors would feast tonight.

Turning north once more, the weary men and women had lost time in their race to outrun the Persians. The sun began to drop, its light becoming more muted, with a strong wind picking up across the open steppe, cutting into the faces of the riders. They would have to keep going if they were to put enough distance between them and their enemy, which would mean setting up camp in the dark.

In the fading light, they almost rode straight into the hide walls of an encampment. Three low yurtas, similar to their own, set up in a triangle, with a thick layer of snow on their flat tops. These tents had been here a while. That theory was confirmed when the riders discovered four empty carts and about forty horses tethered in the centre. But all the steeds lay on the ground, half-covered in snow. Frozen and starved. Dead.

An eerie feeling travelled down Kelermes's body. It was a terrible sight to behold that scattering of dead horses. This place felt very wrong. He turned to Orik and saw the same fear echoed in his friend's expression. Not something he had ever seen on Orik's face before. No one spoke for a moment. There was just the sound of the wind howling across the plain, and the billowing *flap, flap, flap* of the tent walls. Kelermes issued a silent prayer, calling on Tabiti to protect them from evil spirits.

With hand gestures, Aristeas gave a silent order for four warriors to check inside each of the yurtas simultaneously. He and Orik were among four to check one of the tents. Kelermes unsheathed his sword and stood to the side of the entrance with Orik. Agar and Tevtar stood on the opposite side. What would they discover inside? Dead bodies? Armed warriors? Kelermes could accept either of those possibilities. But he had the feeling it would be something far worse, and he could tell from his comrades' expressions that they, too, were unusually wary. Aristeas gave a low whistle – the signal to enter – and the four of them brandished their weapons, pulled aside the entrance flap, and stepped inside.

CHAPTER FOURTEEN

Before long, Alexandre and Nadia came out of the cold and into the warm kitchen. Maddy and Isobel were still at the table where he'd left them what seemed like hours ago. But it couldn't have been that long, surely. The girls rose to their feet.

'What happened?' Isobel took Nadia's hand and led her to an empty chair. 'Sit down. Are you warm enough? No, you're freezing. Maddy, could you get her a blanket?'

Maddy nodded and left the room, returning a moment later with one of the woollen throws from the sitting room. She held it out to Isobel who draped it around Nadia's shoulders.

'Do you want some tea?' Maddy asked Nadia.

'No.' Nadia shook her head. 'Do you have milk?'

'Milk on its own?'

She nodded.

'Warm milk or cold?'

'Warm is good,' Nadia said through chattering teeth.

As Maddy set about warming a mug of milk, Isobel gently questioned the girl. 'What happened?'

In reply Nadia turned to look at Alexandre, her cheeks flushed, her eyes still wet with tears.

'Do you want me to tell them?' Alex asked. The poor girl probably didn't want to talk about it again.

Nadia nodded and bowed her head, pulling the blanket tight around her shoulders and sinking down further into the chair.

'It would seem that our friend Travis attacked her,' Alex said.

'No!' Isobel cried. 'I mean, *Travis*? Are you sure? He's a sweet, harmless boy. Surely there's been a mistake.'

'I not lie,' Nadia said.

The microwave pinged, and Maddy took out the mug of milk, not bothering to check its temperature. She plonked it in front of Nadia and glared at Alexandre. 'Alex, can I talk to you for a minute?'

Alex nodded and followed Maddy out of the kitchen. She closed the door behind them and led Alex deep into the hallway to ensure they wouldn't be overheard.

'Really?' Maddy hissed. 'You really believe Travis would attack someone?'

'I know it doesn't seem likely...' he began. The problem was, Alexandre believed it really was all too likely. The girl was so mesmerising that it was easy to think she wanted you to kiss her, to hold her, to do more. Travis had obviously misread the situation. But he couldn't tell Maddy about Nadia's effect on himself. Not without her getting the wrong idea.

'It's ludicrous, is what it is,' Maddy said. 'She's obviously lying.'

'We shouldn't jump to conclusions. Why don't I pay Travis a visit? Get his side of the story.'

'Good idea. So what are we supposed to do with Nadia? Shall I drop her back to her place?'

'I don't think she has a home? She said she had nowhere to go. No money.'

'Really? Her clothes are expensive, and she looks really, I dunno, groomed, and rich.'

'Why don't we let her stay here tonight?' Alex said. 'In the meantime, I can speak to Travis and then we'll sort something out for her tomorrow.'

'That could be awkward,' Maddy replied. 'Won't she wonder why all the shutters are closed in the morning? Anyway, it's dangerous here – there are vicious vampires hunting us, in case you'd forgotten.'

'All the more reason to keep her safe here in the house. I'll pay Travis a visit now. You stay and be nice to her.' Alexandre pulled Maddy in close and kissed the top of her head, breathing in her scent. He must have been mad to be almost seduced by nothing but a pretty face. Madison was his girl. Now and forever. No blonde temptress could ever change that. 'I love you,' he said. 'Don't ever forget it.'

She looked up and smiled, her pale eyes softening. 'I love you, too. So much. And of course, I want to help Nadia, I just think we've got a lot on at the moment – understatement – and she's a complication we could really do without.'

'But surely we should help someone in trouble.'

'Of course, I'm not saying we shouldn't. It's just...' Maddy's face clouded over. 'We don't even know this Nadia person and now she's staying the night.'

Alex didn't understand why Madison was so unwilling to help. She was normally such a generous, kind person. She'd been the first person to forgive Leonora after her betrayal, so why now was she being so uncharitable to someone in need? 'It won't be for long, Madison. Just until we find out what happened with Travis, and make sure she's safe from harm.'

'As if Travis would hurt a fly,' Maddy snapped.

'Shh, Nadia will hear you.'

'So?'

Alex raised his eyebrows, his temper flaring. 'I'll go now and speak to Travis.'

'Make sure you don't accuse him.'

Alexandre grunted in reply.

'You won't, will you?' she asked, her tone softening. 'Don't forget, he's our friend.'

'Your friend, maybe,' Alex mumbled, instantly regretting it.

'What's that supposed to mean?'

'Nothing, nothing. Let's not fight. It's not our argument, it's theirs.'

'So why is she staying here then? I really don't trust her.'

'We're going around in circles. Let me question Travis and we'll see what's what.'

'Fine.'

He bent to kiss her goodbye, but she turned away and his lips met the side of her head. What had just happened? Why were they arguing? Madison was being impossible. Nadia's face came into his mind, and he swallowed hard. No, she was just a sweet girl in distress who needed a little support. That was all there was to it.

It didn't take Alexandre long to reach the converted Cotswold-stone terrace where Travis rented his small one-bedroom flat. And it took a second for him to ascertain that no one was home. He slid around the back of the buildings to where Travis's van was parked up. The boy was asleep inside the vehicle with his hair and face pressed up against the driver's window. His breath making a silver-grey bloom on the cold clear glass.

Alex rapped on the window, right next to Travis's ear. He expected Travis to wake with a start, but the boy didn't stir, so he tried the door handle. It clunked and opened, spilling Travis into Alex's arms. Travis groaned, mumbling something unintelligible as Alex leant him back against the van, holding him upright by his coat lapels. He smelled of mildewed sleep.

'Travis, wake up,' Alex snapped, shaking him lightly.

'Nadia,' Travis said, his eyes still closed.

Alexandre briefly wondered if he was drunk, but he couldn't smell any alcohol. Perhaps he'd been drugged? But he couldn't be sure. Losing patience, Alex lightly slapped the young man's face.

'Ow!' Travis's hand went up to his cheek as he opened one eye, followed by the other. 'Alex, mate, whaddya do that for?'

'I'm sorry,' Alex replied, loosening his grip on Travis's coat. 'You were unconscious. I thought you might be drugged or drunk.'

'What?' Travis gave himself a shake and rolled his shoulders, stepping away from the van and still rubbing his cheek, which was now the colour of a holiday sunset. 'Unconscious? Drugged? I was asleep. You didn't have to hit me so hard, mate. I feel like I've been clobbered by the Incredible Hulk.'

'Again, I apologise,' Alex said, not feeling sorry at all. 'Why aren't you at home? Why are you asleep in your van?'

'Oh, er, I'm always falling asleep in my van. It's nicer than my flat. Warmer, too.'

'I've come to talk to you. To ask you some questions... about Nadia.'

'Nadia?' Travis flushed and instantly appeared shifty. His eyes lowered and he cleared his throat.

'Yes, Nadia. She's made some serious accusations against you, Travis.'

'*What?*' His eyes widened momentarily. 'What are you talking about?' Travis scratched his head, his fingers becoming momentarily snarled in his matted blond hair. He gave a fake yawn, which looked to Alex like he was stalling for time.

'Come on, you know what I'm talking about.'

'Alex, I don't know what she told you, but—'

'Travis, are you going to tell me the truth, or do I have to shake it out of you?' Alex narrowed his eyes and leant in closer to Travis, who shrank back against his van. Alex felt bad for trying to intimidate the boy, but he didn't have time for games. He wanted the truth.

'You're quite a scary dude, Alex. Did anyone ever tell you that?'

'Maybe once or twice.'

'Where's Nadia now?' Travis asked.

'At home, with Madison. But she doesn't want you there.'

'Christ, did Nadia tell Maddy?'

'Ah, so you admit there is something to tell!'

Travis dropped his shoulders. 'Can we get back in the van? It's freezing out here. Not that the van's much warmer, but it's better than outside.'

Alex nodded impatiently. He went around to the passenger side, as Travis climbed back into the driver's seat.

They each slammed their doors, and Alex waited for Travis to start talking.

'I don't want Maddy to think I'm a bad person,' Travis began. 'She's my friend.'

'Madison doesn't think you're a bad person. She thinks Nadia is lying. I, however, do not.' Alex felt his anger rising as he thought about what Travis had done.

'Nothing like this has ever happened to me before in my life. I mean, I know I'm not the best with girls, but I don't usually get that sort of reaction. I don't... I don't even really know what happened.'

'Whatever you did frightened the life out of her. You should be ashamed.'

'I... All I did was kiss her. Look, I dropped Taff and Kerri home, and then I drove Nadia back to hers.'

'She has a place?' Alex interrupted. 'A home?'

'Um, yeah, just up from the fire station in one of those ex-council houses.'

'Do you have the address?'

'Why is that important?' Travis asked.

'Because she told me she had no home. Do you have her address?'

'No. I mean, she asked me to drop her at the bottom of the road. I didn't get a chance to see which house she lives in.'

'So, what happened? You kissed her...'

'Yeah. And, for the record, she kissed me back. And she was into it. Into me. She didn't pull away or anything. She was amazing. Like some kind of goddess. I couldn't believe she liked me. Anyway, I asked if she was going to invite me in for a coffee. But she said no. That her flatmate wouldn't like it. So I leant in for another kiss, but this time, she stopped me and said she'd better go. It's a bit embarrassing, but I took her hand, and kissed it, and then I leant in to try for a last goodnight kiss. She totally freaked out. She went mad and started really pushing me away. Hitting me. Then, she jumped out of the van and started running. I would've gone after her, but I thought she might get even more freaked out if I started chasing after her. So I stayed where I was. It was weird. Like a switch had been flipped. One minute she was all over me, the next she couldn't wait to get away. I promise that's all that happened. I didn't do anything bad to her. I swear.'

Travis was ashen-faced now. He looked as though he might cry. He sounded very convincing, like he really believed what he was saying. But then so had Nadia. The girl had been terrified. Alex didn't know who to believe. Perhaps it had all been an innocent misunderstanding. The girl was stunning, and the way she looked at you made you feel like you had to protect her, like she wanted to be held, and kissed. He could understand how Travis had been drawn to her. But the fact was that he had terrified an innocent woman, and that was inexcusable. Even if it had been a misunderstanding. The guy had crossed a line.

'You scared her. So, now, you need to stay away from her,' Alex said. 'You need to stay away from all of us.'

'What! But Maddy's my friend. You can't stop me from—'

Alex lowered his voice to a deep hiss. 'I said, you need to stay away. Are we clear?' He stared at Travis until he finally looked him in the eye. Until he finally got the message that Alex wasn't messing about. That he was deadly serious.

'Fine. But I didn't do anything wrong.' Travis glared at him. It was the first time Alexandre had seen Travis anything but amiable.

Alexandre didn't bother to say goodbye. He slid out of the van and made his way back to Marchwood, skimming the damp ground, his thoughts a blur, not really any clearer about the truth of what had actually happened.

But at least Nadia would be safe now. Well, as safe as she could be in a houseful of vampires, with even worse things waiting outside.

CHAPTER FIFTEEN

SCYTHIA, 514 BC

As Kelermes stepped into the yurta with his fellow soldiers, it took his eyes a moment to adjust to the darkness within. There was no warmth in here. No fire had been lit recently. No warriors cried out, brandishing weapons to attack. The tent appeared empty.

He took a further step, deeper into the dark space. Bedrolls lay on the ground, disturbed but unoccupied. He and his comrades began searching the yurta more thoroughly, checking the sleeping areas and taking note of the state of the place. They confirmed that there were absolutely no people here at all. No bodies. There were, however, weapons still hanging from the walls, along with many possessions – loot, clothing, armour, keepsakes and bedrolls – all still in place. This was certainly an encampment of Scythian warriors, just like themselves. But where were they? And, more importantly, would they ever be coming back?

Kelermes stooped to pick up a belt off the floor, running his thumb pad across the fine engraved belt plate. No one would voluntarily leave a treasured item such as this behind. There were shields, swords, daggers, bow cases, coats, boots and more besides. Everything was freezing. The whole place had the bleak air of abandonment. A milk bag hung by the entrance, next to a side of uncooked meat, both frozen solid. Whatever had happened here, it wasn't a recent event.

The interior of all three yurtas had now been thoroughly searched, and the warriors collected outside, feeling it was, at last, safe to talk.

'What has happened here?' Lohant cried. 'Where is everyone?'

'Kidnapped?' Abaris speculated.

'Shall I light a fire?' Abaris's wife, Savlius, asked. 'Are we to remain here for the night?'

At this suggestion, there was a great outcry. It was clear no one relished the idea of remaining in this ghost camp. Kelermes himself shivered at the thought and hoped their leader would feel the same.

'Quiet!' Aristeas commanded. 'We will not stay here. Something bad has happened, and I do not believe it would be wise to tempt any lingering spirits with our immortal souls. But, before we leave, we must gather everything up and bring it with us. We cannot leave a Scythian camp here for our enemy to use. I would prefer to burn the whole camp down, but such a huge fire would give our position away. There are empty carts. Let's pile everything into them, including the yurtas. I'm sorry. I know we are all weary, but the sooner we get it done, the sooner we can move away from this place and set up a camp of our own. Savlius, yes, you may light a fire, but not outside; it must be inside one of the yurtas. We're still too close to the Persians, but we do need to warm up, and so do the horses if we are all to survive the night. Cover the dead horses with snow, first. Hopefully, they will stay buried until spring.'

Kelermes would have preferred it if they simply abandoned everything here and set up their own camp far from this cursed place. But he knew that Aristeas spoke sense. It would be foolhardy to hand the Persians a ready-built place of shelter. And so, although none of them relished the task ahead, no one argued with their leader's orders.

Within minutes, Savlius had a good fire going inside one of the tents, where she also dispensed warm milk to the warriors. They hoped the plume of smoke escaping through the crown of the structure wouldn't be seen by their enemy. Everyone worked hard to strip the yurtas of their contents, piling everything neatly inside the carts with practiced ease. Reluctantly, Savlius damped down the fire before the final tent was dismantled and packed away. The carts were assigned to the strongest, least weary horses, and finally, they were ready to leave.

'One more hour of fast riding,' Aristeas said, 'and then we can rest for the night. I imagine the Persians will already have set up camp, so at least we should be safe from ambush tonight. But we need to move away from this place, and hope that whatever happened here will not happen again.'

With a weary, cold, and aching body, Kelermes swung himself onto Tabi. He hadn't the heart to make the mare kneel for him in the snow. The animal was unhappy, he could tell. 'Not long now,' he soothed, patting her neck. She hung her head, unmoving. 'I know how you feel,' he added.

With a rattle of weapons and a creak of carts, the warriors moved out. Kelermes was so cold and tired, he barely registered the next hour on horseback. It seemed as though he moved in a dream, the grey darkness heavy on his shoulders, the icy wind biting down. Startled out of his torpor, at last, he heard the shouted cry to halt. Finally, they were permitted to stop and set up camp for the night. There would be no celebratory feast, for they were all too weary. But there would, however, be warm fires, a few bites of fresh-cooked meat, followed by wonderful, wonderful sleep. That is, if he could persuade his stiff, icy joints to obey him and move, so he could dismount.

· · ·

The following morning, Kelermes awoke early with a leaden heart. He dragged himself out from under his hide determined to leave the tent before everyone else awoke, in order to avoid having to talk to anyone. The last thing he wanted was to witness Laodice and Lohant breakfasting together, getting used to their upcoming status as man and wife. Or, even worse, pitying looks from Orik and the others. Kel gave a low growl and reached for his weapons belt. Enough self-pity. Get up and get out of here.

It had snowed again in the night – a blessing to cover yesterday's tracks. But now the sky was clear, not quite blue, but heading that way. Yesterday's strange events seemed a distant memory. The discovery of the abandoned encampment meant they had now gained extra weapons, carts and yurtas. Aristeas was a good leader; he would ensure it would all be distributed fairly. Before the arrival of the others, Kel took some dried meat for his breakfast and then melted some snow to splash his face, trying and failing to shake off his dull mood.

Breakfast over, the warriors fed their horses a few handfuls of corn, and broke down the camp in record time. It wasn't long before they were all on the move again.

A couple of hours into the journey, Kel spotted an encampment up ahead – a large settlement of small tents with penned livestock. Perhaps these nomad farmers would trade them a few flasks of *koumiss* – a cup or two of fermented mare's milk would be welcomed by all at this evening's belated feast. They'd have to warn these farmers to move on. Tell them that the Persians would be coming through soon. That it wasn't safe here.

As they drew closer, Kelermes noticed dead sheep lying in the pens. A situation that would normally never be left unchecked by their owners. The remaining goats and sheep bleated pitifully. A feeling of dread passed over the young warrior, and he locked eyes with Orik in a look of apprehension. What was going on here? This didn't have the feel of a normal raid or enemy attack. Livestock would never be left penned and unguarded – not in such inhospitable territory. Any food or shelter would be commandeered immediately. Could this be a repeat of last night's strangeness?

Once the Scythian warriors were in arrow-firing range, Aristeas brought his hand up to halt everyone. He indicated that Lohant and Abaris should approach the settlement to investigate. 'Circle the place first,' he commanded. 'Check the snow for recent tracks. Everyone else, stay put, and have your arrows ready.'

With his bow in hand, Kelermes strained his eyes to see if he could spot anything or anyone. But it was difficult to tell, as each grouping of tents was huddled together, obscuring much from an outsider's eyes. Anyone or anything could be hiding within. Daylight made the place less foreboding than last night's deserted encampment, but there was still a wrongness about the place that made Kelermes's flesh crawl.

Minutes later, the two men returned from their recce.

'Empty,' Lohant grunted.

'Same as before,' added Abaris. 'No one's there. But all the possessions remain. Not much, I'll grant you, but food and tableware, clothing and weapons are all still in the tents.'

Everyone murmured with uneasy surprise.

'Any recent tracks?' Aristeas asked.

'None,' Abaris replied. 'The snow is virgin all the way around. Whatever happened here, happened before today.'

'So, if there are no tracks, there's no point searching the area for survivors,' Savlius remarked.

Aristeas took a breath and looked around at his men and women. 'We cannot take this camp with us like we did with yesterday's. But I still don't want to leave it for the enemy to use.'

'Sir,' Kelermes interrupted.

Aristeas turned to the young warrior and nodded for him to continue.

'How about we take just the weapons, and maybe the animals with us for food? We could collapse the tents and hope the snow covers everything before the Persians come through. Even if it doesn't snow again, the tents will be harder to spot if they're lying flat on the ground.'

'Good enough,' their leader replied. 'Quickly, though. We've had enough delays.'

Kelermes was pleased his suggestion had been heeded. With a proud swelling in his chest, he, Orik and Agar entered one of the small dwellings together. But his proud moment soon disappeared – a family must have lived here, for there were child-sized boots and clothing, as well as a hide crib. It was a sad situation. A family's home about to be dismantled and forgotten. Where were these people? Would they ever return? What had happened here? Kelermes scanned the small space but found nothing the warriors would want or need. He said a prayer under his breath, hoping that whoever had lived here was now safe. Although he very much doubted it. The soldiers laid the abandoned belongings flat on the ground, removed the tent poles and collapsed the dwelling. Glancing around the camp, Kelermes saw that everyone else had done the same. They kicked drifts of snow over the flattened settlement and, with a little rearrangement, were able to bundle the few remaining living creatures into one of the wagons.

Mounted and ready to continue north once more, Aristeas called his soldiers around. Kelermes nudged his horse closer in, earning a few dirty looks from some of his brethren. But he wanted to easily see and hear his leader and didn't mind about ruffling a few feathers.

'I have a feeling these will not be the only abandoned settlements we will encounter,' Aristeas began. 'Something has happened here that is not easily explainable. I would have guessed at raiders, but no possessions have been taken. Persians? But they haven't reached this far north yet, and there are no bodies of the slain. No blood on the snow or in the tents. Slavers? Perhaps. But again, why would they leave behind valuable weapons and livestock? No, something else has happened here, and we must be on our guard, more so than usual. If anyone sees or hears anything out of the ordinary, no matter how trivial it may seem, I want you to report it to me immediately. Is that clear?'

'Yes, sir,' the warriors replied.

'And we need to find a survivor,' Aristeas continued. 'Someone who can tell us exactly what has gone on here. Most importantly, we will make a sacrifice of these creatures tonight.' He nodded towards the newly rescued animals in the cart. 'We must appease the gods if we are to prevent such a thing happening to ourselves.'

At this, there were murmurs of approval. Kelermes instantly felt guilty that he had earlier suggested taking the animals for food. Of course, they should be given to the gods. He hoped the deities would not take offence at his selfishness. Aristeas cast a long look over his warriors, catching each of their eyes with a meaningful gaze. When his gaze landed on Kelermes, the young soldier flushed with embarrassment and regret at his earlier suggestion. No one seemed to have picked up on his error, but it didn't stop him feeling terrible about it.

Aristeas lifted his chin and gave a nod. 'Now, let's move out.'

Leaving the second ghost camp behind, Kelermes prayed fervently to the gods. Begging them to forgive him for suggesting he and his comrades keep the animals for themselves rather than sacrificing them. He offered up anything they wanted in return. He didn't notice the jewel-blue sky or the ice-cold air. Instead, he kept his head bowed low, and prayed for an end to the strangeness of the past twenty-four hours. His gods had looked after him thus far, and he implored them to continue to protect him, assuring them that he was truly their servant. That they could count on him for anything.

Would he and the others find more of the same deserted encampments ahead? What did it mean? Were the gods displeased? Kelermes felt nervous, inadequate, unsettled. Laodice had been right to discard someone as unworthy as he. He couldn't blame her for choosing another. It was just a shame that she had turned to Lohant of all people. As Tabi walked through the snow, Kelermes sank down in his seat, feeling like an imposter. He should have remained a farmer's son. This time yesterday, he had been proud and confident, ready to fight with his love by his side. Today he was alone, having displeased the gods, and displeased his beloved.

CHAPTER SIXTEEN

While Alex was out, Maddy and Isobel attempted to "entertain" Nadia. But Maddy wasn't in the mood and Nadia wasn't exactly the talkative kind, so it had been awkward and uncomfortable in the kitchen, trying to be hospitable to their strange and beautiful guest. Nadia hadn't wanted to talk about herself at all. She hadn't been rude exactly; she just hadn't been engaging. It was as though she was half-asleep. She made no attempts at conversation and, when Isobel eventually asked if she'd like to go to bed, she'd said she wanted to wait until Alex got back, to see what had happened with Travis. Maddy could understand that. She would be interested to hear what had happened herself. She and Isobel kept darting glances at each other over the girl's head. It seemed like they'd been sitting in the kitchen forever. She hoped Ben was having a more fun evening than they were.

As the clock ticked steadily towards 1.30 a.m., Maddy slid into exhaustion. All she wanted to do was crawl into bed, cosy up to Alex and fall asleep. She regretted snapping at him earlier. She'd been a cow. He'd only been trying to be kind to someone in need. When he came home, she'd say sorry, and hopefully, everything would be okay again.

Isobel suddenly stiffened and turned her head. Alex must be returning. Sure enough, a couple of minutes later, the back door opened and closed, and Alex walked into the kitchen bringing a cool swathe of night air into the room. As always, Maddy's heart lifted at the sight of him. She worried when they were apart, and now she felt even more foolish and petty about their earlier disagreement. Would there ever come a time when they could live a life untroubled by danger? He gave her a smile that made her feel like they were the only two people in the room. Unfortunately, they weren't.

'Did you find him?' Maddy asked. 'Was he home?'

'What did Travis say?' Nadia asked. 'Did he tell you truth? Or did he lie?'

Alex scratched at his chin, a gesture Maddy recognised. He was thinking about what to say – considering his answer. Isobel patted the chair next to her and Alex sat down heavily. He looked from her to Maddy, and finally to Nadia. 'Travis is upset.'

'Oh, *Travis* is upset.' Nadia spat out the words. Maddy was a little shocked at her outburst, considering the fact she'd hardly said two words over the past hour. Now, her eyes flashed, her face alive with anger.

'Let me finish,' Alex said gently.

Nadia tilted her head and tossed one side of her hair, waiting for him to go on.

'Travis is upset because he himself is unsure what happened. He said he kissed you, and you kissed him back.'

'Yes,' Nadia said. 'I already told you this.'

'But then he said when he tried to kiss you again, you started hitting him.'

'He tried more than kissing, and I told him, no, but he not listen.'

'Okay,' Alex said. 'I think it sounds as though it could have been a misunderstanding.'

'No,' Nadia said. 'He tried to attack me.' Her eyes filled with water, and she bit her lip.

'Did he hurt you?' Maddy asked.

'No, but—'

'I agree with Alex,' Maddy said. 'It sounds like a misunderstanding. I know Travis, and I promise you he's a good guy.'

'He is not good guy.'

'He wouldn't do anything deliberately to hurt you. He just really liked you,' Maddy said.

'You not believe me. Maybe I should go to police.' The tears were running down her face now.

Maddy had to admit, Nadia did seem genuinely upset. Belle had moved around to put an arm around the girl.

'Don't worry,' Alex said. 'Of course we believe you. We'll make sure nothing bad happens to you. You can stay here as long as you like.'

Maddy caught Alex's eye and tried to convey exactly what she thought of his generous offer for the girl to stay in their house. But his firm expression told her that his mind was made up and Maddy didn't want to call him out on it, no matter how annoyed she was by it. They were stuck with the girl for now. Madison felt mean and ungenerous again. It wasn't that she didn't like Nadia – she didn't even know her. It was more a combination of her loyalty to Travis, and this girl's demands on Alex, plus the fact that they were in the middle of a deadly war with ancient creatures, and not forgetting that her brother had just become a vampire. What a mess. She sighed heavily.

'You not want me here,' Nadia said, her anger evaporating. She gave Maddy a sad smile. 'I go.'

'What? No.' Nothing like a guilt trip to make Maddy feel even worse. 'No, no, of course you're staying. I think I'm just tired. It's late, we should all get to bed. We can talk more in the morning.'

'I go,' Nadia said, scraping her chair back and standing up. 'I'm sorry for trouble.'

'No, please,' Maddy said, also standing. 'You've had a shock. Whatever happened tonight, it obviously upset you, and that's not good. You need to be with people. Stay tonight, and we'll sort the rest out tomorrow.'

'Madison's right,' Isobel added. 'Come, I'll take you up to one of the guest rooms.'

'You are sure?' Nadia looked from Isobel to Maddy to Alex.

'Yes,' Alex said. 'You're staying. No arguments.'

'Thank you.' Nadia bowed her head and followed Isobel out of the room.

Maddy walked around the table to Alex, and he pulled her into his lap. She curled into him and felt some of the tension leave her body. 'You're tired,' he said. 'Let's go up.'

'I'm sorry about earlier,' she said.

'Me too. I don't want to do anything to upset you.'

Well, inviting beautiful strangers to spend the night isn't exactly the right way to go, was the reply on Maddy's lips. But she instantly squashed it. 'I think our nerves are strained after... everything. Do you think Ben should come back in now? Will he be okay out there?'

'I think Ben is the most okay out of any of us,' Alex replied. 'Those three will be having a good time. Let them have their fun now. Tomorrow we can be safe and sensible, and start planning.'

'What about Nadia?' Maddy murmured, her eyes closing.

'I don't know. Let's forget about her tonight. Right now, I'm going to carry you upstairs to bed.'

'Sounds good to me.'

At last, in the shuttered darkness, she snuggled down in bed under the heavy brocade covers, her body finally relaxing. Alex lay next to her, leaning back against the pillows, playing idly with her hair.

'Are you sure Ben and the others will be okay?' she murmured through a stifled yawn.

'Perfectly fine.'

'And Nadia?'

'I'm sure she'll be fine, too.'

'What are we going to do about her? Surely, she must have somewhere else to stay.' Maddy couldn't let it go. She had visions of the girl staying with them for weeks.

'She can stay tonight, and we'll sort something out for her tomorrow.'

'I suppose so. I'm still in shock about Travis.'

'I think Travis is also in shock about what happened.'

'What do you mean?' she asked.

'Nothing. Go to sleep now. You need to rest, to gather your energy, and... *achoo!*'

'Did you just... sneeze?' Maddy glanced up at Alex, but it was too dark to catch his expression.

'I suppose I did.' Alex touched his nose and wrinkled it slightly. 'That's odd. I've never sneezed before. Well, not as a vampire anyway.'

'Do you feel okay?' Maddy asked. 'You can't be getting a cold, can you? Or maybe you have vampire hay fever.' She grinned. It was strange to hear such a human sound come out of her immortal vampire.

'Very droll. No, I feel fine.' But Alex promptly issued another sneeze. Followed by another.

'That's a bit worrying,' she said, putting a palm to his cheek. 'You can't get ill, can you?'

'No. The only illness I've ever had was the sleeping sickness. And I don't feel tired at all. Or weak. It's probably nothing. Just some dust.'

But Maddy's initial amusement at his sneeze was being

replaced by something less welcome. An icy tendril of fear crept up her spine accompanied by all kinds of dark thoughts. She pushed herself up, cupped his face in her hands and kissed him. If anything happened to Alex, she knew she wouldn't be able to bear it. Love was a gift, but it brought so much worry that she sometimes wondered if it was worth it. At least if it was just her on her own, she wouldn't have to face such blind fear every day. Fear of something happening to the ones she loved. Sometimes it was crippling.

'Alex, are you sure you're okay?' she whispered.

'Of course.' Maddy heard the amusement in his voice. 'It was just a few sneezes. Nothing to worry about.'

But Maddy wasn't convinced. Something wasn't quite right. In fact, something was most definitely wrong.

If Nadia thought anything about the shutters being closed in the daytime, she didn't remark on it. Maddy chewed on a piece of toast while Nadia sat at the table sipping a glass of milk. She wore the same clothes she had on yesterday, and Maddy felt bad that she hadn't offered to lend her some fresh ones. But, then again, Maddy was five foot nothing, and Nadia must have been at least five ten. Maddy's clothes would have been nowhere near the right size. She'd have been better off wearing something of Alex's. But there was no way Maddy was offering any of *his* clothes.

'You didn't tell me we were having visitors.' Esther sniffed as she walked into the kitchen and dumped her dripping shopping basket on the counter top. She untied her wet headscarf and patted her hair. 'It's bucketing down out there.'

'Esther, this is Nadia. Nadia, Esther,' Maddy said without too much enthusiasm.

'Hello, Esther,' Nadia said, her voice barely a whisper.

Esther gave another sniff. 'How long will you be staying?'

Maddy replied for her. 'We're not sure. Nadia had an upsetting experience last night, so she might be staying today while we sort it out.'

'Fine. It would be nice to be informed of these things.'

'I'm informing you now,' Maddy said. There was no need for Esther to get all persnickerty with her. She didn't want the girl to be staying here either. But sometimes – most times – you didn't get what you wanted. Maddy snuck a glance at the housekeeper as she huffed around the kitchen. Maybe Esther would be able to get some information out of Nadia. Maddy wondered if she should take Esther aside and fill her in. Esther glowered at the back of Nadia's head and muttered something unsavoury under her breath. *No.* Maybe not.

The others were currently downstairs in the basement planning their trip to Turkey, and Maddy hadn't been happy about being stuck up here with Nadia. Isobel had suggested that Maddy should be the one to chaperone the girl as she was the only human, and what would happen if Nadia wanted to go out? The vampires couldn't risk opening any external doors in the daytime, and it could get awkward, not to mention dangerous. Maddy saw the logic in this but still didn't see why she should be left out of everything. She'd suggested that Esther could keep an eye on Nadia.

'Esther? You really want to leave her to the mercy of Esther?' Alex had replied with a smirk. She realised that Alex was right. Maddy wasn't the best suited to the job but leaving her with Esther would just have been plain cruel.

So, now, here she was babysitting an unwanted houseguest while all the important decisions were being made without her. Added to that, she was still worried about Alex. Although he hadn't sneezed again, he had been very sniffly this morning, even to the extent that he had needed a handkerchief. The

SHALINI BOLAND

others had noticed it, too. But no one seemed to be taking it seriously.

'What do you want to do this morning?' Maddy asked Nadia. 'Stay in? Go out? Watch some TV?'

'I don't mind. Why the others are not here?'

'They're all busy today. It's just you and me, I'm afraid.'

'You have no work to go to?' Nadia asked. 'No school?'

'Not right now,' Madison replied, bristling slightly at Nadia's dismissive tone. Maddy had left full-time education when she inherited the Marchwood estate. She had no job either and had simply been enjoying the freedom to do what she wanted for the first time in her life. She supposed she would like to do something meaningful at some stage in the near future. But, recently, she hadn't exactly had time to think about anything other than Alex, Ben and the other Marchwood vampires. Things had been... busy.

'All day the others are occupied?' Nadia asked.

'Yes. They're out.'

'Ah, okay. We stay in and talk, if you like?'

Maddy was surprised. Nadia didn't seem like the talkative kind. But, okay, maybe this was an opportunity to learn what *really* happened last night. 'Let's go into the lounge.' Maddy tilted her head in the direction of Esther, and Nadia nodded.

They got up and left the room, leaving Esther muttering away about extra mouths to feed and rooms to prepare. It was chilly in the living room, but Maddy couldn't summon up the energy to fetch another sweater or light the fire, so she switched on a couple of lamps, curled up in an armchair and hugged a cushion instead. Nadia sat opposite on one of the sofas, her legs crossed gracefully, her hair shining like white gold in the lamplight.

'You feeling better today?' Maddy asked.

'A little better, thank you.'

'Good. That's good.' Maddy tried to wrack her brains for

conversation. Small talk. Anything, as the rain drummed down on the shutters like machine-gun fire.

'How long have you and Alexandre been together?' Nadia asked.

Maddy thought about her answer, remembering back to the previous Christmas, to when she and Alex first met, him cowering under the gleaming blade of the axe she held over his head. 'Just over a year,' she replied.

Nadia nodded. 'It is love?'

Maddy nodded her head once.

'Alexandre said you had argument last night.'

Did he indeed? Maddy chewed the inside of her lip. 'Nothing serious,' Maddy replied. 'Just a tiff, you know? We made up last night.'

'Good. He is a good person. You are lucky.'

'I know. And Travis is a good person, too.' She probably shouldn't have brought it up, but she still couldn't believe her friend was capable of assaulting someone. She ploughed on. 'Are you going to take it any further?'

'How you mean?'

'Are you going to the police?'

She shook her head. 'They will do nothing. My word against his. Can I stay here for very short time? One day, or two? Then I leave.'

Maddy swallowed. She wanted to help the girl, but she also felt loyalty to Travis. 'Don't you have anywhere to stay? No friends or family?'

'Not a safe place, no. This is your house? Or is Alexandre's house?'

'Mine,' Maddy said, feeling very privileged all of a sudden.

Nadia nodded and looked impressed.

'You can stay here for a day or two, if you like,' Maddy added impulsively. She couldn't very well throw her out, even though she didn't entirely trust her. 'Until you get sorted. Where are you from? I mean, which country?'

'I was born in Ukraine, but I live in Romania for most of my life.'

'Do you miss it?'

'Sometimes...' She shrugged. 'You are English, yes? Born here?'

'Yeah. Born in London,' Maddy replied with a strange stab of something like homesickness for the city she grew up in. 'But I've been told I'm Eastern European on my mother's side.'

'Yes. I can see this,' Nadia said, fixing her with an unnerving stare. 'You have a wolf's eyes.'

Maddy raised an eyebrow, not quite knowing what to make of that comment. Well, if she was a wolf, Maddy thought Nadia was a sleek cat. Perfectly groomed and at ease. Quite different from the shivering, terrified girl she'd been yesterday. 'Will you go back to Romania? Or stay in England?'

'I don't know. I decide later.'

The shutters rattled, making Maddy jump. 'Sounds like there's a storm blowing out there.'

Nadia nodded. 'Yes, a storm. It will be bad, I think.'

CHAPTER SEVENTEEN

SCYTHIA, 514 BC

The afternoon passed without incident. Periodically, Aristeas would send a lone soldier to scout ahead for settlements, or to check behind for the approach of their enemy, always hoping to spot a small detachment of Persians they could obliterate. But there was no sign of either ghost camps or Persians, just the bright sun reflecting off the snow-crusted earth. A flat landscape stretching ahead and behind as far as the eye could see. Perhaps all would be well. There was little chatter, each person deep in their own thoughts. The creak of the carts, the clink of harnesses and weaponry, and the soft step of the horses. These sounds became hypnotic. The familiar rhythm of the journey.

Two further days passed in this way. Steady progress away from the Persians, and deeper into the Scythian heartland. With every mile, the warriors grew less ill at ease. The dark memory of the abandoned camps fading with every step. They caught game and roasted fresh meat each night – no big feasts, merely a hurried meal before bedding down for the night. More snow fell, but it wasn't too heavy, and it had the added bonus of covering their tracks.

Head bent, hypnotised by the white landscape and the steady muffled tread of the horses' hooves, Kelermes tried not to dwell on anything personal. If his thoughts turned to Laodice, he would push her from his thoughts and think instead of how he would try to be braver in battle, and how he would be more pious, less selfish and pray more to the gods. Thank them for protecting him and his people. He would learn by Aristeas's example. There was a true warrior. He had no wife, and it didn't seem to worry him. He was content only to lead. To fight. To do everything in his power to ensure the safety of his soldiers. Kelermes could learn from the man. He could model himself on their leader. Forget fanciful notions of raising a family with the woman he loved.

'Am I interrupting your thoughts?'

Startled by her soft voice, Kel's heart sped up, and he raised his head, turning to find Laodice by his side, their mares in step with each other. Was she still angry with him? He couldn't tell.

'I'm sorry I behaved so badly to you the other day,' she said.

Not angry, then. Her words were a balm to his aching heart, and he had to give himself a shake to ensure he hadn't slipped into a waking dream.

'What you did at the battle was selfless and caring,' she continued. 'Orik told me what really happened. About Lohant stealing your kill, while you were more concerned with making sure I kept my life. Can you forgive me for the awful things I said? For the terrible way I acted towards you?'

At her words, Kel's nerve endings tingled with new life. Laodice was asking his forgiveness. She didn't hate him anymore He silently thanked all the gods, and also gave a silent thank you to his friend for interceding on his behalf.

'Kel,' she said, 'please speak to me. I'm truly sorry.'

He realised that he hadn't replied to her yet. That she was staring at him with unshed tears in her eyes.

'You have no need to apologise,' he began.

'Of course I do. I behaved terribly.'

He held out a hand to stop her. 'What I did, loosing that arrow to kill your foe, was presumptuous and arrogant. You had no need of my protection. I can see that now. You are more than capable of despatching your enemy without interference. It is I who should apologise.'

'But no!' she cried. 'That's just it. The Persian almost killed me. I was losing badly. I only managed to stab the brute by a stroke of luck. He could have easily overpowered me, and you were there to make sure he didn't. Straight after I killed him, I was still consumed with battle rage and with relief for my narrow escape. I truly thought I had been about to die. That he was going to kill me. The relief when I killed him instead turned to shock when I saw your arrow pierce his head. I wasn't thinking clearly. If I had been thinking, I would never have accused you of trying to take credit for my kill. I know you would never do such a thing. I really do know you, Kel. Better than I know anyone else.'

They stopped riding then. Their mares standing side by side as the others continued moving forward without them.

'When I saw you ride off with Lohant, I wanted to die,' Kelermes admitted. 'I couldn't bear the thought of you and he—'

'Shh.' She reached for his hand and gripped it. 'Are we reconciled? Do you truly forgive me for the way I behaved?'

'Of course I do. Like I said, there is nothing to forgive.'

'Thank you. And I will never be angry if you should try to save me again,' she said. 'As long as you let me do the same for you.' She smiled, and her smile was warm enough to thaw his bitterness and hurt. Enough to make his heart sing with the promise of a longed-for future. Suddenly he was filled with the desire to remove all doubt from their relationship.

'Laodice, will you be my betrothed?'

'Yes, Kelermes. Yes, I will.'

Her reply took him from darkest doubt to the pinnacle of happiness. Kelermes couldn't conceal his smile. He felt as though he had grown several inches, that he was floating on clouds. That his steed was a winged creature that had taken him soaring to the heavens. This was everything he had ever wanted.

The following morning, after the best night's sleep he'd had in months, he was shaken awake by Orik. 'Up, you lazy lout,' his friend cried.

Kelermes's body was still lodged in sleep, unwilling to relinquish rest, but he sat himself upright anyway, eyes closed, his mind still half submerged in dreams. Taking a deep breath, he rolled his shoulders back and forth, stretching his arms, then reaching down to massage his stiff neck.

'Get up, Kel,' Orik said. 'Aristeas is itching to be off, and he'll have no problem leaving you behind if you're not ready.'

With an enormous yawn, Kelermes snapped open his eyes and jumped to his feet, clapping his tall friend on the shoulder and glancing around the tent. Orik was right; everyone else was already up and out. Last night, they had all piled into one yurta, not having the desire or energy to erect the whole camp. This morning, only Kel and his gear remained inside. 'Why didn't you wake me before?' Kelermes demanded. He couldn't believe he'd slept late. He was usually the first up. It was humiliating to be the last.

'It was a novelty seeing you all curled up, asleep,' Orik teased. 'You looked so sweet with your thumb in your mouth, like a baby. How could I disturb such a pretty sight?'

Kel gave Orik a friendly shove. 'Fool. Help me get my stuff.'

'Get it yourself. I'm going to take a piss, and then I'm getting some breakfast before it all disappears. Hurry if you want any – you know what greedy sons of asses those animals are.'

Kelermes cursed and pulled on his boots. 'I need to get my

things sorted first. Get me some meat. The lean part; I don't want a hunk of bone and gristle.'

Orik made a rude gesture, grinned and left the tent. Now Kelermes was alone, the events of yesterday hit him anew. He realised that all was good. And now he saw that things were about to get better – here came Laodice with a skin of steaming warm milk and a huge hunk of cooked antelope. The aroma of meat made Kelermes's mouth water, as did the sight of his bride-to-be. Suddenly he felt fully awake.

'What goddess is this?' Kelermes sighed. 'I knew there was more than one reason I was marrying you.'

'Don't get used to it,' she retorted. 'Breakfast in bed every day is not an option. But I thought I'd better bring you something – the others would have shovelled the lot into their greedy gobs if I hadn't grabbed this piece. It's for both of us to share.' She tore off a strip of meat with her teeth and handed him the rest.

He kissed her cheek and took the food. As he ate, it seemed as though a night's rest had improved the flavour. He took another bite and handed the meat back to her. 'Mm, it's good,' he said, wiping his mouth with the back of his hand. She nodded and smiled. Kelermes smiled back and thanked the gods for such a good woman. He was ready for the day ahead, and for their future together.

It was only their third day of travelling, but already so much had happened on their journey. Today's comparatively monotonous trek felt anything but, as a swirl of emotions eddied around Kel's body – relief, excitement, but most of all, love for his betrothed, and a deep contentment that his life was beginning to take shape. To take root. He no longer felt like an outsider. Over time, he had proved his worth to his leader and his brothers and sisters. He had come to belong to this respected band of warriors. Through marriage, he would further cement that bond, and his children would be born as warriors. They would surpass his achievements and be secure in their places. Kelermes had had to overcome many obstacles simply to earn his place here, but he was through the worst. He was protecting his people and his land. This was his life, and it was good. And it would only get better with the wedding celebrations ahead. Finally, everything was coming together.

CHAPTER EIGHTEEN

The spell was woven, and everything was set in place. The creature was confident that it would capture Alexandre tonight. There was no reason for anything to go awry. With centuries of practice, it knew how to spin a sticky web and beckon its prey.

Had it judged everything correctly? Had it given the coven leader enough time? It thought so, but the ancient creature had never acted with quite this much haste before. Had never needed sustenance quite as desperately. Centuries of drought had taken its toll.

There was no choice. It would have to be tonight, lest its very existence be put in jeopardy. It was weakening by the minute, by the second. But if it could hold on just a few hours longer, it would finally reap its reward.

CHAPTER NINETEEN

The hum of conversation washed over Alexandre like rushing water over rocks. It was an important discussion – one that he should be leading – but his mind was elsewhere. Alex stood by the piano in their basement sitting room, gliding his fingertips over the dark polished wood as Belle, Jacques, Freddie and Ben tried to agree on some kind of plan to stop the Cappadocians. Ben paced the rich carpets while the others stayed seated, but Alex's thoughts were upstairs with Madison and with Nadia. That girl unsettled him. He was drawn to her in a disturbing way. She needed to go before he... but no, he mustn't even allow himself to think such a thing. Twice now, no, three times he had been disloyal to Madison in his mind. Was he really so feckless and shallow? The girl he loved was being eclipsed by a stranger. Possibly a lying stranger. One who had cast aspersions on their friend. And yet, she had an innocence about her. She gave off an aura of needing to be protected.

She and Maddy were up there now, talking. Normally, his vampire senses would allow him to hear every word. But he couldn't concentrate now, not with so much chatter going on around him down here. Madison had made it clear that she didn't want to keep Nadia company. That she didn't quite believe the girl's story. But why would Nadia lie? What was there to gain? Madison was a naturally wary person. She'd had to be careful all her life. Let down so many times, was it any wonder she was slow to trust? Alex tried to focus his mind back on the proceedings around him.

'We have to lay some kind of trap,' Ben was saying. 'We could lure them in just before dawn and let the sunlight kill them.'

'Yes, but how exactly would we do that?' Isobel answered. 'We need a specific plan.'

'I haven't worked that part out yet, but it'll come to me,' Ben replied, his eyes shining. He was enjoying this all a little too much. Alex shook his head in frustration. However you looked at it, the ancient vampires outmatched them on every level. They could never hope to defeat them without help.

'We'll go to Turkey and ask Aelia to join us,' Alex said. 'There's no point in planning anything until we hear what she has to say. She is the key to all this.'

'What about UV lamps?' Ben began. 'We could—'

'No,' Alex cut him off. 'It's too dangerous. Those creatures are far too strong. They could overpower us and use the lamps against us. I've been over every possibility, and everything is too risky. We tried once before and failed. We were lucky to escape with our lives last time. I won't risk your lives again.'

'Don't forget,' Jacques said, 'Leonora was working against us last time. Sharing our plans. Putting us at a disadvantage. Sorry, Freddie, I know she's your sister, but she did put us all in danger.'

'It's okay, I know,' Freddie replied, his expression darkening. 'We won't have a spy in our midst this time.' His words were tinged with a bitterness that hung in the air.

A brief silence cloaked the room while they each remembered Leonora's betrayal. Alex was still furious about it. Furious and disappointed. He had trusted her fully. She had been like a sister to him, but he supposed that had been the problem. She had loved him, but not in a sisterly way. Her jealousy of Madison had driven her to do the unthinkable. Alex shook away the unwelcome memories.

'All the same, we'll need Aelia's help,' Alex said. 'We'd be foolish to proceed without it.'

'I agree, brother,' Isobel replied.

'So we should leave as soon as possible,' Jacques said.

'We should go tomorrow,' Ben said. 'I've never even been abroad before. I can't wait to see another country.'

'I'll book our passage,' Alex said. 'Freddie, are you agreed?'

Freddie gave a brief nod, his eyes still clouded with sadness, his shoulders hunched.

'Maybe we could try to find Leonora while we're there,' Isobel offered. 'Perhaps she's had a change of heart...'

'No,' Alex said, his head snapping up. 'She's gone. She made her choice, and it was the wrong one. We simply can't trust her anymore.'

'I know she was wrong,' Freddie replied. 'But maybe Isobel's right. Maybe my sister has changed. I only hope...' He paused.

'What? You only hope what?' Alexandre asked.

'I only hope we won't have to face her... in some kind of battle. She was wrong; with every fibre of my being, I know she was wrong, but I could never physically harm her. And I'm sure she still cares for my well-being.'

'None of us would willingly harm her,' Alex said. 'She was part of our family. She still is. But her judgement was severely lacking.'

'She wouldn't fight against us, surely?' Isobel said.

'Let's not worry about that now,' Alex replied. 'I'm sure we won't have to face her. But if we do... well, we'll deal with it at the time.'

Ben suddenly stopped his pacing. 'I don't have a passport!' he cried. 'How long does it take to get one?'

'You won't need a passport,' Jacques said.

'What? Of course I will. You can't leave me behind. I'm coming and you won't stop me.'

'Calm down, Ben, my friend,' Alex said.

'You won't need a passport,' Jacques said with a snort of laughter. 'Just a nice, cosy packing crate.'

'Uh?' Ben frowned.

They waited for the information to sink in.

'Oh, yeah, course.' He finally grasped the logistics of their travel arrangements. 'I'll be in a crate. Does that mean we'll be in the hold? Won't I get to sit next to a window and see us taking off?'

''Fraid not, Benny boy,' Jacques replied.

'Oh well. I can cope with that... I suppose.'

'It's done.' As morning turned to afternoon, Isobel confirmed their passage to Turkey. They had chartered a private jet for the following day. Maddy, Morris and Esther were booked on as passengers; the others would be cargo, in the form of five wooden crates containing "statues".

Alexandre didn't relish the idea of returning to Cappadocia so soon. But they had little choice if they were to have any hope of leading free and happy lives. Hopefully, this time next week their troubles would be behind them, and they would be back home, safe. He didn't want to think about what had to happen between now and then.

He was looking forward to going upstairs and seeing Madison. He was missing her. Just looking at her face lifted his spirits and made him believe that they would all be okay. He knew how lucky he was to have found her. Or rather, how lucky he was that she had found *him*. She had made his vampire life bearable, wonderful even. He smiled to himself and touched his fingers to his lips. He needed her now. It was a physical ache.

How had she been today with Nadia? He hoped they had got on all right. Madison hadn't been downstairs even once to see him today. Perhaps she was punishing him for leaving her out of their decision-making. But he hadn't had much choice. Someone had to look after their guest, and she was the only one able to do it.

The others chattered around him, but Alexandre still couldn't concentrate. His brain was muzzy. It must be the stress of everything. He blinked and shook his head. And sneezed. Again. Thankfully, no one noticed. A tiny seed of concern skipped across his mind, but there was no room to think about it. First and foremost, he had to focus on their trip. He could think about his health when they returned.

'Travis,' Alex said.

'Did you say something, brother?' Jacques asked.

'I can hear Travis's infernal van on the drive. He's coming to the house.'

'We can't go up yet,' Isobel warned.

'What does he want?' Jacques asked.

'To talk to our guest, I should think,' Alex replied. 'I'm not staying down here while he sweet-talks Madison into believing his story.'

'Are you sure Travis did anything wrong?' Ben asked. 'I like him. I don't think he'd hurt anyone. Not on purpose.'

'I don't know,' Alex replied. 'But I'm not taking a chance either way. Madison and Nadia may need my help.' He walked towards the basement steps.

'Just wait,' Isobel said. 'You won't be helping anyone if the shutters are open and you're exposed to sunlight. You can go up if and when it sounds like they're in trouble.'

Alex made a low growl in his throat and threw his sister a look of disgust. But he knew she was probably right. He didn't believe Travis was dangerous, just hormonal.

Belle dimpled her cheeks as he turned away from the stairs.

Alex ignored her smile and began pacing the room, eager for the night to fall.

The clock ticked, as the day unwound. Outside, the wind groaned and the rain hammered against the shuttered panes. Earlier, Maddy had roused herself to light a fire, so at least the room felt cosy now. But conversation had stopped ages ago, and Madison had moved past the awkward stage to being well and truly bored. Nadia was engrossed in some hefty Russian book she'd found in the library while Maddy flicked through local magazines, skim-reading articles about home décor and Christmas recipes. She was dying to find out what the others had been discussing all morning, but she wouldn't go down-stairs, because a) what would happen if Nadia came looking for her? And b) she was still pissed off with Alex for making her wait up here.

Through the howling gale came the chime of the doorbell. Jolted out of her bored stupor, Maddy got to her feet. Nadia raised her eyes from her book, a look of worry skittering across her features.

'Wait here. I'll see who it is,' Maddy said.

'What if it's Travis?'

'Do you want to speak to him? Maybe it would be good if you cleared the air?'

'No.'

'Okay. Stay here, then. If it's Travis, I'll tell him you're not here.'

The doorbell rang again. And again.

'All right, all right, I'm coming.' Maddy left the sitting room and headed towards the front door. She opened it and put her hand up to ward off the spray of rain that showered her face.

A figure pushed past her into the hallway. 'Hey!' Maddy cried.

'Where's Nadia?' It was Travis. He shook his head like a wet dog, covering Maddy with another fine spray of rainwater. Maddy pushed the door closed against the gusting elements.

'Travis, what the hell's going on? What did you do to that girl?'

'Nothing. Nothing bad, that is. Where is she? I need to clear this up face-to-face. Your boyfriend thinks I'm some sort of sex offender. All I did was kiss the girl and now I'm public enemy number one. It's all a misunderstanding.'

'Calm down, Trav, I'm on your side. I think it's better if you go home and forget the whole thing. It'll blow over in a day or two.'

'No. I want to see her. Alex said she was staying with you. Where is she? In the lounge?' Travis pushed his fingers through his dripping hair and wiped his wet face with the backs of his hands. 'Nadia!' He turned and strode into the sitting room.

'Travis, wait! She doesn't want to...' But it was too late. Maddy followed him, partly regretful, but partly thinking it was probably better if they sorted this out once and for all. Plus, hopefully, it would mean that Nadia could leave. Entering the room, she gave Nadia an apologetic look, which was met with a scowl. 'Sorry,' she said uselessly.

'Maddy, could you leave us to talk for a few minutes?' Travis asked.

Madison glanced from Travis back to Nadia. 'Do you want me to stay?'

'No, it will be okay,' Nadia said. 'You can wait outside door. I hear what he has to say.' She placed her book down on the coffee table, re-crossed her legs and folded her arms. She didn't look happy. But she didn't look scared either.

Maddy left the room and stood in the chilly hallway. Travis closed the door behind her with a click. Maddy shook her head, cleared a space on the hard-backed wooden settle, and sat down, her chin in her hands. Travis's voice came through the wall, his tone low and pleading. Maddy sighed. She wondered what had actually happened between them. Could Travis have taken things a step too far? Or was Nadia lying? What was happening downstairs? And why was she sitting alone in the freezing hallway of her own house, not being included in any of it?

As dusk skimmed the edges of Marchwood House, Alexandre was finally able to leave the basement. He hadn't realised just how much it had meant to him to have all the windows shuttered in the daytime and have the run of the house. He had missed that freedom today. They all had. Before going to see Madison, he threw the back door open wide and breathed in the crisp night air, his shoulders relaxing and his mind calming a little. Would he ever get used to the dark restrictions of his new life? But the memory of sunshine was now all tangled up with the fear of pain and burning. This cool darkness would have to suffice.

Hearing the others climbing the stairs to join him, he re-entered the house and went up to the first floor to find Madison sound asleep in their room. He smiled. She must be exhausted after everything. It was good she was catching up on her rest. But where was Nadia? She wasn't in the house anymore. Funny that he hadn't sensed her leaving. But then he hadn't really been on form today. He felt out of sorts. He didn't like to wake Maddy, but there was too much to discuss to leave her sleeping. He wanted to know how her day had been, and to tell her of their imminent travel plans.

'Madison,' he crooned, sitting on the bed. She lay on her side on top of the covers, her breaths slow and regular, her cheek slightly flushed and her brow smooth, black hair splayed over the cream pillow. 'Maddy, wake up.'

'Hmm?'

'It's me, Alex.'

'Alex?' She stretched and turned, finally opening her eyes, returning his smile.

'Hello, sleepyhead.'

'What? Oh, I drifted off. I don't remember... I must've been tired. Still am.' She frowned. 'Actually, I feel like crap.'

'How was today?' Alex asked.

'Today? It was okay. I was talking to Nadia, and then... um, I don't really remember. What's the time?'

'It's after five.'

'*What?* But that means I've slept all afternoon.' She sat upright and hugged her knees to her body.

'It's okay. You must have needed the rest.'

'But—'

'Don't worry about it.'

'I don't even remember having lunch.'

'Come down and eat then,' Alex replied, pulling her close and planting a kiss on the top of her head.

'Yeah.' She rubbed at her eyes and gave Alex a smile.

'Where is our controversial guest anyway?' he asked.

'Um, I, er... I don't know. Isn't she downstairs? Or in her room?' Maddy had a vague memory of something important, but she couldn't quite remember.

Alexandre shook his head. 'She's not in the house. But I heard Travis arrive earlier.'

Maddy frowned, her nose crinkling. 'Yes, that's right. How could I have forgotten? He came to see her, and they were talking in the lounge. The last thing I remember is sitting in the hallway waiting for them to sort things out. Strange, but I don't even remember coming upstairs.'

'That *is* strange.' Alex felt a jolt of concern deep in his chest. Madison appeared to have blanked out a whole afternoon.

'Nadia must've got fed up waiting for me to wake up. But I wonder where she went. Maybe she and Travis patched things up.'

'Maybe Esther knows,' Alex said with a frown.

'Is Esther still here?'

'No, she's gone home, but I can head over to her place and ask.'

'I'm sorry. I had one thing to do – look after Nadia – and I didn't even do that right.'

'Come on, let's go downstairs. You should eat, and I should go out to look for her.'

'I hope she's okay. I'll call Travis. See what he has to say about it.'

Alexandre was worried about Madison. She was obviously exhausted. It was a pity she couldn't have a few days to relax and gather her energy before they left for Turkey. But there was no time, and he couldn't leave her here without his protection. Not that she would even allow that to happen. He would have to ensure she got enough sleep and ate enough good food to keep her going. Her eyes had closed again, her breathing deepening as she lay against him.

'Madison,' he whispered.

'Mmm?'

'Are you going back to sleep?'

'What?' She sat up and blinked. 'No, I'm awake. Let me jump in the shower, and then I'll give Trav a call. I'll see you downstairs in ten minutes.'

'Very well.' Alex reluctantly let go of her hand as she left the room, running his fingers over the spot on his palm where her flesh had briefly warmed his.

CHAPTER TWENTY

SCYTHIA, 514 BC

At last, tonight, the warriors were due to distribute the spoils of their previous skirmish. So Laodice would finally have the opportunity to present her Persian scalp and claim her right to wed. Kelermes decided that tonight would also be an appropriate time to ask Aristeas for formal permission to marry Laodice. To have a partner in battle, in bed and through life would be the most wonderful thing. His previous worries were almost forgotten. He really had no cause to be anxious or feel inadequate, for he would soon have his bride. And perhaps, if the gods looked upon him favourably, he would also soon have children. A family to love and fight for.

With the darkening of the sky, Aristeas's hand finally came up, and he gave the order to halt. They would begin setting up camp for the night. The excitement of the warriors was palpable – the anticipation of tonight's feasting and, of course, the distribution of loot. All three yurtas were to be raised, plus the bathing tent. This would be a good night.

Kelermes dismounted and removed Tabi's blanket and bridle. He would rub her down and feed her before seeing to his own needs. She was tired and needed pampering. She'd served him well these past few days. Laodice joined him, seeing to her own steed with the same attention. Occasionally, they broke their concentration with glances of love and barely concealed excitement.

'Cut it out, you two,' Orik said, ambling over. 'Your happiness is making me sick. Kel, you're as smug as a king with two queens.'

'One queen is all I need,' he replied.

Laodice grinned. 'Don't worry, Orik, we'll find you a woman.'

'No thanks. I'm happy as I am.'

'That's a good idea, Lae. You are tasked with finding Orik a suitable mate,' Kelermes said with a grin, as he gently worked at a particularly stubborn tangle in Tabi's tail. He had to do something to repay his friend for healing the rift between him and Laodice. For saving her from a lifetime with Lohant.

'Didn't you hear me?' Orik replied. 'I said I didn't want a mate.'

'Ignore him,' Kelermes interrupted. 'He doesn't know what's good for him. A woman is what you need, Orik my friend. Although, who would want a fellow with a face like the back end of a goat, I have no idea. Ow!'

In response, Orik had hurled his water skin at Kelermes, striking him on the side of the head. Tabi shied away, and it took Kelermes a good few seconds to soothe her.

'Fine,' Kelermes grumbled, rubbing his head. 'No need to overreact. I'll grant perhaps you're marginally better looking than a goat's backside. What do you think, Laodice? Is his face more like the back end of a goat or a cow? A horse, perhaps? No offence, Tabi.'

Orik dived forward and tackled his friend to the ground where they began to tussle with good humour, throwing worse and still worse insults at one another. Tabi reared and bucked, nearly kicking Kelermes in the face.

'Cut it out, you two,' Laodice said. 'Tabi isn't impressed, and neither am I.'

The other warriors threw glances their way, shaking their heads and smiling. All except Lohant, who glowered and strode off.

Orik now had Kelermes in a headlock. 'Never mind me,' Orik growled. 'You, Kelermes, my friend, have a face like a Persian's arse. Say it!'

'Never!'

'Say it: I, Kelermes, have a face like a Persian's arse.'

'Get off me, you dung beetle, you frog-faced... frog-faced...'

'Frog-faced...?' Orik grinned at his friend's inability to finish the sentence.

'I can't think of anything hideous enough to describe you,' Kelermes replied in a strangled voice, his airways under pressure from his friend's vice-like grip. The irony was that Orik was tall, well-built, and very handsome indeed. Any woman would have him as a husband in a heartbeat. But Orik was in no hurry to take a bride.

'I can stay like this all night,' Orik said. 'So, repeat after me: I, Kelermes, have a face like a Persian's arse.'

'All right, I'll say it: You, Orik, have a face like a Persian's argh!' Orik put more pressure on his friend's throat. 'Get off me, Orik,' Kelermes croaked. 'Are you really trying to kill me, your only friend in the entire world?'

'Say it. Properly. I, Kelermes, have a face like a Persian's arse.'

'Loosen your grip a little,' Kelermes whispered. 'I... can't... speak... like... this.'

Orik obliged, allowing Kelermes to draw in a breath.

'All right, then,' Kelermes began. 'We, Kelermes and Orik, have faces which could in certain lights resemble the arse-end of a Persian.'

Orik hooted with laughter and released the half-strangled

Scythian. 'Fool,' he said, jumping to his feet and sauntering back to his horse.

'Frog face,' Kelermes replied, massaging his neck and swallowing. He spied Orik's discarded water skin on the snow-covered ground next to him, picked it up and took a few long draughts of the icy liquid, before lobbing it back at his friend with the intention of hitting him on the back of the head. Without turning around, Orik raised his hand and caught the bag before it struck him. 'How did he do that?' Kelermes murmured to Laodice, shaking his head at his friend's lightning reaction.

Within the hour, all the warriors, bar a couple of lookouts who had drawn the short straw, were gathered around a dancing fire inside the largest yurta. Two small deer were roasting on a spit, and everyone's cup was full to the brim with *koumiss*, an alcoholic drink made from fermented mare's milk. Kelermes sat cross-legged next to Laodice, enjoying the warmth of the fire on his skin, his hands and feet now tingling with heat. Flame shadows danced on Laodice's face, and his heart leapt at the thought they would soon be together. The hum of chatter and laughter was broken by their chief who got to his feet and clapped his hands for silence. Within moments, an expectant hush fell over the warriors. No sound but the crackle and spit of the fire, and the faint sigh of the wind outside.

'I want to thank you all for your loyalty and valour these past weeks,' Aristeas began. 'I know I am a demanding leader. I expect nothing less than your willingness to lay down your lives for your homeland. I am lucky to have men and women such as you under my command. I ask and you give. I speak and you obey. You always exceed my expectations. You are brave, honest and true. You are my brothers and sisters, and I commend you.'

At this, there was a pause. Then, everyone rose to their feet and cheered, stamping their feet, whistling and clapping. They took up the chant: 'Ar-is-te-as, Ar-is-te-as, Ar-is-te-as.' The chant grew louder and stronger and faster until their leader's name dissolved into another round of cheering. After a few moments, Aristeas smiled and held his hand up for quiet again. He gestured to the gleaming mound of loot piled up on a blanket before him.

'While we wait for the meat to cook, we will drink, and I will reward your valour handsomely. Bring me your hard-won scalps and you shall choose your payment from the Persian booty in front of me. Anything remaining will be shared equally among us all. All warriors who have slain a foe this past week will come and stand to my right. The rest of you will sit where you are.'

This was the announcement Kelermes had been waiting to hear, and he closed his fingers more tightly around the bag containing the head of his enemy. He had his eye on a Persian dagger, and perhaps one of their long spears – he wouldn't use it himself, but they always fetched a good price. Proudly, he and Laodice made their way across the tent, past the fire, to stand next to their leader and await their turn.

Unsurprisingly, Abaris was called up first. Already standing next to Aristeas, the second-in-command turned to his leader and pulled out of his bag one bloody head, followed by another. He stood and held them aloft by the hair, one in each hand. The tent erupted into more cheers.

'Two of our enemy slain by Abaris!' Aristeas shouted above the noise. 'You may choose four pieces in payment, my friend.'

Abaris bowed and returned the gruesome heads to his bag. Later, they would be skinned and cleaned up, the skulls decorated and turned into bowls or drinking vessels. It was a well-known fact that warriors absorbed the power of their enemies by drinking from their skulls.

Abaris stepped over to the pile of loot, running his fingers over bows, spears, clothing and other precious items. His wife, Savlius, pointed at a pair of Persian shoes, their toes curled up into a point. Abaris grasped them and raised his eyebrows to his wife. She shook her head and jabbed her finger downwards. Abaris moved his hand and pointed at a dull-looking item beneath the garish shoes. At this, Savlius grinned and nodded. Her husband frowned, pulling at the item, dislodging a sword from the pile, which clattered dangerously to the ground, narrowly avoiding skewering his foot. Abaris executed some fancy footwork which elicited laughs from those close enough to see what had happened. Still clutching at the item his wife had pointed out, he gradually pulled it free from the mountain of booty, and everyone gasped, including Kelermes. It had first appeared to be a simple leather belt, but as it slithered out, Kelermes saw that its belt plate was massive, and made from pure gold, with some kind of intricate engraving upon it.

Abaris's grin now matched that of his wife. He held it up to his chief who nodded and clapped him on the back. 'A good choice. It is yours.' As Abaris handed it to Savlius, Aristeas added, 'Or perhaps I should say, it is your wife's.'

Hoots of laughter broke out while Abaris flushed red with embarrassment and scowled at his wife.

'Choose again,' Aristeas urged.

Kelermes watched carefully as Abaris made his next selections. The man stooped to lift the sword which had almost claimed one of his toes. He also chose a decent bow and a quiver of arrows.

Next was the turn of Lohant. Kelermes gritted his teeth to stop himself crying out that the man was a dishonourable thief and deserved none of the loot. The man had no shame, but Kel wouldn't allow him to tarnish the night's shine. He could afford to be charitable. Lohant was unimportant. He let the man bask in borrowed glory, for Kel had something far more valuable than that Persian scalp. He had his heart's desire.

More warriors were called. And then, finally, it was the turn of Laodice. He squeezed her hand before she left his side and watched as she approached their leader. A hush fell over the gathering. She pulled the Persian's severed head from her bag and held it out for all to see. Her eyes shone as she spoke.

'I present my third scalp. A Persian soldier killed by my blade. I will not take compensation for my kill. Instead, I request the right to marry.' Her voice rang out, steady and clear.

'Laodice,' Aristeas replied, 'you are as strong a warrior as I have ever seen, and I am proud to have you in my company. Of course I shall grant you the right to marry. Your husband-to-be is a lucky man. You shall also take your pick from the loot.'

'Thank you.' She returned the grisly head to its bag, gave a small bow of respect and stepped over to the dwindling pile where she chose a golden-yellow embroidered tunic. A choice most uncharacteristic of her. Laodice wasn't usually one for frivolity. Kelermes would have laid bets on her selecting a new weapon rather than clothing. Returning to his side, he could tell she was embarrassed by her choice. 'It's for our wedding,' she muttered to him. 'I want to wear something other than my soldier's garb.'

Now it made sense. 'You'll look beautiful whatever you wear,' he replied, making her flush an even deeper red. But now his name was being called, so he made his way to Aristeas. With a pounding heart, Kelermes realised that this was an important moment in his life. One that he would never forget.

'I have one scalp to present,' he said. 'But first, I would like to formally request permission to wed Laodice. She is willing, and we ask your blessing.'

'Two young, fierce warriors with the desire to make a union.' Aristeas stepped forward and put his hand on Kelermes's shoulder. 'Of course you have my blessing. As soon as we reach the next encampment, we shall request the presence of an *enaree*, and you shall be married. We will all be honoured to celebrate with you.' Aristeas turned to Laodice and crooked his forefinger. She stepped towards him, and he held the betrothed couple's hands together, raising them up in the air with his own. 'We wish you health, joy and love. All the gods' blessings and a scourge on your enemies.'

'All the gods' blessings and a scourge on your enemies,' everyone repeated, toasting the couple with their cups raised. A cheer rose up throughout the yurta, and it filled Kelermes's heart to see his leader and comrades celebrate his good fortune with him. His head was light with liquor, love and happiness. He did not think he had ever felt this full up with joy before. Surely this had to be the best moment of his life. A sign from the gods that he and Laodice were blessed.

Later, sitting together at the darkened edge of the yurta, Kel and Laodice had managed to find a space away from the drunken congratulations and teasing jibes of their comrades. Kelermes leant against the sturdy felt wall, and she lay back with her head against his chest, her warm fragrant scent filling his nostrils. He felt sharp desire and buried his face in her hair, thinking of how to phrase the question that hovered on his lips.

'Will you ride now into the night with me?' he finally asked. 'Away from our brothers and sisters? I want to be alone with you. Now that we are betrothed. I want to look at you without feeling the eyes of others upon us. I need to be with you.'

She lifted her head from his chest and turned to face him. He caught his breath at her smile. She stroked his cheek and kissed his lips, meaning it to be a soft, quick brush of lips. But instead, he pulled her to him and kissed her deeply, feeling the pull of his body towards her. She responded immediately but broke it off too soon.

'We only have a short time until we are married,' she replied. 'Let's wait. I think it is right to wait, don't you?'

At that moment, he didn't think it was right at all. He thought it was unutterably wrong to wait. He knew it would be the hardest thing in the world to step away from her. She was water to quench his brittle thirst. Sunshine to warm his frozen bones. But after her gentle denial, he knew that step away he must. So he gently pushed her from him and sprang to his feet. If he didn't get out of there, he may do or say something he would regret. She had asked him to wait, and he would respect her wish. But, by the same token, he couldn't bear to be in such close proximity to her tonight. It was torture to look at her and not be able to kiss and touch. To possess.

'Of course,' he said. 'As you wish. We will wait. We will be married soon enough.' His voice had taken on a stiff tone, and he saw the hurt in Lae's eyes. His manner had swiftly turned gruff and formal. So different from their easiness a few moments before. He was foolish. He should never have asked her to go out alone with him. Laodice wasn't like that, and she had probably felt hurt by his request. 'I, er, I am tired,' he said. 'Enjoy the rest of the celebrations. I'll see you in the morning.'

'Kel...' She stretched a pale hand out towards him, but he ignored it.

'Goodnight, Laodice.'

He strode out of the tent. What was wrong with him? They had only just reconciled, and now he had messed up their perfect evening. If only he'd kept his mouth shut. What must she think of him? The freezing air outside made his mind spin, and he was suddenly made aware of a night's worth of alcohol swirling around his head and stomach, mixing thoroughly with his foolishness and regret. Curdling. Turning to nausea.

CHAPTER TWENTY-ONE

The phone rang six times before going to voicemail.

'Travis, it's Maddy. Call me back as soon as you get this.'

She threw her phone onto the bed and began towel-drying her hair. Alex had gone downstairs. She hadn't even asked what he and the others had discussed today. How could she have forgotten something as important as that? She'd go down in a minute and find out exactly what their plans were. Her phone began buzzing. She dropped the towel and grabbed the juddering piece of metal.

'Travis?'

'Hey, Mads, I just missed a call from you.'

'Where's Nadia?'

'Thought she was at your place.'

'What happened this morning when you came to see her?'

There was a pause on the other end of the line.

'Travis?'

'Nothing. Nothing happened. We talked, and she made it clear she didn't want to see me again, so I guess that's that.'

'Didn't she leave here with you?'

'Nope.'

'Oh.' Travis sounded genuine enough. But it was strange that Nadia had disappeared without even saying goodbye. 'How did she seem when you left her?'

'Dunno really. She didn't say a lot.'

'Was she angry? Upset? Scared?'

'No. She was just... distant. Cold. Told me she didn't want to see me. That if I bothered her again, she'd call the police. Talk about overreacting.'

'Okay. Well, will you call me if you hear from her again?'

'Unlikely. But, yeah, sure. I'll call you.'

'Cool. I'm sorry it didn't work out with you two.'

'Maddy?'

'Mm?'

'You do know I never did anything to her.'

'Course.'

'Because you're one of my best friends, and I don't want there to be any weirdness.'

'The only weird thing around here is you – in a good way.' Maddy smiled.

'Yeah, I'm a regular freak show.'

'Speak soon, weirdo.'

'Bye, Mads.'

Maddy ended the call and stuffed her phone into the pocket of her hoodie. She still felt out of sorts, but maybe that wasn't surprising given that she was still recovering from her kidnapping ordeal, not to mention Ben's horrific brush with death. She should go downstairs to see how her little brother was doing. Find out what plans the others had made, and see whether or not she agreed with them.

'Where are the boys?' Maddy asked, walking into the kitchen, where Alex and Isobel were deep in French conversation. The divine smell of cheese on toast wafted out from the grill.

'Good evening, Maddy.' Isobel stood to kiss her on each

cheek. 'How are you feeling? Alexandre said you slept this afternoon.'

'I'm okay. Just a bit tired. Where's Ben?'

'The boys went outside to run around. Ben wanted to practice his new-found skills before we leave tomorrow.'

'Tomorrow?'

'I meant to tell you,' Alex chipped in. 'We're going to Turkey tomorrow to see Aelia.'

'Who? Who's going?' They had better not think of leaving her behind.

'All of us, including Morris and Esther.'

'Okay,' Maddy replied, pulling out a chair. 'That's good.' She was glad they were doing something proactive. Nevertheless, her stomach still flipped over with nerves. To be returning to the place of her kidnap so soon was... daunting.

'I'm glad you approve,' Alex said, a smile playing on his lips. 'I want us all to stick together. Last time, we were separated, and that's when things fell apart. If we can stay together, we'll be strong. But, Madison...'

'What?'

'When we're there, if I ask you to do something to remain out of danger, I will need you to do it without argument or question. You are fearless and strong, but you are no match for a vampire. I cannot have you in harm's way again.'

'I was a pretty good match for a cavern-load of vampires last week.'

'I'm not denying you are resourceful and brave. But your luck can't hold forever. Be sensible. I won't be able to think straight if I'm worrying about you.'

'Nobody asked you to worry about—'

'Here.' Isobel put a plate of grilled cheese sandwiches in front of Maddy.

Maddy sighed. 'Thank you, Isobel.'

'My pleasure, ma chere. Now, let us not argue. Alex,

Madison will not needlessly place herself in danger. Will you, Madison?'

'No.'

'Good.'

Moments earlier, Maddy had felt ravenous, but on hearing the news of their imminent departure, she had suddenly lost her appetite. Alex may have called her fearless, but that wasn't entirely true, no matter how much she protested.

'Careful that doesn't poison you, Madison. My sister isn't famed for her culinary skills.'

'Shut up, brother, or I may slide you under the grill, too. Toasted cheese, followed by toasted vampire.'

'I'd like to see you try.'

Isobel sat down with a deep sigh.

'What's up?' Maddy asked.

'I was remembering when my life consisted of soirees, needlework, pianoforte lessons and taking tea with Maman and her friends. Now we fight vampires and plan strategies to save our very lives. It is not what I envisaged for my future.'

'I am sorry, Belle.' Alexandre bowed his head.

'It cannot be helped, brother.'

'I take full responsibility. Maybe you *should* slide me under the grill with your bread and cheese concoction.'

'Much as that sounds appealing, it will not return me to my own life but will merely crisp up your skin a little.'

Alex shifted his chair up so he could wrap his arms around his sister. 'I know I am a poor substitute for Maman and Papa, but I will do my best to fill their shoes. And, after this situation is dealt with and we are out of danger, I will throw you a magnificent party. What do you say?'

'I'll hold you to that promise, Alexandre.'

Maddy nibbled a corner of toast and smiled across the table. Isobel and Alex had certainly lost as much – if not more – than she and Ben had.

'It's Nadia.' Isobel turned to her brother. 'The girl is back. She's out there, and in trouble once more. Shall I go this time?'

'No. I'll go.' Alex stood. 'At least we know where she is now.'

'We can't take her in again,' Maddy said. 'Not if we're all going to Cappadocia tomorrow. I could book a hotel for her while we're away.'

'Let me fetch her, and we'll talk about it.' Alex came around the table and kissed her. 'I won't be long.'

Maddy tried to keep her uncharitable thoughts at bay while Alex left the house, but she really wished they'd never met Nadia and her drama-filled life. Especially as Alex seemed to be constantly at her beck and call.

The chill air brushed across Alexandre's skin, as he crossed the grounds of Marchwood towards the scent of Nadia's tears. He was troubled to find himself pleased at the girl's return. There was something about her that drew him in... *Like a moth to a flame,* he thought wryly. Despite her sadness, she shone brightly, a source of troubled fascination.

Moments later, he found Nadia walking along a narrow country lane, about a mile and a half from Marchwood. She wore the same jeans and sweater she'd had on the previous day, and her face was tear-streaked, her hair tangled. The rain had eased from earlier, but a fine persistent drizzle had ensured that she was soaked. Alex slowed as he approached her along the dark, sodden lane.

'What happened?' he asked, stifling a sneeze.

The girl looked up, startled, and then appeared disinterested. She carried on walking towards him, her head bowed.

Alex tried again. 'We were worried about you. We didn't know where you'd gone. Madison was concerned.' He came to a halt as she approached.

'Madison was not concerned.' Nadia snapped her head up.

'I should think she was glad when I left. Why you are here, Alexandre?' She came to a halt and glared at him.

'We've been out looking for you. Like I said, we were *all* worried.' This girl was an enigma. Alex couldn't work her out. She was angry, sad, vulnerable... and beautiful.

'Why do you care?' she asked, her voice now as soft as the rain.

'I... well, of course we were all worried about you. Nobody likes to think of someone alone and upset.'

'But, you, Alexandre.' She took a pace towards him. 'Why do *you* care?'

Alex could see she was trembling. Shivering with the cold. 'Why don't you come back to the house and get warmed up? You must be freezing.'

'You are kind to me,' she said. 'It is always *you* who are kind to me.'

'Did Travis upset you again? I heard he came to the house earlier.'

'I not care about Travis.'

'Come back to the house.' Alex reached out his hand. She stepped closer, but instead of letting him take her hand to lead her back to Marchwood, she put her arms around his body and rested her head on his shoulder. Alex felt a shock of pleasure as her body melded to his. His arms automatically went around her slender body... to comfort her, nothing more, he told himself.

She gave a stifled sob.

'Nadia, there's no need to cry. We will help you. Whatever the problem is, we can sort it out.'

'You don't know what it is like to have nothing,' she whispered. 'I have no one to care for me. Nobody.'

'You'll find someone. You're beautiful and interesting.'

Nadia looked up at him through rain and tear-soaked lashes, her lips slightly parted. 'You think I am beautiful?'

Alex caught his breath at her beauty. Did she really not know how incredible she was? 'Of course,' he replied. 'Nobody in their right mind would not find you beautiful.'

'It's so cold,' she whispered.

He tightened his arms around her. Just to stop her shivering. Yes, he was a cold vampire with no body heat, yet he still felt the instinctive human need to protect this vulnerable girl, to encircle her. He reasoned that it was a chilly December night, and she was in distress. But then Alexandre took a breath and was blindsided by the warm scent of her hair. It smelled divine. The lost fragrance of summer meadows. Of daylight and childhood. The promise of everything he had ever wanted. It made him dizzy with longing.

Rational thought fled. Alex placed a finger under her chin and tipped her face towards his. And then he kissed her. It was a kiss that spread like fire through his whole body, making him wild. And she was kissing him back, arching her body against him, raking her nails through his hair. He lifted her off the ground, and she wrapped her legs around him. A whooshing sound exploded in his head. Some part of Alex was screaming at himself to stop, but he couldn't. This girl was everything. She was incredible. She was... life, death, the universe. He gave himself over to her until he didn't know who he was anymore. Didn't care if he lived... or died.

CHAPTER TWENTY-TWO

SCYTHIA, 514 BC

Kel stumbled towards his tent, but halfway there he changed his mind and stopped. There was no chance of sleep coming to him now. He was too out of sorts. The sounds of revelry had followed him outside – chatter, laughter, and drunken song. But Laodice hadn't come after him. He didn't blame her. He had acted like a fool. The glow of the torches was dim out here, but somehow there was enough light to see the outlines of their camp – the tents, the wagons, the sleeping horses. Kelermes gazed up at the sky. The snow clouds had moved away. Their feathers of cold would return soon, no doubt, but for now, it was a clear night with a bright moon casting ripples of light across everything, including his upturned face.

Bowing his head, he made his way across to the horses, lurching through the camp, and cursing when he banged his ankle on the sharp corner of a cart. His mare whickered a soft greeting and he patted her neck.

'I'm such a clod,' Kel muttered to his steed, hearing the drunken slur in his voice. 'An inebriated fool. Is she angry with me, Tabi? What do you think? Of course she's angry. Of course she is. I asked her to be alone with me before we are wed. What was I thinking? And then I walked out of the tent, as though she's the one at fault. I shouldn't have left her. I'll go back...' He turned but quickly changed his mind again. 'No, I can't see her now. I'm too drunk. I'll say something stupid. We'll end up arguing. We'll talk later once I've sobered up and my head clears. I'll apologise and I'll make it right.' He leant against his horse, resting his head against hers, his eyes closed. 'Thank you, Tabi, my friend. You always give good advice.'

His thoughts turned again to his bride-to-be. To her face, her mouth, her body. 'No,' he said, jolting himself from his reverie. 'This is no good. I need to stop thinking of her. Tabi, let's go for a quick ride. Do you mind? It won't be for long; I know you're tired. Just a quick gallop to get air in my lungs. To shake the girl from my thoughts.'

Tabi nudged his shoulder, and he ran his hand over her velvet nose. She wasn't wearing her bridle, but he didn't need one anyway – they weren't heading anywhere in particular. Kelermes untied her, clicked his teeth and the placid mare dropped down on one knee without complaint, to let him slide onto her back. Tabi stood, and he gave her flanks a squeeze. She responded with a snort and made her way through the camp until they faced the dark night ahead of them.

Without a thought for the dangers of the steppe, Kelermes dug his heels into her side, startling the mare into a reluctant sidestepping canter. As the icy night air passed across his flushed skin, Kelermes relaxed, and so too did Tabi. He goaded her into a gallop, and they moved as one over the snowy plains, on and on, deeper into the lonely steppe. Beneath an inky sky studded with cold stars, man and beast flew across the earth.

He couldn't tell how long they had travelled, or how far they had come. But eventually, they came to a stop. Tabi was panting heavily, and so was he. He patted her warm neck and murmured praise, his voice sounding both small and loud in the vast quiet plain. Wondering how far they had travelled, he guided Tabi around so they faced in the other direction, looking back the way they had come. All he could see about him now was the black of the night and the white of the ground in an unending three-hundred-and-sixty-degree sea of moon-washed snow. The camp was too far away to make out its light. He was alone under the stars, and it felt good. Liberating. The effects of the koumiss had completely worn off, and he now felt calm and clear-headed. No longer frustrated or melancholy. This ride out was exactly what he had needed. He smiled and thanked the gods for giving him clarity.

'Time to go back,' he said.

Without further prompting, his mare flattened her ears and headed back to camp, the sound of her hoof-beats merging with his heartbeats. Some time later, Kelermes felt a small jolt of relief as he spotted the faraway lights of their camp glowing in the distance. He had never entertained the possibility of becoming lost out here. They had their own tracks to follow back, and he and his horse both had keen senses of direction, but it was still a welcome sight to see the safety of the camp ahead. Tabi must have sensed his surge of confidence, for Kelermes felt her relax and put on an extra spurt of speed.

The lights ahead grew larger and brighter. Home was in sight. Kelermes smiled, keen to return to Laodice and put things right immediately. He would apologise for walking off, and she would forgive him, and all would be well.

The camp was now about five hundred yards away, and Tabi slowed to a canter, and then to a trot. But suddenly she gave a whinny and reared up, almost unseating Kelermes.

'Whoa there, girl.' He leant forward and squinted ahead, but they weren't close enough to camp for him to see anything amiss. He urged the beast to a complete stop and stroked her neck to calm her. He heard the whinny of horses up ahead, but no shouts or cries or anything that could be construed as an attack. Kel's first instinct was to rush into the camp, dagger in hand. But he stopped himself at the last minute, asking what Aristeas would do if he was here. His leader would assess the situation before blindly charging in.

Staying well back from the camp, Kelermes guided Tabi around its perimeter, using the moonlight to see if there were any fresh prints. After a full circle, he came to the conclusion that there were no prints in or out of the camp, other than those he himself had recently made heading northwards away from the camp, and those his company had made earlier this evening when they had first arrived at this place to set up camp.

Now he had to gather his courage, and steel himself to get closer. To see if anything really was amiss, or if it was merely his imagination playing tricks on him. But Tabi shied away each time he tried to urge her forward. Eventually, he slid off her back and attempted to coax her on by whispering entreaties, and murmuring how brave and good she was, but she wasn't having any of it. She wore no halter or bridle, so there was no way of physically leading her forward.

'You'll have to stay here by yourself then,' he whispered, exasperated. Foolishly, he'd left his weapons inside the camp. The only thing he had to protect himself out here was his grand-father's dagger. He crouched down to slide it out from the strap around his calf, feeling comforted by its weight in his hand. He tried not to think about worst-case scenarios. Perhaps Tabi was being irrational. There was nothing else to suggest anything was amiss. But a creeping chill was already working its way down Kelermes's back, and it was nothing to do with the frigid night air. He didn't dare think of Laodice. Of anything bad having happened to her. He took a step away from Tabi, towards the camp. Then another and another.

The squeak and crunch of snow beneath his boots sounded thunderous as he approached the muted lights – the fire must still be lit in the main tent, the torches around camp still burn-ing. No longer the warm, welcoming sight of moments earlier, suddenly now the lights appeared cold and threatening, perhaps concealing something unknown and unwelcome. But surely it was only his mare's skittishness that had spooked him. Chances were that he would return to find everything in order. After all, he hadn't been away from camp for that long. Not long enough for an ambush, surely. Not long enough for... something else.

Ten yards out now. He gripped his dagger more tightly. The scent of horse dung and cooked meat reached his nostrils. Nothing unusual about that. More snorts and whinnies from the horses in camp.

Kelermes reached the first yurta – his sleeping quarters. He skirted the exterior and put his ear to the felt wall. He heard no sound within, but that didn't necessarily mean anything. Perhaps they were all asleep in there. The walls were thick. Thick enough to mask the sound of his comrades' snores. He worked his way silently around to the entrance. The flap was closed, but he didn't dare draw it back. If an enemy was inside, he didn't want them to know he was here. Instead, he crept to the rear of the yurta and dropped to the ground. Peeling up the heavy hem of the tent, he rolled inside and held his breath. It was dark, cold and completely silent. He knew straight away that there were no warm sleeping bodies in here. In the pitch darkness, he made his way to the entrance and drew aside the flap, letting the moonlight trickle through. Kelermes turned back to regard the interior. Everything was as it should be, apart from the fact there were no people. He tried not to draw comparisons with the ghost camps they had come across a few days earlier.

Swallowing down a wave of fear, Kelermes attempted to rationalise the situation. Perhaps everyone was still in the main tent. Or maybe they were in the bathing tent. But why, then, was the camp shrouded in this eerie silence? As he made his way over to the main yurta, he passed the horses who were still tethered in the centre of the camp. Their ears flicked back and forth, and they snorted in greeting. They were still spooked, but now he was here their panic had subsided. He stroked Laodice's steed, murmuring soothing words. But he had little time for these beasts now. He had to find his betrothed.

Kelermes continued on to the main yurta where he'd left Laodice only a couple of hours earlier. He made out the glow of the fire within, but no sounds emanated from the structure. He kept the rising terror in his gut under control. There was no need to give into it yet. There was still hope. Yet Kel knew in his heart that he would find the tent deserted. He didn't even bother to be stealthy this time but drew back the tent flap and stepped inside. Kelermes smelled death, but there was no trace of it. No bodies. No one.

The fire still smouldered, the dying flames giving out an echo of heat, a faint crackle and spit. Odours of burnt meat and stale koumiss hit him – a memory of earlier, richer aromas. Persian loot lay strewn about the floor along with empty cups, gnawed meat bones, and discarded cloaks and hats. But of his brethren there was no sign. A flash of yellow caught his attention, and he strode over to the spot where he'd left Laodice. The golden tunic she'd chosen to wear on her wedding day lay discarded on the floor. She would never have left it here voluntarily. It was payment for her scalp. A precious item hard-won.

He gathered it up, tucked it into his belt and fled the yurta, running now to the bathing tent. Inside, all was darkness, the fire burnt out. A faint trace of steamy warmth infused with the scent of herbs lingered in the air. But here was the same as the rest of his camp – deserted. The whole camp was deserted. No friends, no enemies, no bodies, no bloody mess of battle or skirmish. There was no sign here of a flesh-and-blood foe. This must be the work of evil spirits. Kelermes said a whispered prayer to the gods to protect him. Fear rippled from the tip of his scalp down his spine. Tabi had felt the wrongness, too, which is why she had refused to come within fifty yards of the camp.

Kelermes now left the bathing tent and tore through the whole place again, looking inside each of the yurtas, checking the carts, the horses, making a sweep of the whole perimeter. But there was nothing. No one. Nothing but silence in the star-encrusted night. He can't have been away from camp that long. Not long enough for everyone to disappear. There must be someone left here who knew what had happened. Who could tell him where everyone had gone. How was it that he himself had heard nothing, seen nothing? No screams or cries had reached his ears while he was riding. No fleeing soldiers or enemy had crossed his path.

'No,' he whispered. 'No,' he cried. 'No!' This time, he yelled, heedless of enemy or evil spirit who might hear his cries. This must be a bad dream. A nightmare brought on by too much koumiss, by the strong vapours of the bathing tent. This was not reality. How could it be? He belonged to a feared Scythian warrior company. They were his friends, his family. He was betrothed. What should he do? He couldn't transport their camp and belongings on his own. No, he refused to allow this ghost camp to become his new reality. He would search for his brethren. They couldn't have gone far. He and Tabi would find them. He would rescue them from whoever or whatever had abducted them.

Shivering with cold and shock, Kel untethered the horses and watched them head off into the darkness, glad to be free of this cursed place. He'd had no choice but to free them. They would die if he left them here. He acknowledged that they would probably die anyway. Next, he hastily attached his bow, quiver and sword to his belt. Then, without looking back, he left the camp and headed to where he'd left his horse.

'Tabi!' he called. 'Here, girl! Tabi!' He glanced wildly around but couldn't see his mare anywhere. Had she deserted him? 'Not Tabi, too,' he whispered. 'Not my faithful friend. Tabi, where are you? I need you.' It hadn't occurred to him to take one of the other steeds, and now his own had vanished. He stood in the empty, cold night, closed his eyes, and bowed his head. He didn't know where to go. He must leave the camp and search for his brethren. But which direction should he take? There were no tracks to follow. It was as though everyone had simply been spirited away. And how far could he hope to get on foot? It was hopeless.

CHAPTER TWENTY-THREE

Dying... I must be dying.

Alex lay on the cold wet grass. His skin burned with fever, and yet he felt so cold. Like ice. Ice and fire. He shivered. His teeth chattered. What had happened? Why did he feel so awful? His body was soaked with rain and sweat. He didn't even have the strength to open his eyes. They ached. His whole body ached. Maybe if he slept, he would feel better. Yes, sleep would be good. If he could let the darkness take him for a while, perhaps he would wake up feeling better? Or perhaps he would not wake up at all...

Ben had persuaded Jacques and Freddie to practice their fighting skills with him that night. Not that they had needed much persuasion. They would need to be at their sharpest if they were leaving for Turkey tomorrow. Ben was at a disadvantage, being the one with the most to learn. If they came face to face with hostile vampires, Ben didn't want to be the weakest link.

'Don't worry about not being able to do it,' Freddie said to Ben. 'If you hesitate, they'll have the advantage.'

'You know all those video games you play?' Jacques said.

Ben nodded.

'You can do it all for real. Those punches, spinning kicks, karate slices? You can do all that and more. Give it a try. Step out onto the lawn and I'll come at you from the woods. Don't hold back.'

Ben nodded again, his face splitting into an excited grin. He knew the real thing would be different. Scarier. But right now, he was eager to try out his moves.

He flexed his vampire muscles and rolled his shoulders back and forth in preparation for his brothers' attack. For *brothers* was how he thought of his vampire family, and it gave him a warm feeling just thinking the word. The two older vampires had gone deep into the trees. While Ben awaited their return, he enjoyed the sensation of cold rain on skin, without any of the human discomfort he might previously have felt. The icy air gave him energy rather than goosebumps.

Freddie and Jacques had separated out. They were going to come at him from different angles. Ben smiled. He'd be ready for them. He'd already worked out how he would disable them. He'd use a mixture of Super Smash Bros. moves, mixed with some Street Fighter combos.

Jacques emerged from the woods first. He came from the right, with a roar that made Ben forget any strategic thoughts. Instead, he put his head down and charged at the blond-haired vampire. They clashed on the grass and rolled about two hundred yards before sliding away from each other and then quickly regaining their footing. Jacques's smile was hilariously evil, his eyes narrowed and challenging. Ben laughed before charging at him again, but this time, there was no collision. Jacques had disappeared, and was now sliding towards him from behind, gouging a deep line in the grass before knocking

Ben's feet out from under him, like a dirty football tackle. Ben instantly recovered and sprang to his feet. He flew through the air to meet the new threat of Freddie shooting towards him from the left. Ben's hands went for Freddie's throat, but Freddie kicked him in the stomach and sent him careering back into Jacques.

Ben was excited to discover that none of the punches or kicks seemed to really hurt him. They just kept him from doing what he wanted to do. Once the fear of being hurt (and of hurting his friends) was eliminated, he began to feel infinitely more confident. This time, he rolled off Jacques, picked him up by the back of his coat and launched him across the lawn towards the house. 'Nice move!' Jacques called back over his shoulder as he flew through the air.

Freddie was already almost upon him again, but Ben side-slipped him at the last minute, throwing a combination elbow jab to the kidney and a kick to the back of the knees, knocking him to the ground. He finished by leaping onto his back and attempting to pin him in place.

'Looks like I was going too soft on you, Benny boy,' Freddie said, throwing him off, while springing to his feet and twisting around to face him.

'You can go as hard as you like,' Ben retorted. 'I'm ready for you nineteenth-century losers.'

Freddie grinned. 'Enough trash talk. Fight.'

But Ben felt the change as soon as it happened. A subtle shift in atmosphere, a darkening. Freddie and Jacques felt it too... *danger*. Alex was in distress.

'Mon frère!' Jacques cried out, and then he was gone. Freddie gave Ben a troubled look, and then he too disappeared. Ben hesitated only a fraction of a second before following on behind. They were headed outside the grounds to the road beyond. Isobel had joined them, skimming the ground until they reached Alexandre.

Ben knelt at his side with the others. Alex wasn't dead, but he had been hurt in some way. He was different.

'Is it the sleeping sickness?' Belle cried. 'Is he infected?' She put a hand to his forehead, and opened an eyelid, but it instantly closed again. 'He's shivering! But he feels hot. How can that be?'

'Has he been attacked?' Freddie asked.

'I don't know what's happened, but we should get him home,' Jacques said, narrowing his eyes and scanning the area. 'It's not safe out here.'

'He only left the house to find Nadia,' Isobel said. 'She was out here, upset, wandering alone again. And now she's gone. I can't sense her anywhere.'

Ben stood and tried to see if he could feel her presence, but she was nowhere around. 'Shall I see if I can find her?' he asked.

'I'll come with you,' Freddie said. He turned to the twins, their blond heads bowed over their brother's body. 'You two take Alexandre back to the house. Ben and I will get the girl and see if she knows what happened. I hope she hasn't been harmed. Could Travis have taken her? Or could it have been vampires?'

'I didn't sense Travis anywhere around this evening. And there were no vampires here tonight either,' Jacques said. 'We would have known if there were.'

'Someone, or something, has done this to Alex,' Isobel said. 'He wouldn't have collapsed for no reason.'

Freddie turned to Ben. 'We'll search for her, but we must stick together whatever happens. We don't know what did this to Alex. Your sister would kill me if I let anything happen to you now.'

'No, we should split up,' Ben argued. 'We'll cover more ground. I can take care of myself.'

Freddie narrowed his eyes, his usually placid features hardened by worry. 'Alex thought he'd be all right out here alone, yet look where he is now. And he's stronger than any of us. Come on, there's no time to argue. We stick together, no arguments. Let's head away from town to begin with. We can double back later if we don't find her.'

Ben gave a brief nod, somewhat relieved that he wouldn't have to head into the night alone, not feeling quite as brave as he'd sounded.

He and Freddie took off, heading west, but could find no scent of Nadia in the chill night air. At last, he and Freddie came to a stop by the butter-coloured walls of a large country house, its occupants all sound asleep. 'I don't understand,' Freddie said, a frown crumpling his forehead. 'There's no trace of her in the vicinity. She can't have left that long ago.'

'She must have had a car,' Ben said. 'Either that, or she was taken by someone.'

'Even so, we would've had some sense of the direction she'd taken. Some lingering scent of her. But there's nothing. Not a hint.'

'Shall we turn around and head east?' Ben asked.

'I suppose we'll have to. We're finding nothing here.' Freddie stared at Ben for a moment.

'What?' Ben asked.

'It's strange that this isn't strange,' Freddie said. 'It's almost as if you've always been this way. One of us, I mean.'

'I know,' Ben replied. 'I'm almost worried that it feels so normal. I thought I'd be freaking out a lot more.'

'And how are you feeling after the attack? Those vampires the other night. It must have been terrifying for you.'

'I'm trying not to think about it. It happened so fast,' Ben said. 'When I remember it now, it's like it happened to someone else. Do you think the people who attacked Alex are the same vampires who attacked me?'

'I don't think so. It couldn't have been vampires tonight, or we'd know about it. But... it doesn't seem to have been humans either.'

'Maybe Alex just got ill.'

'Vampires don't get ill.'

'Sleeping sickness?'

'I don't know. When we had the sickness, it came on gradually, over weeks and months. This, tonight, was sudden. And he's really ill, shivering and feverish. Not simply sleeping. Come on, we have to try to find Nadia before dawn. Hopefully, she'll shed some light. Maybe she saw something.'

They doubled back and made their way further east. But, again, there were no sightings of the girl. It was as though she had vanished into the night. Back at Marchwood's gates once more, Ben suggested visiting Travis. 'He might know where she is.'

'Good thinking,' Freddie replied, clapping him on the back.

Travis answered his doorbell within twenty seconds. His face fell when he saw who it was. 'Oh, I thought you might be Nadia. Never mind.'

'Sorry, bud,' Ben said. 'I guess that means you don't know where she is.'

'Can you show us where she lives?' Freddie asked.

'Why? What's happened? I thought she was staying with you guys,' Travis said, stepping outside to join them.

'She was,' Freddie replied. 'But she left sometime this afternoon. And then she reappeared, upset, wandering near Marchwood again.'

'I think she's either got problems or she's playing some kind of game,' Travis said, shaking his head. 'I mean, I really like her and everything, but she has serious mood swings. One minute she's into me, and the next minute she hates me.'

'Let's check out her place, make sure she's okay,' Freddie said. 'Where does she live?'

'When I dropped her off yesterday, I didn't see the actual house. I waited in the van because I wanted to see her get safely inside, but she just stood there, waiting for me to drive off. So I did. I'm not sure she even lives here. I think she might be homeless.'

'Can you show us where you dropped her?' Freddie asked.

'Sure. Yeah. The van's parked round the back. I'll drive you.' He checked his pockets for his keys and pulled the front door closed behind him.

They all sat up front as Travis started up the gravelly engine and pulled out of the narrow back lane. 'Have you got her number?' Ben asked.

'No, she hasn't got a phone. Can you believe that?' Travis said, shaking his head. 'Why was she upset again? You know it was nothing to do with me this time, right? I haven't seen her since this morning, at your place.'

'We don't know what the problem was,' Freddie replied.

'Didn't you ask?' Travis said, raising his voice to be heard above the engine, and crunching the gears into third.

'No, Alex was the one talking to her.'

'Alex?' Travis didn't look too happy about that. 'So didn't he ask her what was wrong?'

Neither Ben nor Freddie replied. They were getting into awkward territory now. They didn't want to mention that Alex was unconscious; it would lead to too many questions.

'Well?' Travis persisted.

'We don't know anything, really,' Ben said. 'We thought we'd look for her first. We didn't really get a chance to speak to Alex properly.'

'Oh, right.' Travis's scowl deepened. It only took a couple of minutes to reach their destination. The three of them got out and approached the small square yellow brick houses, peering up at the windows. But Ben could tell she wasn't in any of them. A quick glance at Freddie's darkening brown eyes told him that his ancestor agreed.

'Should we start ringing doorbells?' Travis asked. 'Maybe we should call the police?'

'No, no,' Ben replied. 'I'm sure she'll be fine.'

Travis stopped walking and looked at them both through narrowed eyes. 'There's something funny going on here. Are you telling me the truth? I'm getting a weird vibe off you two.'

'What do you mean?' Ben said. 'We came to you because we thought you might have seen her. You're getting a weird vibe because you're worried, that's all.'

'Yeah,' Freddie interjected. 'Tell you what. Why don't you stay here and start knocking on doors. We'll drive around, see if she's still on the streets. But chances are, she's tucked up safely in bed by now.'

'Yeah... I guess. How did you guys get here? Did you drive? Are either of you old enough to drive anyway? Where's your car?'

'Freddie's car's just up the road,' Ben lied, cutting him off. 'Text us if you find her. We'll do the same.'

Ben and Travis quickly exchanged mobile numbers; Ben had to consciously slow his fingers down on the keypad so Travis didn't think he was some kind of freak. It felt tortuously slow doing things at human speeds. After what seemed like an age, Ben and Freddie finally left an anxious and slightly confused Travis knocking on the doors of some very sleepy, irritated occupants, knowing full well that he wouldn't find Nadia in any of the houses. Ben did feel a little guilty, sending Travis on a wild goose chase, but they had to ditch him. It was no good. They weren't going to find the girl tonight. They had to get back home and hope and pray that Alex was going to be okay.

Once again, Maddy had been left behind like a spare part. Left to pace the kitchen without a clue what was happening out there. Half of her was worried sick, but the other half was frustrated and angry. Living with a houseful of vampires was enough to make anyone insecure. They were faster, stronger, and seemed to know about everything before it even happened. Madison, on the other hand, was like a stupid, slow, uncoordinated child who knew nothing and could do nothing... about anything.

First, Alex had gone off to find Nadia *again*. Now Isobel had fled the house in a panic. Oh, and, of course, she made sure to tell Madison to *stay where she was, and don't worry*. Hah! What a ridiculous thing to say. She might as well have told Madison to worry herself stupid and have a panic attack. Well, there was no way she was sitting around in an empty house wondering what was happening outside. She'd tried everyone's mobile phones in succession, and each one had gone straight to voicemail. Honestly, what was the point of having a phone if you weren't going to even answer it?

She grabbed her coat and keys, and strode out through the back door, slamming it behind her. The security lights flashed on, illuminating the side of the house and grassy bank. Maddy tried not to think about who or what could be skulking about in the darkness. If there were hostile vampires around, the others would surely know it. Just the same, her heart pounded like a jackhammer as she strode towards the garage.

Fumbling for the keys in her pocket, she pressed the tiny remote, and the garage door whirred upwards. Next, she clicked the button on her car key. The Land Rover lights flashed on, and the alarm beeped off. Maddy would feel much better once she was sitting behind the wheel with the doors locked. Not that locked doors could stop a vampire taking her, or killing her, if it wanted. She blew out a breath, trying to quell her panic. What was wrong with her? Why was she suddenly so jittery? She'd coped with a lot worse over the past few weeks.

Isobel had fled the house so fast. Did that mean that Alex

was in trouble? Or Ben? Maddy wrenched open the door and climbed into the vehicle. Her head felt swimmy and strange. She really did feel like she was going to pass out. No. She must pull herself together. This was no time to go to pieces. Maddy tried to summon back her earlier anger; *that* would keep her going until she knew everyone was safe. Alex had said that Nadia was in trouble, but he hadn't said how she was in trouble, or where she was. They couldn't be far, surely. She would just have to drive around until she found someone who could tell her what the hell was going on.

It didn't take her long to find them. She turned right at the end of the driveway, onto the Tetbury road and after less than a minute's drive, her headlights illuminated two hunched figures on the grass verge. She slowed the vehicle. The figures turned towards her. It was Isobel and Jacques, and they were bent over something... or someone. The feeling of panic returned, her fingers clammy and sticky on the steering wheel as she wrenched it to the left and parked on the opposite verge. She almost fell out of the Land Rover, leaving the lights on and the engine running. Who was the figure on the ground? Nadia? Not Ben or Alex. Please.

'It's okay,' Jacques called out. 'He's alive.'

'Ben?'

'Alexandre,' Isobel replied.

Maddy crossed the empty road and pushed the two vampires aside. She sank down to her knees and took in Alex's pale features. Touched her fingers to his cheek.

'He feels hot! Shivery. Is he ill?' Maddy asked. 'How can a vampire be ill?'

'We don't know,' Isobel said. 'We were just about to bring him back home.'

'Put him on the back seat,' Maddy said. 'I'll drive.'

Jacques and Isobel did as she asked. Jacques sat in the back with his brother, and Isobel got in beside Maddy.

'Where are Ben and Freddie?' Maddy asked, sliding the gears into first and executing a clumsy five-point turn. 'Do they know what's happened? Do they know about Alex?'

'They've gone to look for Nadia,' Isobel explained, filling her in.

As Maddy listened, her fingers took a vice-like grip on the steering wheel. That girl. It was something to do with that girl Nadia. She knew it. She should've trusted her initial instincts and insisted that they have nothing to do with her.

CHAPTER TWENTY-FOUR

SCYTHIA, 514 BC

Standing in the silent night, horseless and friendless, Kelermes turned to Artimpasa, the celestial goddess, to guide him. Lifting his face upward to the stars, he beseeched her to help him. 'I am no soothsayer or enaree, but please hear my prayer. Help me to find Laodice and Orik, and the rest of my brethren. Which way should I go? North? South? East? West? I am your humble servant. Please give me a sign.' He waited, staring into the endless sky. What did he expect his goddess to do? Light a trail for him with her stars? What if she gave him a sign but he was too stupid to interpret it? What if she had abandoned him?

Kelermes felt a soft, warm breath at his ear, and he whirled around. His chestnut mare stood at his shoulder, her dark eyes full of a fear and sadness that matched his own. But, briefly, he felt a burst of happiness at her return, and kissed her warm nose. The mare knelt of her own volition, and he swung up onto her back. 'Where are they, Tabi? Take me to them.'

He gave Tabi her head, and she set off northwards. As they gradually left the camp behind, Kelermes's head became a whirl of confusion. Fear lapped at his body in waves. He clung onto Tabi like she was his last link to normality. He knew her homely scent, and how it felt to move across the earth on her back. Everything else – the night, the air, the darkness, his aloneness – felt strange and terrifying. As long as he kept moving, he wouldn't have to think about Laodice, about Orik. He wouldn't have to think about what had happened back there. He wouldn't have to wonder if the thing that had happened to his tribe, would also happen to him.

Tabi kept going, her breath becoming laboured. Kelermes knew she would have to rest soon, but he dreaded that moment. The moment they would stop moving and he would have to think about what to do next. Part of him wanted to get as far away from the unseen threat as he could, but a stronger part knew that he would have to seek it out. To find whatever had taken his beloved away. To confront it, and destroy it, or be destroyed.

Numbed by cold and exhaustion, Kel stopped thinking. His mind became loose, hovering on the verge of sleep. So when he saw a shape in the distance, it didn't really register at first. It felt as though he were seeing it in a dream. A slow-moving image on the edge of his subconscious. Tabi whinnied, jolting Kelermes from his stupor. He rubbed at his eyes and focused on the shape up ahead. Was it an animal? A Persian? Something more sinister? Tabi hadn't slowed down or shown any alarm. In fact, she had put on a spurt of speed, as though she wanted to catch the thing.

Despite a recent veil of cloud, the moon gave out enough light for Kel to deduce that the shape appeared to be a lone horse with a rider. Closer still, he could tell the rider was wearing Scythian clothing. A warrior slumped low over his steed's neck. Could it be one of his brethren? Whoever it was moved slowly and didn't appear to have spotted Kelermes approaching from behind.

'Hey,' Kelermes called. 'Hey, you there!'

The rider sat up and turned his head. Kelermes gave a start. He knew that face.

It was Lohant.

Never had Kel been so pleased to see the man. But Lo didn't appear to have recognised him. The look in his eyes was one of shock and fear. Lohant was urging his mount from a walk to a canter. He was trying to get away.

'Hey! Lohant, wait. It's me, Kelermes!'

The fool kept going. Kel was completely awake now, determined to catch up to his comrade. Tabi was exhausted, yet she still managed to find some extra speed. She had more stamina than Lohant's mount, who had slowed to a trot, even though her master was urging her on, swearing and yelling at her to go faster.

Kel had almost reached them. He was only a few lengths behind. 'Lohant, stop! It's me, Kelermes!'

This time, the man must have heard, for he turned his head and stared hard. Finally, he wheeled his horse around and Kel was able to give Tabi a much-needed break from their pursuit.

'Kelermes? Is it really you?' Lohant's voice was low and incredulous. His eyes wild and staring.

Kel smiled at the man, a weary grim smile, but a smile, nonetheless.

'I thought you were all taken,' Lohant said. 'I thought everyone was gone. Did you escape? Do you know what happened to them? Is anyone else alive?'

'I was hoping you could tell *me* what happened.' Kel slid off Tabi and patted her neck. She hung her head, exhausted.

'How did you get away?' Lohant said, dismounting. He strode up to Kelermes, suddenly grabbing him by his shoulders. 'It is you, isn't it? It really is you? I'm not dreaming, am I? Or dead? Is this the afterlife? Am I still alive?'

'Lohant, listen to me; did you see what actually happened back there?'

'Of course I saw!' Lohant let go of Kel's shoulders. The wild, haunted look in his eyes made Kelermes nervous. The man was chewing on his thumbnail, casting his eyes around. 'They could be here any minute. We should keep moving. We managed to escape them, but they'll find us if we stay put.'

'Who? Who could be here? Who will find us?' Kelermes cried. 'Was it the Persians? Did they attack?'

'I only wish it were the Persians. Those mongrels I could deal with. But no. Did you not see? Were you not there?'

'No,' Kelermes replied. 'I didn't see. Tell me what you saw. What happened back there?'

'Demons,' Lohant whispered, sending a spike of fear through Kel's body. 'They came from nowhere, and then suddenly they were everywhere. They could be stalking us now. They'll take us while we stand here talking about it. We must go.' He climbed back onto his horse.

'Wait!' Kel needed an explanation of what had happened. 'Where is Laodice? Did she manage to escape?'

'Laodice? I don't know.'

Kel glared up at the man. He wanted to pull him off his horse and throttle him. 'You *must* know. You must have seen something. You were there.'

'Yes, I was there. But where were *you*? You still haven't said.' Lohant's voice lost its fearful tone and turned to suspicion. 'Why are *you* still alive? I always thought there was something off about you, *runt*. Are you in league with them? Is that how you got Laodice to change her mind and choose you? Did you make a pact with the demons? Did you sell us out?'

'Are you mad?' Kel said, taking a step backwards. 'I don't even know who or what the demons are. I love Laodice, so why would I wish her harm?'

'Hmm.' Lohant stopped his verbal attack and wheeled his horse around. 'We need to keep going,' he muttered. 'It's not safe here.'

Kelermes swung back up onto Tabi and came alongside
Lohant. 'All right, we'll keep moving. But we can't go too fast, or
the horses won't make it. They're already too tired. If we keep
going, will you, at least, tell me everything that happened back
there?'

Lohant gave a nod, and the two mounted warriors moved off
in step. 'Just before it happened,' Lohant began, 'I was in the
main yurta joking with Abaris. I can't even remember what we
were laughing about. We heard cries of alarm from outside. We
thought we must be under attack from the Persians, so we took
up arms and went out to take a look. But we saw no one. Then I
heard cries coming from the bathing tent. These weren't yells of
alarm or even fear, you understand, but cries of pure terror. You
know our men and woman, Kel. You know their bravery, so
what would make them so afraid? Abaris charged off in the
direction of the cries. But I waited, looking around, trying to
make sense of what was happening. And then I saw them –
demons.'

'How did you know they were demons?' Kelermes asked.
'Could they not have been Persian soldiers? Or another mortal
enemy not yet known to us?'

'No, they were not mortal. They were not like any enemy I
have ever seen. They had human form, yet they travelled across
the ground at such speed you could hardly see them. It was as
though they flew. Snatching our men and women out of the
yurtas and taking them away to who knows where. They had
evil grins on their faces, but they were silent, issuing no war
cries or threats. And their teeth! They had these teeth and... it
was as though these demons were...'

'What?' Kelermes asked 'As though they were what?'

'It looked as though the demons were drinking the blood of
our comrades. They sank their teeth into our brothers' flesh and
drank their blood. Our soldiers tried to hack at the creatures
with swords and shoot at them with arrows as they were carried

away. Alas, our weapons did nothing to them. For a moment, I was paralysed. Terrified. I don't mind admitting it.'

'What did you do?'

'Do? There was nothing to do. I could see our weapons were no good against those creatures. I jumped on my horse, and I got out of there. They could have caught up with me if they wished. But they didn't give chase. I don't know why. I thank the gods that I was so lucky.'

'You ran?' Kelermes cried. 'You left everyone to face the demons alone?'

'You would have done the same if you'd seen them.'

'No! I would not! I would have at least tried to stop them. What about Lae? What happened to her? Did you even look for her? I know you had feelings for her. Surely you wouldn't have left without even trying to see if she was still there. You could have taken her with you. Saved her.'

'I... I didn't see her.'

'You mean, you were too busy saving your own hide to think about looking for her.'

'No... No. I mean—'

'Where did the demons take them? Which direction did they go?'

'They didn't go in any one direction. They came across the snow, and also from above. Like a swarm they came, and they left just as quickly. If you'd been there, you would have seen what it was like. You'd have known that there was nothing I could have done. It happened so fast. Like a dream. A nightmare. Where were you, anyway? Why didn't the demons take you? Why didn't *you* help out?'

'I was away from the camp. I went for a ride to clear my head.'

'On your own? What about Lae? Why did you leave her alone? It was your betrothal day. I would have thought you would be stuck to her side.'

'I... we... I'd said things to her that I regret. I went to clear my head and then I came back to apologise. But when I returned, everyone was gone.'

'So, you argued and left her on her own. No wonder you're blaming me. You feel guilty for abandoning her.'

'I'm not blaming you. And I don't feel guilty! I didn't abandon her. I didn't know the demons would come.' But Kel knew Lohant was right. He had left Laodice alone, all because he couldn't control his own desires. He had as good as killed her. And, of course, it would have to be Lohant who had escaped. Of all the people, why did it have to be this surly fellow who was the only one of his tribe left? Why couldn't it have been Lae, Orik, or Aristeas who had survived? Because they would never have run off to save their own skin. That's why. Only someone like Lohant would flee.

'We should look for them,' Kel said. 'There must be some kind of trail to follow. We should go back. I should never have left the camp. I wasn't thinking straight.'

'No,' Lohant replied.

'If you're too cowardly to return, I'll go back on my own.' Kelermes brought Tabi to a halt and reined her around.

'I am no coward,' Lohant growled. 'What I say is wise. Going back is not a good idea. What can we achieve, the two of us? Nothing. We'll get ourselves killed for no reason. Either that, or we'll die of hunger and exhaustion. Our horses will never make it.'

Kelermes knew the man was right, but it still felt wrong to be heading away from camp, while the others were... were what? He didn't even know what terrible fate had befallen his comrades. Were they still living?

'We'll find an enaree,' Lohant said. 'Someone who knows what we're dealing with. We can't take on a host of demons alone. If our whole tribe was no match for them, what makes you think you can rescue Lae on your own? You're a fool if you think you can do it without help,' Lohant sneered.

For the second time that night, Kel wanted to knock the man from his horse and beat him senseless, but, unfortunately, he realised that Lohant was right.

They travelled at a sickeningly slow pace through the cold darkness – clouds had gathered quickly, taking away the moon's guiding light, and threatening more snow. Dawn brought little respite – the day beginning as a cold, grey affair. No sunshine, just a biting wind and a few whirling snow flurries to add to their misery. The horses plodded, and Kelermes knew that if they didn't rest and eat soon, he and Tabi wouldn't last much longer. The men were too tired even to argue with each other; they barely spoke. Too exhausted and hungry to even think.

By midday, Lohant's horse refused to go any further. She stopped, and no amount of kicking or cajoling would induce her to move. Lohant slid off her back and tried to lead her, but it was no use.

'Let's rest,' Kel said. 'The horses need to sleep. So do we.'

Lohant nodded. If Kel had had the energy, he would have attempted to build some kind of shelter from the snow. He cursed his lack of foresight at having left vital supplies back at the camp. Such necessities as a thick hide to lie on, fire sticks, food and extra clothing. Now he and Lo were forced to sleep side by side to conserve heat. They lay on one of the horse blankets and covered themselves with the other. Within less than a minute, Kelermes felt the wet snow seep up through Tabi's blanket, and through his clothing. He closed his eyes with the grim knowledge that he would probably never wake up. But, at that moment, he didn't have the strength to care.

CHAPTER TWENTY-FIVE

Was this hell? It certainly felt like it. His skin was clammy. Hot, yet cold. And a drum pounded in his head. As he tried to bring his hand to his brow, he felt the stabbing of a thousand knives from shoulder to wrist, like splintered bones digging from the inside out. Alex whimpered and let his arm drop back onto the twisted sheets. He realised it wasn't just his arm; he was aching all over, his stomach cramping, and his throat dry as the Cappadocian desert. In short, he didn't believe he had ever felt so awful in all his life, and that included the time he was turned into a vampire.

'Alex?' A voiced pierced his misery. Madison was here.

He wanted to open his eyes, but his eyelids were stiff and unyielding, like rusted metal.

'Madison.' Alexandre mouthed the word, but no sound came forth.

'Alex, are you awake?'

He felt her breath on his cheek.

'Maddy,' he tried again. This time, a faint whisper emerged.

'Alex, are you okay? Can you talk? What's the last thing you remember? You went out to see Nadia. She was upset. What happened to her? Was it vampires? Were they attacking her?'

Her voice sounded too loud, but at the same time, it sounded fuzzy and strange. It felt like he was underwater. He couldn't focus on her words.

'Alex, what happened?'

And then he remembered.

Alexandre broke out in an even colder sweat as the memory of what had happened returned. The girl. Nadia. He had... Oh my God, he had *kissed* her. How could he have done such a terrible thing? What had he been thinking? With immense effort, he turned his head away from Madison, glad his eyes were still closed so he didn't have to look her in the eye. Afraid she would guess what had occurred. He loved Madison. That other girl meant nothing to him, so why had he done it? What had possessed him?

What had happened after the kiss? Here, his memory went a little hazy. Had they taken it further? God forbid he had slept with the girl. He didn't think he would have done such a thing, but the lust and longing he had felt were beyond anything. The feelings now came back to him with the force of a hurricane, but whereas last night he had been consumed by them, now he simply felt disgusted with himself. And now... now he was paying the price. Perhaps this was punishment, a physical manifestation of guilt.

'Alex.' Maddy's low voice interrupted his self-loathing. 'Alex, look at me. Can you open your eyes?'

He tried again. This time, his eyes inched open, to rest on the armoire. As his vision swam in and out of focus, he reluctantly turned to face her. She peered down at him, the expression on her face fracturing his heart into a million pieces. She, so tender and loving. And he, so undeserving and worthless. A tear squeezed itself from the corner of his eye, and he let it slide down onto the pillow.

'You must take some of my blood,' she said. 'It'll make you strong again. Make you better.'

He shook his head. How could it hurt to shake one's head? But it did.

'Please, Alex. It's the only way. It doesn't hurt me, only makes me a bit weak. And I can deal with that.' She thrust her wrist under his nose, but he didn't even feel thirsty. All he wanted to do was sleep. 'Take it!' she cried.

'No. I cannot.'

'Please,' she begged. 'I hate seeing you like this, Alex. What's happening to you?' He wouldn't do it, and turned his face away. She climbed off the bed and went over to the dressing table, rummaging around in one of the drawers. Eventually, she must have found what she was looking for, for she came back and sat on the bed. He caught the silver glint of metal – nail scissors.

'No!' He gave a weak cry and put his hand out to try to stop her, but he was too late. She had used the point to slice her wrist.

'Holy crap!' she squealed, before adjusting her expression. 'It's okay, it doesn't really hurt that much, it was just... just a bit painful for a second or two.'

'What have you done, Madison?' He sighed. 'Go and bandage it up.'

Crimson droplets now dripped from her skin, staining the sheets.

'I will not. Look – I've stabbed myself in the wrist for you, so you can bloody well drink it. Don't tell me I've done this for nothing, okay?'

How did this girl have the power to make him smile, even when he felt like death? 'Very well,' he replied. 'Put the wound to my mouth and I will have one sip. And then you will bandage it. Okay?'

She held her wrist to his mouth, but he didn't even have the energy to sink his teeth in. Instead, he licked and sucked at the blood. But its taste did nothing to satisfy him. In fact, it made him feel even worse, if that were possible. Could he have caught the sleeping disease again? He prayed that was not the case. But, sleeping sickness, or not, all he knew was that he was so tired, he couldn't keep his eyes open a moment longer.

Once her seat belt clicked shut, and they lifted into the air, Maddy closed her eyes. She hadn't slept for over twenty-four hours and she didn't think she'd be able to sleep now, but she'd give it a try, she needed it. The plane climbed through multiple layers of white cloud, eventually breaking out into a jewel-bright sky. Her ears popped, and she gave a shiver. Her brain spooled backwards and forwards like an old video cassette, loose and spongy, not able to hold onto any coherent thought for more than a second or two. Reaching across, Maddy pulled down a couple of the window shades and shook out the soft chequered blanket on the seat next to her, spreading it over her body and pulling it up to her chin. She closed her eyes again, hoping against hope for an hour or two of oblivion. Morris sat opposite, his mouth slightly open. Sleep had arrived instantly for him. Well, good. At least one of them would be capable of rational thought when they arrived. She sighed, gave up thoughts of sleep and opened her eyes again.

After Alex had fallen sick, their plans had changed. With much toing and froing, begging and cajoling, arguing and plead-ing, it had been decided that Madison and Morris would be the ones to travel to Turkey. They were hoping that two mere humans arriving in the country would pass undetected by the Cappadocian coven. It wouldn't be safe for the other March-wood vampires to go to Turkey. Not without Alex. Their pres-ence would stir up too much attention.

Having chartered a private jet to Cappadocia, she and Morris were now going alone to beg Aelia for help. Perhaps the woman would have some idea of what had happened to Alex. Hopefully, she could save him. If not... Maddy couldn't entertain any thoughts of *if not*. Aelia was their best and last hope. Maddy couldn't keep away the unbearable possibility that Alex was dying, and that they didn't have much time left. Her stomach fell away at the thought.

Would any of them ever be able to live normal lives? Okay, well, maybe not *normal*, but uneventful would be nice. To be able to do regular things, like go for walks, go to the movies, and have a laugh. They'd managed a few months of normalcy at the end of the summer, but then it had all gone downhill after she'd been kidnapped at the ice-skating rink. Now they were deeper in trouble than ever before. At least Ben was safe... for now. She should stop dwelling on all the bad stuff. Take one day at a time. One hour at a time. If she looked any further ahead, all she could see was scary stuff – uncertainty and danger.

So, they'd get to Turkey, find Aelia and ask for her help. That was the plan. After that... she would have to wait and see.

After a restless night's sleep at the hotel, Madison awoke early and met Morris for breakfast in the restaurant. It was only two days until New Year's Eve, and the whole hotel was decked out with lights, baubles, and gaudy decorations. But, besides the waiting staff, she and Morris were the only ones in here. No one else was crazy enough to get down here for 6.30 a.m. during the holidays. Maddy had been taken aback by how busy it was last night at dinner, with throngs of European and American tourists enjoying their winter break. Maddy had felt so far removed from all these relaxed holiday makers, eyeing them with jealous fascination until Morris had had to tell her to stop staring. What must it be like to live a normal life, blissfully unaware of the existence of supernatural creatures? People didn't have a clue what was going on under their very noses. Under their very feet. Beneath the bedrock lurked a vast thrumming city of evil. These tourists wouldn't have tucked into their dinners quite so heartily if they'd known the truth.

There had been a message from Isobel yesterday when they'd landed, informing them there was no real change in Alex's condition. That, if anything, he was worse. That Maddy needed to find Aelia quickly and pray she could identify what was wrong with him. No pressure, then.

Her appetite was seriously diminished, but she knew she had to eat, so she helped herself to a cup of tea and a single slice of toast. Morris, on the other hand, loaded up a couple of plates from the buffet. He headed back to their table and put one of the loaded plates in front of Madison. She eyed the mountain of hot food with a lack of enthusiasm.

'Eat it,' Morris said. 'Long day ahead of us. You'll be no good to Alex if you run out of energy.'

Maddy screwed up her face but did as he asked, plucking a fried egg off the top of the piled-up plate, plonking it onto her buttered toast and spearing a bite-sized amount onto her fork. It tasted pretty good, and she grudgingly murmured her thanks.

Morris made short work of his full-English breakfast, and so, to her surprise, did she. By seven o'clock the two of them were ensconced in their hired jeep setting out towards Aelia's cave. Maddy smiled inwardly, thinking what an unlikely pair they made. He, a fifty-something-year-old ex-army Gloucestershire groundskeeper, and she, a multimillionaire teenage orphan. This was not in any way, shape, or form how she had envisaged her life unfolding.

The ice-glazed lunar landscape jolted past the windows of their jeep. The snow had melted a little since they were last here, which made the going somewhat easier, but a few rogue snowdrifts still clung to the shadows. Morris seemed to know where they were headed, so Maddy didn't interfere. Neither of them said much, but it was a companionable silence. They both knew why they were there.

The pale morning sun shone bright enough that Maddy wished she'd remembered to bring her sunglasses. She squinted and gave an involuntary shiver. Those ancient and terrifying vampires, Mislav and Sergell, were probably in their underground city right now. If they knew she was here, they would have no hesitation in sending out their minions to kill her. She was glad she and Morris had decided to wait until dawn to venture out. Although the long night had seemed to last forever.

'Are we nearly there?' she asked, feeling like a child.

'Maybe an hour more,' Morris replied.

'I hope Aelia still lives there. What shall we do if she's gone?'

'Cross that bridge when we come to it.'

Maddy's heartbeat thudded over the engine noise. The last time she was here, she had been threatened, chased and almost killed. The memory of it brought bile to her throat. She put her hands on the dashboard and took a deep breath. A cold sweat swept across her brow.

'Stop the car.'

Morris glanced across at her and did as she asked. Once they were stopped, Maddy opened her door, slid out of the vehicle and heaved her guts up onto the snow. So much for a nourishing cooked breakfast. After a moment, Morris passed her a bottle of water. She took it gratefully and swished the cold liquid around her mouth before spitting it out.

'Sorry,' she said.

'Nothing to be sorry about. Feeling a bit queasy myself. Maybe you were right; we should have stuck with the toast.'

She was grateful for his understated sympathy. After taking in a clean lungful of frigid Cappadocian air, Madison climbed back into the jeep and gave Morris the nod to continue. At least her stomach felt more settled, despite their continued juddering and jolting progress. Sipping at the water, Maddy tried to empty her mind. Thinking about everything wouldn't do her any good right now.

As the sun's rays spread across the landscape, Morris pointed ahead. 'See that cliff? That's it, that's where we're headed. Do you remember it? Probably only take us another ten minutes to get there. You feeling any better? Or do you want to wait in the jeep while I go in?'

'I'm fine.' Maddy couldn't wait to get there. The image of Alex's face was seared into her mind – his pale skin covered in a sheen of sweat, his chattering teeth and shivering bones. Nothing like the indestructible Alex she knew and loved. Maddy prayed Aelia would be in the cave. That she would be able to help Alexandre. She had to.

CHAPTER TWENTY-SIX

SCYTHIA, 514 BC

When he awoke, Kelermes didn't know where he was. His mind felt foggy. His memory, hazy. It didn't feel like morning, and this didn't feel like the sleeping tent. It felt like somewhere else. Somewhere unfamiliar. Strange herbal aromas permeated the air. It was warm here, comfortable beneath the thick bed coverings. He opened his eyes and pushed himself into a sitting position with some effort. He was weak. Glancing around, he saw that he was inside a yurta. A fire blazed in the centre, and bright rays of sunshine flooded in through the open crown of the tent to meet the flames, bleaching their orange glow. Not early morning sunshine – more like midday or early afternoon.

The memory of what had happened suddenly enveloped Kel.

Laodice.

Would he ever see her again?

First, he must find out where he was. Whose yurta he had slept in. Before falling asleep in the snow, he had thought he was about to die, and now he found himself in this strange sun-filled tent. And where were Lohant and the horses? Had they survived? Kel pushed back the covers and stood up, his legs a little shaky, his throat parched with a thirst that suddenly overtook all other thoughts. He glanced around, spying a leather bag hanging from the felt wall. He took out the stopper, sniffed the contents, then tipped a little onto his finger and gave it a lick. Mare's milk. Perfect. After a few satisfying swigs of the liquid, his thirst abated and he felt less woozy. He replaced the milk bag and tried to take stock of his situation.

He was wearing a loose robe. Someone must have undressed him and put him into this garment. It was finely made, from hemp, embroidered and adorned with felt applique. It was a Scythian robe, of that much he was sure. Hopefully, that meant he was among allies. He glanced around with a jolt of panic. Where was his bow? His sword? There was no sign of his weapons belt or his clothing. He leant down and with relief felt his grandfather's dagger still strapped to his calf. At least they – whoever they were – had left him with his blade. He slipped it out of its sheath and gripped it in his right fist.

'Ready for battle, my friend?'

Kel whirled around, heart pumping double time. Before him stood a tall, androgynous man with a broad smile upon his painted face. He wore flowing robes and held a willow wand in his right hand. Kelermes realised he was in the presence of an *enaree*.

'Where am I?' Kel asked, lowering his weapon and bowing his head, careful to temper his request with respect. The Enarei were revered soothsayers. They could divine the future and interpret the will of the gods. It would not do to anger or offend this priest.

'The gods have seen fit to send you and your comrade to the royal court,' the enaree replied with a hint of irony. 'You are currently residing in one of the royal tents.'

'Royal?' Kel looked up for a moment, stunned by the soothsayer's revelation.

'Yes.' The enaree inclined his head and gave a smile. 'A

couple of days ago, while returning from a recce, the Royal
Cavalry almost trampled you both to death as you lay sleeping.
They saw you and your companion in the snow and, at first,
thought you dead. But one of you made a noise, and they
realised you were alive – barely – and that you were fellow
countrymen. Warriors. So they brought you here.'

Kel took in this information, hardly believing their luck.
From a snowy grave, they had been rescued by royal soldiers.
The goddess Artimpasa had indeed been listening to his
prayers. To end up in the royal encampment was a chance in a
million, for the Scythian people had no cities, no towns, no
permanent settlements. They were a kingdom of nomads,
hunting and warring across their lands. Roaming the steppe
with its endless sea of snow and grasses, and vast skies. Even
Scythian royalty lived in this manner, making it near impossible
for their enemy to seek them out and destroy them. They were a
people who could not be displaced, for they owned none of the
land and all of the land.

With his head bowed once more, Kel asked, 'Do you know if
my horse survived?'

'It is interesting that you would enquire after your horse,
before asking about the well-being of your companion,' the
enaree replied.

Kel flushed. The enaree must think him a terrible person.
'Of course I am concerned for Lohant. Please reassure me that
he lives.'

'He lives,' the enaree replied. 'Your horse, alas, does not.'

Kel felt another blow to his heart. A lump formed in his
throat at the thought of his gentle Tabi. His eyes filled with
water. Thankfully, his head was bowed so the enaree could not
see his reaction. He prayed his tears would remain unshed and
not drip traitorously onto the floor. For a Scythian warrior to cry
was unthinkable. First Laodice and his tribe, gone. And now his

faithful steed, dead. All that was left of his previous life... was Lohant.

'I am happy Lohant lives,' Kel said, not altogether untruthfully. Then, he recalled something the enaree had said. 'Forgive me, but did you say the Royal Cavalry discovered us two days ago? Have I been sleeping for two days?'

'Yes. Your comrade awoke last night. But you were in need of a few more hours rest.'

'There is something...' Kelermes began.

'Speak,' the enaree said.

'I am sure you are already aware of this, and my comrade must have already mentioned it, but the Persians have crossed the Silys. They are right now marching north.'

'Yes, Lohant told us of their approach, and of your engagement with them. An army of that size, in this weather, will take at least a few more days to reach us. We will be moving out soon. I hope you are fit enough to travel.'

'I'll be fine,' Kelermes replied. 'There is something else... something harder to explain.'

'You mean the blood demons?'

'Yes! Have you seen them? Did you escape from them? Did they have any captives? My betrothed, she—'

The enaree held out his hand to stop Kel's questions. 'We have not seen them. But we know they are close. They have wrought devastation on our people.'

Kelermes opened his mouth to interrupt, but the enaree stopped him again. 'No. We will talk of demons later. Now, you must rest again. Do you feel quite well?' the enaree enquired. 'You are pale. You should sit.' As the enaree gestured towards his bedding, a wave of dizziness overtook Kelermes. He took a step back and crashed down on the covers.

'Sorry,' Kel whispered. 'I feel a little...'

'You need to eat. I'll have some food brought in.' As the enaree turned and left the room, Kel lay down on his side and closed his eyes. The dizziness had receded, but he did feel weak and hungry. Overriding his physical discomfort was an ache of despair. Why was he still alive? Why had he been saved yet again from impending death? What did he have left to live for? A week ago, he would have been euphoric to find himself in the royal encampment, a guest of the king, no less, with the king's enaree who might have agreed to marry him and Laodice. But now... now what did any of that matter? Kel didn't know anyone here. His life wasn't here. He had no love for Lohant. Everything from this day on was pointless.

Some time later, Kelermes was brought briefly out of his gloom by the arrival of a young woman bearing a platter of food. Food such as he had never seen before – meats and cheese, fish, and other delicacies he didn't even recognise. After eating his fill, the same woman returned with Kelermes's clothes. The garments were stiff and reeked of smoke and cooked meat – they must have been dried beside a fire.

'Thank you,' Kelermes said. 'Do you have my weapons, too?'

'They are safe,' she replied, head bowed.

'May I have them? I feel undressed without my belt.'

'I am sure they will be returned to you soon.'

Dressed once again in his familiar clothing (minus his belt), and with food in his belly, Kelermes felt some strength return to his body. He decided to leave the confines of the yurta and take a look outside at the royal encampment. He ran his fingers through his hair and beard, attempting to untangle a few knots, then gave up. He wasn't here to impress anyone.

Peeling back the heavy tent flap, the cold air made him catch his breath, a stark contrast to the stuffy warmth of the yurta. The light outside had dimmed, and dusk had almost arrived, but the camp was far from gloomy. As he stepped beyond the tent and gazed about him, Kel saw that his own yurta was one of many, of differing shapes and sizes. Torches had been lit outside each, and open fires blazed before richly

dressed people who were talking, laughing and eating. He had
better take note of the position of his own yurta, for the encampment seemed so vast that he was likely to become lost.

Walking about the place, he saw many of the king's soldiers
with their decorated uniforms and chain mail jerkins. There
were also many noblemen and noblewomen, as well as children
and servants. Scores of horses, cattle and other livestock were
penned here. It was all Kel could do to stop his mouth hanging
open. This royal camp had a feeling of permanence that Kel had
never seen before. Surely it would take longer than a few days
to dismantle everything. How would they manage to get going
quickly if they needed to flee their enemy? As he walked
through the camp, no one paid Kel any mind. He wondered
again how far north they were from the Silys River. How far
they were from the approaching Persians. How far from the
demons.

Bursts of raucous laughter sounded up ahead. Kel walked
past a group of women tending to a stew pot and saw the source
of the merriment – a group of the king's soldiers squatting on
the ground playing knucklebones. It was a game Kel often
enjoyed. A game he was particularly skilled at it. Or perhaps it
was simply a matter of being lucky. He took a few paces closer
to get a better look. To see who was winning. Another cheer
rose up from the group, and Kel glanced at the man who seemed
to be scoring all the points. It was Lohant.

But it was a Lohant Kel had never seen before. This
Lohant was laughing, his eyes shining. This Lohant garnered
looks of respect from these royal soldiers. He was making them
laugh, throwing out friendly insults. And there were children
at the man's back, touching his shoulders and urging him on to
win. They were *admiring* him. How had this sullen and unlike-
able fellow managed to win round the royal soldiers in just
one day?

The man in question happened to look up at that moment

and catch Kel's eye. After the briefest darkening of expression, Lohant beamed up at him. 'Look who lives! It's the runt!'

Kel scowled as everyone laughed at the nickname. But a couple of the soldiers made a space on the ground for him to squeeze in. He felt appraising eyes on him as he squatted in the circle with the other men.

'This is my comrade Kelermes,' Lohant continued.

Everyone nodded in his direction. One soldier turned to him and said: 'I hear you were thrice lucky, my friend.' This statement was met with murmured agreement.

'Thrice lucky?' Kelermes asked. 'How so?'

'Firstly, you were discovered half-dead in the snow by our comrades and brought back to life. Secondly, you were saved from a Persian brute by Lohant's sword. And thirdly, you were lucky enough to be away from your camp when the demons came, leaving Lohant here to fight them off single-handed.'

At his comment about Lohant's bravery, Kelermes almost laughed. *Leaving Lohant here to fight them off?* What had the man been telling these people? Lies by the sound of it. Lohant certainly hadn't admitted to them that he'd been a quivering wreck who had abandoned his comrades at the first sign of the demons; fleeing the scene with no intention of trying to find his missing brethren. And then, a blatant lie about saving Kel from a Persian? These soldiers had lapped up Lohant's stories, believing every word. They seemed to adore him. Kel was dumbstruck.

'He's a quiet young pup, isn't he?' another soldier added, nodding in Kel's direction. The man turned to Lohant. 'Are you sure this one is really a soldier?'

The men laughed.

Kelermes stood, offended by everything he was seeing and hearing here. 'I have been a warrior with Aristeas for almost two years,' he said stiffly, 'and I have taken twenty-one scalps. All Persians. I regret that I was not at my camp when the demons attacked, but had I been there, I would have fought hard to save my brothers and sisters. Unlike some—'

'Settle down, brother,' Lohant said, cutting him off. 'I know it wasn't your fault. Enough of the serious talk. Come and show your skill with the knucklebones. These fellows will change their mind about you when they see you play.'

This was something new – Lohant being nice to him. Of course, it was only to stop him telling everyone the truth about Lo's cowardice. About how the man had left everyone behind. Gods only knew what other lies he had spun here. Kelermes decided that Lohant could have his glory if he wanted it. Kel wouldn't contradict him, but he didn't want any part of it either. He didn't care what these people thought of him anymore. All he wanted was to find the demons so he could get Lae back.

'Where is your enaree?' Kel asked the soldier next to him. 'I need to speak with him. It's important.'

'Kel,' Lohant interrupted. 'Relax. Play a game with us. We're seeing the enaree after sunset. You can speak to him then.'

'Thank you, but I don't feel in the mood for games.' Kel turned and walked back towards his yurta, leaving the soldiers to their obviously low opinion of him. The sound of their laughter followed him back to his tent. He put his hands to ears and gritted his teeth. Surely Lohant couldn't sustain this hero charade forever. He would slip up, and then everyone would see him for what he really was. A coward. A snake. Kelermes needed to banish Lohant from his thoughts and concentrate on what was truly important here – finding his beloved and bringing her back to his side. Nothing else mattered.

CHAPTER TWENTY-SEVEN

Despite having been in Aelia's cave only a week ago, the place was nothing like she remembered. Back then, a cosy fire had cheered the place, and the aroma of Aelia's cooking had made it feel like a well-loved home. Today, the cave felt cold, damp and abandoned, the lingering scent of stale food making Maddy feel mildly nauseous once again.

Morris held a hunting knife in his right hand and shone the torch across the empty stone floors and walls with his left. It was obvious no one was staying here at the moment. Aelia had left.

Maddy didn't blame the woman for leaving. Her safe haven had been compromised. Maddy wouldn't fancy living out here all alone while a vicious coven of vampires was out for your head. Even if Aelia did have superhuman strength and carried the devastating sleeping sickness in her blood, Maddy was sure there were ways the vampires could despatch her if they wanted to – which they very much did.

'What now?' Maddy asked. She was trying not to dwell on the fact that Aelia was probably Alex's best hope for recovery.

'I'll light a fire,' Morris said, sheathing his knife and tucking it back into his boot.

'Why?' Maddy asked. 'There's no one here. She's obviously moved out. We're wasting our time.'

'You got any other leads on where she might've gone?'

'No,' Maddy replied. 'But we could ask around.'

'You know her last name? Or whether she still calls herself Sofia, or Havva, or Aelia?'

'No.'

'Well then. We'll light a fire and take a look around the place. See if we can find something to point us in the right direction.'

'I guess so.' She knew he was right, but impatience gnawed at her.

'There's wood over there in the corner. Once we get the fire going, it'll warm us up and shed some more light on the place.'

Maddy took the torch from Morris and shone it in the direction of the woodpile.

'Kindling's fairly dry,' Morris said, picking up a bundle of twigs. 'The logs might smoke a little, though.'

'Want any help?' Maddy asked.

'Just keep the torch steady.'

Madison watched as the groundskeeper made short work of creating a bright and crackling fire. She edged closer, enjoying the surprisingly fierce heat, eyes watering as a thin plume of smoke curled towards her. Dancing flames of orange light illuminated all but the darkest corners of the cave.

'There, look.' Maddy swept the torch beam along the rock walls. 'Are those wooden torches?'

'Well spotted, lass.'

One by one, they removed the torches from their wall brackets and used the fire to light them, the sharp scent of pitch making Maddy screw up her nose. Once the torches were all flaming away and set back on the walls, the whole cave swam with light.

However, over an hour spent searching the cave revealed

nothing of any consequence. Maddy had known it would be fruitless. They needed to be out there, looking for Aelia, asking around. 'Alex is really ill, Morris. We can't afford to be hanging around like we've got all the time in the world.'

'We're not hanging around, Madison. We're being methodical, and careful. If we go racing around the place half-cocked, we'll tip those vampires off to our arrival. We need to go steady if we want to get results.'

'Can we, at least, drive somewhere that's got a signal so I can call home and find out how Alex is doing?'

'We'll search the cave one last time. Then we'll go.'

'Again? Why? We've looked at every square inch of the place.'

'Better to be safe than sorry. We could've missed something.'

'Trust me,' Maddy muttered, 'we didn't.'

'Don't get snippy.'

'*Snippy?* Is that the polite word for it?'

Morris inclined his head. 'It's a word the missus would use for it.'

'I'm pretty sure Esther would call me a lot worse than that.'

'No, Maddy.' Morris raised his voice enough to make her look up at him. He continued but softened his voice again. 'Esther thinks the world of you and Ben. You're like family. You *are* family. Snippy or not.'

Maddy blinked. Morris had never been one to talk about things like this. Emotional stuff.

'So,' Morris continued, 'as I was saying, we'll have a last look round here, and then we'll go.'

'After we've looked, *then* can we start asking around for her?'

'Not today.'

Maddy opened her mouth to object, but Morris raised his palm to silence her. 'We've to get back to the hotel before dark.

You know how dangerous it is to stay out any later. Night falls quickly this time of year. We can ask in the villages first thing tomorrow. Discreetly. See if anyone knows where the lady might be.'

'But what about Alex? By tomorrow, he might be even worse.'

'Yes, and you'll be no good to Alex if that Mislav fella takes you back underground.'

'We'll be careful. And anyway—'

'This isn't up for discussion,' Morris said, his easy-going tone disappearing.

He and Maddy jerked their heads around simultaneously as a voice cut through their disagreement. It sounded like a hesitant greeting in a foreign language.

A young man had entered the cave. He looked Turkish. Tall and dark, with a friendly enough smile.

'Hello,' the man said, switching to English.

Morris took a couple of steps so he was positioned in front of Madison. She tried to sidestep him, but he put his hand back to keep her in place.

'Hello,' Morris returned the greeting.

Maddy noticed the stranger slipping something into his pocket.

'Morris,' Maddy hissed in his ear. 'I think he's got a gun.'

'Noted,' Morris murmured.

'Good day,' the man said, raising his empty hands in a placatory manner.

'Who are you?' Maddy called out from behind Morris. She was capable of looking after herself and was irritated by Morris's attempt to shield her from this stranger.

'Hello, I am Derin.'

'Morris Foxton, pleased to meet you.' Morris took a step forward and held out his hand.

As the men shook hands, Maddy stepped out from behind

Morris, this time, meeting with no resistance. 'Madison Greene,' she said.

'Ahh, Madison.' The man gazed at her with recognition.

'Sorry, do I know you?' she asked, surprised.

'No, no. We haven't met, but you know my aunt. I am Derin, Sofia's great-nephew.'

'Sofia's nephew? Can you prove it?' Morris asked.

'Prove it?' The man's smile increased. 'Yes. You can come to the house to meet her.'

'Really?' Madison felt the first stirrings of hope since they'd arrived in Turkey.

'Wait a minute,' Morris said. 'No offence, but how do we know you're telling the truth?'

The man pointed to the fire. 'Can I warm up? It's cold out there.'

'Did you come alone?' Morris asked.

'Yes,' Derin replied, following Morris as he led the man towards the fire. 'I came on my motorbike, but I wheeled it the last part of the way. I saw your jeep outside and didn't want you to hear my approach. I didn't know who I'd find in here.' Derin crouched in front of the flames, removed his gloves and began warming his hands.

'Did I see a weapon on you earlier?' Morris asked.

Maddy held her breath. Was it all about to go off? Or could they trust this stranger?

'Yes,' the man replied. 'I have a gun. Unfortunately, my aunt insisted upon it. I don't know why. I don't like the things.'

'Will you let me have it for now?' Morris asked. 'As an act of trust?'

Derin hesitated. 'I am not a threat to you. My aunt said Madison was her friend.'

'All the same,' Morris said. 'We can't go anywhere with you if you're carrying a gun.'

'Why don't you put it at the back of the cave?' Maddy

suggested. 'Then none of us will be armed.' She crossed her fingers against the lie, remembering the knife Morris had stashed in his boot.

Morris nodded his approval. 'That would be acceptable.'

'Okay. I'll do that,' Derin said, a wary look in his eye. He walked to the rear of the cave, throwing glances behind him as he went. He reached the underground spring and placed the weapon behind a rock before returning. Morris made him stand still and then proceeded to pat him down.

'Thank you for your trust,' Morris said. They resumed their positions crouched around the fire. Maddy angled a couple more logs on the top, showering sparks into the smoky air. 'What brought you out here to the cave?' Morris asked.

'My aunt,' Derin replied. 'She's been away for a while, but she returned last week, and insisted we come out here each day to check if anyone was here, looking for her.'

'*We?*' Maddy said. 'I thought you said you were alone.'

Derin turned to face her. 'Yes, I'm alone. But my brothers and I have been taking it in turns to come out here and check the place each day. *Only in the daytime*, my aunt says, *only in the daytime.* So we come in the daytime and we check. She gave us some names of people who might show up here. Yours is one of the names, Madison. I don't know what all this is about, but she insisted it was important. Nobody argues with my aunt.' He shrugged and smiled. 'I confess, I thought she might be getting a little muddled. But now, here you are. It turns out she might not be losing her mind. Although I have no idea what she wants with you.'

'Just because she's old, doesn't mean she doesn't know what she's talking about,' Morris said. 'Your aunt is a unique and incredible lady. You'd do well to remember that.'

Derin nodded, wearing a slightly bemused expression at Morris's defence of his elderly relation. 'It's a good fire,' Derin said. 'I'm warm enough. Shall we go?'

Maddy and Morris nodded, rising to their feet. 'I'll put out the flames,' Morris said. Maddy realised that Derin probably didn't even know who or *what* his aunt really was. She'd also be willing to bet Derin didn't even believe in vampires. She only hoped he'd be true to his word and take them to Aelia. They didn't have any time to waste.

CHAPTER TWENTY-EIGHT

SCYTHIA, 514 BC

Still seething from his encounter with Lohant and the royal soldiers, Kelermes strode through the camp intending to return to his yurta, barely concentrating on the direction in which he was heading. The sun had almost set completely, and Kel had to finally admit to himself that he was lost. The camp dwellers had all disappeared inside their tents now, and there was no one to ask for help. He was starting to feel chilly, tired and hungry. Disconsolately, he skirted around another tent. Before him sat a huge, wide yurta. Obviously, this had to be the main feasting tent. Two royal guards stood at its entrance. Kel approached to ask for directions, as they eyed him with unfriendly stares. But, before he had a chance to open his mouth, someone stepped out of the yurta. It was the enaree.

'What are you doing out here?' the man asked. 'You should be resting in your tent. Come with me. I'll take you back.'

The enaree began walking, weaving through the maze of tents and animal pens, with Kelermes keeping pace. As they walked, Kel decided to take advantage of the opportunity to speak to the soothsayer alone. He hadn't had a proper chance to ask his advice yet.

'May I speak to you of the demons?' Kel asked, continuing without waiting for an answer. 'I must find them, and rescue my tribe, if it's not too late. My betrothed, Laodice, she is gone and I—'

But infuriatingly, once again, the enaree stopped his questions with a raised hand. 'There's no use asking me this now. Tonight, I will ask the gods, and they will tell us what to do. They will know how to proceed.'

'Tonight?' Kel asked.

'Yes. Two hours after sunset, we will gather at the feasting tent and make a sacrifice. I will ask the gods about the blood demons, and we will act accordingly. You will also be in the presence of the king and queen, so forget your questions now, and rest. And Kelermes, you must also forget whatever is angering you. It is not important.'

At the priest's words, Kel's anxiousness and anger subsided. He had waited two days, so two more hours wouldn't hurt. Anyway, he was exhausted. He needed the time to gather his energy.

'Here we are.' The enaree pointed ahead to a small yurta.

Kelermes recognised it with a relieved sigh.

'I will leave you to your rest. Your maid will guide you to the feasting tent at the correct hour.'

'Thank you,' Kelermes said, meaning it.

The soothsayer nodded and turned away with a swish of his robes, disappearing into the darkness. With a yawn, Kelermes entered his tent. Another short sleep and he would be ready for the night ahead... he hoped.

Two hours later, Kelermes found himself being led into the largest yurta he had ever been in. It was the one he had seen earlier that day – the feasting tent, its interior lavishly decorated with flaming torches, carpets and dried garlands. Kel gazed about him, trying not to appear too overawed by everything. In the centre, a fire pit had been lit with a small fire burning a heady and fragrant incense. Around the outside sat what looked like the entire population of the royal encampment. Hundreds of people sitting cross-legged, talking in murmurs and whispers like the swishing of the steppe grasses in autumn. But what really drew Kel's attention was the tableau at the far end of the yurta. Seated upon two carved golden thrones were the rulers of his people – King Idanthirsos and Queen Opiya.

At first, the young monarchs appeared to be golden statues. They sat motionless and erect, bright and shining. But, on further inspection, Kelermes realised it was their clothing that made them seem this way, embroidered as it was with hammered-gold motifs – stars, discs, rosettes, squares and rings. These Scythian royals wore gold rings upon all their fingers and carved bands around their wrists. Their elaborate neckpieces had been carved with griffins, horses, swirls and flowers. The figures were dazzling and otherworldly. Kelermes was mesmerised.

Kel's maid ushered him forward, closer to the monarchs than he was expecting. He turned to look at the girl for confirmation, and she nodded, encouraging him forward, pointing to a carpet right at the front of the circle of people. She then stepped back and disappeared into the dark edges of the yurta, leaving him to pick his way through the seated crowd, who drew back to let him past. Lohant was also seated at the front, his eyes alight with excitement, and he gestured to Kelermes to join him.

Once Kel was seated, the crowd seemed to grow quieter, and quieter still, until the whole place was silent, save for the hiss and spit of the fire. The two warriors found themselves directly in front of the king and queen, with only the low fire separating them from their monarchs. Kelermes hardly dared breathe. He could be imagining it, but it looked like the rulers were staring directly at him and Lohant. He swallowed and prayed he wouldn't do anything mortifying like pass out, or cough uncontrollably. He knew he shouldn't be staring either, so he hastily looked down.

The ground in front of the fire appeared to be moving. Or perhaps it was just the shadow of the flames. No, it was definitely moving. Something was gradually rising from the hide-covered floor. A loose, swirling shape that grew, and grew, until it stood before them – a man in flowing robes holding a willow wand...

The enaree.

The soothsayer gazed at Lohant and Kelermes. The hairs rose on Kel's neck and arms. How had he appeared from nowhere? Was this magic? He had heard tell of a soothsayers' powers but had never witnessed them first hand before. The silence in the yurta was overpowering.

Then the enaree spoke.

'Brave Scythians, we are at war. Constantly. The Persians, the Cimmerians, the Black Cloaks, the Assyrians.' As he spoke each enemy's name, he dropped something into the fire making it flare up each time with a brief white explosion. 'But we are now under attack from something far worse – blood demons.' This time, he threw something into the flames that made them rise up almost to the roof, glowing red and black, hissing, spitting and crackling, as though he had conjured the very demons he spoke of from the fire. Kelermes found himself gasping and drawing back from the flames along with everyone else. Even the king's and queen's composures seemed rattled by the enaree's display, their eyes widening.

'I have prayed to the gods,' the priest continued, as the fire subsided to its normal state, 'and have asked them to keep us safe. We are spared as long as we stay within the circle of our encampment. But should we venture outside the circle, we will no longer be under the protection of Oetosyrus, God of the Sun, and Tabiti, the Fire Goddess. They alone can protect us from the blood demons. We need the gods' light to banish them.

'Many of our brothers and sisters have not been so lucky. Every day we hear of more disappearing warriors, vanished cattle herders, and deserted encampments. These demons are stalking our people.' The enaree gazed at his rapt and terrified audience.

Here were fierce warriors who went daily into battle without fear of pain or death. But tell them of demons, and the hairs rose on their necks, their eyes widened and sweat broke out on their broad backs, Kelermes included.

'They are stalking us,' the enaree continued, 'because of the prophecy.'

At this statement, there were murmurs of agreement from the crowd. Kel didn't know of any prophecy and looked to Lohant to see if he was any the wiser. Lohant gave Kel a quick shrug of his shoulders. They turned back to the enaree, who continued speaking.

'The last time I spoke to the gods, they told me of this prophecy. A promise that tells of *the bright one*. Of a shining warrior who will hunt out evil and return our lands to us. We still await the bright one, and so we will now honour Oetosyrus with our finest steed. The king's own stallion. Nothing less can be offered to the sun god. Maybe then he will hear our pleas.'

Kel glanced up at King Idanthirsos. He knew something of how his monarch must be feeling. To lose your horse was a terrible thing. But to willingly give him up must be heart crushing.

Through the crowd, led by a well-dressed groom, came the king's steed. Calmly, the chestnut stallion walked towards the enaree, head down, a sight to behold, dressed as he was to match his master in a golden headdress, and strung about with gold chains fixed with shining discs that winked and shimmered in the firelight. Kel knew how important this sacrifice was. The king's horse no less. Surely the gods would hear their prayers now.

What followed was a hard thing for Kel to watch. Witnessing the death of this beautiful creature tore at his heart. The enaree began to strangle the beast by means of a tightening rope and stick. The sacrifice was necessary but terrible to behold. Kel clenched his fists and dug his nails into the palm of his hand. Finally, the deed was done. The horse lay motionless on the ground before the fire. The following hour was taken up with the enaree and his acolytes flaying the dead horse and boiling its flesh in a cauldron over the fire.

The tent grew warmer, and Kel felt his eyes growing heavy. He couldn't allow himself to fall asleep, it would be the gravest insult. The scent of cooking flesh invaded his nostrils making him feel at once hungry and nauseous. He took a breath through his mouth and willed himself to show interest in the proceedings. This was important. He was in the king's tent. He was an honoured guest. Why? He did not know. Perhaps it was due in some part to Lohant's boastful lies. Lohant, who had seen the demons, yet lived to tell the tale.

The enaree had now removed portions of the cooked horse meat from the cauldron and was laying them on the ground by the fire. Offering them up to Oetosyrus and Tabiti. Asking the gods to protect them and guide them. Now the atmosphere in the yurta changed from one of heaviness and fear to one of expectant interest. The enaree was about to divine the future. To make another prophecy and tell his people how they would move forward from here. Everyone sat a little taller and leant forward a little further. Even Kel felt his mind grow sharper, hunger and weariness forgotten for the moment.

A young apprentice brought forward a slim bundle of willow wands and laid them on the ground in front of the enaree before disappearing back into the shadows. The priest knelt to untie the bundle. He placed a single wand on the ground and uttered a prophecy:

'To defeat the blood demons, a worthy warrior will show himself,' the enaree cried.

The soothsayer then placed another wand on the ground, uttering another prophecy:

'This warrior will speak to the gods.'

Everyone else in the room gave a collective gasp. It was unheard of for regular men and women to speak to the gods – they could pray, yes. But to speak directly was an honour reserved for the Enarei alone.

He placed another wand, and spoke again:

'This warrior will beg the gods to protect us from the blood demons.'

Then he placed another wand and uttered another prophecy:

'This warrior will be given gold and gems, livestock, furs and weapons from the king's own stores. Some as payment for his bravery, some as a gift to take with him when he visits the gods.'

Visits the gods? Kel was confused. Would this warrior truly get to meet the gods? It sounded too fantastical.

Then came the final wand, and the final prophecy from the enaree:

'We mortals have tried and failed to defeat the blood demons. The warrior we send to the gods will be both pure of heart and brave in battle. If he is successful, Oetosyrus will send us a hunter to slay the demons.'

The enaree stood and cast his gaze around the room.

'I will do it!'

Kelermes turned to his right and watched in horror as Lohant stood and cried out the words. Kel put a restraining hand on his arm to try to stop him from making this terrible mistake, but Lohant shrugged him off. His eyes glittered as he spoke: 'I was spared once from the demons. The gods must already hold me in high regard.'

Kel couldn't find any words to stop him. The man was an arrogant fool. Surely the enaree would turn on him. And, if not the enaree, then the king must object. And, as Kelermes was his comrade, they would not spare him either. For such an inappropriate interruption, the two of them would surely be put to death.

After Lohant's outburst, Kelermes tried to inch backwards into the crowd. To remove himself from the attention of the enaree, the royals and everyone else. But he and Lo were viewed as a pair. Having been discovered together, they were inextricably bound. The enaree glanced down at Kel and then let his gaze travel up to Lohant.

Without taking his gaze from the broad warrior, the enaree spoke:

'The warrior we send must be one who is pure in heart. Are you this man?'

'Yes,' replied Lohant, his voice steady.

'The warrior we send must be one who wishes to serve his people and save them from this blight on our land. Are you this man?'

'Yes,' replied Lohant.

Each time Lohant said the word 'yes', Kelermes wanted to shout *no!* He wanted to shout that the man was a coward and a liar and a bully and a braggart. But he said none of these things. He kept his silence and watched this incredible travesty unfold.

'Only one who is truly good and brave and selfless will have the ear of the gods,' the enaree continued. 'He will be travelling to beg them to deliver our people from the blood demons. If the warrior is worthy, they will send help. If the warrior is false, he will fail, and the Scythian people will be doomed to live in fear for eternity. Are you the warrior we need to complete this task?'

'I can do it,' Lohant replied.

The enaree put his hand on Lohant's shoulder. 'Then you are chosen,' he said. He drew Lohant to his side and proclaimed to the people:

'This man has fought with the demons and survived. Lohant is our chosen warrior. He was sent to us from the gods. He shall be our messenger to them also.'

The crowd erupted into deafening cheers, rising to their feet and stamping the ground. Even the king and queen rose, nodding their approval.

Kelermes took it all in with a heavy heart. With Lohant chosen, the gods would surely ignore their plea. For the man was not pure in heart. He didn't care about serving his people. All he wished to do was the minimum required, and to then bask in stolen glory. He wanted the adulation and the riches with none of the work. They needed someone like Aristeas or Abaris to be the chosen one. Even Orik. But Lohant? No. What a joke. How could the fate of their people rest on Lohant's shoulders? How could they prize that man – a stranger to them – above the king's own fearsome, loyal soldiers? But it was already decided. Lohant was to be the messenger.

The rest of the evening passed in a blur. Kelermes slouched at the back of the yurta sipping a warm cup of koumiss, watching the proceedings with a drunken eye. Everyone congratulated Lohant, crowding around him, trying to speak to him, to touch, to hug, to breathe the same air as him. If it wasn't such an awful situation, Kel would have laughed aloud. He broke into a twisted smile at the complete absurdity of the situation. If Orik was here, he would have spoken out against Lohant. He wouldn't have let such a travesty occur, but Orik was not here. Orik was gone. The only person who knew the truth about Lohant, who could stop it, was Kelermes. But no one would listen to him. They would merely assume he was jealous.

Now Lohant was being given gifts from the king's nobles – a

golden cloak, a jewelled sword, coins, and more. Next, the enaree presented him to the royal couple. Lohant knelt at their feet. Kelermes couldn't hear what was being said, but he was sure he didn't want to know. Instead, he made up his own conversation: 'My name is Lohant,' he mocked. 'And I'm a total ass. Would you like to rest the fate of our people on my traitorous shoulders? You would? Why thank you. Then, I shall take your jewels and riches, and I shall use you for all I can get, and then I shall fail you.'

Kel sank to the ground, hiccupping, and spilling his koumiss down his front, wiping at the stain ineffectively. In truth, he was no better than Lohant, skulking about at the back of the yurta, refusing to speak out about what he believed to be right. He was glad Laodice wasn't here to witness his misery and failure. She would not be proud of him at all. But she too would agree that Lohant should not be the one to carry out this task. He was not pure in heart. He was too concerned with his own skin to worry about others.

If they had any hope of persuading the gods to help them, if he truly wanted to avenge Laodice and his brethren, then he would have to prevent Lohant from becoming the messenger. He would have to go against the enaree's proclamation.

He, Kelermes, would have to go in Lohant's place.

CHAPTER TWENTY-NINE

Alexandre had spent two days in bed already. Sleeping, with just occasional moments of painful consciousness, too weak to stand for more than a minute or two. The others took turns checking up on him, trying to get him to talk, to drink a little blood, to do anything other than lie in bed like a dying person. Maybe he *was* dying. But he couldn't die. He couldn't leave the others to face the Cappadocians. They needed him. He had to rid himself of this illness and regain his strength. Isobel had said his skin looked grey. A few shades away from death, she'd said. It was an apt description. He certainly felt like death. He felt old, and tired, and squeezed dry. Like the life had been scraped from the very marrow of his bones.

But, worse than the relentless ache in his body, was the churning, gnawing guilt. Disgust still swam through his body, like a rat through a sewer. If ever there was a physical manifestation of guilt – this was surely it.

What had he done?

He knew very well what he had done. He had been unfaithful to the girl he loved. He had kissed another. He couldn't even say why he had done it. Yes, Nadia was a beautiful girl, but so was Madison. And he loved Madison, he did not love Nadia. Hell, he didn't even know the girl. She was a troublesome stranger who had accidentally stumbled into their lives; that was all. Yet again, Alexandre was paying the price for a thoughtless moment of passion. Would he never learn?

Pain in his body and pain in his heart. He closed his eyes and wished for sleep. Perhaps it would be best if he never woke up.

<hr />

Back in the jeep, Maddy and Morris followed Derin's bike through the empty landscape.

'Wish he'd slow down a bit,' Morris said. 'Sorry, Madison, we're going to be bounced around if I'm going to keep up with him.'

'S'okay,' Maddy replied. 'Do what you've got to do.'

Morris changed up a gear and pressed his foot harder on the throttle. Maddy held onto the dash to steady herself. She didn't care about her bodily discomfort. All she wanted was to get to Aelia and find out what was wrong with Alex.

After what seemed liked hours of bone jolting across endless snowy terrain, they finally reached some semblance of a road. Actually, it was just a wide dirt track, but it felt like heaven to pick up some real speed. Finally, Maddy was able to get a signal on her phone. A text had come through an hour ago from Isobel:

No change. Please hurry.

Maddy's heart rate sped up as her eyes skimmed the text, her feelings of anxiousness heightening.

'We have to hurry,' she said, already aware that they were going as fast as they could.

'Alex not any better?' Morris asked, glancing across at Maddy's phone.

'No,' she replied.

'Less than a quarter of a tank of fuel left, and only a couple of hours till sunset,' Morris said. 'I hope it's not much further.'

Maddy chewed her lip and stared at the road ahead.

The sun was bleeding down into the mountains by the time they reached civilisation and a proper tarmac main road. Maddy's eyes were drawn to a tree bare of leaves but hung about with glinting blue-glass charms dangling down like over-ripe fruit. A woman sat beneath the tree and fixed Madison with a stare as they motored past. Alex had told her the glass discs were called *nazar boncuğu* or evil-eye talismans. The locals would attach them to anything perceived to attract greed, envy or ill-will, to ward off the evil eye. As they drove through scrubby little towns, Maddy glimpsed more of the talismans nailed over doorways, embedded into thresholds and displayed in shops, bars and restaurants. She wasn't superstitious but made a mental note to stop and buy one as soon as they were able – they could do with all the luck they could get.

Derin turned right, off the main road. They passed a car hire place, a motorcycle repair shop and a charmless complex of tourist shops and eateries. The road narrowed as they approached a town, its shops and houses rising up around them, set as they were into a steep hillside. The buildings were a mixture of old and new – some flat-roofed, others quaint and traditional with red tiled roofs and pleasing proportions. Pretty bars and restaurants were opening up for the evening, waiters setting tables, lights flickering on illuminating the fast-fading day. Morris switched on the jeep's headlights, as he tried to keep Derin's motorcycle in sight amid the ever-narrowing lanes.

'Night's coming,' Morris stated grimly.

'Do you think she lives here, in this village?' Maddy asked.

'Soon find out.'

They finally came to a stop outside a large square house set deep into the valley, right in the heart of the town. It was pretty much the grandest place they'd seen so far. Almost full dark now, two lamps glowed either side of the stone arched entrance-way. Morris parked up next to Derin's bike and switched off the engine, the ensuing silence a welcome relief after the constant engine noise of the jeep and the excessive roar of the motorbike.

Maddy slid out of the jeep onto the grey block pavement, stretching her limbs before peering up at the building before them. Inside the impressive archway, a set of studded wooden double doors sat above three semi-circular stone steps. The house itself was two stories high, with a balcony set into the centre of the house above the entrance. Green-leafed ivy clung to the lower windows, valiantly holding on through the chill of winter. Maddy shivered and smiled hesitantly back at Derin, who had dismounted, now ushering them up the front steps. They removed their shoes in the entrance way and followed him inside.

After they had all freshened up, Derin showed them into a blissfully warm sitting room furnished in a contemporary style. Maddy and Morris sat on a long low corner sofa scattered with jewel-coloured cushions while Derin remained standing, warming his hands over a blazing open fire. They all murmured their thanks to a middle-aged lady who brought in a tray laden with tea and snacks. She exited the room without a word.

'Help yourselves,' Derin said. 'The toasted pumpkin seeds are good, and the tea will be strong and hot. He bent down to scoop up a cup, cradling it in his palms before taking a noisy sip. 'My aunt will be down any minute.'

Right on cue, the sitting room door opened and Aelia walked into the room, eyes bright and alert, softening when she saw Madison. Maddy was overcome with a wave of relief that the old lady was actually here. She had hardly dared hope that Derin had been telling the truth. They could just have easily been walking into a trap. Morris stood, and Maddy followed suit, but she was momentarily stuck for words. There was so much to say, she didn't know where to begin. She hardly knew this woman who had saved her life. In fact, she'd saved all of their lives. And now she would hopefully be saving Alex, again.

'Hello, Madison, Mr Foxton,' Aelia said. 'It's wonderful to see you both again.' She smiled, a warm genuine smile that reached her eyes and encompassed Madison in a sudden feeling of well-being that made her want to run over and hug the woman, but instead Maddy settled for returning the smile. 'Please, sit down,' Aelia said.

Derin spoke to his aunt in his native tongue, a stream of words which Maddy wished she could understand. Aelia nodded along to his monologue before holding out her hand for silence.

'Good,' she said. 'Tea.' She sat in an armchair. Her nephew brought her a cup and placed it on the side table. She said something to Derin in Turkish. It sounded like he was unhappy with whatever she had said. But she spoke again, and he nodded reluctantly.

'I'll leave you in my aunt Sofia's care,' Derin said to Morris and Maddy. 'Perhaps I'll see you later.'

'Thank you,' Morris said.

'Yeah, thanks,' Maddy added.

Derin gave a polite smile and left the room, pulling the door behind him with a click.

'Before we speak,' Aelia said, 'I must ask that you always call me Sofia, and not Aelia or Havva. Sofia is my name at present. It would be confusing and awkward if my family were to hear you address me as anything else.'

Morris and Madison nodded.

'Also, they know nothing of how old I really am, and of my history. They know nothing of vampires and blood plagues, and for that, I am infinitely grateful. I wish to maintain their blissful ignorance.'

Morris nodded.

'We won't say anything,' Maddy agreed.

'Good.' Sofia clapped her hands together.

'How did you know we'd go to the cave?' Maddy asked.

'I didn't know; I just had a feeling,' Sofia replied. 'You seemed to be in a lot of trouble the last time we met, and I thought there was a possibility you might decide to come looking for me. I gave my nephews your names, just in case. They are good boys, but they are rich and lazy, with much time on their hands. I thought it would cause them no harm to do their aunt a favour and check up on the place for me.'

'That was thoughtful of you,' Morris said. 'We didn't think we had much chance of finding you. Not when we discovered you'd moved out of the cave.'

Maddy took a sip of tea. It was very strong. She leant forward and added a spoonful of sugar, stirring the liquid.

Sofia continued: 'If you or your vampire friends need my help, I am prepared to give it. I still feel some remorse that I didn't help Harold Swinton when he asked for it all those years ago. This is some small way of making amends.'

'We're grateful,' Morris said.

'And we do need your help.' Maddy said. 'We're desperate for it.' She took another sip of the tea, but now it tasted too sweet. She placed the cup back down on the glass-topped table.

'Tell me,' Sofia said. 'What can I do?'

'It's Alex.' Maddy's voice began to crack. She took a steadying breath and continued. 'He's ill, and we don't know why.'

'Is he conscious?' Sofia asked. 'Could it be the sleeping sickness again? Perhaps it has stayed in his system. I don't really know if it can be truly cured. Perhaps it lay dormant but has resurfaced.'

'It's not like before,' Maddy said. 'Now he's delirious. He's got a fever. He's hot and cold, sweating. He looks terrible. Isobel says he's getting worse. I don't know what to do.' As she spoke the words, her panic returned to the surface. She'd been keeping it in check ever since they'd arrived back in Cappadocia, but now the reality of things slammed into her with the force of a hurricane. She could lose Alex. He could die. 'Please, please say you can help him.'

'I'm sorry, Madison,' Sofia said, shaking her head. 'I've never heard of a vampire having these symptoms.'

Maddy's hopes plummeted. She had wanted the woman to say she knew exactly what it was. That she knew just how to fix Alex. 'You must know,' Maddy pleaded. 'You're our only hope to help him.'

'Start at the beginning,' Sofia replied, 'and tell me exactly what happened. How did he get to be like this? Perhaps we can figure it out.'

Maddy told her everything she knew. From her brother being attacked and turned into a vampire, to Alex going outside to help Nadia. Sofia's face was impassive throughout her account. There was no sign that she'd had a moment of clarity and suddenly remembered a cure. When Madison came to the end of her short tale, she waited for Sofia to give her some kind of hope.

'I'm not sure,' Sofia said.

'What do you mean?' Morris said. 'Not sure about what?'

'It could be something. It could be nothing.'

'What?' Maddy said, her heart beginning to race. 'Do you know what it is?'

'Something is gnawing at me, but I don't know what exactly.'

'Think,' Maddy said. 'Do you have *any* idea what it might be? Anything we could try?'

'No,' Sofia said with finality, shaking her head. 'No, I don't know what it is.'

'But you just said...' Maddy's frustration was spilling out. It took all her willpower to bite back the expletives hovering on her tongue. The last thing she wanted to do was offend Sofia; she was currently their only hope to help Alex. But the woman was talking in riddles. Contradicting herself and giving Maddy shreds of hope where there may be none.

'Forgive me,' Sofia said. 'I don't mean to cast confusion into the mix. I had thought of something, but it was not a solution. Please, you must give me a moment more to think. Without interruption.'

Morris reached over and patted Maddy's arm, presumably as a warning to calm down. She was so tightly wound, she had to stop herself flinging his arm away. But she surprised herself by heeding his silent advice; she made herself sink back into the sofa and take a deep breath. Rushing Sofia wouldn't help matters. They were here now. She had already said she would help them if she could, so Maddy would have to learn to be patient, and to trust her.

Sofia sipped her tea and stared into the fire. The silence seemed endless. She glanced at Morris. He too was sipping his tea and looking into the fire. Patience was all very well, but this was tortuous. Either the woman knew how to help Alex, or she didn't. If this meditating malarkey carried on for much longer, it was going to drive Maddy to commit murder.

After what seemed like days, but was possibly only minutes, Sofia broke the silence.

'I can do nothing here,' she said. 'I will come with you to England.'

CHAPTER THIRTY

SCYTHIA, 514 BC

Kelermes was woken by the servant girl bringing him a breakfast of porridge and cold meat. She set it next to his sleeping mat and left the yurta. The warm, oaty smell wafted under his nose, encouraging him to open his eyes. The events of last night came to him in a rush. Each day seemed to bring more and more unpleasant news. What new calamities would befall him today, he mused, levering himself into a sitting position. His head began to thump unpleasantly. Last night's koumiss was having an undesired effect. He took a spoon of porridge and swallowed. Not such a good idea. Nausea hit. He needed fresh air.

Outside, white flakes whirled through a thick, grey mist. Kel shivered and clutched his cloak tighter around his shoulders. The snow must have been falling a while, for his boots sank up to his ankles in the fresh powder. Kelermes crunched along, trying to remember which way he'd gone yesterday when he had come across Lohant playing knucklebones with his new comrades. He had to find him as soon as possible. Talk sense into the man. Get him to see that he was not the right person for the task. Perhaps he could bargain with him... promise him something in return.

After an hour or more's searching, and asking around, Kelermes was finally shown by a soldier to an impressive dwelling not far from the main tent. Two of the royal guard stood at its entrance.

'I was told Lohant is here,' Kel said to the men.

The guards remained impassive, staring ahead.

'Lohant? Is he here? I'm his comrade.'

Nothing. No response.

'Lohant!' Kel cried. 'Lohant, You in there?'

After a moment, the tent flap drew back, and the guards moved a pace to the side. Lohant stood before him, a little dishevelled. It appeared Kel wasn't the only one to wake late this morning. 'Morning, runt,' Lohant said. 'What brings you here?'

'I need to speak with you.'

'So, speak.'

'Can we go inside?'

Lohant nodded and stepped aside to allow Kel access to his yurta. It was wonderfully warm inside – the work of a crackling fire – and Kel felt his hands and feet tingle as they began to thaw. A gorgeous young woman sat on the floor, working the tangles from her hair with a comb. She smiled up at Kel. Lohant picked up a cloak, draped it around her shoulders and sent her out. Kel raised his eyebrows but said nothing.

'Here to congratulate me?' Lohant asked.

'Of course,' Kel replied. 'Congratulations.'

'Don't sound so happy.'

'Sorry, hungover,' Kel said, wondering how in the gods' names he was going to broach this delicate subject.

'I too had a skinful last night. But not so much as you, by the look of your face – it's green,' he said with a laugh.

'Are you really going to do it?' Kel asked.

'What? Go and meet the gods? You can bet on it, brother. My name will be remembered throughout history. I'll be the greatest warrior who ever lived. It's a wonderful thing, eh? And I'll be rich. Don't worry, I'll remember who my friends are – even the runty ones like you.'

Kel balled his right hand into a fist, then he took a breath and made himself uncurl his fingers again. He would just have to come straight out with it: 'The enaree said that the warrior must be pure of heart. I don't wish to offend you, but—'

'But, let me guess – you're going to offend me anyway.' Lohant smirked.

'You may be a brave warrior, Lohant, but pure of heart you are not. You bully your friends, you stole my Persian kill – don't deny it – and you fled the camp when the demons attacked. You didn't lift a finger to help save any of our comrades.'

Lohant jerked forward, grabbed Kelermes by the throat and leant into his face, so their noses touched. 'Say just one more word, brother, and I'll kill you here and now,' he hissed, his rank breath making Kelermes more uncomfortable than the increasing pressure on his windpipe. 'Speak these lies to anyone, and I'll have you burnt as a sacrifice to the gods.'

Kel tried to pry the man's hands off his throat, but his grip was too firm. 'Listen,' Kel croaked. 'Please. I'm sorry.'

Lohant suddenly let go, turned away from Kelermes, and began striding up and down the tent, muttering to himself.

Kel rubbed at his throat, wracking his brains for something he could say that might get through to the man.

'What do you want, Kel? Why are you here?' Lohant demanded. Then he softened. 'Are you jealous, is that it? I don't blame you for that. I have been handed the world, and you are left with nothing. But haven't I just told you, I will remember my friends. Stop your accusations and we can both win here.'

'Win?' Kel was astounded by the man's ignorance. 'This is

about our lives. The lives of our people. Our families. Everyone. If the demons keep coming, they will slaughter us all.'

'Yes,' Lohant replied. 'Which is why I am going to speak with the gods. I can convince them to help us. I'm certain of it.' He strode back to where Kelermes stood and took his shoulders this time instead of his throat. 'I will do this, Kelermes. I will be the warrior everyone wants me to be. Have faith.'

Kel nodded. It was clear there was no way of dissuading him – Lohant had convinced himself that he was the chosen one. Short of kidnapping him and keeping him tied up, there was nothing more he could do.

The rest of the day had been one of feasting and excitement for the whole camp – all except for Kel, who spent the day in his tent trying to sleep. To block out the disaster his life had become. He drifted in and out of dreams. Some were wonderfully real dreams of him and Laodice riding across the steppe. And others were nightmares of Persian demons with Lohant's face.

His servant woke him as dusk settled. She must think him a terribly lazy, ill-humoured fellow. He hadn't smiled, or thanked her, or done anything of any worth since he'd arrived here.

'Your warrior friend is leaving tonight to meet with the gods,' she said. 'He's a brave man.'

'Tonight?' Kel asked. So there really would be no further opportunity to try again to change Lo's mind. Kel was surprised they would send their pure-hearted warrior on his quest after dark. Surely it would be better to start a journey in daylight. But there must be some reason for it.

'Yes, tonight. You must get up. Everyone must be there to see him off. It's bad luck otherwise.'

'Thank you for waking me,' Kel said with a warm smile.

The girl blushed and gave an awkward curtsey.

'You may go and get ready,' he said. 'I don't need anything else.'

'If you're sure,' she replied, and scuttled off.

An hour later, Kelermes was standing with all the other inhabitants of the royal encampment, ready to witness Lohant's send-off. The people had formed a circle as they had done the previous night in the feasting tent. The main difference being that tonight they were all standing outside instead of sitting inside. This time, Kel wasn't given a reserved spot at the front, so he squeezed into the middle of the crowd along with everyone else which suited him fine. He wanted no more special treatment.

The sky was strangely light, the night air bitterly cold as feathers of snow continued to fall. Instead of a warming central fire, there was a large pile of dry animal bones and linden bark stacked around a pole. King Idanthirsos and Queen Opiya were seated on their thrones once again, but this time, the enaree was in full view of the people – no sudden magical appearance tonight.

The enaree clapped his hands twice, and a chant was taken up, a low murmuring hum which seemed to emanate from all over. Kelermes glanced around, but none of the people near him seemed to be making the sound. The hum continued as a pure white mare was brought into the circle, her face mask and blanket covered in precious metals and gems. On her back sat a warrior like none Kelermes had seen before. He shone with gold and jewels. Even his blond beard was threaded through with precious gems. He wore a golden helmet, breastplate and sword, and his clothes were of the finest cloth, his boots the finest leather. An array of the most skilfully crafted weapons hung from his belt. Truly, he was an awe-inspiring sight. More stunning than the king and queen themselves. It was hard to believe this warrior could be Lohant. But it really was him. Kelermes could tell the man by the arrogant jut of his chin, and the hard set of his eyes. But, the way he looked tonight, surely the gods would have to take him seriously. He was impressive. He was glorious.

The enaree clapped twice again, and the chant ceased. Silence dropped like a stone. There was just the hush of falling snow.

'Here is Lohant,' the enaree cried, his voice echoing into the night sky. 'He has come to us, a saviour. His name will be remembered, for he has volunteered to meet with the gods. He will beg them to save us from the demon blight upon our lands.'

Lohant raised a hand to the crowd, a victorious expression on his face. The crowd sighed in adoration. The enaree continued:

'This brave warrior has chosen to give up his earthly life to visit the celestial plane. He will leave his mortal body behind and move on to the afterlife.'

At these words, Kel realised with a jolt what was really about to happen. How could he have been so dense? He had thought Lohant was to be sent on a mortal journey to a place here on earth, a place where the gods would actually meet with him. But the reality was that Lohant was to be sacrificed. Yes, he was to meet with the gods. But the only way he could truly meet them was if he was dead.

Even now, four young acolytes were setting light to the dried animal bones and linden bark. They were making a pyre. A pyre for Lohant.

CHAPTER THIRTY-ONE

It felt like they'd been away from home for weeks, but it had barely been two days. Dusk cloaked the air as Morris drove them down the familiar tree-lined driveway. Maddy averted her eyes from the dark, empty deer park, and the terrible memory of that night, concentrating instead on the view ahead, their headlamps illuminating the way. She drank in the sight of home. Her beautiful house, solid and safe, shuttered against a hostile world. She couldn't wait to see everyone. To witness with her own eyes that they were all safe. To hug her brother and tousle his hair. To race up the stairs and kiss Alexandre, and pray that Sofia would know the answer to his sickness.

They didn't have time to fumble about for keys. The front door flew open and before Maddy had even set foot outside the car, she was swept up by her newly strong brother.

'Shortie!' she cried. 'Put me down.'

'Missed you, Mads,' he said, lowering her back onto the driveway. 'I wish I could've come with you. Can she fix Alex?'

'Hold on a minute,' Maddy said. 'I'll introduce you, and then we can go in.'

The others were already gathered in the doorway, awaiting their arrival. Sofia came around the side of the vehicle.

'Good evening,' she said. 'I don't believe we've met. I am Sofia, and you must be Ben.'

'Yeah, hi,' he replied, a little shyly.

'Shall we go in?' Sofia asked.

'You go ahead,' Morris called from the back of the vehicle. 'I'll bring the luggage and say hello to the missus.'

'Thanks, Morris,' Maddy called back.

'Esther's in the kitchen,' Ben added.

'Thanks, lad,' Morris replied.

Maddy led Sofia towards the house. She turned to the woman who appeared completely unruffled by their journey, dressed immaculately in a smart, navy trouser suit, her grey-blonde hair pulled back in a sleek bun. 'Would you mind if we went straight upstairs to Alex?' Maddy asked.

'That's why we're here, child. Lead the way.'

They murmured greetings to Isobel, Jacques and Freddie, their faces drawn in worry. Maddy hugged each of them in turn before leading everyone upstairs to her bedroom.

'Is there any change at all?' she asked as they traipsed up the staircase.

'None,' Isobel replied, her voice tinged with panic. 'Sofia, thank you for coming. Do you know what ails my brother? Can you do anything?'

'I'll take a look at him, but I can't promise I'll know what it is, or how to cure him.'

Isobel cast a worried glance at Maddy, who pressed her lips into a determined line. The doorknob creaked as she turned it and pushed open the door, making her way into the darkened room.

'It's stuffy in here,' she said. 'Ben, can you open the window, let in some fresh air?'

'Sure.'

Maddy strode over to the bed, and turned on the bedside lamp, casting a pool of light over the rumpled bedclothes. Alex lay on his side, half asleep, his breath shallow and rasping, the covers pulled up to his chin, a stream of incomprehensible words trickling from his lips. She put a hand to his head. It was warmer than usual, but at least sweat no longer clung to his brow. She kissed his cheek and pushed a stray lock of hair from his eyes. He stirred at her touch but didn't wake.

An icy gust of wind blew into the room, making the shutters bang and the curtains billow inward. Alex flinched in his sleep, and Maddy glared at her brother.

'Sorry,' Ben called. 'I opened it too much.' He fiddled with the window latch so now it hung open just a crack.

As Sofia joined Madison at Alex's bedside, Maddy stood up and took a step back so the old woman could examine him. Sofia sat on the bed and leant over Alex feeling his brow like Maddy had done a moment before. Then she eased back the covers, lifted his arm, prodded and poked at him. Maddy realised she was holding her breath, willing Sofia to pronounce a hopeful verdict. Turning her head, she saw that the others were also focused intently on the woman. Jacques caught her eye and she managed to give him a brief smile. He looked as terrified as she felt.

'Where is the kitchen?' Sofia stood up and turned to Maddy.

'The kitchen?'

'Yes. Show me the way.'

'Oh, yes, of course. Why do you—'

'Come, there's no time to lose,' Sofia urged as Madison began to make her way towards the door.

'Do you need something?' Isobel asked. 'Some kind of medicine for my brother? I can get it for you.'

'The kitchen,' Sofia repeated.

Madison cast another look back at Alex, reluctant to leave

his side after so long away from him, but Sofia was insistent. Hopefully, it was because the woman knew of a cure. Maybe Alex would soon be well and back to normal. She hardly dared hope. In a rush and a clatter and a blur, they all made their way back downstairs and into the warmth of the kitchen. Morris was sitting at the table while Esther bustled about over the stove. The groundsman rose to his feet as they entered the room.

'There's spaghetti bolognese here for your supper,' Esther said. 'It'll be ready in two minutes. Just enough time for you and Morris to wash your hands. Will our guest be eating, too?' Esther glanced from Maddy to Sofia, and back again.

'Thanks, Esther,' Maddy replied. 'This is Sofia. Sofia, this is Esther, Morris's wife. She takes care of us and the house.'

'Pleased to meet you, I'm sure,' Esther said, not looking or sounding at all pleased to meet her.

'Hello, Esther,' Sofia said, throwing out a charming smile, unfazed by Esther's prickly welcome.

'Erm, Sofia needs some ingredients or something,' Maddy said to the housekeeper.

'Where is the larder?' Sofia asked Maddy.

'The larder?' Esther replied. 'What do you need? I'll get it for you.'

Sofia politely ignored Esther. She glanced around at the kitchen units, took a step towards the nearest cupboard, and pulled it open. Not finding what she was searching for, she began to open more cupboards and drawers. The room grew noisy with the sound of clanking and clattering, as she began removing various cooking utensils and pans. Esther looked on, her mouth hanging open for a second before she snapped it back into a firm, thin line.

Morris took a step back towards the door. 'Best not get involved in this,' he muttered to Madison before taking his leave.

'Esther,' Isobel said, turning to the outraged housekeeper. 'Why don't you take the evening off? We can manage here.'

'What about my spag bol?' Esther snapped.

'Take it with you. Morris must be hungry.'

'But Madison hasn't eaten either. I've made enough for—'

'I'm fine. Not hungry at all,' Maddy replied, her gurgling stomach betraying her words.

Isobel turned off the heat and tipped the bolognese mixture into a bowl while Maddy drained the spaghetti. Between them, she and Isobel managed to bundle the housekeeper out of the kitchen, along with dinner, while Sofia continued to rifle through cupboards and boxes in search of whatever it was she needed.

Satisfied that Esther and Morris were on their way out of the door, Maddy rushed back into the kitchen.

'Are you making a cure?' Jacques asked the woman.

'A cure? No.'

'So, what are you doing, then?' Freddie asked. 'What are you looking for? Maybe we can help find whatever it is you need.'

'I have everything I need, thank you.' Sofia marched over to the sink and began rinsing out the large metal saucepan which had previously held the spaghetti. The water splashed down into the pan, as billowing steam rose up. 'It would be best if you left me alone while I do this.'

'Do what?' Maddy asked.

'I'll call you if I need you,' Sofia said. She turned off the tap and turned to face Maddy and the vampires who all stared at her in hopeful confusion.

'You will let me get to work in here?' she asked.

'I suppose so,' Maddy said.

As they backed out of the room, fresh worry gnawed at Madison. The woman was obviously doing something for Alex in there, so she should be pleased. But why couldn't Sofia just tell them what the hell it was she was concocting? Maddy wanted to barge back in there and demand answers, but Isobel had obviously sensed Maddy's mood and now had her by the arm and was steering her into the lounge with the others.

'Let's give her half an hour,' Isobel said, 'and then we'll go back in and see if she'll enlighten us.'

'This is our house. Our kitchen. She should tell us what the hell she's—'

'Calm down,' Isobel said. 'She can hear you.'

'She's here to help us,' Ben said. 'We should let her do her thing.'

Maddy's shoulders sagged. 'Well, if I'm not allowed in the kitchen, I'm going back upstairs to see Alex. You guys can wait down here. Get me if anything happens.'

Lying on her side on her four-poster bed, staring at his sleeping face, Maddy could almost pretend everything was okay. Almost. But he seemed so vulnerable. She'd never seen him so pale and ill. Even when he'd had the sleeping sickness, he'd had a mesmerising glow about him. Now his skin was waxy, his hair dull and his lips dry and cracked. It frightened her to see him this way. Whatever Sofia was doing down there, she hoped and prayed it would bring Alex back to her. If he survived this, they should sell the house and move to another country. Somewhere where no one knew who they were. Where no one could find them. She couldn't face more battles and threats. She'd had enough of confrontations and near-misses. It just wasn't worth it. All Maddy wanted was for them all to be safe. To live their lives in peace. Was that such an impossible dream?

And now that Ben was one of them, it was more vital than ever that they escape the Cappadocians. Could they do it? Perhaps they could stage their own deaths to stop the vampires coming after them. That's what people did in the movies. And sometimes it worked, didn't it? But Maddy knew very well the reason why her mind was flying off on these tangents. It was to stop herself worrying. To push away the crippling fear. Because to lose Alex was unthinkable.

Maddy sat up. What was she doing up here? She needed to find out what was going on downstairs in the kitchen. This was her house. If Sofia was making a cure, then Maddy needed to know about it. She would demand answers. She swung her legs off the bed. Determined.

As she reached the bottom of the stairs, Isobel poked her head out of the lounge. The French vampire opened her mouth to say something but snapped it shut at a sharp glare from Maddy.

'I'm going to find out what she's doing in there,' Maddy said.

'Very well,' Isobel replied, a scowl clouding her pretty features. 'But please remember, he's not just the boy you love, he's also my brother, Madison. I'm worried about him, too.'

'I know you are. I know. I'm sorry.' As anger and impatience turned to guilt, Maddy felt a tear welling in the corner of her eye.

'Shall I come in with you?' Isobel asked.

'No, it's okay. I'll tell you as soon as I know anything.' Maddy gave Isobel an apologetic smile before walking towards the kitchen.

As Maddy pushed open the door, she was met with a delicious aroma. Sofia had her back to her and was tending to something bubbling on the stove.

'What are you cooking?' Maddy asked. 'I don't mean to be rude; it smells lovely, but I thought you were here to try to cure Alex. Unless it's some kind of medicine?'

'Alexandre isn't sick, as such.' Sofia didn't turn around.

'What do you mean, he isn't sick? Of course he is. You just saw him. He's weak and delirious. I've just been with him. He's worse, if anything.'

'He isn't sick,' Sofia replied. 'He's hungry. Starving, in fact.'

'I tried feeding him. I gave him some of my blood, but he wouldn't take it. He's—'

'He's hungry, so I'm making soup. It's a good nourishing broth, passed down through my family over the generations.'

'I don't understand.' Maddy took a few steps closer to the stove and bent her head over the pan. Whatever it was, it really did smell delicious. She wouldn't have minded some herself.

Sofia stopped stirring the mixture for a moment. She turned to Madison and gripped her arms, a half-smile playing on her lips.

'What? Why are you smiling?' Maddy's heart sank for a moment – maybe the woman was mad. Or maybe... Maddy didn't dare to hope that Sofia had the cure for Alex, but why else would she look so pleased with herself?

'I wasn't going to tell you yet,' Sofia said. 'I was going to wait and see because I'm not one hundred per cent certain. But I can sense how desperate and impatient you are. And I am ninety-nine percent sure I'm correct.'

'What?' Maddy said. 'What aren't you telling me?'

'Listen to me, child,' Sofia said, her grip tightening and her smile growing. 'Alex isn't sick. He doesn't need blood. He is weak and tired and hungry, and he needs good, nourishing soup to build up his strength.'

Maddy stared at Sofia, trying and failing to comprehend what the woman was telling her.

'Madison,' Sofia said, fixing her with a strange stare. 'Alex is no longer a vampire. He is human.'

CHAPTER THIRTY-TWO

SCYTHIA, 514 BC

As the pyre caught light, the aroma of smoke and incense drifted across to Kelermes, mingling with the damp, clean scent of falling snow. The shocking truth of what was about to happen to Lohant settled over him as the enaree continued talking to his people:

'This warrior will step into the flames with his treasures and will leave this earthly life in order to visit the celestial plane. To beseech the gods for their mercy. To ask their favour. To send us *the bright one* in his place. The one who will deliver us from evil.'

The tension mounted. Had Lohant known all along what his fate was to be? Perhaps the man was not as cowardly as Kel had always suspected. Perhaps he really was a brave warrior. No. From the expression on Lo's face, he too had only just this moment understood what was truly about to happen to him. Even from way back here, Kel could see realisation dawning on the man's face. The horror of the truth. Lohant blanched, and a deep fear appeared in his eyes. Kelermes knew without a shadow of doubt that Lohant would never have agreed to become the messenger if he had known what it really involved.

Would he, Kelermes, have still wanted the task if he had known it involved dying? He asked himself the question now, and was amazed to find that, yes, he would willingly have gone in Lohant's place. The demons had taken everything from him – his friends, his betrothed, his future. If left unchecked, the demons could go on to destroy all of Scythia. They could kill his parents. He had to stop them, and if that meant dying to beseech the gods to help them, he would do it. He realised that Lohant must not be allowed to go.

Kel did not pause to think further. He pushed his way through the mesmerised crowd to stand before the enaree and before Lohant's terror-stricken face. Quickly, not giving them enough time to call for the guards to remove him, Kelermes spoke:

'Lohant is a worthy warrior,' he began. 'But I believe it should be I who goes in his stead.'

A ripple of shock ran through the crowd. The king stood, his face a thunderous scowl, but Kelermes felt no fear. He only felt an excitement and a rightness, like this was what he was meant to do. He knew it in his bones and in his very core. He would save his people tonight. He would do it. And not for riches or glory, but for their lives.

The enaree must have seen something in his expression, for he motioned to his acolytes to douse the flames on the pyre, and he bade Kelermes continue. The circle grew silent once more, as everyone waited expectantly to see what the young warrior would say next. Kel took a breath and spoke:

'Yes, Lohant is brave, and you have chosen him to make this journey. But I should be the one to go in his stead, for I have truly suffered at the hands of the blood demons. They took Laodice, my betrothed. The one I love. And I was not there to avenge her. This journey to the gods would be for her. It would be for my chief, Aristeas. For my friend and comrade, Orik. And it would also be for Lohant. He is a warrior who could do much for you here. He would be missed if he left. But I... I would not be missed. The gods would surely listen more favourably to one who has a heartfelt, personal reason to desire the demons' destruction.'

'No!'

Kelermes turned to see the king on his feet, staring at him. It was a terrifying experience. More terrifying even than the thought of dying by fire. He had lived with the knowledge of this mythical man all his life. And now his revered king was glaring at him. Telling him *no*.

'It is my belief,' the king said, 'that personal issues always cloud matters. Your reasons are not strong enough. We have already chosen. We have our warrior, and it is Lohant.'

The enaree approached King Idanthirsos and they consulted in whispers. But it was while they were talking that Lohant decided to speak up:

'If Kelermes wishes to go in my stead, I will not oppose him, for he is my brother-in-arms and I would not stand in his way.'

Kel almost laughed at the relief in Lohant's voice; his pretence at being magnanimous in order to avoid death.

The enaree stepped away from the king with a bow.

'It has been decided,' he said, facing both Lohant and Kelermes. 'You both came to us at the same time. So you will both go.'

Lohant spoke up once more: 'I really think Kel is better suited to this—'

'Hush, now,' the enaree said, staring up at Lohant on his horse. 'It is no longer your decision to make. The king and I have decided.'

Lohant removed his golden helmet and tried to dismount, but the acolytes rushed to his side and held him firmly in place. Kelermes was almost embarrassed for his comrade. The man was clearly terrified, visibly distressed. It was one thing to be brave in battle, but it was something else to willingly step into the flames. He wondered why he himself felt so calm. Perhaps he was not in his right mind after everything that had happened.

As the enaree led Kelermes over to the pyre and drew a rope around his waist, tying him to the post, none of it felt quite real. It was as though he was standing outside himself, watching from above. Lohant was really protesting now, pleading, letting his brave-warrior act drop, so that it was becoming embarrassing for everyone to watch. The crowd began to murmur and hiss.

The enaree was tight-lipped, a dark scowl upon his face. In the end, the soothsayer dragged Lohant from his horse and slit his throat as the crowd jeered. Kel gazed down at Lo's wide, scared, staring, dead eyes, but he felt no fear. Only peace and relief that it would all soon be over.

The enaree came close and lay Lohant's weapons and jewels at Kel's feet, scattering them on the pyre of bones and bark. Then the soothsayer did something unexpected – he kissed Kelermes on both cheeks and whispered in his ear, 'You were always the one, I knew it from the start. I believe in you. You will be victorious. Thank you.'

And now Lohant's body was dragged off, his dark blood smearing the icy ground. His white horse led away, safe from the flames. And it was just Kelermes, tied to the pyre. All eyes on him. Willing him to be successful. The enaree lit the pyre once again, the smoking animal bones catching light much quicker this time.

Led by the enaree, the crowd began to chant: *Mighty Oetosyrus, Mighty Tabiti, we send offerings from our people. We are your servants. We beg you deliver us from the demons. Save us from destruction... Mighty Oetosyrus, Mighty Tabiti, we send offerings from our people. We are your servants. We beg you deliver us from the demons. Save us from destruction.*

As the fire licked up around his boots, Kelermes's greatest sorrow was that he would never again see a Scythian spring-time, with its soft grasses and warbling birds. Never feel the gentle warmth of a new sun on his face. This snowy winter's night was his final view of life. Fire and ice to send him on his way. He prayed that his sacrifice would save his people. That the gods would conjure something good from his ashes. Something far fiercer than he, to send the demons back to hell.

Kel shivered in the icy air. Strange to feel such cold on his cheeks, and such heat at his feet. He gritted his teeth at an intense flash of pain on his leg. It was his grandfather's knife still strapped to his calf – the fire had heated the blade which now pressed into his flesh, scorching the skin. He reached down with some difficulty, but managed to grasp its handle, unsheathing it and holding it flat to his chest. How easy it would be to plunge the blade deep into his heart and end the pain that now tortured his body. To stem the sudden searing shards of agony that made him want to scream out. But he would not scream, and he would not use the knife to end his fear and pain. He was a warrior. He was used to pain. The enaree had told him he must die by fire. And so he would. And then, once he had reached heaven, he and Laodice would be wed. There, it would be springtime, and they would hunt and feast and make love every day. As the flames licked at his thighs, he smiled at the thought of her blue eyes twinkling in the sunshine. Her hand in his as they walked together into the never-ending steppe.

But the image faded as smoke began to writhe its way into his body, thick plumes of the stuff choking him, preventing him from taking in air, taking his mind off the pain of his burning flesh. He must keep the message to the gods in his mind. He must be clear-headed when he reached them. He tried to tell himself that soon this earthly pain would be over, and he would be restored. His body made whole again to stand before the gods. Would they listen to him? Would Laodice be with them, serving the gods in the afterlife? To see her again would be worth this suffering.

Like a mantra, in his head, he chanted his people's plea: *Mighty Oetosyrus, Mighty Tabiti, I bring offerings from our people. I am your servant. I beg you deliver us from the demons. Save us from destruction.* But his mind was closing down, the smoke was too thick, the flames too vicious, the pain too unbearable. He needed it to end. His mind couldn't keep the pain at bay any longer. Kelermes opened his eyes and cried out in agony, the flames up around his face now, closing in to consume the last parts of him. Through their orange burn, he saw the blurred faces of his people. The enaree, the king, the queen, the king's soldiers, he even fancied he saw Lohant, all with their eyes on him, willing his journey to be successful.

The pain and stink of burnt flesh and smoke were momentarily replaced with something else, something beautiful: the smell of fresh snow melting into spring flowers. Kelermes walking barefoot through silken steppe grasses, fish leaping in the Silys. An azure sky and the call of a lark. The touch of soft lips and the heady, apple-blossom scent of fresh-washed golden hair brushing his cheek.

Through the flames, a sapphire-eyed girl embraced him. Where the fire scorched, her touch was a balm. Where the smoke suffocated, her kisses were cool. Where his mind rebelled, her words soothed. Was she his mother? His betrothed? His daughter who never was? The goddess Tabiti? She was all these things and more. She had come from his sacrifice. She was their answer. The creature who would save them all.

She was Hope.

She was the Hunter.

CHAPTER THIRTY-THREE

SCYTHIA, 514 BC

The creature stepped fully formed from the flames, the dying kiss of the young warrior on her lips. His essence now part of her essence. She emerged, bright as day, from the smoke and fire to walk barefoot upon the snow.

The open-mouthed stares of the mortals did not interest her, even though it was their call she had answered. Their desperate chant. Their plea to the gods. She scented what she wanted out there – the demons beyond this circle of light. Her prey.

Out there into the darkness she would go.

CHAPTER THIRTY-FOUR

'What are you talking about?' Maddy shook Sofia's hands away and took a step backwards. The woman had just told her that Alex needed soup because he was now human. But how could that be? 'He's a vampire,' Maddy insisted. 'He does vampire stuff. He's over a hundred years old, he drinks blood, he doesn't go out in daylight, he doesn't look like a human and he bloody well doesn't drink soup!'

Sofia turned away from Maddy, removed the pan lid and ladled a spoonful of the aromatic broth into a shallow blue bowl. 'We'll take it upstairs,' Sofia said. 'See if he wants to try some. Not too much – he hasn't eaten regular food for a long time. It will take him a while to get used to it.'

'Bonkers,' Maddy muttered under her breath, as Sofia placed the bowl on a tray.

'Let's wait and see, shall we?' Sofia replied, with a smile on her lips.

Maddy followed Sofia out of the kitchen, her shoulders sagging with the weight of disappointment. This woman was supposed to be Alex's salvation. Instead, it seemed as though the years had scrambled her brain. Alex a human? What a load of rubbish. Maddy hadn't flown all the way to Turkey and back just for a bowl of soup. She felt like crying.

Instead, she followed Sofia up the stairs and into their bedroom where Alex still lay, in the same position as she'd left him. With trepidation, she edged past Sofia to check on him. To make sure he wasn't... but it was okay, his chest still rose and fell. He was still breathing.

Sofia was trying to clear a space on the bedside table for the tray of soup, but there wasn't enough room. Its surface was cluttered with all Maddy's stuff – books, bedside light, various papers, keys and other bits and pieces. Madison gathered it all up and dumped it on the chest of drawers. Sofia set the tray on the table with a clatter.

'He's still asleep,' Maddy said pointlessly.

'Wake him up,' Sofia replied.

'Isn't it better if we leave him to rest?'

'If he doesn't get some liquid now, he will die. How long has he been like this?'

Maddy did some quick addition on her fingers. 'Three days,' she said.

'Then it's critical he gets this now.' Sofia's earlier smile disappeared.

Although Maddy still didn't agree with the woman's diagnosis, she was infected with her worry, and anyway, what did they have to lose? She bent over the bed, kissed Alex's pale cheek and smoothed his hair away from his face, hoping it would wake him. But he didn't stir. 'Alex,' she murmured. 'Alex, wake up?'

Nothing.

'Alex,' she said, louder this time. 'You need to wake up.'

Madison was forced to take a step back as Sofia edged around her and slid her arm under Alex's torso. She propped him up with ease, plumping the pillows around his head.

Maddy was taken aback by the small woman's strength. She
kept forgetting Sofia was no ordinary human.

Alex's head lolled. His eyes opened for a brief moment
before closing again.

'Alex, it's me, Maddy.'

'Maddy,' Alex croaked, opening his eyes.

'Yes, it's me. Are you feeling any better?'

'Maddy,' Alex repeated, before closing his eyes again.

'He needs nourishment,' Sofia said. 'This is a thin, clear
broth. It will be easy for him to digest.' She took a spoonful of
the liquid and blew gently across it. 'And now,' she said, 'we will
see.'

Maddy held her breath as Sofia trickled some of the liquid
onto Alex's lips. The delicious aroma made Maddy's stomach
grumble. After a heartbeat, Alex's tongue licked at his dry lips.
Sofia held the spoon up once more and tilted the rest into his
mouth. His eyes flickered open and closed as he swallowed the
liquid. Could Sofia be right? Could Alex really be human?
Another spoonful went down, but this time, Alex choked and
coughed, his eyes flying wide open.

'What is that? What am I drinking?' he gasped. 'Who are
you?' He stared at Sofia in fear and bewilderment.

'It's all right, Alex,' Maddy said. 'It's Sofia. From Turkey.
You remember?'

'Sofia? Why is she here? Am I dreaming?' He tugged at the
bedclothes and ran a hand through his hair. 'I feel strange.
What is she feeding me?' Alex turned to Sofia. 'What is that, on
the spoon?'

'It's soup,' Sofia replied. 'To build up your strength.'

'Whatever it is, I need more,' he said. 'It's so good.'

Sofia lifted another spoonful to his lips. Maddy stood and
watched trying to process the fact that Alex was eating actual
food. Could this mean he really was human? Could Sofia be

right? He was gulping the soup down now, anticipating each mouthful she fed him.

'That's enough for now,' Sofia said after a few more spoons.

Alex's eyes widened. 'What? No. I'm still hungry.'

'One more spoon, and then that's it,' Sofia replied. 'You need to eat little and often. Too much, too quickly and you'll be sick.' She let him take one last mouthful before placing the spoon back on the tray.

'What's happening?' Alex asked, his eyes flitting from Sofia to Maddy. 'I feel so strange. Am I dreaming? I thought I was a vampire... or was that the dream?'

Maddy sat next to him, took his hand in hers. His skin was warm, soft and dry, not cold and hard like it usually was. She gave it a soft squeeze and examined his face, searching for proof that Alex really was no longer a vampire. He gave her a tired smile.

'Madison,' he said. 'Am I awake? Or am I dreaming? Is that you?'

'Yes. I'm here. But Alex, there's something else...'

'What is it?'

'You were a vampire, yes. That part wasn't a dream. But Sofia, she thinks you've changed. That you're no longer a vampire. She thinks you're human again.'

Alex withdrew his hand from hers. He put his fingers to his face, gently prodding at his skin. Then, he moved his fingers to his teeth.

'My teeth are changed,' he said in wonder. He blinked. 'And I have been wondering why I can no longer see as clearly. I thought it was because I was ill. My hearing. My sense of smell. All my senses...' His shoulders dropped. 'It is true. I thought I was dying. Instead, I believe I am mortal again.'

Sofia discreetly cleared her throat. 'Shall I leave you both for a while?'

'Please,' Maddy replied. 'If you don't mind.' Her mind spun. Alex was really human. He was okay.

'No!' Alex cried, making Maddy jump. He turned to Sofia. 'Don't go. You must tell me how this happened. How I changed back. I need to fix it!'

'Fix it?' Maddy said. 'Fix what? You *are* fixed. This is a miracle.' The reality of what had happened was just beginning to hit her. If he was human, they could have a proper life together, without danger and without restrictions.

'No, you don't understand!' Alex leant forward, his eyes boring into hers. 'How can I defeat the Cappadocians like this? I am weak. I have no power. I can't protect you if I'm *human*!'

'You're not weak, and I don't need protecting,' Maddy said. 'I didn't fall in love with a vampire, I fell in love with *you*, Alex.' How could she make him understand that this was a *good* thing? 'Remember how sad you were last summer, when you were stuck in the house for hours because of the long days? How you wished you could be human? Now you have that back!'

'Can't you see, it's not a case of what I wish for. It's a matter of safety. I can't look after you if I don't have my strength. This situation makes us more vulnerable.'

'But now that you're human again, they won't bother with you, surely?' Maddy said.

'They'll kill us all,' he hissed. 'And I'll be powerless to stop them.' He turned back to Sofia, his eyes flashing with fear and anger. 'How in the hell did this happen? I need to be turned back.'

'You've had a shock,' Sofia said. 'Eat, sleep, rest, and then you'll be able to think more clearly. But, for the record, I agree with Madison. What has happened is nothing less than a miracle. You have your life back. You are lucky.'

'What I don't get,' Maddy said, 'is *how*? I mean, you can't just stop being a vampire. Something must have happened to you.'

Alex flushed, then closed his eyes, turning his face away from her, his cheek pressed into the pillow.

'What happened?' Maddy said. 'Tell me.'

'Leave him be for a while,' Sofia said. 'He's exhausted. It's a lot to take in.'

'There's something you're not telling me, Alex.' Maddy felt a stab of worry. She knew he was keeping something from her.

'Come downstairs, Madison,' Sofia urged. 'You look like you could do with some of my soup, too.'

Maddy couldn't deny it. She was so far past the point of hunger, she felt faint and nauseous. 'Okay, I'm coming. But I'll be back in a while to talk some more.' She stroked Alex's cheek, but his eyes remained closed – asleep again, or angry, she couldn't tell. Maddy took his hand again. 'Alex, you're not dying. That's the main thing. I thought I was going to lose you.'

He opened his eyes briefly and gave her a small, sad smile, before closing them again and turning his face away.

Back downstairs in the hallway, Maddy turned to Sofia for answers. 'How could you tell he was human?' she asked.

'I will tell you what I know,' Sofia replied. 'But let's tell the others at the same time. Otherwise, I'll only have to repeat myself.'

'Okay,' Maddy agreed. 'And, Sofia... thank you.' Maddy's heart was beating hard with the shock of it all. The shock and the relief.

On entering the sitting room, the others were already standing, waiting.

'We heard,' Jacques said. 'Is it true? Is Alex really okay? Is he actually human again?'

'How is it possible we didn't realise?' Isobel asked. 'Can we see him?'

'Will he be all right?' Freddie added.

'Let's sit here for a while and let Alex rest some more.' Sofia said. 'The boy has had a shock. He needs some time. Madison, get yourself some broth. You look ready to keel over. Bring it in here, and I will tell you all what I believe has happened.'

Maddy rushed into the kitchen, spooned out a large portion of soup and raced back to the sitting room, liquid sloshing down the sides of the bowl in her haste. She was so hungry, she couldn't tell if she was more eager to begin eating, or to hear what Sofia was about to reveal. Once they were all seated, Maddy took a sip of the warm broth. It tasted every bit as good as it smelt.

'So, as you no doubt heard, Alexandre is no longer a vampire.' Sofia gazed at each of them in turn, her voice low and hypnotic.

'How, though?' Isobel asked. 'Will he be all right?'

'I will tell you how I believe it happened,' Sofia replied. 'And I hope he will be all right, but truthfully I cannot guarantee it.'

'What?' Maddy's pulse began to race. 'I thought you said he wasn't ill. I thought you said he was human.'

'Calm yourself, child. I cannot guarantee he will be all right, just as I cannot guarantee any of you will be all right. Human, vampire – things happen. Things we cannot control. But, as far as I am aware, he is a normal mortal being and, as such, he will be fine. Let me tell you all I know, and then ask me your questions afterwards.'

Everyone nodded, heads craned forward and eyes bright, keen to hear the old woman's revelations. The ticking of the clock seemed to grow louder, as though prompting her to continue.

'The girl you told me about – Nadia – I don't think she is a mortal girl,' Sofia began. 'I believe she is a creature, an ancient vampire hunter, known as *the bright one*.'

'Nadia isn't human?' Maddy asked, a bad feeling creeping over her.

'That's what I'm telling you, yes.' Sofia gave Maddy a sharp glare for interrupting. 'She has been called many names over the centuries: *dhampir, glog, perun, svarozic, kresnik, vampire hunter. The bright one* goes by many names. But it is a very rare being, and in all my hundreds of years on this earth, I have only ever heard tell of one other instance where a vampire was hunted by this creature and turned back into a human. They are not usually left alive. Alexandre is extremely lucky he was spared.

'The legend goes, that hundreds of years ago, even before I was born, there lived a race of people called the Scythians. They were fierce warriors, afraid of no man. But they were hunted by demons. Blood demons. Vampires. The vampires were out of control, in danger of destroying their entire civilisation. So, the Scythians called on their gods to send a warrior to defeat them. Their prayers were answered, and a hunter was sent to them. A creature known as *the bright one*, for she was as fair and bright as the Scythians themselves, created as she was from fire and light and snow.

'Although she had the power to do so, *the bright one* didn't instantly slaughter all the demons in a rage of retribution as the Scythians had hoped, instead, she made them love her. And with their kisses she took their power to feed herself, absorbing their essence and leaving them either dead or – in rare instances – human. She brought hope to the Scythian people and gave them a few more centuries of power and glory before their civilisation died of more natural causes.

'Legend says the creature would destroy whole covens at once, growing ever more powerful. But I think, in recent centuries, it must have grown weak from the years of drought. Don't forget, the world's vampires have lain dormant for over a millennium, as a result of the sleeping sickness. Nadia will not have been able to replenish her energy. She will not have been as powerful as she once was. She would have had to stalk Alexandre with care, preserving what little energy she had, making herself extremely desirable to seduce him. Stalking him to discover his weaknesses and using them to its advantage. While Nadia was around, Alex probably wouldn't have felt anything like himself. He would have been gradually weakening, losing some of his vampiric senses. Maybe even succumbing to human conditions.'

'Wait a minute. You mentioned kisses, and *seducing him?*' Maddy interrupted, the implications sinking in. 'You mean...'

'Yes, I am sorry,' Sofia replied. 'The creature receives its power from vampires, but they have to come willingly or it doesn't work. So Nadia will have made herself as beautiful to Alexandre as possible. She appeared vulnerable and hurt because she knew it would appeal to him. Each vampire is different, you see.'

'So, you're telling me that Alexandre is ill because he got it on with Nadia?' Maddy placed her unfinished soup bowl on the floor, suddenly feeling like she was going to throw up. Surely Alex wouldn't have—'

'He will have kissed her voluntarily, yes. Nothing more, just a kiss is all she needs to replenish her energy.'

'Shit.' Maddy sank down into the overstuffed sofa and dropped her head into her hands. A kiss was enough to make her feel sick, hurt, betrayed.

Sofia came and sat next to her, placing her hand on Maddy's arm. 'He was enchanted, bewitched; totally unable to prevent it. This creature possesses an ancient power that no vampire can resist. It was inevitable that as soon as Nadia marked him as her prey, this scenario would play out.'

'It still sucks.' Maddy swiped a tear from the corner of her eye. From what Sofia said, it wasn't Alex's fault, but she still felt betrayed and foolish. She'd spent half a day with the girl, who wasn't actually a girl. That icy creature had probably thought she was an insignificant distraction. Had probably been laughing at her. And how had Alex felt at the time? Had he

wanted to get rid of Maddy so he could be with Nadia? He'd
certainly been insistent that they help her. That Nadia should
stay with them at Marchwood. Maddy had known there was
something up with that girl. She should've listened to her
instincts.

'And what about Travis?' Ben said. 'She must've used him
to get to Alex.'

'Yes,' Sofia replied. 'Everything she did was to get to
Alexandre. And she finally had her way.'

'What a cow,' Maddy muttered.

'At least some good came out of it,' Isobel said. 'My brother
can finally have a normal life. You can be together, Maddy.
Maybe get married, have children. You are so lucky! I wish the
creature had kissed *me*.'

'Maybe she can,' Freddie said.

'What?' Isobel frowned, and then comprehension dawned.
'Oh! Yes!'

'Do you think she would?' Maddy asked. 'She could turn
you *all* back. Oh, Ben, that would be amazing!'

'I've got a much better idea.' They turned to the doorway to
see Alex standing there, shaky and pale, but with fire in his eyes.
He gave them all a grim smile. 'We'll send her after the
Cappadocians.'

CHAPTER THIRTY-FIVE

Alex walked into the drawing room with everyone staring at him like he was some rare creature in a zoo, his legs shaky, his vision blurred. He hated the way his body felt – slow and clumsy, inelegant. His flesh might be weak, but at least his mind felt sharper than it had for a while. He had listened outside the door and heard Sofia tell the others about Nadia and about how he had kissed her. Madison must hate him. He would have to speak to her about what happened. Explain that it had all been a terrible mistake. But, unfortunately, the very girl who had come between them was the one they now needed to help them.

'We must find Nadia,' Alex said. 'She can destroy the Cappadocian vampires for us. After what she did, she owes me.'

'Unfortunately, she owes you nothing,' Sofia replied. 'She is a creature out of time. Not subject to human laws or wishes. You cannot command her or make her feel a sense of duty. And, don't forget, she will be energised now. Almost back to her full strength. More dangerous than before.'

'Well,' Alex replied, 'the fact remains, she's the only one who can help us now. She has the power to turn the Emperor into a mortal and render him helpless. So, I'll just have to make her listen to me.'

'But we don't know where she's gone,' Jacques said. 'I can't feel her presence anywhere near here. Anyway, I don't even think she can be found by vampires; not if she doesn't want to be. She's hidden from our senses. It must be how she was able to stalk you so easily, Alex.'

'Rub it in, why don't you, brother,' Alexandre replied.

'Sorry.' Jacques came over to where he stood. 'I haven't even said how wonderful it is to have you back on your feet. For a while there, we thought you weren't going to make it.'

Alex smiled at his younger brother, feeling a rush of love. Isobel, Freddie and Ben came over, too. Isobel kissed his cheek, Freddie clapped him on the back, and Ben threw his arms around him. Alex choked back unexpected emotion at the boy's affection. Only Madison stayed sitting where she was. Alexandre felt a sharp twisting in his gut. Knowing about the kiss, she really must hate him. What could he do to make things right? It didn't matter that Sofia had said he was powerless to prevent it. The fact was, he had kissed another.

'It's weird to know you're human now, Alex,' Jacques said. 'But you seem different from other mortals. You don't *smell* human, if you know what I mean.'

'That's because he has been a vampire before,' Sofia said. 'He won't be easy prey to any other vampires now. His human scent is masked.'

'That's irrelevant,' Alex said. 'Because, obviously, if we are to go to Turkey with Nadia to finish of the Cappadocians, then I cannot stay like this.'

'What are you talking about?' Isobel asked.

Maddy stood up and glared at Alex before turning to Isobel. 'Your brother has this crazy idea that one of you should turn him back into a vampire. I mean, how can he even think about it!'

'Is this true?' Isobel turned to Alex, her blue eyes wide with shock.

'It's common sense,' Alex replied. As he spoke, his knees suddenly gave way.

Freddie threw an arm around him before he fell and led him over to the sofa.

'You see!' Alex cried. 'I can't even stand upright. I'm useless as a human. Absolutely useless.'

'That's because you haven't eaten anything for three days,' Maddy replied. 'Anyone would be weak after that. In a couple of days, after Esther's fed you up, you'll be back to normal.'

'We might not have a couple of days,' Alex replied, relieved that Madison was at least still talking to him. 'Those vampires could be back at any moment to finish what they started. We need to find Nadia, and one of you needs to turn me back.'

'No, Alexandre!' Isobel cried. 'There is no way I will allow any of us to do it.'

'It's not your decision,' Alex replied.

'I agree with Belle,' Jacques replied. 'It's a bad idea.'

'Sorry, Alexandre,' Freddie said. 'I cannot do it.'

'Ben?' Alexandre turned to the boy.

'Don't you dare,' Maddy snapped at Alex. 'Don't you dare ask my fourteen-year-old brother to turn you.'

Alex glared at her. 'But it was all right for me to turn him into a vampire?' As soon as the words came from his lips, Alex regretted them. He knew he had gone too far. Everyone was staring at him like he was the devil.

'You know that was completely different,' Maddy said, swiping at a tear on her cheek. 'He would have died...'

'Maddy, I'm sorry.' Alex reached out to touch her arm, but she jerked away from him and sat back down.

'I'm sure Alexandre didn't mean to say that,' Isobel said, trying to save the situation. 'He is not himself.'

'Whatever.' Maddy stared down at her knees, tight-lipped and pale.

'I didn't,' Alex said. 'I really didn't mean it. I wasn't thinking. And Belle is right – I'm not myself. I haven't been myself for days.'

'The problem with you, Alexandre,' Isobel began, 'is that you always want to do everything yourself. Why can't you have faith that the rest of us are able to manage things? If we have Nadia and Sofia's help, I'm sure we'll be able to do it.'

'Belle,' Alex said. 'I don't wish to insult you, but all you have ever wanted is a conventional life. I know you don't want any of this. That's why I need to be turned back – so I can take the burden from you. I remember how terrified you were the last time we were in Turkey.'

'Yes, I was scared,' Isobel said. 'But I still did what was required. I still fought those monsters, and I'd do it again. Being scared isn't a reason not to do something.'

'I'm just saying, you don't need to go. I'm more than happy do this, once I'm back to normal.'

'Normal?' Madison said. 'Since when has being a vampire been normal?'

Alex flinched at her words.

'Sorry, guys,' Maddy added. 'But... you know what I mean.'

'Belle will have us to help her, too,' Jacques said. 'Me and Freddie and Ben.'

'Absolutely not!' Maddy cried. There's no way my baby brother is going to fight centuries-old vampires. No way.'

'I agree with Madison,' Alex said. 'Ben is too young.'

'Mads, I'm not a baby. And I'm stronger than you. Just ask Jacques and Freddie how good my fighting skills are now.'

'Before we get deeper into discussions about who is going and who is not going,' Sofia interrupted, 'we need to find Nadia. So, I suggest we stop arguing and concentrate on the first matter in hand – tracking her down.'

'You're right,' Alex replied. 'Of course, we need to find the girl.' He caught Maddy's scowl. 'Madison, can I talk to you for a moment privately?' He turned to the others. 'Give us a few minutes. Please?'

Everyone nodded awkwardly and filed out of the room. Before Isobel left, she gave Alex a meaningful glance, mouthing the word *apologise*, and tilting her head in Maddy's direction. He glared back at her; he did not need relationship advice from his younger sister.

Madison was staring into the dying fire, her back giving off angry vibes. The door clicked shut behind Belle, and Alexandre sighed. He felt like death. His stomach was cramping, his head was spinning, and his whole body ached. Now, he had to make things right with the girl he loved. But she was also the girl he had betrayed and insulted. Could she ever forgive him? He wouldn't blame her if she didn't.

'Madison,' he began.

She didn't respond. Didn't turn her head even.

'Maddy.' He rose to his feet, unsure whether his legs would support him. 'Madison, I'm sorry.' He came up behind her and bent to kiss the top of her head. Her body stiffened below him. 'I'm an idiot. If I could erase this past week I would.'

'It doesn't work like that,' Maddy said. 'You can't just do stuff and say stuff and then apologise. You can't erase the things you say and do with a simple *sorry*.'

'I know. But I don't know how to make things right. Will you please turn around and look at me?' He put a hand on her shoulder, but she shrugged him off.

'Alex, I can't.' She sighed. 'I'm glad you're not ill anymore, but I'm pissed off, and I don't think I can talk to you at the moment; not without saying something I'll regret.' Her words, although softly spoken, were like piercing daggers, each one more painful than the last.

'Very well,' he said. 'I'll ask the others to come back in.'

'Maybe you should go back to bed and rest,' she said, finally turning around. 'You must be tired.' She spoke the words without emotion, but when she glanced up at him there was sorrow in her eyes, and he felt sick with love and regret.

'I've been resting for days,' he said. 'I'll rest again when this is over.'

She walked past him and told him to sit back down. Said that she would fetch the others.

Moments later, Maddy returned with everyone. As they re-entered the drawing-room and made themselves comfortable, Alexandre tried to put his hurt away. He told himself that he would make things right. That he would make Maddy understand that he had no feelings for Nadia. That it had all been a dreadful mistake.

He realised Ben was talking and tried to turn his attention to what the boy was saying. 'Sofia was telling us that the name Nadia means *hope* in Slavic,' Ben said. 'Which is funny, because she really is our only hope, now.'

'She'll only be our hope if we can find her,' Alex replied. But finding Nadia wasn't going to help his relationship with Madison. He worried it would make things ten times worse between them. But if they didn't find her, they would have no chance of being left in peace by their enemy. What an impossible situation.

'So how *are* we going to find her?' Freddie asked. 'And what will we do if we can't?'

'We could see if Travis has seen her?' Jacques suggested.

'She won't have gone back to him. Not now she's got what she wanted,' Alex said.

'We'll have to think about this logically,' Sofia said. 'Think how she would think.'

'She'll be looking for other vampires, won't she?' Isobel suggested. 'Maybe she'll come back here. Maybe she'll want the rest of us?'

'She might,' Sofia said. 'But I don't think so. If she'd wanted you all, she would have taken you already. I'm sure she won't return.'

'Listen,' Ben said, excitement in his voice. 'I think I've got an idea. One that could really work.'

CHAPTER THIRTY-SIX

Maddy sat on the sofa chewing her nails, not really hearing what everyone was saying. Feeling angry and sick and hurt. Why was Alex so determined to become a vampire once again? Wasn't being human enough for him? She could see how he might be seduced by the strength and power of it, but how could they truly be together if he was one thing and she was another? She would grow old, and he would grow tired of her. Leave her behind. Couldn't he see that becoming human again was an amazing opportunity for them? They could have a proper life together. It was the reason she could forgive what had happened between him and Nadia. Because Nadia had set him free from his curse.

But Alex didn't want to listen to reason. He was determined to be in control of everything. And how could he do that if he wasn't the strongest, the fastest, the sharpest. This was all to do with his ego being bent out of shape. He was more concerned about being a vampire than about being with her. Fine. Let him be an idiot. She felt so frustrated with everything she could scream. She should have been celebrating tonight. They had come back from Turkey with Sofia and had found out Alex wasn't dying. That he was human. But instead of being happy, she was reeling from the fact that Alex had kissed someone else (yeah, not his fault, she knew), but mainly she was gutted that he didn't want to remain human.

The others seemed to be listening intently to Ben's idea. Maddy supposed she'd better pay attention. Despite her emotional pain, she needed to know what was going on. There was still so much to be done to keep everyone safe.

'So, I saw this movie on TV,' Ben said, 'and they used CCTV cameras to track someone across the country. Maybe we can do that with Nadia. It's called *facial recognition*.'

'That's a smart idea,' Jacques said. 'But wouldn't Nadia need to be in some official database?'

'That's my point,' Ben said. 'If we had a photograph, it could work.'

'What is this photo recognition thing?' Isobel asked.

'*Facial* recognition,' Jacques said rolling his eyes.

'All right, clever clogs. Sorry if I'm not as technically literate as you, brother.'

'Sorry, Belle,' Jacques said.

'Facial recognition is where computers can recognise and distinguish one face from another,' Ben explained. 'It's pretty amazing – computers can identify someone from a digital image. They compare the facial features between the image and the facial database. Once they get a match, then they know they've found that person. So, if we had a photo of Nadia, the software would scan all the images in its database. If Nadia's face has been captured on CCTV, the software would find a match, and would tell us where she'd been spotted.'

'This new world is something else,' Isobel said. 'You cannot go anywhere or do anything without everything being recorded or captured. I don't think I like it. It's like being in a big prison with no doors. I miss the freedom of my century.'

'Well, we haven't got time to get into the ethics and politics of this now,' Alexandre said. 'We need to get a photo of Nadia. How are we going to do that?'

'Maybe Travis has one,' Jacques suggested.

'He only knew her for a day or two,' Maddy said. 'I'm pretty sure they weren't taking pictures of each other yet.'

'It's worth checking. He was pretty besotted with her,' Freddie said.

Everyone was besotted with her, Maddy thought, but didn't say the words aloud.

'Mads, you should call Travis and ask him,' Ben said.

'Why me?'

'Because he's your friend, and he's more likely to do stuff for you than for any of us,' Ben replied. 'He's always had a crush on you, anyway.'

'Not true,' Maddy said, feeling her face turn crimson. 'But fine, I'll give him a call.'

'Why are you so angry, Mads,' Ben asked, oblivious to the awkward vibes between her and Alex.

Isobel gave Ben an unsubtle kick in the shins. 'I'm not angry,' Maddy replied, trying and failing to replace her scowl with a smile. 'I'm just tired. We've only just got back from Turkey, in case you forgot. I'll give Trav a call, and let you know if I have any luck.'

'What will you say?' Isobel asked. 'He'll want to know why you want a picture of her, surely.'

'I'll think of something.' Maddy dragged herself up from the sofa and went into the hall to get her mobile. It was still in her coat pocket like she thought. She took it with her into the kitchen, wanting to get away from everyone for a minute or two. What she wouldn't give for a long, hot shower, and then to get into bed and sleep. To not think about everything. She hated how she and Alex were being with each other right now, but she didn't know how to fix it.

Travis answered on the second ring. 'Mads, hey.'

It was nice to hear his voice. She missed hanging out with him. 'Hey, Trav, how you doing?' She pulled out a kitchen chair and plonked herself down.

'Oh, you know. Okay,' he replied.

'Sorry things didn't work out with Nadia.'

'Yeah, well, I knew she was too good to be true. Way out of my league. But I also think she was a bit...'

'High maintenance?' Maddy finished his sentence, making him laugh.

'I was going to say troubled. But, yeah, I guess she was a bit full on.'

'Trav, do you know where Nadia is?'

'No.'

'Are you sure?'

There was silence on the end of the phone.

'Travis? You there?'

'What? You think I'm holding her hostage or something? I thought you were supposed to be my friend, Maddy.'

'I am your friend. I just need to find her.'

'Well, I don't know where she is. Believe me, or don't believe me. But that's the truth.'

'I believe you. Sorry.'

'S'okay. It's just, everything's been a bit weird, lately. The whole Nadia thing has freaked me out.'

'Yeah. You and me both.' *If only you knew.* 'Trav, this is a weird request, but you wouldn't happen to have any photos of her would you?'

'Why?'

'I think she stole something when she was here. I need to find her and get it back.'

'Wow, you think she's a thief? How will having her photo help?'

'It's a long story.'

'Want me to come over?'

'No thanks, that's okay. I'm just about to go to bed.'

'Oh, okay. So, the photos...'

'Yeah,' Maddy said. 'Do you have any?'

'I did take some of the two of us on my phone. We were goofing around, you know, happy days.' Maddy wanted to give him a hug, he sounded so down.

'Can you send them to my phone?' she asked.

'But why do you need them?' he asked again.

Maddy could tell he wouldn't let it go. She decided to trust him. 'Travis, if I tell you this, will you promise me it won't go any further?'

'Course.'

At that moment, Isobel came into the kitchen shaking her head at Maddy. 'Hang on a sec, Trav, I'll be right back.' She pressed the mute button and turned to Isobel.

'You can't tell him what we're doing,' Isobel said. 'It's too risky. If he talks...'

'He won't talk. I trust him. Anyway, you shouldn't have been eavesdropping.'

'Sorry, we couldn't help it. It's part of the whole powerful-vampire thing.'

'I won't tell Travis everything. Look, just leave me to sort this out, okay? I won't tell him too much; just what he needs to know.'

Isobel nodded and left the room. Maddy sighed. She still couldn't get used to having a supposedly "private" conversation, yet knowing there were people in the house who could hear every word.

'Sorry about that,' Maddy said resuming her call with Travis. 'I need her photo so I can find out where she is.'

'How you gonna do that?'

'Facial recognition.'

Travis laughed. 'Mads, this isn't the movies.'

No, it's more far-fetched than the movies. 'Well, yeah, I know it sounds a bit over the top, but it's the only thing I can think of to find her.'

'So, do you even have access to that kind of software?'

'Not yet. I'm working on it.'

'Why don't you call the cops?' Travis asked. 'If she stole something, you should report it and let them find it for you.'

'I thought reporting it would be too complicated, what with everything she's accused you of. They'd need to know the whole story. If they found her, she could lie and say bad stuff about you.'

'Yeah, right, of course. Thanks.' He paused. 'Actually, there is someone my brother knows who might be able to help you.'

'Oh yeah?'

'Yeah. This guy. I've never met him, but he's supposed to be this incredible hacker. He might be able to get you into the kind of system you'll need to find her.'

'Trav, that would be amazing! Can you set up a meeting?'

'I can try.'

'For tomorrow.'

'It's New Year's Eve tomorrow. I don't think he'll—'

'Please, Trav.'

'Yeah, sure. Leave it with me. And I'll send you the photos of me and Nadia – they're a bit embarrassing, though.'

'Travis, you're an angel. Thank you.'

Maddy hung up, feeling better than she had all evening. They really were getting somewhere now. Maybe they might actually have a chance of defeating the Cappadocians after all.

Back in the living room, she sat down and began to fill everyone in on the conversation.

'It's okay, Mads,' Ben interrupted. 'We heard.'

'Yes, but did you hear what Travis said about the hacker?'

'Yep.'

'Okay. So, Travis is going to set up a meeting for me to meet this guy tomorrow.'

'I'll come with you,' Alex said.

'No need,' Maddy replied. 'You should rest. It's better if I go on my own anyway.'

'I'll be fine by tomorrow,' Alex said.

'I still think it's better if I go on my own.'

Alex stood up. 'Fine. I'm going to bed,' he said.

'Good idea,' replied Maddy, ignoring his simmering anger. 'You need to build up your strength.' She knew he was mad at her for disagreeing with him, but she wasn't going to back down. If she went to see the hacker alone, she could try to charm him. In the mood Alex was in, he could end up killing the guy if he didn't agree to help them.

'I'll sleep downstairs in the basement tonight,' Alex said. 'You'll sleep easier if I'm not tossing and turning next to you.'

Maddy felt a stab of hurt in her stomach. He didn't even want to spend the night with her. 'Fine,' she said. 'Sleep well.'

The atmosphere in the room was beyond awkward. Everyone murmured goodnight to Alex as he left the room without a backward glance. Seconds later, the door to the basement slammed, making Maddy flinch. How had it all gone so wrong so quickly? What if Alex didn't love her anymore? She still didn't understand his thinking – surely Alex being human was a good thing. But maybe that wasn't the real problem. Maybe he had feelings for Nadia. Maybe Maddy wasn't enough for him anymore.

CHAPTER THIRTY-SEVEN

Madison couldn't let Alex go off to bed like that. There was no way she'd be able to sleep with this kind of bad feeling between them. She stood and made a move to go after him, resolving to be gentler with her words. But Isobel pulled her back.

'Leave him to calm down, Madison. It's no good talking to him when he's like this. He'll come around. He just needs a bit of time. I think he's in shock at what's happened to him.'

'What about me!' Maddy cried, her resolve to be gentler melting. 'Nobody even cares how I'm feeling. Alex kissed someone else. He doesn't want to have a normal, human life with me. These past few weeks, I've been kidnapped, and held hostage, and my brother nearly died, and there are vampires hunting us down. And I'm so tired I feel like I could die.'

The words tumbled out before she could stop them, and then, to her horror, she burst into tears. Proper, sobbing hysterical tears that wouldn't stop. She found herself surrounded by warm comforting arms. Ben, Isobel and Sofia hugged her, while Freddie and Jacques looked on, somewhat embarrassed – not as embarrassed as *she* felt right now. But she just couldn't seem to stop crying. Sofia took Maddy by the hand and led her up the

stairs, murmuring gentle, comforting words in another language
– Turkish, she supposed.

Sofia nudged her into the bathroom and told her to take a
shower. She patted Maddy's shoulder and closed the door
behind her on her way out. Maddy stripped and stepped under
the warm powerful jets, letting the heat soothe her travel-weary
body, the water mingling with her tired, angry tears. When she
finally felt clean, she stepped out of the glass cubicle and
wrapped a thick, fluffy towel around her body. In the bedroom,
she found clean pyjamas on the end of the bed, and when she
slipped under the covers, she found that the sheets had been
changed. There was a fresh glass of water on the bedside table,
and the window was now closed. Sofia was a sweetheart.

Maddy couldn't even think anymore. She closed her eyes
and let sleep overtake her.

Driving to Bristol on her own was not a pleasant experience.
There were about five trillion lanes going into the city, and as
she navigated the tricky roundabouts and junctions, she
thanked God for satnav. Maddy tried to banish last night from
her mind. For now, she refused to think about her problems
with Alex. She would concentrate on today, instead. On getting
this done. Happily, the sun was shining, she didn't get lost and
she reached her destination without mishap, finally parking
outside a converted red-brick warehouse in the city centre.

Travis had texted Maddy the details this morning. The
hacker guy – Tommo (no last name) – hadn't wanted to meet
her, but Maddy had got his address off Travis anyway and had
decided to chance her luck. She figured she'd be able to talk him
round. Maddy had persuaded the others that she could do this
alone. It was only Alex who wasn't happy about it, but then he
wasn't happy about anything at the moment. She sighed and
tried to put him out of her head again. Problem was, she got

terrible fluttery, painful butterflies every time she thought about him. She couldn't eat. Couldn't sleep properly. They would have to sort things out between them soon, or she'd end up a starved, jittery wreck.

Maddy hopped out of the Land Rover and peered up at the building. *Here goes.* She pressed the buzzer and waited.

Nothing.

She pressed it again... and again. Was this going to be a wasted journey?

'What?' An irritated male voice came through the intercom.

'I'm a friend of Travis – Miles's brother. You know Miles, right?'

The voice on the intercom swore.

'Can I speak to you for a minute?' Maddy said.

No response.

'It's urgent. A matter of life and death.'

No response.

'Please.'

The buzzer sounded, and Maddy pushed the door open, relieved he'd at least let her in. The entrance hall was spacious with an old-fashioned elevator. Maddy slid the ornate metal gate open and stepped inside. It took her up to the top floor where Tommo had his apartment.

There was only one door on the landing – he must have the whole floor to himself. The door was ajar, but there was no one waiting there for her. Maddy nudged the door open a little further and peered into the flat. She was greeted by a huge, open space bathed in sunlight. The only furniture she could see was a couch and a couple of packing crates pushed together as a coffee table.

'Hello!' Maddy called out. She spotted a guy at the far end of the room, his back to her, sitting at a desk, surrounded by computer equipment. She walked in. 'Hi, are you Tommo?'

'I told Miles I didn't want to see you, or anyone,' he said

without turning around, his fingers clacking over a laptop keypad. 'Miles shouldn't have given you my address. I'll have to have words.'

'I know,' she said, approaching the figure. 'Don't blame him. He told me you said no, but I really need your help.'

'I don't care what you need. The answer's still no.'

Charming.

The guy stopped typing and swivelled around in his chair to face her. He was small and angry with dark, beady eyes, like a pissed-off ferret.

'I'm really sorry to disturb you,' she said, using her gentlest voice. 'I wouldn't have come if it wasn't an emergency.'

'What part of "no" do you not understand?'

Maddy restrained herself from saying something she'd regret. She was proud of the way she managed to keep it together and remain polite in the face of such rudeness. 'I have money,' she said. 'I can pay you.'

'Not interested,' he said. 'Money isn't my thing, and even if it was, I can get my hands on cash whenever I want.'

'Will you at least hear me out?'

He paused. 'Get me two pints of full-cream milk, a seven-fifty-gram box of Cheerios and a six-pack of salt-and-vinegar crisps, and then I'll think about hearing you out.'

Jeez, was this guy for real? 'Erm, yeah, sure, okay,' Maddy said. 'Where's the nearest shop?'

'Use your initiative.' Tommo turned back to his computer screen, dismissing her.

Little tosser.

'And make sure they're Walkers. I don't want any own-brand crap.'

Ten minutes later, she returned to the apartment with all his requirements and dumped the bag onto one of the packing crates.

'Fridge is to your right,' Tommo said without turning around.

She should pour the milk over the little twat's head, but instead, she walked over to the kitchen area and did as he asked. Groceries put away, she got straight to the point. 'Okay, I've got your shopping for you. So, I need your help. Are you able to hack into the public CCTV networks and find someone for me?'

Tommo swivelled around to face her, checking her out. 'You're cute, I'll give you that,' he said.

'Can you do it?' she asked, ignoring his slimy compliment. She knew she was supposed to be charming the guy, but she just couldn't bring herself to flirt with him. He was way too irritating.

'Yeah, I can do it,' he replied. 'But I'm not going to.'

'Look, I know you said you don't want money, but I can pay you whatever you want.'

'Told you before, I'm not interested.'

'Okay, not money. So, what do you want?'

He stared at her, and she had the horrible feeling he was going to ask for more than she was willing to give.

'What I want,' he said getting to his feet, 'is for you to get out of my flat and leave me alone.' He pointed to the door.

'I got your shopping for you,' she said, trying to contain her temper, 'so how about you try to be a little more polite? Maybe just say you'll think about it.' She couldn't seriously have wasted her morning driving over here, just to get some loser geek boy some cereal.

'I can't remember the last time a bunch of shopping equalled an illegal hack,' he said.

'Is it because it's illegal? Is that why you won't do it?' Maddy asked.

'I don't care about the law. I'm just not in the mood.'

'So, that's it then?' Maddy said, her frustration rising.

'Looks that way.'

'You won't even think about it?'

'Just leave. And close the door on your way out.'

Maddy stormed over to the kitchen, got the milk out of the fridge and stuffed it back into the carrier bag along with the rest of her purchases.

'Oh, come on now,' Tommo said. 'Leave the shopping where it is.'

'It's not *your* shopping,' Maddy replied heading towards the door, carrier bag swinging from her hand.

'I said, leave it,' Tommo yelled. 'Put that stuff back.'

'Make me,' Maddy replied.

'Look, I'm agoraphobic,' he said. 'That's why I asked you to get the shopping. I don't like going outside and there weren't any Tesco delivery slots left.'

'Tough,' she said, and marched out of the door, leaving it wide open.

Tommo wasn't big on New Year's Eve. Fireworks and socialising and all that crap just wasn't his thing. Instead, he was waiting to go online with his gaming mates. Their clan had a serious mission tonight, and he couldn't wait. It was what he lived for – the game. Nothing else mattered. The outside world was irrelevant.

The visit from that girl today had unsettled him. Granted, she was pretty, but she'd stared at him like he was dirt on her shoe, so who cared how good-looking she was. She was just like everyone else – disdainful, stuck-up and not worth a second thought. It was a pity she hadn't left the shopping, though. His online grocery delivery wasn't coming until the day after tomorrow and he only had half a box of Cheerios left.

He wandered over to the kitchen and ferreted around for a

clean bowl, but they were all encrusted with week-old gunk. He should really get around to washing up. Either that or buy a dishwasher. Giving up the search for a mould-free bowl, he washed out a mug and dried the inside on the hem of his sweat-shirt. He poured in some cereal, and the last of the milk. No clean spoons either, so he begrudgingly rinsed one under the tap. He'd eat this, and then it should be time to go online.

Tommo took his mug of Cheerios over to his desk and began eating. Over the crunch of cereal, he heard distant fireworks. It wasn't even eight o'clock yet, and already people were celebrat-ing. Why was everyone so eager to get to next year, anyway? Were their lives really so bad that they needed to constantly look forward to tomorrow and next week and next month and next year?

Hold on... that noise? He had thought it was fireworks, but...

The hair on the back of Tommo's neck began to prickle. He realised that the popping sound might not actually be distant fireworks. It might be something a lot closer – like maybe a light tapping at his window.

Tommo placed his mug and spoon down on the desk, and carefully finished chewing the contents of his mouth. From the dark window, his own scared reflection stared back at him. Surely he must have imagined the noise. His apartment was four floors up, and there was no balcony. No tree with branches that could be scraping against the window. But there it was again. A rhythmic *tap, tap, tap*.

Tommo pushed himself away from the window, his chair rolling backwards over the parquet floor. The tapping had now been replaced by a squeaking sound. What the... Was that a circle appearing on the window? Yes, someone was drawing a large circle on the window with their fingernail! He had to be hallucinating. Maybe the milk was off, and he was coming down with food poisoning.

Just then, the circle of glass moved. It tipped out of the

window and crashed onto his computer monitor. Tommo jumped up in terror, as the glass slid down the monitor and landed with a thud on his desk, unbroken. A rush of frigid air flew into the apartment. Tommo gasped, too scared to run or even scream.

He had to get out of here. He had to leave the apartment. But he hadn't left the apartment in weeks.

Someone or something was out there in the darkness. An arm reached through the empty circle of air. He must be dreaming. This had to be a hyper-real nightmare. Tommo panted in fear, pushed the chair out of his way and backed up against his front door. Someone was climbing through the window. Coming to get him.

In the blink of a cursor, that someone appeared in front of him, staring down at his face with murderous eyes. Tommo shrank back even further, trying to melt into the wooden door, wishing he had the courage to open it and run away from whoever *this* was.

'Who are you?' he squeaked. 'What do you want? Take whatever you need. Just, please, don't hurt me.'

'Tommo,' the man said. How did he know his name? This man wasn't like anyone Tommo had ever met before. He was blonde and pale, with piercing eyes and the whitest teeth. He looked like a character from one of his games. He wasn't quite a *man* either. More, a boy. But the scariest boy he'd ever seen. Young and old at the same time. Like an angel, or a devil. Not... human.

'You had a visitor today,' the man-boy continued, his voice a hissing whisper. The trace of a foreign accent.

'A visitor?' Tommo repeated. He felt as though he was watching himself from above, his mind divorced from his body.

'Yes. A girl.'

'She came here, yes,' Tommo stammered.

'She asked you to do something for her. But you said no. Why did you say no?'

'I... I... can do it. If you want me to do it. I can do what she asked. The CCTV thing. It's not, it's not a problem at all. I can do that.'

'Now.'

'Yes, yeah, sure. It... it might take a while, though. A few hours at least. First, I have to hack into the network, and then who knows how long the software will take to find a match. It might not even find a match. What happens if it doesn't find a match?'

'A photograph has been sent to your phone and to your email. Email back when you find a match.'

'Yeah, sure, sure. Erm, what, what happens if I can't find a match?'

The man bent down, so his face was millimetres from his own. 'Do you see the hole I made in your window, Tommo?'

Tommo nodded.

'Look at it,' the man said. He took hold of Tommo's chin and turned his face towards the window, to the newly made hole. The man's hand was hard and cold like ice. Not like a human hand at all.

'I can see. I can see the window, and I can see the hole.'

'Good,' replied the man. 'It's a long way down, Tommo. A long way down.'

Tommo felt sick. He felt the Cheerios working their way back up his gullet.

'Remember,' the man said, letting go of Tommo's chin. 'Find the girl in the photo.'

And then the man was gone. Just like that. Gone. And Tommo's Cheerios finally made a reappearance all over the parquet floor.

'How do you think he's getting on?' Freddie asked the others for the umpteenth time.

Everyone was waiting in the lounge for Jacques's return. Maddy had filled Morris and Esther in on everything that was happening – about Alex becoming human and their plans to find Nadia.

'I wish it could have been me doing it, tonight,' Ben said. 'I'm sure I would've been scarier than Jacques. I've watched way more horror movies. I would've known exactly what to do to freak that guy out. And after he was so rude to you, Mads. He deserves it.'

'How long has he been gone?' Isobel asked.

'Only half an hour,' Maddy replied. 'He won't be back for ages.'

'He's coming!' Freddie and Ben said together.

A minute later, Jacques breezed into the drawing room, his eyes bright, his smile wide.

'Well?' Ben asked

'Did he go for it?' Isobel added.

'Of course he did,' Jacques replied. 'He was terrified. I was brilliant. I hope I didn't overdo it, though. He really was quite petrified.'

'I feel sorry for him,' Isobel said. 'I don't think we should have done it.'

'You wouldn't say that if you'd met him,' Maddy said. 'Anyway, we had no choice. It was either give Tommo a little scare, or we all die.'

'But, still, it just sounds as if he's lonely,' Isobel said.

'Fine, I'll send him a kitten as a thank you,' Maddy said. 'And a crate of Cheerios.'

'Cheerios?' Isobel frowned.

'Doesn't matter,' Maddy replied. Although she hadn't admitted it, she did feel a little bad at how they'd treated Tommo. True, he'd been super-rude to her, but then he'd admitted he was agoraphobic. Maybe she would send him that crate of Cheerios after all.

Madison's gaze rested on Sofia who sat in the corner on a wingback chair taking it all in. She was one of those people who didn't speak much. She only said what needed to be said. Otherwise, she held her tongue. Maybe that was because she'd lived for such a long time. She didn't feel the need to fill the room with all her thoughts. After all, she had all the time in the world to get her point across. Maybe she didn't feel that pressing, mortal need to make her mark.

And Alex. He was quiet, too, which was most unlike him. Sulking? Angry? Maddy couldn't tell. His expression was guarded, and he hadn't so much as glanced her way all evening.

'Do you think he'll find Nadia?' Alex asked his brother.

'If he doesn't, it won't be through lack of trying,' Jacques replied. 'I gave him some strong motivation.'

'Maddy, you and Alexandre should try to get some sleep,' Isobel said. 'We'll wake you if Tommo locates her.'

'Good idea,' Esther said, getting to her feet. 'I'll make you some hot chocolate to take to bed.'

Maddy glanced over at Alex again, wondering where he was planning to sleep tonight. How had things gone so wrong that he couldn't even bear to be in the same room as her? But then, she supposed she had pushed him away earlier. Had she been unfair?

'No hot chocolate for me thanks, Esther,' Maddy said. 'I'm going straight to sleep. Isobel, you will wake me, won't you? The minute you hear anything.'

'Of course.'

'Night, everyone,' she said, finally catching Alex's eye. But he just gave her an unreadable look and turned away.

CHAPTER THIRTY-EIGHT

Alexandre couldn't work out if mortal sleep was a blessing or a curse. It felt good to fall into oblivion for a few hours, but waking up was painful, and his basement bedroom was lonely. Madison obviously needed her space right now, so he had thought it best to sleep down here until she forgave him. Assuming she ever would.

'Sorry to wake you, brother,' Isobel said, her voice warm in the darkness. 'There's an email.'

'From the hacker?'

'Yes.'

'I'll be straight up.'

Isobel left. Alex turned on the light and glanced at the clock – 5.35 a.m. He stretched and jumped out of bed, giving himself a shake and taking a few deep breaths. Hopefully, this was the start of it. Their chance to escape the Cappadocians forever.

In the drawing room, everyone gathered around Maddy's iPad. Esther and Morris were still asleep upstairs, but the rest were here, eager to see if Tommo had delivered. Madison opened the email. There was no message; just three attachments. She tapped the first one.

The image had been taken from a security camera. It showed a blonde girl in a dark wool coat walking out of what appeared to be a hotel decorated with Christmas lights. Three liveried doormen stood to the side. The girl in the image looked remarkably like Nadia, but the camera wasn't close enough for Alex to be entirely certain.

'Is that a hotel?' Ben asked.

'Looks like it, but I can't see what it's called,' Maddy replied.

'Open one of the other attachments,' Freddie said.

Maddy did as he asked. In this image, the name of the hotel was clear: CLARIDGES.

'Is that in London?' Ben asked.

'Yes,' Alex replied. 'Claridges was around in my day.'

'She's got good taste,' Isobel said. 'Claridges was something special even back in the nineteenth century. A hotel frequented by royalty.'

'Do you think it really is Nadia?' Jacques asked.

'Open the last attachment,' Sofia said.

Maddy did as Sofia asked. This final image was a close-up of the girl's face.

'It's her,' Alex said, unsure at how he felt looking at Nadia's features once again. The last time he had seen her, they had been kissing. Certainly, he didn't have any feelings for her anymore... if he ever did. No. The only emotion he felt now was anger. A simmering, bubbling anger. But they needed her help, so he'd have to keep it under control.

'I can't believe Tommo did it,' Maddy said. 'He actually did it.'

'Told you I'd get him to help us,' Jacques said.

'When were these images captured?' Sofia asked.

Maddy re-opened the first attachment. The timestamp read: *Mon* 20.47.

'Last night!' Ben said. 'That means she's probably still there now.'

'We should try to find out what name she's checked in under,' Sofia said. 'We'll need to know the room number.'

'I'll ask Tommo,' Jacques said. 'He'll get the information for us.'

Jacques was right. Tommo came back to them with the information almost straight away. Someone had checked into to one of Claridges' terrace suites on December 28th under the name of Ms Seraphine Sholeh. A hallway security camera had captured Nadia leaving the suite.

'Is that her real name, do you think?' Isobel asked.

'I doubt it,' Alex replied. 'Maybe she doesn't even have a real name.'

'Those names both mean *fire*,' Sofia said. 'Seraphine is taken from the word seraphim, meaning *fiery one*. Sholeh is the Persian name for fire. So, regardless of whether it's her real name or not, we can at least be sure it's her.

'What do you think she's doing there?' Jacques asked.

'Isn't it obvious,' Isobel said. 'She got what she wanted – energy and power from Alexandre – and now she's checked into a chic hotel to relax and enjoy herself. It's what I would do.'

'We know it's what *you* would do, Belle,' Jacques replied.

'No,' Sofia said. 'She is an ancient creature. She is not concerned with modern-day luxuries. This is *the bright one*. She is more at home on the wild frozen steppes of Eastern Europe. She's not a cossetted modern-day being who needs warmth and room service.'

'So, why's she in a five-star hotel, then?' Maddy asked.

'Why not,' Sofia replied. 'London is the centre for international travel. She will be planning her next move. Deciding where to go next. For her, it is all about the hunt. We don't have much time if we want to catch her. She could leave at any moment. We may already be too late.'

'Then we should leave now,' Alex said.

'It's almost morning,' Jacques replied. 'I can't believe that we're trapped here for eleven more hours. We'll have to wait until this evening.'

'It might be too late by then,' Alex said. 'I'll go.' Maybe there was at least one upside to being mortal – he was no longer restricted by the sun.

'It's too dangerous to go alone,' Isobel said. 'We need to all stay together. Safety in numbers.'

'I agree with Isobel,' Sofia said. 'Although time is of the essence, it's not wise for you to go on your own, Alex. Nadia is dangerous. We don't know enough about her. We'll just have to hope she's still there by this evening.'

'Very well,' Alex replied, too weary to argue further. 'In that case, I might go out. Get some fresh air. I've been cooped up for days. I feel like a bear in hibernation.'

'Good idea, brother,' Isobel said. 'You do look very peaky. Don't go too far.'

He gave her a wry smile and went downstairs to fetch an extra sweater. Being human and feeling the cold again was very inconvenient. He thought about asking Maddy to join him on his walk, but he couldn't face more rejection. Instead, he grabbed his coat, keys and phone, and left the house by the back door, the pre-dawn air making him catch his breath and shiver.

It was still dark out, but close enough to sunrise to be safe from vampires. Alex shoved his hands inside his coat pockets and walked across the wide patio at the back of the house, down the steps onto the frozen lawn. The outside security lights had come on, illuminating his way, but he felt an urge to walk in darkness, so he headed away from the house, towards the distant gates beyond the garden's maze.

Strange to be outdoors knowing the sun could rise at any moment, but that he would be safe from its rays. How would it feel to be outside in daylight again? At this moment, he didn't even care about that. So many thoughts raced around his head. He could do with someone to talk to, but the boys were too immature, Isobel was too judgemental and Madison...

She still didn't appear to be talking to him. He'd have to fix it. He couldn't let their relationship deteriorate further. But there never seemed to be a good moment. After everything that had happened with Nadia, he couldn't blame Maddy for hating him. Nadia wasn't who he wanted. Far from it. She wasn't even a real person – she was a lone creature trapped in a centuries-old cycle of power, life and death.

How could he explain to Madison that the kiss had happened without warning? Had he meant to kiss her? He didn't think so, but the memory was too confused. He couldn't seem to get it clear in his head. He remembered feeling sorry for the girl and giving her a hug to warm her up because she was shivering. But the rest of it was a blur. Sofia had said Alex had been powerless to stop it happening, but did Maddy believe that? If it had been Madison kissing a tall, handsome, blond man, he knew he wouldn't be forgiving. He'd be insane with anger and jealousy.

What a mess.

If he needed any proof that he still loved Madison, it was right here in his gut – a constant, churning worry that something would happen to her. That the Cappadocians would come for her again. Or that Nadia would do something to her. He had to keep Maddy safe. Keep her away from these dangerous creatures. Alex was so weak now, that if anyone decided to attack Madison, he wouldn't be able to do a damn thing about it. How could he stop her going to London, straight into the lair of that *thing* – or whatever she was? Maddy was so stubborn, she would never listen to him. He would have to think of something else. Another way to keep her from Nadia, or Seraphine, or whatever her name was.

On the advice of Sofia, Maddy spent the day trying to rest – an impossible task given the level of tension in the house. The place had the atmosphere of an electric storm. She lay on her four-poster bed, her skin itching, her brain whirring, pushing Alex from her thoughts every time he crept in – which was often. She tried and failed to sleep, to read a book, read a magazine, watch TV. Her mind couldn't settle to anything. Instead, she put on some music and gazed out through her bedroom window, the iron-grey sky seeming to sink lower and lower, adding to the heavy, claustrophobic feeling inside the house.

The others were busy organising accommodation for their London trip, as well as a private jet to take Nadia to Turkey. 'I know she hasn't agreed yet, but it's better to be prepared,' Sofia had said. First, they had to hope that she was still at Claridges.

As morning turned to afternoon, Maddy threw a few clothes into a bag. Once night fell, they would be leaving for London. All of them, including Morris and Esther. They had decided it was better for them all to stay together – bad things tended to happen when they split up.

Once the sun had set, everyone gathered on the front drive and began loading their bags into Maddy's Defender. They would travel in convoy. Morris had just gone to fetch his Volvo from the garage.

'Where's Alex?' Ben asked.

'I'll get him,' Jacques offered. A few minutes later, he returned, frowning. 'I searched every room, but he's not in the house or garden.'

Maddy had a bad feeling.

'I can't sense him anywhere,' Isobel said.

'Yes, but we haven't been able to sense him properly since he was turned back into a human. It's like his scent is masked.'

'I told you earlier,' Sofia said. 'You can't track Alexandre any longer. He may be human, but he now shares Nadia's essence, and she is a master of stealth.'

'Great,' Jacques replied.

Morris brought the navy Volvo up to the front of the house, its headlights blinding Maddy momentarily.

'Everyone ready?' Morris asked, getting out and stowing the last couple of bags in the boot.

'We were just wondering where Alex has gone,' Isobel said.

'Alex?' Morris replied. 'He left for London early this morning. Took his motorbike. Said he'd like to get a head start. Bit nippy for a bike this time of year, but he insisted.'

Maddy stared at Morris stupidly while everyone started talking at once, blaming themselves, blaming Alex. But Maddy couldn't speak. She felt hollow. She should have realised he'd go off and do his own thing. It was typical of him. Now they were all worried sick. She pulled out her mobile and called him. It went straight through to voicemail.

'Alex, it's me. Would've been nice if you'd let us know you were going without us. Anyway, I hope you found her. Call me back.' She ended the call and shoved the phone back in her pocket, her fingers trembling.

Central London at night looked like a glossy postcard – Christmas lights, sleek and shiny cars, black cabs, red double-decker buses and throngs of people wrapped up against the icy air in warm coats and bright scarves. The place was humming. Maddy stared out of the window at the blurry scene, the knot in her stomach growing harder. She should have guessed Alex would try to fix this on his own. She'd left countless voice and text messages – they all had – but he hadn't replied to any of them. She had to hope it was because he'd run out of battery or lost his phone. And that there wasn't a more sinister reason for his silence.

It was almost a shock when they reached Mayfair and finally arrived at Claridges Hotel. Walking into the beautiful red-brick building, Maddy felt like she was in a slow-moving dream. Would they find anybody here? Nadia? Alex?

Sofia crossed the black-and-white-chequered marble floor and went straight over to the reception desk while the others waited in the lobby beneath an enormous, glittering chandelier. The four vampires looked unruffled, beautiful and glamorous, while Maddy felt crumpled and tired looking, along with Esther and Morris.

Five minutes later, Sofia returned to them. 'They called Nadia's suite,' she said, 'but there was no reply. She's here, though. I can sense her. And I have the feeling she's expecting us.'

'What about Alex?' Maddy asked. 'Can you tell if he's here, too?'

'I don't know,' Sofia replied. 'We'll ask Nadia in a minute. Follow me.'

They took the lift to the top floor. Maddy's heart pounded as the elevator rose. *Please let Alex be there.* She felt as though she was being swept along by everyone else, a collective force all after the same elusive thing – peace.

Sofia used her instincts to guide them to Nadia's hotel suite. The door stood ajar. Everyone paused outside except Madison who pushed the door with her fingertips and walked in. The others followed.

Inside, the rooms were freezing. Maddy strode through a dining area which opened out into a large sitting room. Nadia stood there with her back to them. She was barefoot, wearing a white silk dress, gazing through a set of French doors, her hair billowing out behind her. The doors were wide open to a roof terrace, welcoming the chill north wind into the room – the reason for the suite's arctic conditions. Nadia must have heard them come in, but she didn't turn around or acknowledge their arrival.

Maddy shivered and pulled her coat tighter around her body.

'Nadia,' Isobel said. 'It's us. Isobel, Madison and—'

Nadia pulled the French doors shut with a bang and turned to face them. Even with the doors shut, the room still felt like an icebox. Maddy wouldn't have been surprised to see icicles hanging off the ceiling. Although freezing, the suite was warmly furnished in an art-deco style, with light oak floors, neutral sofas and plush armchairs.

'Why you are here?' Nadia demanded.

'We know who you are, Nadia,' Maddy said. 'And we know what you did to Alex.'

'Yes,' Nadia replied.

'Yes?' Maddy said. 'Is that all you've got to say?' She could feel her core temperature rising as anger threatened to take over. Sofia put a warning hand on her arm.

'Where's Alex?' Maddy asked.

'Alexandre is not here,' Nadia said.

'But he *was* here, though?' Isobel asked. 'Earlier?'

'No,' Nadia said. 'I have not seen Alexandre since the other night.'

'What are you talking about?' Maddy said. 'You must have seen him. He left this morning to come here. He should've been with you hours ago.'

'Maybe he didn't intend coming here,' Nadia said. 'Maybe he just left.'

'What have you done with him?' Maddy snarled. 'You better not have hurt him.'

'Who are you to come in here and question me?' Nadia said. 'If I wanted hurt Alexandre, he would be dead already. I like Alexandre. Be happy I leave him alive for you.'

'Yes,' Maddy replied. 'We all know how much you like

Alex. You seduced him. You kissed him.' Madison heard how childish and bitter her words sounded, but she couldn't help herself.

'You love him, yes?' Nadia said.

'None of your business. But... yes.'

'So, go. Look for him. Don't waste your time and mine.'

Maddy couldn't tell if Nadia was trying to trick them. If she really did know where Alex was, or if she was being truthful.

'You.' Nadia turned to Sofia. 'You are different. What are you?'

'Where is Alexandre?' Sofia asked. 'Please tell us. We don't want to cause you any trouble. All we want is Alexandre.'

'What are you?' Nadia stepped closer to the woman, tilting her head to the side as if trying to work her out.

'I am nothing to interest you,' Sofia replied.

Maddy's heart leapt as her phone pinged. She stared at the screen, relief flooding her body. 'You guys, it's a text from Alex.'

Everyone instantly transferred their attention from Nadia to Madison.

'Oh my God!' Maddy cried. 'Oh no. *No!*'

'What? What is it?' They crowded around as Maddy held her phone up so they could read the text:

Looking for someone?

But worse than the message was the photo accompanying the text. An image of Alexandre in a dark room, his eyes closed, a single light shining on his pale face... with a female vampire sucking the blood from his neck.

CHAPTER THIRTY-NINE

The brutal image of Alexandre swam before Maddy's eyes. It would have been too easy for her to collapse sobbing in a heap on the floor, but she couldn't fall apart now. She was done with crying. Alex needed her to focus. To find out where he was and work out how they were going to get him back.

'Let me see that photograph,' Morris said.

Maddy handed him the phone, the image still burnt into her retinas. Alex, a human. Alex, a captive. Alex being fed on by a vampire. He had been right, and she had been wrong. If they had agreed to do as he'd asked, and turned him back into a vampire, he would be safe right now. The Cappadocians would never have been able to capture him. At least he would have had a fighting chance.

'It looks like he's in a bedroom,' Morris said. 'Could even be a hotel room. I'm guessing he must still be in England.' He turned to Jacques and Freddie. 'If he's in London, maybe you could find him.'

'He is not in London,' Nadia said. 'I would know.'

Everyone started talking at once, speculating, arguing,

trying to work out what to do next. Maddy took her phone back
from Morris and began typing:

What do you want?

She sent the text and waited. Within twenty seconds she
received a reply:

*You must all come to us, or he dies. Painfully. Even your busy-
body housekeeper and groundsman. We want you all* ☺

It was the smiley face that made Maddy want to vomit.

'Look at what they've written,' Maddy cried, holding her
phone out so Nadia could see. 'Please help us. You must feel
something for Alex. You let him live. Don't let that be for
nothing.'

'Mads, what is it?' Ben said. 'What did they say?'

Their frantic conversation faded, and everyone turned to
Maddy. She sank down onto the sofa and stared up at the faces
of the people she loved. 'They want us all to go to Cappadocia,'
she said, 'or they'll kill Alex.'

Isobel snatched the phone from her and read the text. She
passed it to everyone. 'We have no choice. We must all go to
him,' she said. 'We must rescue my brother. But how will we do
it? Surely, they will kill us all!'

Nadia turned to Sofia once more. 'What are you? Why do I
not know what you are? You tell me. Why are you different?'

'It's a long story,' Sofia said. 'I will tell you, but first, will you
help us?'

'Help you?'

'Alex has been taken,' Maddy said. 'By ancient vampires in
Cappadocia.'

'You are lying,' Nadia replied. 'There are no ancient
vampires in Cappadocia. I would know of them.'

'I'm not lying,' Maddy said. 'There's a whole city of them. Hundreds. All old and powerful. They've been there for centuries. They've got Alex, and they want us dead. If you come with us to Turkey, you'll see. You can have them all. It would be good for you, and good for us.'

'Why you are telling me these lies?' Nadia said, approaching Madison, her eyes narrowed. 'Do you think I don't know every inch of this world? I have travelled to every village, every city, every acre of countryside. I have climbed mountains and swum to the remotest islands. I know there is no coven of which you speak.'

'Maddy's telling the truth,' Jacques said. 'It's where we were turned.'

'I don't believe your story,' Nadia said. 'You all leave, now. Not you,' Nadia said, turning to Sofia. 'You stay and tell me what you are.'

'All right,' Sofia, replied. 'But you must let everyone else stay while I tell you my tale.'

'Very well. Sit. Talk,' Nadia said.

Sofia sat in an armchair. Maddy didn't want to sit down. She was too impatient to get moving. To get Alex back. But it looked like they weren't going anywhere until Nadia had heard Sofia's story. And then they somehow had to persuade her to accompany them to Cappadocia. She was their only hope at getting Alex out alive. So, Maddy perched on the arm of the sofa and chewed her thumbnail, willing Nadia to tell the tale quickly.

As Sofia began her story, Nadia stood in front of her, examining the woman as though she were some rare artifact.

'I am old,' Sofia began. 'Not as old as you, Nadia. But old enough. My homeland is Cappadocia in the country now known as Turkey. Fourteen hundred years ago, my people were taken by a coven of ancient vampires. The largest coven you have ever seen. There were hundreds of vampires. Maybe even thousands. The creatures had built an underground city to protect themselves from the sun. They tricked my people and kept them captive down there as slaves. But most were shut in dark cells and taken out periodically to feed on. Like animals, they were bred, penned and then slaughtered.'

Maddy had heard this story before, but it still sickened her to hear of how Sofia's people had suffered.

'I was not captured, but I knew of my village's fate. I had to do something. I was apprenticed to a healer, a woman who had seen these blood demons before, in her own country. She made a plague to kill them. We didn't know if it would work, but I had to try. So, I infected myself with the plague and let the vampires drink from me. It was awful. A nightmare made real. But it worked. The plague spread. The vampires grew sick. Soon, they were all rendered unconscious. The world was free from the blood demons. Humans were safe from vampires... until Alexandre was woken up just over a year ago by Madison here.

'As for me, I walked out into the sun, intending to kill myself, for they had turned me into a vampire, too. And I did not wish to become a slave to the blood. But, instead of dying, I became like this. Strong. Immortal. But no longer a vampire.'

'You!' Nadia hissed. She hauled Sofia from her chair, pulled her to her feet and thrust her face up close to hers.

Maddy was shocked at Nadia's reaction; she gasped, unsure what to do or say.

Sofia looked afraid. She tried to pry Nadia's hands from her shoulders, but the vampire hunter was too strong. 'What?' Sofia cried. 'What have I said?'

'*What have I said?*' Nadia mimicked, pushing her back down into the armchair. '*What have you said?*' Nadia grabbed a table lamp and flung it across the room. Then she picked up a side table and hurled it at the window with such force that it splintered into pieces. Next was the turn of a wooden dining chair which she smashed against the wall. Everyone, including

Maddy, had now backed away from the crazed creature, bewildered and scared by her sudden anger. Sofia remained in the armchair, watching nervously.

As Nadia paused in her destruction of the suite, Sofia bravely spoke: 'Please, will you tell me what I have said to make you so angry.'

'It is not what you said,' Nadia began, 'it's what you did. For centuries I journeyed. I look everywhere for sustenance. But there was nothing for me. No vampires to sustain me. No prey. No hunt. I grew weak, I could hardly move. Just existing – *existing*, you understand? Not for days, not weeks, or years, but for centuries. So weak, I could barely see. But I could still feel. Yes, I felt everything. My mind was active. I thought I would be destined to live forever like that. And it was all. Your. Fault.' She lifted Sofia out of the chair by her hair. 'You took my prey from me!'

'Wait!' Maddy rushed over to where they stood while Nadia's eyes flashed with fury, Sofia cowering before her. 'What was Sofia supposed to do?' Maddy demanded. 'The vampires were slaughtering her people. Did you expect her to do nothing? To just watch while they killed her friends? Her family?'

'To die is nothing,' Nadia said, letting go of Sofia. 'To live for eternity a helpless creature, as I did, was torture. It wasn't until last year that I begin to sense vampires on the earth once more. I dragged myself here to London and I found one wretched creature who gave me the little energy I needed for the hunt. Then I found Alexandre. But... I am changed. I am not the powerful being I once was.'

'I am sorry,' Sofia said. 'Truly, I wish I'd known of your existence back then. You could have helped destroy the Cappadocian coven. Things would be very different now.'

'Listen,' Maddy said. 'You had a really shit time, Nadia, I get that. But don't you see, this is your chance to make a new start. To boost your power, or whatever it is you do. You hunt vampires, right? So, if you want powerful vampires – coven leaders – well, the ones who have Alex are ancient and far more powerful than any in this room. Their leader is a Byzantine emperor, over one thousand years old. He's the one who turned Alex.'

Was it Maddy's imagination, or did Nadia's skin light up for a second? It looked like she was glowing. The others must have sensed something, too, because they all took an almost imperceptible step back.

'So,' Nadia said to Sofia, 'this is why I not sense coven in Cappadocia – because they were all unconscious from your plague.'

'Yes,' Sofia replied. 'Madison is right, though. This is your chance to restore your power.'

'And you want me to help Alexandre.'

'Why I should help you?' she sneered.

'Because, if it wasn't for me waking up Alexandre, you'd still be living in torture with no vampires to feed off.'

'How you wake him?' Nadia asked. 'You are just a young girl.'

'I'll tell you, but will you help us?'

Nadia's eyes narrowed and she took a step towards Madison.

Maddy stood her ground. 'Don't forget, if you help us, you'll have a whole city of ancient vampires to hunt.' The shrill ringing of a phone made Maddy jump. It wasn't her mobile. It was coming from the sideboard behind her – the hotel phone. 'Do you want me to get it?' Maddy asked Nadia.

The creature lifted one shoulder; an almost imperceptible movement that Maddy took as a yes. Maddy lifted the phone from its cradle. 'Hello?'

It was a man from hotel reception enquiring if everything was all right. They'd had complaints of shouting and banging coming from the suite.

'Yeah, everything's fine,' Maddy replied. 'Sorry, just celebrating a friend's birthday. We'll keep it down.' She replaced the handset.

'We have a plane waiting,' Sofia said. 'Will you come?'

'Fine,' Nadia replied. 'We go.'

Maddy exhaled, her heart still pounding.

'And you will tell me the story of how you woke Alexandre.'

'I will,' Maddy replied. At last, she felt as though the tables might be turning in their favour. With Nadia on their side, they, at least, had a fighting chance.

It was the deep of night. Sometime after midnight, but not close enough to dawn. Their convoy of hired jeeps traversed the icy Cappadocian terrain. To be back in this ancient, snowy land again so soon was more than a little unsettling. Madison felt tied to this terrifying place. Every time she managed to leave, something or someone seemed to drag her back. She'd be happy if she never had to set foot on Turkish soil again. In any other circumstances, she would have found it a beautiful country. But all she had known here was cold terror, the threat of death hanging over her. And now they were going willingly to the scariest place on the planet. A hell on earth – the vampires' underground city.

No one spoke. All thoughts turned to what lay ahead. There was just the thrum and roar of the jeep engines, the smell of leather upholstery, and the frigid darkness beyond the windows. Maddy's stomach twisted up in knots. What was happening to Alex? Could Nadia ensure everyone's safety? She may be powerful, but she was just one single being against who knew how many vampires. One hundred? One thousand? More?

Ben sat next to her. Unusually silent. What was her baby brother doing here on this suicide mission? How had she allowed him to become involved in all this? She wished she'd been able to leave him behind in England. But to leave him alone was just as dangerous as to bring him along. She took his hand in hers, his skin a cold, hard reminder of what he had become. He turned to her, and her breath caught in her throat at how beautiful and young and vulnerable he was.

'Hey, Shortie,' she murmured. Regular human ears wouldn't have been able to hear her words above the engine noise.

'Hey, Mads,' he replied.

She turned away and continued staring out of the window. Willing them to arrive so they could get this over with, one way or another.

After a time, the jeeps came to a stop. The engines quieted, and silence enveloped them all. Maddy's heart pounded, and she had to take a couple of steadying breaths. This time, it was Ben who took *her* hand.

'Don't worry, Mads,' he said. 'I'll look after you. I'm just as strong as them now.'

She wished that were true.

'We need to get out of the vehicles,' Sofia said from the front of the jeep. 'Can you see them?'

Maddy peered ahead, through the windscreen. Her legs began to tremble, and Ben squeezed her hand a little tighter. Outside, in the darkness, illuminated by the jeeps' headlamps, stood a welcoming committee. Five unsmiling vampires.

The creatures were dressed in ancient robes which billowed in the night air. Their faces white as chalk, their lips stained red. They stood, still as statues. This was it. No turning back now.

Maddy gave herself a shake. They had come here to rescue Alex, and so that is what they would do. They were three humans, four vampires, and two immortal beings with powers that could be used against their enemy. This was no time to be afraid. She turned to Ben and gave him a smile.

'Let's kick their asses,' she said.

Ben gave a lopsided grin. But she could see his nerves beneath the bravado.

Within moments, they were all outside under the clear night sky. The Cappadocians didn't speak. As one, they turned and walked towards a rocky outcrop. With movements too fast to see, they had shifted a massive boulder, exposing an opening in the ground. One by one, the five vampires disappeared. Sofia followed. Then Isobel and Nadia. Jacques took Esther in his arms and carried her down. Freddie took Morris, and Ben took Maddy. His arms wrapped tight around her as they dropped vertically into the belly of the earth, landing with a soft thud in total darkness below. The shock of their sudden descent made her stomach clench and her head swim, the smell of earth and decay thick in her nostrils.

They moved at speed through the dark tunnels, her feet not touching the ground, just a rush of air over skin, hair flying, eyes watering.

And then they arrived.

Their journey here had been so fast, Madison hadn't been able to register her surroundings. But now, recovering her breath, she took it all in. She found herself standing next to the others at the front of a dimly lit hall. A cavernous space built to hold hundreds, with pillars, arches and faded paintings on the walls. Like a church or temple.

Ahead of them, seated on an ornate throne set high upon a raised dais, a male vampire with a young face surveyed them. But his youthful looks were deceiving, for he radiated a power that made Maddy's body tremble. His eyes were blank. Lifeless. Reptilian. Wearing a crown and clothed in gorgeous purple-and-gold robes from a bygone time. This was the Emperor.

To his right stood two creatures. Madison recognised them. Vampires she had hoped never to set eyes on again: Mislav and Sergell. She shuddered. The last time she had seen them,

Mislav had given Sergell the order to rip out her throat. She swallowed and prayed there wouldn't be a repeat performance.

The five vampires who had escorted them here flanked Maddy and the others. So, was it just these eight vampires in total? Maddy didn't think so. The hall was built to hold hundreds, if not thousands. Why bring so few to such a massive space? She turned her head to glance over her shoulder and had to bite her lip to stop herself crying out. Behind her, throngs of the creatures had now entered the hall. She couldn't tell how many, but there were certainly more than one hundred. More than they could hope to overcome.

Where was Alex?

Sofia's voice broke the silence:

'Good evening, Mislav. Good evening, Your Imperial Highness.'

Maddy marvelled at the woman's bravery. The last time Sofia was down here, she had been a young girl. She had incapacitated these powerful beings and saved her people from a life of terror and slavery. What must she be feeling? Was she scared to be back?

Her voice rang clear and steady. 'Everyone has come just as you asked,' Sofia continued. 'Now, where is Alexandre?'

'Aelia,' Mislav said. 'Or should I now call you Sofia? What are you doing here? You are a fool to come back. I don't believe you were even invited.'

'Do I need an invitation?'

'Don't go getting any ideas about spreading your vile blood plague among us. After all, we have now discovered how to cure it. Sunlight. A very clever cure. The last one we'd ever think of. Your threats won't work on us anymore.'

'Who said anything about that,' Sofia retorted. 'We are here for Alexandre. That is all.'

'Silence!' The Emperor rose to his feet, his cold gaze encompassing all.

Mislav bowed.

'Bring him,' the Emperor said, his voice high and reedy, like the boy he appeared to be.

At the far end of the hall, to the left of the dais, through an archway, three figures approached. Two female vampires supporting a semi-naked man. His head bent, his hands bound, his torso, neck and arms covered in puncture wounds. From small red dots to gaping bloody gashes.

It was Alex.

'Oh no!' Maddy cried out, unable to keep silent. 'Alex, what have they done to you?' She rushed forward but felt herself pulled back. It was Sofia, restraining her. Telling her to wait. To be calm. But how could she be calm when Alex had been so mistreated, when he was there and she couldn't go to him? She felt waves of anger and tension from Isobel, Jacques, Freddie and Ben. A palpable feeling. They hissed and bared their fangs. She kept telling herself at least he was alive, at least he was alive. But the state he was in, who knew how long he had left.

'Calm yourselves,' Mislav said. 'He is not badly hurt. Not yet, anyway.'

At this, the other Cappadocians laughed, sly whispering chuckles that swept over Maddy's skin and chilled her bones.

Alex was led towards Maddy and the others. And that was when Maddy had another shock. One of the female vampires with Alex... it couldn't be...

It was.

'Leonora!' Freddie cried. 'What have you done?'

CHAPTER FORTY

Leonora glanced across at her brother. A brief flicker of sorrow in her eyes. She and her companion let go their grip on Alex and left him swaying next to Morris, who put a supporting arm around his body, preventing him from collapsing to the ground. Leonora moved to join the crowd of vampires behind them.

Madison was horrified at the thought of Leonora having anything to do with the wounds inflicted on Alex. Had she really fallen so far? Had she become loyal to the Emperor at the expense of her friends and family? Maddy had tried to make excuses for her ancestor's behaviour in the past. But not this time. There was nothing that could forgive this kind of betrayal.

Maddy slipped around the others to be by Alex's side. She took his hand in hers, stroking his cheek and trying to make eye contact, but his head lolled, and his eyes widened briefly before half closing once again as he leant into Morris for support. Nadia stood to Maddy's right, but she hadn't even attempted to make any kind of move yet. Maddy wondered what she was waiting for. And if she could even be trusted to do what she had promised.

'There,' the Emperor said. 'You now have your Alexandre

returned to you. But you must realise that we cannot allow any of you to leave.'

'That was not the deal,' Sofia said.

The Emperor waved away her words with the flick of his wrist. 'We make no deals here.'

'You said you would kill Alexandre unless we came,' Sofia said. 'Well, we came. So you cannot kill him. Unless your word cannot be trusted.'

'Very well,' the Emperor replied. 'We will not kill Alexandre. We will kill the rest of you instead. And Alexandre can watch. Then we shall turn him back into one of us so he can live through all eternity in suffering and pain for the loss of his loved ones. Is *that* a better deal? I think so. And you need not think you can escape. The exits to this hall have been barred and locked. You will die here, today.'

As the Emperor spoke, Mislav stepped down off the dais and began walking towards them. Maddy gripped Alex's hand more tightly. Was this it? Was he going to kill them now? But Mislav's eyes appeared to be locked only on Nadia.

'You,' he said to her. 'I do not recognise you. And yet, there is something familiar... I feel as though I know you.' He moved swiftly across the floor, coming closer, his gorgeous robes rustling as he moved.

'Now would be a good time to do your voodoo thing,' Maddy hissed at Nadia.

'Not yet,' she murmured. 'Wait.' She took a couple of steps forward, away from Maddy and the Marchwood Vampires.

Maddy took a deep breath as Mislav approached. The memory of his viciousness still fresh in her mind.

'Why did you bring this girl here? Who is she?' Mislav asked them, without taking his eyes from Nadia's face. 'You cannot think much of her to put her in such mortal danger. For surely you knew that you were travelling to your graves.' He now stood directly in front of Nadia, while she gazed at him, expressionless. 'Quite exquisite,' he said. 'I will enjoy today. More so than I thought.'

Sergell left the Emperor's side to join Mislav. 'Yes, sir. I agree. This one is quite mesmerising.'

'What are you doing?' Mislav snapped. 'Get back up there. Did I ask you to accompany me?'

Sergell reached out a hand towards Nadia, ignoring Mislav. 'Who are you, child? What a beautiful creature.'

Mislav tore his gaze away from Nadia's face to glare at Sergell. 'Get back to where you were,' he ordered. Again, Sergell ignored him. 'Did you not hear me?' Mislav hissed. 'I said get back.'

'Yes, of course,' Sergell finally replied. 'Forgive me, sir. But she is enchanting, is she not?'

'Go back, Sergell,' Mislav said, his voice low, his eyes slits. 'I'm warning you.'

'Yes, sir.' The vampire reluctantly backed away, but he couldn't drag his eyes from Nadia's face. Barely half a dozen paces away, he stopped, rooted to the floor just staring at her. Then, strangely, he began to move back towards Nadia once again.

Maddy's jaw fell open as she watched Sergell's disobedience. Mislav would not be amused. A strange mood had descended upon the hall. A mood of crackling tension, as though everyone was holding their breath. Waiting. A pause in proceedings.

As Sergell reached Mislav's side for the second time, the senior vampire's patience ran out. He shoved Sergell backwards. But, as he did so, several more vampires began to gather around him, also mesmerised by Nadia.

'All of you, get back!' Mislav swatted them away, without taking his eyes from Nadia. The vampires momentarily came to their senses, shaking their heads and walking off, dazed. The tension in the hall was so high, it felt almost unbearable, like a bomb about to go off.

Despite Mislav's warnings, like moths to a flame, the other Cappadocians could not resist Nadia. Once more, they began to edge forward. Mislav lost his patience again and struck the one closest to him. To Maddy's surprise, this lowly foot soldier struck Mislav back. And now a kind of violent dance began. Another male vampire approached Nadia, a rapt expression on his face. He began to stroke her cheek, and then her hair. As a female came forward to take Nadia's hand, the male vampire grabbed the female by the throat and began to shake her. Now the two vampires were locked in combat.

Mislav snarled at the gathering creatures who were still attempting to get closer, whilst also trying to prevent others from approaching. It was descending into a proper fight – a chaotic and violent attempt to reach the source of their desire: Nadia. But throughout all this, the great hall remained strangely hushed. Only snarls and hisses. No yells or screams, or the kinds of sounds you'd expect to hear during a battle.

Now that the vampires were otherwise occupied, Maddy and the others had begun retreating towards the back of the hall. Maddy and Morris supported Alex between them, but Ben immediately took over, scooping him up in his arms, carrying him with ease. As they crept away from the battling, mesmerised Cappadocians, Maddy couldn't seem to tear her eyes from the scene.

Mislav had somehow managed to fight off the other vampires to briefly come within reach of Nadia once again. He smiled in triumph and tried to touch her face. But as he did so, she reached forward, and faster than the human eye could see, she snapped his neck. Maddy gasped. Mislav was still standing, but his head was bent at an impossible angle, hanging down over his chest. Nadia then broke both his arms and legs, twisted them up, and kicked his body across the floor. Her face remained impassive. The hall was now cloaked in silence apart

from the gurgling, whimpering sounds coming from the back of
Mislav's throat. Nadia had broken and bent his body so badly
that – vampire or no vampire – the man must be in agony. His
eyes were wide and staring, disbelieving.

Maddy was shocked at the brutality of it. Yes, Mislav
deserved everything he got, but to witness it first-hand was
horrific. None of the other vampires made a move to help him.
In a matter of seconds, the mood in the hall had changed. A
moment ago, the vampires had been desperate to reach Nadia.
Now they had all seemed to come to their senses. Fear had
taken over, and they began to back away from her.

'Madison!' Nadia called out. 'You must all stay back! Turn
away and press yourselves to the back of the hall.' Earlier,
Nadia had warned them it would be too dangerous for the
Marchwood vampires to remain close by. That she wouldn't be
able to protect them from herself. She had told them that under
no circumstances were the vampires to look at her. Maddy's
heart sped up. This was it. What was Nadia about to do?

In the centre of the hall, Nadia's skin began to glow. Not a
brief glimmer, like before in the hotel room, but a bright, warm
glow as though lit by a fire from within. Her eyes darkened from
sky blue to deep red, like burning coals. Her hair began to move
as though blown by the wind, the bright tresses fluttering up
and down. But Maddy realised her swirling hair was no longer
simply hair – instead, it had erupted into a mass of yellow
flames. In fact, her whole body was burning! Crackling and
whooshing. Lit up like a Catherine Wheel, Nadia had become a
creature of fire.

As the vampires became increasingly more fearful, she took
a step towards those closest to her. They took a step back. And
then she struck. She pulled three of them at once into her
flames and set them alight, cutting them down with a long
dagger that she had pulled out from a strap around her calf. The
other vampires flew into a terrified panic, trying to escape this

flaming, vicious creature who, only seconds earlier, had been a source of desire.

Nadia wielded the dagger like it was part of her body. Slicing and twirling in a dance of death, the blade now glowing as red as her eyes. She moved so swiftly, that she seemed to appear everywhere at once. Her flames reaching almost up to the vaulted ceiling high above their heads. The vampires were truly terrified now. Screaming and flying in all directions. But Nadia was too fast. She blazed through the hall in a fury, taking all the vampires into her flames, one by one. Turning them to ashes in seconds.

Within moments, they were nearly all dead. Incinerated by a single swirling, dancing, burning, killing creature. The only vampires still left alive were Mislav – a sickening mess of blood and bones – and the Emperor, who remained on his throne, his hands clenching the armrests.

Nadia's flames had died down a little now. She took two paces towards Mislav and dropped into a crouch on the stone floor, her flames disappearing with a final flicker. 'If you kiss me,' she crooned, gazing into his pitiful eyes. 'I will stop the pain.'

Maddy grimaced at the sight of the twisted creature of bone and skin. How Nadia could even consider kissing the ruined vampire was beyond her.

Mislav closed his eyes. Nadia tenderly put her lips to his and kissed. Her skin took on an extra brightness that made the entire hall glow. Madison was mesmerised. The girl really was beautiful. So beautiful it almost made her want to cry. In a brief second the spell was broken. Nadia broke the kiss and drove her dagger into the place where Mislav's heart should have been. To Madison's surprise, instead of turning to dust, Mislav's chest shed crimson blood. Nadia had made him human before killing him. The living vampire was now a dead mortal. She used Mislav's robes to wipe his blood from her blade, then she stood, her attention turning to the last of the Cappadocian vampires. The coven leader. The Emperor.

He stood and regarded her from the dais. He must be incredibly powerful to have escaped her flames so far. Or maybe Nadia had planned it this way – saved the best until last.

'Do you know who I am?' the Emperor asked Nadia, his thin voice echoing. He glided down from the dais to face her.

She stood, silent.

'I am the most powerful creature you will ever encounter,' he said. 'I am centuries old. I have slain great leaders, conquered armies and squashed nations. And you think that your fiery little display will intimidate me? Those creatures you burned were merely my foot soldiers. I have the strength of the night and the power of blood and shadows. The might of centuries. I could crush you if I wished.'

Nadia laughed and took a step forward. She hit the Emperor on the side of his head with the hilt of her dagger, knocking him to the ground, and then she kicked him in the face. It was obvious that her blows had hurt him. He clutched his head and face and stared at her in shock and bewilderment. Nadia raised the dagger again, blade down, ready to strike a death blow.

Maddy should have let Nadia finish him like she had finished the others. But she suddenly had a better idea.

'Stop!' she cried out.

Nadia turned to Madison, her face so radiant that Maddy had to look away.

'Please stop!' Maddy repeated. The others remained at the back of the hall, safe from Nadia's killing powers. But Madison approached the glowing creature, her heart in her mouth, terrified, but compelled to continue. Nadia's eyes had changed back from red to blue, giving her a more human aspect, but she still radiated an electrifying power that made the hairs on Maddy's neck and arms stand up. The incapacitated Emperor was oblivious to Madison, his eyes still trained upwards on Nadia.

'Nadia,' Maddy said, unsure how safe she was from her.

Nadia's eyes were back on the Emperor.

'Nadia,' Maddy tried again, her voice louder this time.

'Madison,' Nadia acknowledged her without turning around.

'Please don't kill him,' she said. 'The Emperor. Don't kill him.'

'You want I should spare this one? The most powerful of them all. That is not why I came here.'

'I don't want you to "spare" him exactly.' Maddy murmured what she would like Nadia to do to the Cappadocian.

Nadia threw back her head and laughed. 'Yes,' she said. 'Yes. I agree. That would be fitting.' She smiled and twirled her knife. Its handle was intricately carved. Its blade long and curved.

'That looks old,' Maddy said, drawn to the beautiful dagger.

'It is older than I,' Nadia replied. 'But just as powerful – the only blade that will pierce a vampire's flesh. It belonged to the one who sacrificed his life for me.'

Maddy turned her attention towards the back of the hall, checking on the others.

'They may come forward,' Nadia said. She stood and turned, beckoning Sofia and the others over. They made their way across the hall, footsteps echoing. 'I will not harm them. I brim with power now,' Nadia said, her eyes shining. 'More power than I have had for centuries.'

Sofia reached them first, stepping behind Nadia to keep an eye on the stunned Emperor. For all his claims of power, he was now injured and outnumbered, and he wasn't going anywhere. But it was best not to take any chances. As the others drew closer, Maddy saw that someone else was with them – Leonora.

'I see *you're* still alive,' Maddy spat. 'How can you live with

yourself after what you did to Alex? You said you loved him!'
Maddy stumbled over to her brother who still carried a barely
conscious Alex in his arms.

'I'm sorry, Madison,' Freddie said. 'But Leonora is my sister.
No matter what she's done, I couldn't leave her to die with the
rest.'

'No. I understand that,' Maddy said. 'But how could she
have hurt Alex?'

'You cannot think that I wished to harm Alexandre,'
Leonora said. 'I would never have willingly—'

'It doesn't look that way to me,' Maddy said. 'Have you seen
him? Are you responsible for those marks and gashes on his
skin? Did you drink his blood?'

'They... they gave me no choice,' Leonora said. 'But, I have
paid for it. I feel a weight of guilt. My time here has been more
terrible than you can imagine.'

'Not as terrible as Alex's,' Maddy replied. 'Don't ask us to
feel sorry for you.'

'No, of course not. I was wrong. This place is not what I
thought it would be. It is evil.' She bowed her head. 'These
vampires have no humanity left. They are nothing like us. I was
used by them. I know that now. I won't deny I enjoyed the
blood, but not at this cost. I never wished to cause such suffering.' Her voice broke and she choked back a sob. 'I never wished
to become what I am.'

Maddy believed she was sorry, but she still couldn't forgive
her for what she'd done to Alex.

Leonora turned to Nadia. 'My brother has just saved me
from your fire, but he was wrong to do so. I deserve to die.
Please kill me, for I fear I cannot live with what I've done.'

'Nora, no!' Freddie cried.

'Freddie,' Leonora whispered. 'I have missed you terribly
these past days. I have missed England. I want... to go home.
Not to Marchwood as it is now. I just wish to be free. To not

have to fight against my vampire nature every second of every day. It is exhausting.'

Freddie turned to Nadia. 'Will you help her?' he asked. 'Will you do for my sister what you did for Alexandre?'

Nadia smiled at Freddie and then turned her gaze back to Leonora. 'You will not have to fight your dual natures any longer,' she said. 'You can return to your brother as his real sister. His flesh-and-blood sister. Not the demon you have become. You have too much darkness in you, Leonora. Let me bring back your light.'

'My light?' Leonora said.

Pulsing with energy, Nadia leant forward to place a kiss upon her lips. Moments later, Leonora swooned and Freddie gathered his sister up in his arms.

Maddy imagined that this must have been what it had been like between Alex and Nadia. It was nothing to feel jealousy over. It was simply what Nadia was born to do.

'Thank you,' Freddie said to Nadia. 'I only hope the old Leonora is still in there, somewhere.'

Nadia bowed. She turned to Maddy. 'And this one?' She nudged the Emperor's body with her foot. 'You still want him alive?'

Maddy nodded.

'What!' Isobel cried. 'You can't let him live. Surely—'

'Don't worry, I've got a plan for the Emperor,' Maddy said, cutting off her objections. 'Call it a gift for Alex, once he's recovered.'

'Is that wise?' Isobel replied.

'Trust me,' Maddy said.

There was a moment of silence as they all realised that they had won. That it was finally over.

'Can we go home now?' Esther asked. 'This damp is playing havoc with my knees.'

'Yeah, sure we can,' Maddy replied, feeling an inappropriate urge to laugh. Esther and Morris were brave and loyal, and were somehow still undaunted by all they'd seen tonight. She owed them – again.

'Go then,' said Nadia. 'Back to your small island.'

'Thank you,' Maddy said. 'You saved our lives.'

Nadia inclined her head.

'What will you do now?' Maddy asked. 'Will you come back with us? You're welcome at Marchwood.'

'No. I go.'

'Before you go,' Isobel said. 'Can I beg one last favour?'

CHAPTER FORTY-ONE

TWO DAYS LATER

This cold, black morning in January was considered to be one of the worst days of the year. That dead time after Christmas when spring is too far away to look forward to. And, on the worst day of the year, the last place anyone would wish to be was this no-go council estate in South East London. A dead-end place. Devoid of hope. A vista of grey concrete, burnt-out cars and dark underpasses. No one would come here willingly. No one would feel glad to be here.

Except maybe Alexandre Chevalier – Frenchman-turned-Englishman. Victorian-turned-Gen Z. Human-turned-vampire-turned-human, again. Yes, Alexandre was decidedly pleased to be here. An ember of hope flared in his chest as he opened his door and stepped out of the van. He stared through the darkness at the deserted street, at the shards of broken bottles glinting under the orange streetlights. At the sweet wrappers stuck to wet kerbstones. At the discarded needles and dog ends. To him, this place was absolutely perfect.

Here. Now. This was where it ended.

He glanced at his watch, and then up at the dark sky. He had timed it perfectly. Sunrise was just twelve minutes away.

The rainclouds had dispersed like the weather app had predicted they would. And Alex was quite optimistic that all would go as planned.

He walked around to the side of the van, trying to ignore the biting cold. The temptation to wear the parka Maddy had given him was overwhelming as the icy January wind cut into his mortal skin. But for this occasion he had opted to wear a beautifully tailored suit – and a navy blue parka would ruin the effect. He was regaining his life and to do so he had to feel right. He had to be his nineteenth-century self – that arrogant well-dressed young man who had confidence and style. Who had his whole life ahead of him. The life that was taken away.

Well, now he was about to take it back.

He yanked at the van door, and it slid open with a loud, echoing *whoosh* in the otherwise silent street. Alex hopped up into the back of the van and stared for a moment at the long wooden crate. With frozen fumbling fingers, he untied the straps that secured it to the wall. Then, he took up the crowbar and pried open the lid. With a splintering of wood, the lid came off, and Alex gazed down at the occupant.

Dark, cold eyes gazed back at him. Alex swallowed down a spark of fear, reminding himself that this creature couldn't hurt him now. That he was too weak. Too puny to do any damage. But it was still the face of his nightmares.

'Out you get,' Alex said.

The creature blinked.

'I said, *out*.' Alex hoisted him out of the crate. He hardly weighed a thing. This once-powerful Byzantine Emperor was now at his mercy. His hands bound with silver chains.

'I am weak now,' the Emperor hissed. 'But I will feed, and then you will pay for your disrespect.'

Alexandre ignored him, nudging him out of the van and onto the dark street. The Emperor stumbled over his hem and tripped into the gutter. Filthy rainwater splashed up and soaked one side of his ancient robes. He pushed himself to his feet again and tried in vain to reposition his crown with his tied hands, but it now sat lopsided on his head.

'What is this place?' the Emperor asked, staring about him, a faint glimmer of apprehension in his eyes. 'Where are we?'

'London,' Alex replied.

This powerful being couldn't have been more than sixteen or seventeen when he was turned. His face, although cruel, was so young. It almost gave Alex pause for thought. Almost, but not quite. His looks belied his age. He was a two-thousand-year-old monster. Maybe even older. This creature deserved no sympathy. Alex pushed him forward, guiding him towards the centre of the street.

'I am disappointed,' the Emperor said, as he stumbled ahead of Alex. 'I thought you would have had the courage to face me in Cappadocia where we first met. Instead, you have slunk back to hide away on this miserable island once more.'

'I don't care if you're disappointed. I did what was necessary.' Alex drew a knife out from his jacket pocket.

'You cannot harm me with that child's toy,' the Emperor sneered. 'Even these chains won't hold me once my strength returns. I am too old and too powerful for silver to contain me.'

'You may not be scared of the blade or the chains,' Alexandre said. 'But we only have' – he glanced at his watch – 'about two minutes until dawn.'

The Emperor's haughty expression faltered. He glanced to his left and to his right, presumably looking for somewhere to run and hide. Somewhere safe from the sun's lethal rays.

Alex laughed. 'There's nowhere for you to go. This is it. This grotty, squalid little corner of the universe is where you will finish your days.' The Emperor stared at Alex in disbelief. He dodged left and then attempted to run in the opposite direction, but in his weakened state he could barely stand, and Alex was easily able to grab hold of his cloak and pull him back into a firm embrace.

'No,' the Emperor said in disbelief, his voice rising even higher. 'No. You cannot do this.'

'Look ahead, Your Imperial Highness,' Alex said. 'The sky is lightening. You'll soon be able to see this place lit up in all its glory.' Alex loosed his grip on the Emperor and watched as he sank to the ground, covering his face, folding himself into the pavement to escape the first rays of morning.

'Take me back to the vehicle!' the Emperor screamed. 'Take me into the darkness. Save me, and I will make you rich and powerful beyond your wildest dreams. You can live whatever kind of life you want. Your wish will be my command. I guarantee your safety from all our kind for now and always. You have my word. The word of an emperor.'

Alex laughed again. 'You should hear yourself,' he said. 'Look at you. You murdering, evil piece of filth. You killed thousands of innocents. You mocked their terror. Treated them with disdain and ignored their cries for mercy. So, why then should I grant you mercy?'

'I'm sorry,' the Emperor sobbed. 'I'm sorry. Please, take me back into the darkness, before it's too late. I am your maker. Your father. That should count for something.'

'You are *not* my father,' Alex spat. The very idea that this pathetic, evil creature could be in any way related to him made his skin crawl. 'Stand up,' Alexandre ordered.

'No. I cannot. The sun is rising. I can see the light. I will burn.'

'You will not burn,' Alex said. 'You will not burn because you are no longer a vampire.'

'Of course I am!'

'You know that I am human again,' Alex said. 'Well... surprise! So are you.'

'*No.* This cannot be true.' The Emperor grew still.

'So, how do you explain the fact that you are cowering on the ground under the rising sun without so much as a scorched eyelash.'

The Emperor took his hands away from his face and tentatively raised his head, gazing up towards the sunrise. As the pink blush of light illuminated his almost translucent skin, his black eyes squinted in terror and wonder.

'I cannot believe it,' the Emperor said, letting out a breath. 'I am staring at the sun.'

Alexandre untied the silver chains around the Emperor's wrists and put them in his pocket. 'These were just for show,' he explained. 'Silver has no effect on humans. But blades do. I'll show you.' Alex took hold of the Emperor's curled fist, spread it flat and sliced across the soft flesh of his palm with the point of the knife. 'More proof that you are mortal.' The boy whimpered in pain and brought the wound to his mouth.

'I am weak!' he cried. 'I am human! What have you done to me? How did you do this?'

'That girl you were so disdainful of back in Cappadocia,' Alexandre said.

'What girl?'

'You know the one.'

'The golden-haired girl?'

'That's right,' Alex replied. 'Her name is Nadia. She is *the bright one*. Have you heard of her?'

'The bright one? The *hunter*?'

Alex nodded. 'She took our power. You and I are both mortal once again.'

'Then we are both doomed,' said the Emperor, his voice flat.

'No,' Alex replied. 'You are wrong. I am happy to be human.' Alexandre realised that he was finally ending this. The Emperor truly no longer had the power to hurt him and his family. It was an exhilarating feeling. 'You have no power over me. I no longer have any ties to you. You, however, are very much alone, Your Imperial Highness.'

A car screeched around the bend and came to a stop about a hundred yards away from them, partially blocking the sunrise. The muffled sound of a deep bass line could be heard from its interior. Through the car's windscreen, Alex saw a group of young men. Restless, angry-looking youths who stared at him, and at the Emperor, and especially at Alex's shiny new van.

'It looks like we've got company, so I'm going to go now,' Alex said to the Emperor.

'*Going to go?* Going to go where?' The Emperor's eyes widened, as he stared from Alexandre to the newly arrived car. The doors opened all at once and a pounding beat spilled out from the car along with four men. Two with their hoods up, one in a baseball cap and the fourth with a malicious grin that could lead to nothing good. The Emperor scrambled to his feet and turned back to Alex. The expression on his face was that of a terrified child.

Alexandre almost felt sorry for him – almost, but not quite. Again, he remembered the horrors that this being had inflicted upon so many. Alex's own parents were dead because of this creature and his coven. He had posed a mortal threat to him, to Madison, and to their families. He had almost destroyed their lives. No, he couldn't feel pity. Alex hardened his heart.

'I'm going home now,' he said.

'But what about me?' the Emperor asked. 'You cannot leave me in this place. Take me back to my city. Take me anywhere else but here. I will reward you well.'

'Goodbye,' Alex said, tucking his knife back into his pocket. 'I heard there might be snow on the way later. You'll need to wrap up. Those robes are no good for a human in the northern hemisphere. And your crown is impractical.'

'Please,' the Emperor said, falling back down to his knees. 'I beg you.'

'I'll bet you've never said those words before,' Alex said. 'But I have a feeling you'll be saying them a lot more before today is over.'

Alex turned and walked back towards his van, ignoring the Emperor's continued pleas. Ignoring the taunts and jeers from the youths. Ignoring the cries and the laughter. He got into his van and, without looking back, drove away, back home towards Marchwood.

CHAPTER FORTY-TWO

TWO MONTHS LATER

He was running in the rain, his feet pounding the concrete of the narrow Gloucestershire lanes, and he was enjoying it. Alexandre never knew that running could be so therapeutic, allowing him to order his mind and push his body.

This morning, like every morning since coming back to Marchwood, he had woken before dawn and stepped outside to run, and to witness the sunrise. Today's was a gradual lightening of clouded skies rather than a dramatic display of colour. But any kind of daylight was still a novelty. Sunrise, sunset and every shade of light in between. From dull grey mornings and rain-soaked afternoons to bright winter days laced with ice and snow. Alexandre needed to be outside. To inhale each day as if it were his last.

Now that he was mortal again, every second was precious, every moment a jewel. Yes, he had lost his vampire strength and senses, but he had also lost the restrictions that blood and daylight imposed. He was freer than he had ever been. And he was determined to feel strong again. So, he ran and biked and swam and climbed. Building up his strength, inside and out.

Alexandre checked his watch. It was almost 7 a.m.; time to

head back to the house. After his run, he would go upstairs, get showered and then slide back into bed with Madison. Their bodies warm. Human. The same. This was his comforting morning routine.

Life was as perfect as he could have ever imagined it to be. Yes, he had scars – the marks on his neck and torso would never completely fade. And he still couldn't shake the sadness he felt over the loss of his century. The death of his parents. The betrayal by Leonora. But didn't everyone have something they carried around with them? An invisible suitcase that was best left closed.

He reached Marchwood's wrought-iron gates and turned into the driveway. Alex felt a little weary this morning, but he wouldn't let himself slow down. Not yet. He would run to the end of the tree-lined driveway, and then he would walk the final two-hundred yards. He passed by the deer park. Soon they would have a new herd. Ben was sorting it out. The boy had been devastated by the loss of their deer. Alex could still picture the carnage in his mind. An image he wished he could forget. This time, the new deer would be safe. Nadia had seen to that.

Now that the Cappadocians were dead and gone, they could all relax. Alex had been wrong to think he could have defeated them by himself. He had needed the others' help. Without them, he would be dead right now. His foolish pride had prevented him from seeing clearly. But he now realised that he needed his family as much as they needed him.

Isobel, too, had become mortal. Nadia had turned her before they left Turkey. He had never seen his sister so happy. She had even enrolled in a college course – something to do with dress designing. She was excited about the future. As well as a husband and babies, Belle wanted a career. That was something this century would let her have.

The boys, however, had chosen to remain as vampires – for now at any rate. Ben, Jacques and Freddie were enjoying their powers too much to give them up. Madison and Isobel had objected at first. There had been arguments, long silences and tears. But eventually, they had come to a compromise. Nadia would return in three years' time to turn the boys back. They would have three years to enjoy their strength, and pretend to be superheroes. He couldn't blame them. They were young and adventurous. Such powers were a hard thing to give up. Alex had already had two colds and a vomiting bug since becoming mortal – he hadn't missed these fleshly weaknesses.

But remaining a vampire would never have been a good outcome for him. He would have had to watch Maddy grow old, and one day die. He would have ended up powerful, but alone. This way, at least, they got to be together properly.

He felt as though he had died twice and yet been allowed to return twice. First, he had died in the Cappadocian caves all those years ago and had come back a vampire, mourning the death of his human life. Then he had foolishly mourned the loss of his vampire life. He was truly blessed to have his mortality back, and he wasn't going to waste it on regret.

Being human again was like a weight lifting from his shoulders. Madison had been right. To be given his mortal life back was a gift. He could now concentrate on being Alexandre. But he could be the Alex he wanted to be. Not the sensible engineer his father expected him to be, or the fearless vampire he thought his family needed him to be, but simply the man he always knew he could be. The one who would find his place in the mortal world. The one who could discover his passion and live a full life with the girl he loved.

Madison lay in bed waiting for him to return. Her vampire. She smiled to herself. Even though Alex was mortal again, she still thought of him as a magical being. The one who had changed

her life. She couldn't believe how mad she had been at him for
what had happened with Nadia. He had been as much a victim
as she. More so. But it was okay, because now she was going to
make it up to him. She had a surprise planned.

———

Rising up through the clouds was an odd experience. His ears
felt as though they were full of air. Everything sounded muffled.
And his stomach kept dropping away, which was most discon-
certing.

'I feel strange,' Alex said. 'Is this normal? This heavy feeling
in my head?'

'Don't worry, it's the air pressure,' Maddy replied. 'Anyway,
you've been on a plane before.'

'Yes, but either as a vampire in the cargo hold or as a human,
sedated. Never on a private jet with a beautiful girl.' He
grinned. 'Are you blushing, Madison?'

'No.'

'You are. I made you blush. Beautiful, gorgeous, stunning
girl.'

'Shut up, Alex!'

He laughed. 'Learn to take a compliment. I'm only speaking
the truth.'

'Thank you,' she said, her cheeks still crimson.

Alex took her hand and brought her slender fingers to his
mouth, breathing in the scent of her skin. She leant back in her
seat and closed her eyes, a smile playing on her lips. He leant
across and kissed her neck, enjoying the sound of her sighs.

'Will we be there soon?' he murmured in her ear.

'No clues, Alex. I already told you. Just enjoy the flight.
You'll just have to wait and see. And I've briefed the pilot and
cabin crew not to tell you anything, so don't even think about
asking them.'

Alex growled in frustration and turned back to the window. He had tried to guess where she could be taking them. A fancy hotel, a beach holiday, skiing, a lakeside retreat? As long as it wasn't back to Cappadocia, he didn't care where they went – although he wouldn't mind visiting Sofia again; she was truly an amazing lady. They were climbing out of the clouds now into the bluest sky he had ever seen, the brightness of the sun as dazzling as a diamond. He could never have imagined that it would be so clear up here. That above the clouds was this whole other world of sky.

As the plane continued on its mysterious journey, Alex and Maddy chattered about Marchwood, about Isobel, and Ben and the others. About nothing and everything. After the seat belt sign turned off, they were served champagne and canapes. Then, a while later, coffee with chocolates. Alex's taste buds had been going crazy ever since he'd become mortal again. Everything tasted incredible, but so strong. He could only manage a few mouthfuls of anything, apart from plain food like pasta. Oh, and soup. He loved soup.

Before they knew it, the steward told them to fasten their seat belts again. They were beginning their descent. Back down through more grey rainclouds – not a beach holiday, then.

The landing was thrilling and loud. Alex felt like a kid, he was so excited. And then he saw the welcome sign written across the airport terminal building:

Paris le Bourget

Alex turned to Maddy. 'You brought me to Paris?' His chest tightened and his stomach was suddenly filled with butterflies. He hadn't been in Paris since 1881. Since before his trip to Turkey with Maman and Papa. Before... everything.

Madison bit her lip. 'I hope I didn't make a mistake,' she said. 'I thought it might be a good thing to do. To come back...'

'Of course,' he said with false jollity. 'Of course. It was a really thoughtful thing to do.'

'You don't want to be here, do you,' Maddy said, as they taxied down the runway, slowing to a stop. 'We can turn around and go back if you like. I'm sorry. I can see by your face that you're freaked out. I was nervous about doing this,' she said. 'About bringing you back here. It's too overwhelming, isn't it?'

'It is overwhelming, Madison,' Alex replied. 'But in a good way. In such a good way. I will admit, I never thought I would return home again. The thought scared me. But now I am here. I think it will be good.'

'Are you sure?' Maddy asked. 'I'm such an idiot.'

'You are not an idiot. And yes, I am one hundred per cent sure.'

'It's raining,' she said, looking out at the drizzle. 'I had this image of bright sunshine. Paris in the springtime, you know?'

'I don't care about the weather,' Alex replied truthfully. 'It rains a lot in Paris, so I feel properly at home.' He kissed her nose. 'Stop looking so worried. Come, let's get off this contraption and see my city.' He took her hand, and they exited the plane.

To hear his native language being spoken all around him in the airport terminal gave him goose bumps. Made him shiver with the memories. Ghosts of people long gone – friends, family. All gone. He shook himself. No point in thinking that way. They got into the car that was waiting to take them wherever they were going. He didn't ask Maddy any more questions about their destination. It would most likely be a nice hotel, a good base for exploring the city. He would show her around – as long as it hadn't all changed too much. As long as he still recognised it.

In the car, Alex was almost scared to gaze out of the window. To discover how his Paris looked today. Scared it would let him down. That it wouldn't be everything he wanted it to be. Everything he remembered it to be. That the beat of his city's heart would have altered irrevocably.

Back then, it was horse-drawn carriages, omnibuses and crowds of people. Today, it was cars, taxis and buses. But there were still crowds of people here. The roads were just as wide, the avenues still as grand. He saw smart men, chic women, bustling shops and steamed-up café windows.

An image came to him, clear as glass, of sitting with his family eating lunch in a café on a busy shopping street in Saint-Germain-des-Prés, a Bohemian part of the city frequented by intellectuals and philosophers. He remembered feeling embarrassed because Isobel had been babbling on about shopping and soirees in a loud voice, when everyone around was discussing the meaning of life and the world at large. Alex had ended up gazing out through the rain-streaked café window dreaming of adventure while listening to the rattling of carriages and the rumbling of huge omnibuses as they splashed water across the pavements onto shoppers and street-vendors. He couldn't remember his exact daydreams that day, but he was certain they had not featured vampires, immortality or powerful legendary creatures.

He realised the car was heading south-west. It all looked so distinctly *French*! He hadn't realised how *English* England was. Not until he came back here and saw his place of birth. A seed of joy began to grow inside him, and he felt a smile escape from his lips. One he couldn't contain. He was here! He knew this place. He knew it like the back of his hand. From his mind, he conjured the memory of the oyster peddlers, newspaper sellers, pickpockets and pedestrians all jostling for space on the crowded nineteenth-century Parisian streets. Was it really so different now?

'Are you sure you're okay, Alex? You look a little out of it?'

'It's just... memories. You know. Thinking about my life

here, my family and about how it used to be. I was also thinking how my mother and father would have loved you.'

'Liar,' Maddy said, a grin across her face. 'They would have been horrified by me, and you know it.'

'Well, all right. They would have disapproved at first. But once they got to know you, they would have adored you.'

'I wish I could have met them.'

'I wish it also.'

Maddy rested her head on his chest, and Alex ran his fingers through her dark, silky hair, bending to kiss the top of her head. This girl was everything. The fact that she had done this for him meant more than he could express. It was the most thoughtful gift. They had gone through so much, the two of them. It felt strange to finally be allowed to relax. To enjoy each other's company instead of running, chasing, hiding, fighting, worrying. All those things which had become their normality for such a long time.

She tilted her head up and smiled. How was it that his stomach went into free fall every time she smiled at him? He rubbed his thumb across her bottom lip. But it was impossible to touch her lips and not then kiss them. Heedless of the driver and what he might think, Alexandre dipped his head to kiss Madison. A slow kiss full of heat and promise. A kiss that set fire to his nerve endings and charged the air around him with static. He was in danger of losing his mind over this girl.

The car had stopped, and the driver cleared his throat. Maddy drew back. 'I think we're here,' she said, a slight tremor in her voice.

'Bien, I'll tip the driver.'

'Okay.' Maddy slid across the seat and stepped out onto the rain-slicked pavement.

Alexandre counted out a few notes, giving the driver a generous tip. The man gave a grunt of thanks. Alex had forgotten how dismissive the drivers were in Paris. Whether car or carriage, some things never changed. He'd missed it.

Stepping outside to join Maddy, Alexandre suddenly stopped dead in the middle of the road where a shiver ran across his shoulders. He knew this street. He knew it – Rue Saint-Honoré. Was it a coincidence? Or had Maddy brought him here on purpose?

'Come out of the road, Alex,' she called to him. 'You'll get run over if you stand there.'

It was as though she was speaking from a long way away.

'Alex?' She came to him and took his hand, guided him onto the pavement as he stared up at the house in front of him.

'But this is...'

'Yes.'

'...my house. The house I grew up in with Maman et Papa. Our house.' Goose bumps prickled his flesh.

'Yes,' Maddy replied, her face turned up towards his.

'You know where I lived,' he said, unable to take his eyes off the building. 'How did you know?'

The cab sped off. Now it was just the two of them standing outside Alexandre's old family home.

'I can't believe it.' Alex couldn't stop staring. 'Who lives here now?' His heart dropped a little as he realised it was now someone else's home. 'It used to be one big house back then,' he explained. 'But I suppose it must have been converted into apartments by now or, God forbid, offices.'

'Alex,' Maddy said softly. 'I hope you don't mind, but... I bought it. It's your house again... if you want it?'

Alexandre blinked up at the building. 'My house? What are you talking about?' His heart began to pound.

'I wanted to do this for you. So you could stay connected to your past. So you wouldn't lose touch with everything. Jacques and Isobel helped me. It's furnished almost exactly the same as it was in 1881, with all the modern additions, of course. We don't have to live here all the time, but it's yours and Jacques's and Isobel's, anyway.'

Alexandre couldn't believe what Madison was telling him. He hadn't let himself think about Paris, about his family home, because those memories had been too painful. But now she was telling him that his past could become his present. That he could make new memories here. With her. With all of them.

He desperately wanted to go inside. Was dying to see everything again. But he was scared at the same time. Madison pressed something into his hand. He looked down. It was a silver key.

'Shall we go in?' Maddy asked.

Alexandre swallowed as tears threatened to fall. He blinked them back, excited and yet terrified to step over the threshold into his old life. With trembling fingers, he slotted the key into the lock and turned it, pushing the door open into the grand hallway he hadn't seen in over a century. Alex exhaled. It looked exactly as he remembered it – *home*. A calm feeling settled over his shoulders.

Maddy slipped past him and beckoned him through into the drawing room where he could now hear a piano playing an uplifting melody that Isobel had always favoured back when they lived here.

As Alex walked into the beautiful room his mind was instantly transported back to 1881 as he saw that Belle was actually here in person, seated at their grand piano, wearing one of her best gowns. She lifted her gaze and gave him a smile of pure happiness as she continued to play, and called out, '*Surprise!*'

He turned at the sound of other voices joining hers. And there were Jacques, Freddie, Ben and Leonora standing at the window with Esther and Morris, their faces wreathed in smiles as they noted his astonishment.

It was no good, Alexandre could no longer prevent the tears

from sliding down his cheeks at the rush of joy he felt to finally be back home in his beloved Paris with everyone he loved. He felt the warmth of his family surround him, and even imagined he could see the proud, loving faces of his parents seated in their favourite chairs.

'I cannot believe you did this for me,' Alexandre murmured to Maddy. She smiled up at him, her eyes bright as he bent to kiss her, his heart filled with love for this girl who had changed his life.

A LETTER FROM SHALINI

Dear reader,

Thank you so much for reading *Hunted*. I hope you've enjoyed the Vampires of Marchwood series.

If you'd like to keep up to date with my latest releases, just sign up here and I'll let you know when I have a new novel coming out.

www.secondskybooks.com/shalini-boland

I loved writing these books, especially all the historical parts. Truthfully, I'd never even heard of the Scythian people until I started researching ancient civilisations, wanting to find a race with customs and folklore that would complement my story. But I found myself being drawn into their history, wondering what it must have been like to live such a nomadic life when most of us today are so concerned with putting down roots.

I love getting feedback on my books, so if you have a few moments, I'd be really grateful if you'd be kind enough to post a review online or tell your friends about it. A good review absolutely makes my day.

When I'm not writing, reading, walking on the beach or spending time with my family, you can reach me via my Facebook page, through Twitter, Goodreads or my website..

Thanks so much,

Shalini Boland x

KEEP IN TOUCH WITH SHALINI

www.shaliniboland.co.uk

facebook.com/ShaliniBolandAuthor
twitter.com/ShaliniBoland
goodreads.com/shaliniboland

ACKNOWLEDGEMENTS

THANK YOU

To my husband, Peter Boland, who helped me shape this series, made me endless cups of tea, bought me chocolate and helped with the fight scenes (not literally).

To my wonderful beta readers: Amara Gillo – best mum ever (who's devastatingly no longer in this world but who continues to inspire me every day) and Julie Carey, who's read every single one of my books.

To all my gorgeous friends and writing support network online from back when I first wrote this series a decade ago, including: Johanna Frappier, C. Reg Jones, B. Lloyd, Samantha Towle, Suzy Turner, Amanda Cowley, Robert Craven, Poppet and Sessha Batto.

To my wonderful publisher, Natasha Harding, for believing in the series and working her magic on these characters. I'm forever grateful for your talent and patience. I cannot thank you enough.

To the dedicated team at Second Sky. Jenny Geras, Ruth Tross, Jack Renninson, Sarah Hardy, Kim Nash, Noelle Holten, Melanie Price, Mark Alder, Alex Crow, Natalie Butlin, Jess Readett, Alexandra Holmes, Emily Boyce, Saidah Graham,

Lizzie Brien, Occy Carr and everyone else who helped relaunch this book.

To Madeline Newquist for your fantastic proofreading skills. Thank you to designer Eileen Carey for an incredible cover.

To Jordan Spellman at Tantor Audio and narrator Henrietta Meire for creating fabulous audiobooks for the series.

To all my lovely readers who take the time to read, review or recommend my novels. It means so, so much. And to all the fabulous book bloggers and reviewers out there who spread the word. You guys are the absolute best!

To my wonderful dad who we lost when I was thirteen. He loved reading to me back then, and when he got sick, I used to read to him.

To my incredible family and friends who are always there to ease me back into the real world when I emerge from my writing cave – I love you!

Printed in Great Britain
by Amazon